Highest Praise for
John Lutz

"John Lutz knows how to make you shiver."
—Harlan Coben

"Lutz offers up a heart-pounding roller coaster of a tale."
—Jeffery Deaver

"John Lutz is one of the masters of the police novel."
—Ridley Pearson

"John Lutz is a major talent."
—John Lescroart

"I've been a fan for years."
—T. Jefferson Parker

"John Lutz just keeps getting better and better."
—Tony Hillerman

"Lutz ranks with such vintage masters of big-city murder as
Lawrence Block and Ed McBain."
—*St. Louis Post-Dispatch*

"Lutz is among the best."
—*San Diego Union*

"Lutz knows how to seize and hold the reader's imagination."
—*Cleveland Plain Dealer*

"It's easy to see why he's won an Edgar and two Shamuses."
—*Publishers Weekly*

Chill of Night

"Since Lutz can deliver a hard-boiled P.I. novel or a bloody thriller with equal ease, it's not a surprise to find him applying his skills to a police procedural in *Chill of Night*. But the ingenuity of the plot shows that Lutz is in rare form."
—*The New York Times Book Review*

"Lutz keeps the suspense high, populating his story with a collection of unique characters who resonate with the reader, making this one an ideal beach read."
—*Publishers Weekly*

"A dazzling tour de force . . . compelling, absorbing."
—*St. Louis Post-Dispatch*

"A great read! Lutz kept me in suspense right up to the end."
—*Midwest Book Review*

Night Kills

"Lutz's skill will keep you glued to this thick thriller."
—*St. Louis Post-Dispatch*

"Superb suspense . . . the kind of book that makes you check to see if all the doors and windows are locked."
—*Affaire de Coeur*

In for the Kill

"Brilliant . . . a very scary and suspenseful read."
—*Booklist*

"Shamus and Edgar award–winner Lutz gives us further proof of his enormous talent . . . an enthralling page-turner."
—*Publishers Weekly*

CHILL
OF
NIGHT

John Lutz

PINNACLE BOOKS
Kensington Publishing Corp.
www.kensingtonbooks.com

PINNACLE BOOKS are published by

Kensington Publishing Corp.
119 West 40th Street
New York, NY 10018

All Kensington titles, imprints, and distributed lines are available at special quantity discounts for bulk purchases for sales promotions, premiums, fund-raising, and educational or institutional use. Special book excerpts or customized printings can also be created to fit specific needs. For details, write or phone the office of the Kensington special sales manager: Kensington Publishing Corp., 119 West 40th Street, New York, NY 10018, attn: Special Sales Department; phone: 1-800-221-2647.

Pinnacle and the P logo are Reg. U.S. Pat. & TM Off.

ISBN-13: 978-0-7860-2194-9
ISBN-10: 0-7860-2194-2

First Printing: November 2006
First Printing (with excerpt from *Mister X*): September 2010

10 9 8 7 6 5 4

Printed in the United States of America

For Eunice Pope

Vengeance is in my heart, death in my hand,
Blood and revenge are hammering in my head.
—Shakespeare, *Titus Andronicus*

Render therefore to all their dues.
—Romans XIII.7

None are so desolate but something dear,
Dearer than self, possesses or possess'd
A thought, and claims the homage of a tear.
—Byron, *Childe Harold*

1

Things are never as they seem.

The area was supposed to be clear, marked off with yellow NYPD crime scene tape, but Beam caught a glimpse of movement behind one of the parked cars and moved toward it.

One step, that was all he'd taken, and the figure hiding behind the parked Mercedes was off and running toward the garage exit. Beam could see by the way he moved that he was young, teens or twenties. Beam had just turned fifty-three. Convert that difference in years to distance, and there was a lot of it to make up. Still, Beam was on the run and gradually gaining.

The victim's body had been removed, and the crime scene unit and other detectives had left. It was part of Beam's method to hang around alone at a murder scene and take in what he could in the immense silence and stillness that followed violent death. Now and then, he discovered something.

He'd sure as hell made a discovery this time—probably the shooter.

His feet pounding the concrete floor, Beam yelled, "Halt! Police!"

That seemed to speed up the guy, a skinny kid dressed in jeans, a dark watch cap, and a black jacket, flailing his arms, and with long legs that could eat up the ground. He was making for the vast rectangle of light that was the exit from the garage to freedom, where he'd be lost in the crowded New York streets. Beam couldn't risk taking a shot at him and would soon be outdistanced. The probable killer of the garage attendant, and he was getting away.

Can't let that happen!

Beam had seconds to act or he'd lose the angle, and his bullet might ricochet out onto the sidewalk.

"Halt or I'll shoot!"

Should it be a warning shot at the concrete ceiling? Or should he try to bring down the fleeing man before it was too late? One of those split second decisions you read and hear about in the media.

"Stop, damn it!"

The suspect lifted his knees higher, trying to draw more speed from his adrenaline-jacked body.

Beam stopped, spread his feet wide, and raised the revolver and held it before him in his right hand, bracing with his left.

Decision time.

But not for Beam.

The fleeing man suddenly skidded to a halt, at the same time whirling and dropping to one knee. It was a graceful, dancer's movement made possible by youth.

He shot Beam.

It was like getting whapped in the thigh with a hammer.

Beam was on the hard concrete floor without knowing how he got there, fire pulsing in his right leg. He craned his neck and peered toward the garage exit and saw that the kid was getting away.

Rubber screeched out on the street, and there was the dull sound of impact. A woman shouted something over and over that Beam couldn't understand.

He reached for his two-way. If the damned thing would work in the garage, he could get help, maybe nail the bastard on the street.

Then weakness came with the pain.

Then darkness.

Beam thought, *Lani* . . .

2

"What's it been, bro?" Cassandra Beam asked. "A week?"

"Nine days," Beam said. That was how long since he'd been released from the hospital into a bright spring day. His right leg still ached and wasn't as strong as his left. He'd lost twenty pounds while laid up, and his clothes hung on him as if they were somebody else's.

He was wearing a pale gray shirt with the sleeves unbuttoned and folded neatly halfway up his forearms. His face was so gaunt as to be almost vulpine, with blue eyes that could charm or cut steel, and an intensely curious, slightly lopsided expression due to a missing right earlobe that had been bitten off in a saloon fight his rookie year as a cop. Beam looked like a guy who'd been dragged bumping and thumping through life, resisting every inch.

The bullet fired in the parking garage had done only minimal damage to the bone, so he'd be able to walk soon without a cane. He was having lunch at Fostoria's, on Central Park West, with his sister, Cassie, who was a psychiatrist with her office nearby. A long way from downtown, where they'd spent their childhood.

The restaurant's tables were small and round, with lacy

white tablecloths, and the place was filled with brilliant winter sunlight. They were waiting for their server to bring them their orders of croissant sandwiches. It looked to Beam as if everyone in the restaurant was eating something on a croissant.

Their table was by the window, and both had been watching people stream past out on the sidewalk. It was easier than talking.

"You were thinking about retiring anyway," Cassie said.

She hadn't done well in the gene pool. Unlike Beam, who was tall and rawboned, his older sister was short and blocky, in a sturdy way that dieting would never change. Her eyes were darker than his, too, staring at Beam now from beneath black bangs.

"Thinking about and doing are two different things," Beam said.

Cassie gave him her gap-toothed smile. "You're telling *me* that?"

Beam had to smile back. "Sorry. Sometimes I forget what you do for a living."

"Getting shot, so soon after Lani, it was like a one-two punch."

"Is that psychoanalyst talk?" Beam asked. "A one-two punch?"

Cassie took a sip of lime-flavored bottled water. "I'm not talking like an analyst now. More like a sister. Not that I don't think analysis wouldn't help you, but it should be done by another professional."

"I'll get through it," Beam said. His wife of twenty-three years, Lani, had for reasons unknown leaped from the high balcony of her friend and business partner's apartment, where she was attending a cocktail party and charity fund raiser. It was five months later when Beam had been surprised by the suspect in the parking garage, while investigating the robbery shooting of the attendant, and was shot in the leg. The shooter, who turned out to be twenty-two years old, with an impressive record of armed assault and burglary, had been struck and killed by a car in the street outside the garage exit. Beam's final collar.

Not the best way to end the career of legendary New York homicide detective Artemis Beam, the cop who'd made his reputation understanding and hunting down serial killers. He'd been kicked up to the rank of captain and unceremoniously pensioned off. Since then he'd had to use pills to help him sleep, and awake he wandered alone and uneasy in the shifting world of the retired.

Cassie was the first to tell him he'd never been one to adjust easily. She had a seer's gift for spotting trouble even before it appeared on the horizon, and she'd known Beam's retirement was going to be hell. As usual, she was right.

Beam still grieved for Lani.

Beam's leg still hurt.

Beam still missed the hunt.

Here came the croissants.

3

It felt like butter.

Lois Banner stood in front of the bolt of rich fabric and again ran her fingertips over it along the barely discernible warp of the material that was so incredibly soft despite its high wool content. It was dark gray, with a faint black splatter pattern, and would be perfect for some of the fall lines she'd seen at last week's fashion show. *Evening in Paris* was the name the supplier had affixed to the material, and Lois thought they had it right. That was what the soft fabric reminded her of, her earlier, not-so-innocent years in the city that lent itself to sin.

Lois herself was a former fashion model, almost forty now, and twenty pounds beyond her working weight. But she would still look good in some of the clothes due in the shops next season. In fact, she would look fantastic. Her features were still sharp, her eyes a brilliant blue, and her dark hair was skinned back to emphasize prominent cheekbones that looked like swept back airplane wings. As a model she'd been considered exotic. She was still that, if she dressed for it. Which happened less and less often.

Lois preferred to spend time tracking fashions and buying the wonderful fabrics that her customers, gained from longtime business contacts, would purchase wholesale to make the most of what was new. And always, in the world of fashion, something—the most important thing—was *new*.

The main office of Fabrics by Lois was on Seventh Avenue. This fabric warehouse and showroom was on West Forty-sixth Street, in the loft of a building that housed offices below. Though most of the bolts of fabric were stored vertically to maximize space, at five feet, ten inches, Lois was the tallest thing in the unbroken area with its vast plank floor. It was evening and dark outside. The Forty-sixth Street end of the loft was shadowed but for dappled light that filtered through unwashed windows and skylights. The rest of the area was dimly illuminated by original brass fixtures suspended on chains from the high ceiling. Lois would not abide florescent lighting—*the cruel tricks it played on colors!*

She was dressed simply and casually in black slacks and blouse this evening, and wore white Nikes, no socks. On Lois, the outfit looked even more expensive than it was.

A breeze played across her bare ankles, as if a door had opened. But the loft was accessible by elevator. The only door was to the fire stairs that ran down the south side of the building.

The subtle change of temperature jogged Lois' memory. She glanced at her Patek Philippe watch, a gift from a long-ago admirer. Almost eight o'clock, and she was due to meet a buyer for drinks at nine. She barely had time to get to her apartment, shower, and change clothes.

Time to lock up. But she couldn't resist running her fingertips one more time over *Evening in Paris*.

A slight noise made her glance to her left.

She gave a sharp intake of breath. A shadowy figure stood silently among the tall fabric bolts. *Almost like someone standing watching in a corn field.* The bucolic image surprised Lois and, through her fear, unpleasantly reminded her of her childhood in Ohio. She belonged here! In New York or Paris or Berlin. She was no longer the early version, the early Lois Banion, who was no more.

"Who—" she began in a strangled voice.

The figure, a man, stepped forward, and she could see in his right hand a bulky object which she recognized as a gun with a silencer attached to its barrel.

Lois forced herself to speak. "If you want money, there isn't any here."

The man said something she didn't understand.

"What?"

"Justice," he said softly, and raised the gun as if to point it at her like an accusing finger.

"My God," she said in a small girl's voice, "what have I done?" *What haven't I done?*

Oh, Jesus, what haven't *I done?*

The gun jumped in the man's hand, and she felt a fire and then a numbness in her chest, and she was on the floor. Terrified, she tried to get up and found herself entangled in fabric. Tried to get up. Tried not to die. Tried to get up.

The light was fading. She was staring up at one of the dangling brass fixtures, and it was like a distant star, moving even farther away.

There was no pain, she realized. *Incredible! No pain!* For that, at least, she was grateful.

If there's no pain, why should there be fear?

Evening in Paris enfolded and embraced her like a warm, welcoming shroud.

4

To his friends and enemies, Artemis Beam was simply "Beam." Ella, the waitress at the Chow Down Diner on Amsterdam Avenue, thought of him as "Over hard." The way he liked his eggs. The way she figured he was.

Beam sat in his usual booth near the window, where he could look out on the street over coffee and his folded *Times,* at people who had places to go in a hurry. He had no particular place to go, but he thought that if need be, he could still get somewhere in a hurry. Though he walked with a long, limping lope, the truth was that the leg didn't hurt much anymore, and he was still in pretty good shape and could move fast.

Another truth was that Beam hadn't been eased out of the NYPD four months ago only because of the gunshot wound. Politics had been involved. Beam had never been in his element within a bureaucracy—which the NYPD was—and had stepped on the wrong toes.

The resultant trouble had been all right with Beam, except that his job was at least partly the cause of his wife Lani's bouts of depression. Almost a year had passed since Lani's death leap from the apartment balcony near Lincoln Center.

Beam was still grieving for his wife, still trying to come to terms with the hard fact that she was actually gone, that the dark winds of her tortured mind had finally claimed her, and that in part it had been his fault. Because of who he was, because of not quitting the department sooner, because of all the things he hadn't done and all the words he hadn't spoken and she would now never hear. She had left him behind in a cold world that denied him peace and comfort.

Still feeling the effects of the Ambien he'd taken last night to get to sleep, he sipped his coffee and gazed out at the crowded sidewalks and stalled morning traffic on Amsterdam Avenue.

New York. His city, like clustered Towers of Babble, that he used to protect, that he still loved. Where he was born to a Jewish father and Irish mother, and, with Cassie, raised on the Lower East Side. His father, who'd been a cop.

The city still needed protection, needed to be set right again and again because that was its raucous, rowdy, and sometimes deadly nature.

The hell with it! Not his problem anymore.

Beam was getting accustomed to not thinking about his past, but it still scared the hell out of him to contemplate his future. His future alone.

He still didn't mind stepping on toes. And he didn't feel like being involved again with the NYPD.

He knew Andy da Vinci was going to ask him to do both those things.

Beam's eyes narrowed at the invasive morning light beyond the window. There was da Vinci, picking his way like a nifty broken-field runner through the stalled traffic before the signal at the intersection changed, engines roared, horns blared, and he might be run down and over and dragged. He was grinning, obviously relishing the challenge.

Dumb! Beam thought, but he liked da Vinci. It was just that needlessly risking a life wasn't Beam's game.

"Topper?"

Ella was standing next to his booth, holding the round glass coffee pot, staring down at him with a questioning look on her long, bovine features.

"Sure," Beam said.

Horns honked wildly outside. Da Vinci hadn't quite made it all the way across and was really dancing now, his moves a graceful series of passes within inches of bumpers and fenders. He was still grinning, now and then waving, or flipping off an irate driver.

"Look at that idiot," Ella said, staring out the window as she poured coffee into Beam's cup. "He's gonna get himself killed."

"Bet not."

"You're on."

"I know him," Beam said. "He's on his way here. Pour him a cup of coffee. I know he'll want one."

"You don't mind," Ella said, "I'll wait till I know it's necessary."

And she did. Da Vinci was safely up on the sidewalk before she brought another cup from the nearby counter and poured.

"Mine?" da Vinci asked, pointing to the steaming cup, when he'd pushed inside the diner and slid into the booth to sit across from Beam. There were perspiration stains beneath the armpits of his otherwise pristine white shirt. It was going to be a hot summer.

"Yours. And on me."

Da Vinci flashed his handsome grin and shook hands with Beam. "It's good to see you again, Cap."

"No longer a captain," Beam said.

"Hard not to think of you that way."

"The waitress and I had a bet about whether you'd make it across the street."

"Ah! And you had faith in me."

"I knew you," Beam said. "And by the way, I still think of you as Deputy Chief da Vinci."

"Good."

Da Vinci skipped cream but dumped three heaping table-spoons of sugar into the cup. Still living dangerously.

"Had breakfast?" Beam asked.

"Naw. Never eat it. My stomach doesn't like it. What I came here for's to talk."

"My stomach doesn't like that," Beam said.

Da Vinci sampled his coffee and smiled. He was hand-some enough to be an actor, dark wavy hair, slightly turned up nose, strong chin and clear gray eyes. Young Tony Curtis, Beam thought.

Da Vinci was in fact the youngest deputy chief ever in the NYPD. He was clever and shamelessly ambitious, but at least he was up front about it. Despite his sometimes brash and manipulating manner, Beam liked him. Da Vinci had proven himself incorruptible and dedicated, two virtues Beam admired. It was also rumored that eight years ago da Vinci, as a young motorcycle cop, planted a "throw down" gun after pursuing and shooting to death a Mafia enforcer without giving him a chance to surrender. The thug had deliberately run down and killed an assistant DA's six-year-old daughter. A review board had, without winking, cleared da Vinci of any wrongdoing. That was fine with Beam.

"Better talk before you run out of coffee," Beam said.

"Doesn't matter. The waitress will top off my cup."

"Not if she thinks I want you to leave."

"Don't kid yourself, Beam. Women love me, with or without coffee. I give her the word and she might chase you away."

"Doesn't a deputy chief have more important things to do than yak with an old retiree in a diner?"

"That's for damn sure. Which means the old retiree oughta be wondering what it's all about."

"Give my friend some more coffee," Beam said, as Ella passed close by the booth with her pot.

Da Vinci sat silently and watched as his cup was topped off. He didn't seem at all out of breath from playing dodge with the traffic. Must still be in pretty good shape.

"Two words," da Vinci said, when Ella had left. "Serial killer."

"Not my favorite words."

"But nobody was ever better at getting inside their sick minds. Especially the vigilante types who think they're righting some terrible wrong."

Beam knew what da Vinci was talking about. Four years ago Beam had hunted down and nailed Reverend Death, the city's last vigilante serial killer, who had been murdering porn shop owners whose establishments the city seemed unable to shut down.

"We got one who might be cut from that same sanctimonious cloth," da Vinci said. Two days ago a woman named Lois Banner was shot and killed in her fabric warehouse. Two weeks before that a tax attorney named B. Eder was whacked."

"What's the *B* stand for?"

"Nothing. Like with Harry S. Truman."

"Nobody ever called Truman '*S.*'"

"Doesn't matter. Two weeks before B. Eder, an exercise equipment salesman named Harry Meyers was murdered." Da Vinci sipped coffee and looked at Beam. "All of the victims were shot."

"With the same gun?"

"No doubt about it. A serial killer. The media hasn't tumbled to it yet."

"They will soon. The NYPD does nothing better than leak information."

"So it won't be long before they leak the letter *J.*"

"Is it something like Truman's *S* and the victim's *B*?"

"No, we think it stands for something. At the scene of each murder was a capital letter *J.* Lois Banner's employees discovered her body under some kind of fabric, and a red cloth *J* had been cut out and placed on the corpse."

"All the *J*s cut from red cloth?"

"No. But they're all red. The attorney had red marking pen on his forehead. The exercise salesman had a red *J* torn out of a magazine ad tucked in his breast pocket."

"But you don't know what the *J*s stand for?"

"We're not sure. But Eder was Jewish. Meyers wasn't, but his name could have suggested in the mind of the killer that he might have been. Same way Banner, though her real name was Banion."

"Anti-Semitism. Nasty."

"If that's what's going on. Some kinda religious or political nut." Da Vinci stared at his coffee cup, as if he didn't like its contents, then placed the cup on its saucer and stared across the table at Beam. "I don't really give a frig about the why of it, Beam. I just want the bastard stopped."

"Why not give this knotty problem to a working homicide detective instead of one who's happily retired?"

"You're not happily retired. And you happen to be the best at this kind of investigation. And I'm gonna be honest with you. You break this case, as I know you will, and I'll get credit for putting you on the scent. I could make chief."

"Being nakedly ambitious becomes you."

"I also think you're a certain kind of cop, Beam."

"The kind you are?"

"Yeah, only much more so. What I think of your kind of cop is that they're Old Testament cops. Now and again, they play God. You got a reputation for bending the rules, even the law, in the interest of seeing justice done. And as you're already retired and more or less don't give a shit, you'll bend whatever you have to in order to nail this letter *J* scumbag."

Beam had to smile. "I'm more used to being called a dinosaur than God."

Da Vinci shrugged. "God is a dinosaur."

Beam thought he better not ask what da Vinci meant by that. Didn't want lightning to strike the booth.

"You do this thing, Beam, and you'll be on a work-for-hire basis, have a captain's status, and all the resources of the NYPD at your disposal. And I'll assign you a team of detectives."

Da Vinci bolted down the rest of his coffee, making another sour face, then stood up from the booth.

"This where you ask me to think about it?" Beam said.

"Naw. You know I know that you know."

"That I'll do it," Beam said.

Da Vinci smiled. "I'll have Legal draw up a contract."

"Nothing in writing," Beam said.

"That's not the way it works."

"That's the way I work."

Da Vinci's grin widened and he shook his head. "Okay. Dinosaurs never had anything in writing."

"I'll work this case my way, out of my apartment."

"Why?"

Beam shrugged. "I'm retired. But I do want access by computer to NYPD data bases."

"Easy enough. But you're gonna need those investigators."

"A couple of good ones," Beam said. "And some added uniform help if and when I need it."

"You mean you're not gonna wrestle this guy to the ground yourself?"

"Let me think on that one," Beam said.

"Okay, we'll meet again and I can give you more details."

Da Vinci grinned, saluted, then turned and strode from the diner. Beam watched him cross the street the other way, toward his illegally parked car. There wasn't much traffic just then. Da Vinci seemed to wish there were some.

"What was that all about?" Ella asked, standing by the booth and clearing away dishes.

"Extinction," Beam said.

* * *

Beam's bedside phone that night was insistent, piercing his sleep with its shrill summons, not letting him sink back each time he rose toward the real world.

He reached out in the darkness, noticing that the luminous hands of his wristwatch had edged past midnight, and found the receiver. He drew it to him and mumbled hello. Terrible taste in his mouth.

"Cassie, bro," said the voice on the other end of the line. "Just thought I'd call and tell you about this dream I had."

"I wasn't dreaming," Beam said, annoyed, "which is rare for me."

"It was about you."

"Great." He wasn't in the mood for one of Cassie's hazy prognostications.

"I think it was about you, anyway. Had to do with biblical figures. In a place with tall stone columns, like a temple. I could make out faces. One of them was yours. The dream was about betrayal."

Beam waited, exhausted. "That's it?"

"It was vague. Piecemeal. Like most of my dreams. But you were in it. You and someone close to you—I'm not sure who, or if it was a man or woman."

"Tall stone columns. Maybe Julius Caesar. Brutus is gonna stab me in the back. Kinda thing happens to me all the time."

"You weren't Julius Caesar, bro. Biblical, but not Roman."

"And I'm gonna be betrayed by someone close to me? Like Jesus?"

"No. You were Judas."

"Terrific."

"Hey, you know how dreams are, all mixed up. Probably means nothing."

"Thanks for calling."

"No problem."

Try getting back to sleep after that.

5

New York had been leaden-skied, cold, and gloomy all week, and the man who entered the Waldemeyer Hotel looked like a product of the weather.

He was medium height, wearing a dark raincoat spotted from the cool drizzle that had just begun outside. Ignoring the bellhop's half-hearted attempt to relieve him of the single small suitcase he was carrying, he paused just inside the revolving glass doors, glanced around, then trudged across the lobby toward the desk.

A whiff of mold made everything seem damp. Though small, the Waldemeyer had once been one of New York's better hotels. It had been in decline for years. People wanted to stay closer to the theater district now, or to upscale shopping or Central Park. Fewer wanted to stay in Tribeca, in a fading small hotel that had once housed celebrities who wanted to visit town incognito. Tribeca was becoming more desirable, but not for the Waldemeyer. The rehabbing and construction in the area would soon catch up with demand, and the struggling hotel would fall even further victim to commerce and skyrocketing real estate prices. The ancient, ten-story Waldemeyer was in too valuable a location to be saved. It would doubtless be razed to make room for something that would generate higher taxes.

Grayer and almost as old as the Waldemeyer, Franklin, behind the desk, watched the man approach, sizing him up. An average looking guy, but there was something about him that drew and held the eye. He hadn't bothered to unbutton his raincoat, and he seemed oblivious of the faded red carpet, oak paneling that needed waxing, potted palms that had seen better days, marble surfaces that were stained and cracked. His face was composed, his eyes unblinking and sad. He was here, in the Waldemeyer, but his mind seemed to be somewhere else.

It occurred to Franklin that more and more of the hotel's guests wore distracted looks. Sad was the word that persisted in Franklin's mind, as the man did a slight dip and put down his suitcase out of sight on the other side of the desk.

"I've got a reservation," he said. "Justice."

Franklin gave him a smile and checked on the computer. "Yes sir, we've got you down for one night." Something in the man's eyes kind of spooked Franklin, so what he heard next was no surprise.

"I'm not carrying credit cards, but I can pay cash."

"Cash is still good here, sir." Franklin couldn't help glancing across the lobby, out to the street, thinking maybe there was a woman lurking out there who would soon enter the hotel and nonchalantly make her way upstairs. Justice had the earmarks of a guy on a guilty pleasure trip with the baby sitter or his wife's best friend. Or maybe it would be a guy. The world had changed since Franklin started as a car parker at the Waldemeyer thirty-five years ago.

"It'll be in advance," the man said, pulling an untidy wad of bills from his pocket and peeling off the exact amount of the room rate.

"Best way, sir." Franklin had him sign a registration card.

"Room five-oh-six," he said, forgetting the man's name and glancing at the card as he handed over a key, "Mr. Justice."

"There should be a package for me," Justice said.

Franklin checked beneath the desk, and sure enough there was a small box wrapped in plain brown paper, hand addressed to the hotel in care of a Mr. I. Justice.

"Came in today's delivery," Franklin said, and handed over the package, which was heavy for its size. He saw that it was marked book rate. Guy might be a writer. They stayed at the Waldemeyer sometimes.

Justice thanked Franklin, tucked the package under an arm, then hoisted his suitcase and walked toward the elevators. A cheap vinyl suitcase, Franklin figured, and the way Justice was carrying it, moving so balanced, it couldn't be very heavy.

Okay, Franklin thought, whatever the guy's game, it was fine with him. Whatever was making Justice edgy in a deadpan sort of way, it was none of Franklin's business. In fact, it didn't really interest him. Didn't interest him much what might be in the package, either—could be pornography, or not a book at all but a vibrator, or one of those blow-up dolls. No matter. In Franklin's job, you learned to submerge your curiosity.

As soon as Justice had stepped into an elevator, and the tarnished brass arrow above its sliding door started its hesitant journey toward the numeral five, Franklin turned his attention back to the newspaper he'd been reading.

More shit in the Middle East. Always.

After a while he forgot about watching for a woman entering the lobby and going straight to the stairs or elevators.

After a while, he pretty much forgot about Justice.

The guest in the raincoat had decided on traveling under the name Justice because it seemed apropos, though "Vengeance" might have done as well.

He laid the half-packed suitcase on one side of the queen-sized bed, then removed his coat and his sport jacket and stretched out on his back on the other side.

But he couldn't relax.

Suddenly unable to lie still, he sat up on the edge of the mattress and reached for the phone directories in the nightstand drawer. It took him only a few minutes to find what he was looking for in the Queens directory. Davison's Dent and Paint, an auto body shop on Filmont Avenue.

He sat with the directory spread open on his lap, staring at the phone number. He could call the repair shop now and probably talk to Elvis Davison, who owned and operated the dent removal and paint business. Who a year ago had sexually molested and murdered Justice's four-year-old son, Will. Davison, who, acquitted despite overwhelming evidence, had walked smiling from the courtroom. Who'd returned to his family and business and life as usual after an unpleasant but brief interval, while Justice and his wife April walked from the courtroom into hell.

Elvis Davison, who was right now, since it wasn't quite closing time, probably concerned mostly with pounding out dents and matching paint colors. Davison, the child molester and murderer, free because the police had searched his apartment with a faulty warrant.

Davison, who had killed what was bright and pure in a dismal, cruel world.

Davison, the man Justice was here to kill.

After the trial, Justice and April had thought the tragedy might somehow make them closer. Couples who shared grief at least shared something. Perhaps they might lessen each other's burden of pain.

They'd instead discovered that grief was a thing you could almost reach out and touch and feel grow, if it weren't for your terror. Even though two people rather than one desperately wanted it to leave, it didn't go away any sooner. Instead it loomed larger, feeding off the agony of two rather than one. It did drive Justice closer to April. It drove April further and further away.

Justice's wife, the murdered Will's mother, lived now more on antidepressants than food. When she wasn't taking pills, she drank. When she wasn't drinking, she was downing pills. Two psychologists and a psychiatrist had been unable to make her grief bearable. Unable to sleep, she roamed the house at night, and she roamed Justice's dreams.

He slid the phone closer to him and punched out the code for an outside line. Then he called, but not the number of Davison's Dent and Paint. He called his home.

April picked up on the third ring and said hello. He could tell from the slow slide of her voice that she was heavily medicated.

At first he said nothing, then simply, "It's me."

"Why aren't you home?" She sounded disinterested, everything obscured by her fog of medication.

"I told you I had a business trip. I'm in Cincinnati."

"Cinciwhat?"

"—Nati. In Ohio."

"That's right, a business trip. I forgot."

"You okay?"

"What's okay? Who the hell's okay?"

"April, have you had supper?"

"Not suppertime," she slurred.

She was right, he realized. He was an hour ahead of her in New York. She was in their apartment in St. Louis.

"I'll eat somethin' later," she said, obviously not meaning it. She'd have a drink later, or take a pill. Or take too many pills, as she had more than once.

He thought of telling her where he really was, what he was going to do. She would approve, he was sure. At least she wouldn't disapprove. She was beyond caring, beyond hoping. He wasn't. Not quite yet. She could pull out of her pain and grief, as he could. Someday. Possibly. It might help them to know that Davison was dead, that he'd paid for what he'd done to their child.

But would she recover from her grief without Justice— her husband?

"You still there?" she asked.

"Always," he said.

She didn't answer. He could hear her breathing into the receiver, maybe sobbing. He wanted to be there to comfort her. Should be there.

"April?"

"Yeah?"

"Promise me something."

"Why not?"

"Make yourself a pizza for supper. We've still got some in the freezer. Put one in the microwave. Will you do that? Eat something instead of . . . Will you put in a pizza?"

"Oh, sure."

Yeah.

"Whatever we do," she said, "we can't bring back Will. It won't *un*happen."

Why did she say that? Can she somehow know where I am? What I'm intending to do?

Her voice, heavy with medication, came over the phone. "Like the prosecutor said, there's no way to unring a—"

"I know what he said!" Justice interrupted.

"The bastard was right."

"The bastard was," he said after a while.

"I'll put in the pizza," she said, and hung up.

Justice replaced the receiver, stood, and went to the dresser, where he'd placed the package he'd picked up at the desk. He peeled off the brown wrapping paper, opened the box inside, and from wadded newspaper used as packing material he withdrew a .45 caliber revolver. It had belonged to his father, who'd been an avid hunter, and who had bought the gun at a hardware store in Iowa, before permits were required and firearm sales recorded. Justice didn't hunt. After his father's funeral six years ago, he'd left the shotguns and rifles to be disposed of by the estate, and for some reason had kept the revolver.

Now it seemed like fate, helping him to make up his mind to come here and kill Davison, so he'd mailed the gun, loaded, ahead to the hotel, telling the postal clerk it was a book, hoping it would make it through security. It had. Now it was in Justice's right hand. Now he could point it at Davison and squeeze the trigger.

Now it didn't seem so much like fate that he should be here. The simple fact was, while he might not care what happened to him after shooting Davison, he still very much cared what happened to April.

And he knew what would happen to her.

He placed the gun back in the box and stuffed the newspaper around it before closing it and using what was left of the brown paper to rewrap it. Then he put his raincoat back on.

Outside the hotel, he found a trash receptacle and dropped the box into it. Since rain was falling heavier, the sidewalks were less crowded than when he'd arrived, and he was sure no one had seen him. And even if they had, he was simply a man disposing of some trash, perhaps the small box that had contained a gift he'd received, or simply something he'd purchased down the street and that was now in his pocket.

Feeling a relief that surprised him, he saw that his hand, that had so recently held the gun and was now wet from the rain, was trembling. He crossed the street to a diner and had a tuna melt and french fries for supper.

The next day, he checked out of the hotel and returned home to St. Louis to watch his wife continue her ever deepening spiral into depression.

6

Bev Baker was forty-eight but looked thirty-eight. She stood nude before the steam-fogged full-length mirror in the bathroom and watched the exhaust fan clear the reflecting glass to reveal a woman still wet from her shower. Her breasts were lower than a girl's but still full, and what Lenny Rodman, in that way of his, had just called bouncily bountiful. Her long legs were still curvaceous, her hips and thighs slim, her abdominal muscles taut from daily workouts. Her auburn hair was wet and tousled. Her smile was wicked.

Aging nicely and not a bad package, she decided, and one Lenny certainly appreciated, which is what made her appreciate Lenny.

Lenny was in the bedroom on the other side of the door. Bev figured he was still lying back in bed, smoking a cigarette, even though it was a no-smoking room. Lenny didn't like obeying rules, which was part of what had led him to the midtown Manhattan hotel room for sex in the afternoon with Bev. The other part was Bev.

It wasn't the first time they'd enjoyed an afternoon assig-

nation. Three months ago Lenny, thirtyish and handsome as
a soap actor, had come into Light and Shade Lamp and
Fixture Emporium and asked to see the buyer, who was Bev,
who was also head of the sales department. She'd had an argument with her husband, Floyd, that morning, and was still
smarting from some of the insults he'd sent her way. In retro-
spect, she knew that was what had made her vulnerable to
Lenny, who could spot a broken wing like a hawk.

Floyd was almost fifteen years older than she was, and his
increasing absence from home and her bed, his constant whin-
ing about his heart condition, were symptoms of what Bev
knew was a failing marriage. It was why she insisted on continuing working, though Floyd was retired now, with a decent
pension and Social Security, and they could get by comfortably if she stayed home. But Bev didn't want to stay home,
cooped up in a one-bedroom New York apartment—not with
Floyd. They both understood that was the reason she continued
to work. Floyd had become disinterested except for when he
wanted to be verbally abusive. But he wasn't dumb. He knew as
well as she did that their marriage was headed for a train wreck.

Bev could be insulted only so much, and ignored only so
long. What happened with Lenny seemed so natural, she
wasn't sure if he'd seduced her or vice versa. She'd listened
carefully to what he had to sell that day, in her office right off
the display floor. He was handsome in a smooth way, with
lazy eyes and an easy smile, and full of bullshit from the
get-go. It seemed he'd made a deal to purchase hundreds of
obsolete fire extinguishers, which he'd had made into "nov-
elty lamps." He was now trying to market them discount because of increasing demand and decreasing storage space,
due to a rental dispute.

Bev could be a charmer herself. Never bullshit a bullshitter,
she told Lenny, but in a nice way, not using those exact terms.
He got the message, and with his sexy grin admitted he was
stuck with a warehouse full of fire extinguisher lamps and
needed to sell them cheap or he'd have to give them away.

"Have you always been in the lamp business?" Bev asked.

He settled back in his chair and crossed his legs real cool-like, the drape of his gray slacks saying they were well tailored. Lenny knew how to dress the part. Something Bev liked in a man. Some of the stuff Floyd had been wearing lately looked like it came from a retirement home fire sale. And if she told him about it . . . well, never mind.

"Before this I was in the coffee table business," Lenny said. "I made this deal with a cemetery near the Hudson that was being moved. They weren't going to reuse the damaged marble slabs that rested on top of the coffins."

"Why on top?" Bev asked.

"That's to keep the coffins from rising to the surface when the water table gets higher during the wet seasons. Good, beautifully veined marble. So I bought them, ground and polished them, and put some fancy legs on them for coffee tables."

"How'd they sell?"

Lenny smiled. "What would look good on them would be those fire extinguisher lamps."

"The ones I'm going to buy?"

"You serious?"

She glanced at her watch. "You want to go to lunch, we'll talk price."

His hooded gaze traveled over her body, lingering on her breasts. She was sitting behind her desk, and she knew he was wondering what her legs were like. He wouldn't be disappointed. *Legs, I got.*

"I'm picking up the check," she said. "Company business."

"Then I can't say no."

"I know the feeling," she said.

That fateful lunch had been three months ago. The fire extinguisher lamps still sat in the showroom, unsold. If anyone else had been head of sales, they would have been priced down and out or junked.

"You die in there?" Lenny called, from the other side of the bathroom door.

"No, out there, with you."

Bev didn't bother with a towel as she opened the door and went into the bedroom to let Lenny see what she'd been looking at in the mirror. She got the result she expected.

"C'mon back to bed with me," Lenny said, snuffing out his cigarette in a room service glass he was using as an ashtray.

"It's almost two o'clock, Lenny. I've gotta get back to work." Bev moved toward where her clothes were folded on the chair near the bed. Too near. His hand closed gently but firmly around her wrist. She pretended to struggle but didn't really pull away. "I just took a shower, Lenny."

"You took one, you can take another in no time. You're already undressed for one."

She laughed. "I don't think a shower's what you have in mind."

He pulled her toward the bed. "Mind reader, you."

At twenty after three they left the hotel together. It was one of the big chain hotels, the lobby was crowded, and it was midday in Midtown. No one paid much attention to them.

Out on the sidewalk, after the dim room with its closed drapes, it seemed unusually bright and sunny. While the doorman was standing with one foot on the curb and the other in the street, trying to hail a cab, Lenny kissed Bev on the cheek. "Gonna ride back to work?"

"No. It's a nice day. I'll walk." A cab veered toward the curb and the doorman stepped out of the way, then opened a back door.

"I thought you were late."

"I am. I'm also sales manager."

Lenny grinned as he lowered himself into the cab, simultaneously tipping the doorman. "Must be nice being boss," he said.

"It sure is some days, around noon."

She watched the cab pull out into heavy Midtown traffic. Lenny lifted a hand, so a wave went with his grin.

Bev began striding along Fifty-first Street, a tall, attractive woman, well dressed but with her hair, fluffy from the hotel drier, mussed by the breeze as soon as she crossed the intersection. She drew appreciative stares, even a honking horn that might have been for her. She might be married to Floyd, but she wasn't a fossil like Floyd. Not yet by a long shot.

Halfway back to Light and Shade, she got the feeling she'd been getting too often lately. It was a prickly uneasiness, like a slight pressure on the back of her neck, and sometimes when she turned around it was as if there might have been someone there if she'd only turned faster. Once, when Floyd was out of town with his golf buddies, and she'd come home from work exhausted and kicked off her high heels and fallen into a leather armchair, she could have sworn the cushion was still warm, as if somebody had been sitting there and left only minutes before she arrived. It was creepy, and she had an idea what it might be.

Floyd suspected something and had hired someone to investigate her. A detective.

Bev almost grinned at the thought. If Floyd wanted a divorce, he could have one. They had an iron-clad pre-nup, so there was no logical reason he should hire a detective other than to satisfy his curiosity. No monetary reason, anyway.

Of course, there were other reasons and other kinds of satisfaction. Floyd didn't get it up very often these days, but he still had an active mind.

Hell with it.

Bev crossed the intersection against the light, taking her time even though traffic up the block was bearing down on her. If anyone honked she'd give him the finger. That was the kind of mood she was in.

But no one honked.

7

Even though he'd taken a pill, Beam didn't sleep well.

His dreams were a jumble of images. Lani leaping without hesitation from a balcony high in the night, da Vinci smiling at him and holding out a badge, swastikas, pale stone buildings with columns, people lying dead with red letter *J*s on them, da Vinci again, still smiling, pointing at something on the sidewalk, something that had fallen.

He awoke after a dream of waking and finding someone had taped red ribbons all over the room. Ribbons in bows, in loops, simple strands of ribbons.

When he sat up and switched on the lamp, he almost expected to find them.

But it was his bedroom as usual. Their bedroom. He remained sitting up in bed, wondering what dark specter of the mind had plucked his wife from the balcony. Witnesses had said she'd put down her drink at the charity function cocktail party she was attending, then walked calmly and resolutely out to the twenty-fourth-floor balcony. She'd been alone out there, and apparently she'd simply let herself fall over the railing into space. The railing had been higher than her waist, so it couldn't have been an accident. Something like that, something so . . . monstrous and profound, what had moved her to do it?

Beam had been sure things had changed between them, but was that true? Had it been more that things had finally come to a head? Had it been the death of their only child, so long ago? Had all the years of doubt and wondering that any cop's wife endures finally taken its toll?

The fact was, when people committed suicide without leaving notes, they left agonizing, unfinished business behind. Questions that would never be answered. Guilt that might never be firmly affixed. Their survivors had to learn to live with uncertainty, and get used to being haunted.

Uncertainty was something that had always bothered Beam. Lani had known that about him, yet she'd chosen her anonymous and eternally mysterious death.

Or might it have been an accident? Somehow . . .

He knew he wouldn't be able to get back to sleep. Light brighter than the lamp was beginning to show around the edges of the closed drapes. Glancing at the clock radio by the bed, he saw that it was quarter to five. Morning enough, he thought, swiveling on the mattress so he could stand up. He caught a glimpse of himself in the mirror, still lean and strong but with undeniably more fat collecting around his waist, musculature still there, but now that of a fifty-three-year-old man. There on his right thigh was the scar where the bullet had been removed, a pink-edged pucker about two inches in diameter. He ran a hand through his mussed gray hair and looked away from his image. *Getting older fast.*

Well, at the same speed as everyone else. Some solace.

Usually he showered and shaved, then walked to the diner where he had breakfast. The walk was part of his physical therapy to regain at least some of the wind and endurance he'd lost to his injury. He experienced normal stiffness and joint aches at first when he climbed out of bed—he hadn't been easy on his body over the years—but nothing connected to the gunshot wound actually hurt anymore. And he knew he should be pleased; his endurance had improved considerably. But it was only months since Lani's death, and to Beam she was still beside him, still in his dreams and his life awake. He knew she would be for some time to come.

Retirement might have been a good thing if Lani were still alive, but now retirement was like a disease. That was one of the main reasons Beam had accepted da Vinci's offer to take over the serial killer investigation. Beam desperately, *desperately*, needed something to do, needed to be useful, needed something to displace his grief, at least temporarily.

When he was showered and dressed, he looked out the window and saw that a light rain was falling.

Instead of walking, he decided to elevator to the building's garage and take his car.

The rain had stopped by the time Beam finished breakfast. He was paying at the register, when he glanced out the Chow Down's window and saw da Vinci standing with his arms crossed and staring at Beam's parked, gracefully aging black Lincoln.

"How come you drive a behemoth like that in New York?" he asked, when Beam emerged from the diner.

"I drove it this morning to keep the rain off me."

"You managed to find a space right in front. I half expected to see an NYPD placard on your dash."

The air smelled fresh from the recent rain. The street and sidewalks were still wet. A few of the cars and cabs swishing past still had their wipers working.

"I figured you'd come around again," Beam said.

"Of course. Want to go back in for some coffee and conversation?"

"Let's drive and talk," Beam said, and stepped off the curb to get behind the wheel of the Lincoln. He and Lani had bought the car new ten years ago, with money she'd inherited from her wealthy family in Philadelphia. Lani had been rich with her own money when Beam married her. That bothered a few of his fellow cops, but the circles her wealth allowed them to travel in had been useful to Beam. He could talk to people otherwise inaccessible without a warrant.

As soon as he pressed the button on his key fob, the doors unlocked and da Vinci was climbing into the other side of the car. Beam settled into the plush leather seat and fastened his safety belt. As he started the engine, the car began to chime, and he noticed da Vinci wasn't using his seat belt.

"You forgot to buckle up," Beam said.

"Never do."

"Shame on you." Beam pulled out into traffic. The warning chime finally stopped. "We making progress?"

"Computer guy will be at your place tomorrow afternoon. He'll make sure you're plugged into the department network," da Vinci said.

"He didn't say 'plugged into' I bet."

"I didn't talk to him personally, but you're probably right. They think in terms of ports. The thing is, we don't want there to be any glitches."

"We don't," Beam agreed, swooping the big car around a corner to beat a traffic signal.

"This old boat's amazing," da Vinci said. "You don't even feel the potholes."

"It's like new. We didn't drive it much. I mostly drive it now to keep up the battery."

"Anybody ever mistake it for a limo?"

"Sometimes. When I tailed or staked out suspects, I wore my eight-point uniform cap and they thought I was a chauffeur."

"I never asked you," da Vinci said, "do you happen to be Jewish?"

"My father was. My mother wasn't."

"Was your father of the faith? Wear a yarmulke, all that stuff?"

"He went to synagogue for a while, then he drifted away

from religion. I asked him why once, and he said he'd lost his faith in Korea, and it took him a while to realize it."

"He was a cop, wasn't he?"

"Sergeant, Brooklyn South."

"Didn't he—"

"He ate his gun," Beam said. *Didn't leave a note.*

"Shit deal. Korea? The job?"

Beam knew what da Vinci was thinking, that people close to Beam tended to commit suicide, as if he carried an infection.

"That when you joined the department?" da Vinci asked.

"You know all these answers," Beam said.

Da Vinci smiled. "I guess I know most of them."

"I dropped out of college and joined the Army, became an MP, then applied at the NYPD when I got out."

"Because of your father?"

"I'm not sure. It seemed the natural thing to do."

They drove without talking for a while, the big sedan seeming to levitate over bumps.

"I'm giving you Corey and Looper," da Vinci said.

"What's a Corey and Looper?"

"Detectives, and good ones. Looper's early fifties, gone far as he's gonna get in the department and knows it. He's a good cop, but he's burned his bridges behind him, far as promotion's concerned."

"What's his flaw?"

"Too honest. Nobody trusts him."

"And Corey?"

"Nell Corey. Coming off a nasty divorce. Hubby used to bounce her around. Woman's got her faults."

"She's a foul-up?"

"More a don't-give-a-damn type. Mind of her own. But only sometimes. Then there was that business with the knife?"

"She stabbed her husband?"

"Not that I know of. A security tape outside a convenience store in Queens caught her beating up a suspect with unnecessary force. What the tape didn't catch was that during the struggle the suspect pulled a knife, which was later picked up by one of several onlookers."

"It's happened before," Beam said.

"Probably happened that time, too. But since the knife never turned up, it doesn't officially exist. At base, Corey's a solid cop, and a talented detective. Trouble is, without that knife, she's permanently screwed. And knows it."

Beam neatly swerved left and squeezed the Lincoln through a space between a van being unloaded and some trash piled at the curb. It was tight enough to make da Vinci wince.

"Andy," Beam said, "is there somebody in the department who doesn't want this endeavor to succeed?"

"Sure, lots of them. Because of me. They think I'm coming on too fast. You know how it is, I'm a young Turk. Look like and act like one, anyway."

The last part was true, Beam thought. Though in his forties, da Vinci might pass for thirty. He was too young looking, good looking, and blatantly ambitious to be universally popular. It was as if a small-market TV anchorman had somehow gotten hold of an NYPD shield and was aggravating the piss out of his betters.

"Am I gonna get cooperation when I need it?" Beam asked.

"Oh, yeah. I got the push to make it happen. I've got allies, Beam."

"You must."

"You don't wanna ask who they are. I will say this: they see you pretty much the way I do."

"Which is how?"

"They know your reputation as a bad ass who can't be bought or bumped off course, that *nothing* will stop you."

Not even the law.

Beam remained stone faced as he shot through an intersection barely in time to avoid colliding with a cab that had run the light. Da Vinci flicked a glance out the windshield but showed no emotion. There was a toughness and drive beneath all that smooth banter, cologne, and ass kissing. In truth da Vinci was one of the main reasons why Beam had agreed to take on this assignment. Not only did he rather like the brash, manipulating bureaucracy climber, but he still owed da Vinci for being willing to put his ass on the line seven years ago in Florida. The way it worked out, he hadn't had to, but it was the willingness that counted. A lot of life was favors owed, favors paid.

A bus hissed and paused in the traffic coming the other way, a billboard-size sign featuring a Mets star pitcher in full windup on its side. Beam hadn't been to a ballgame in years. Looking at the sign, he felt his stomach tighten, a pressure behind his eyes. *Florida* . . .

The bus roared and moved on.

"Send me Corey and Looper," Beam said, "along with copies of the murder books on the three killings. I don't want to waste any more time."

"I'll arrange it," da Vinci promised.

They'd circled the neighborhood and were approaching the diner. There was a break in traffic, so Beam took the big Lincoln up to sixty and abruptly spun and locked the steering wheel and brakes simultaneously. The car rocked and skidded to face the opposite direction, then sedately double parked so da Vinci had room to open the door and get out on the passenger's side.

Throughout the maneuver, da Vinci had braced himself with his feet against the floor and his hands on the dashboard.

"Somebody oughta call a cop!" an elderly woman pushing a wire basket cart full of grocery bags yelled over at them from across the street.

"Somebody oughta tell her people call us things all the time," da Vinci said, completely unrattled.

Bev overslept. That was okay; her and Floyd's West Side apartment was only a few blocks from Light and Shade.

Even if she couldn't hail a cab, she could walk it in no time. Breakfast she could make up later, maybe send one of the employees out to pick up Danish and coffee at Starbucks.

She was alone in the king-size bed. Floyd was still in Connecticut on a golfing outing with his buddies. Bev had slept so soundly the covers were only slightly disheveled. She slid both bare legs out from beneath the sheets, then stood up and removed her nightgown, which had somehow bunched its way up around her hips.

In the morning light she examined herself briefly in the mirror. She and Lenny had played rough and she had a few bruises, but nothing Floyd was likely to notice. Not that she cared that much if he did notice; she just didn't want a scene. She was tired of scenes.

The apartment was large by New York standards, furnished with a hodgepodge of furniture and decorated without much style. Except for the lamps. Lamps they had, and good ones. And ceiling fixtures. Bev was proud of the massive crystal chandelier dangling above the dining room table that they hardly used.

She padded nude into the bathroom and took a quick shower, managing not to get her hair wet. She'd dropped by Tina's Beauty Shop and had it done yesterday afternoon after taking off work early. After the wreck Lenny had made of it.

The shower had fully awakened and refreshed her. Yesterday had been a hell of a day, and today she'd better concentrate on work. She knew her business and got the job done, but her attendance record was abysmal. No one from the company had said anything to her, but they might. You could push them only so far. Besides, her job was the one thing in her life she liked. Her job and Lenny.

Bev was fully dressed in her new mauve outfit, seated before a teakwood vanity she'd bought in Mexico and had shipped home, leaning forward and applying just the right shade of lipstick to complement the dress—red, but with the slightest touch of purple—when her heart almost stopped.

She managed to start breathing again and turned to gaze back and up at the figure she'd glimpsed in the mirror. At the hand that held the object that was indeed what she'd first feared. A gun, a small one with some kind of bulky cylinder fitted to its barrel. She'd seen enough TV and movies to know what the object was—a silencer.

Seated on the padded vanity chair, staring up at the intruder, she was aware of her insides melting away, heard a slight trickle, felt a warmth, and knew she'd wet herself. She began to cry, tightening her grip on the chair back with one hand, on the lipstick tube with the other. She begged with her eyes. It was unmistakable, her silent pleading. He did nothing, drawing out the moment. She managed to speak, but her voice caught in her throat and the words came out as a sob.

"What'd I do? For God's sake, what'd I do?"

Then she knew. *Floyd! Floyd must have hired someone to pretend—*

The silencer spat and a bullet *thunked!* through the thinly padded wooden chair back and clipped her spine before smashing through her heart.

The way she dropped and her chin hit the edge of the vanity on the way down, it would have hurt like hell if she'd been alive.

The killer gently pried the lipstick tube from her dead right hand.

8

Beam silently watched the NYPD computer genius da Vinci had sent.

He looked about fourteen and seemed to know everything. It was obvious from the way the kid—actually in his twenties—had handled Beam's five-year-old notebook computer that he knew his stuff. Soon there'd been talk of RAM and giga and mega and pixels while Beam looked on in gray mystification as his computer was upgraded and brought into the present world of tech.

By the time the kid was finished, Beam was patched into the NYPD system and had gone wireless so he could use his computer anywhere in the apartment, or—the computer kid had assured him—various places outdoors, or in certain restaurants and entire areas that were set up for wireless.

"That's damned amazing," Beam told the kid.

"I don't understand why anybody'd ever use a type-writer," the kid replied. "Or how they ever got that complicated machinery to work at all."

"I don't type, either," Beam said.

With a pitying shake of his head, the kid gathered up his

bits and bytes and left. Beam watched him out and down the hall to the elevator.

Beam closed the door and looked at his watch. Almost four o'clock, when da Vinci had told him by phone that detectives Nell Corey and Fred Looper were coming to the apartment to meet Beam to get acquainted and have a strategy session.

Moving out to the middle of the living room, Beam looked around. It was a pleasant room with a hardwood floor, throw rugs, a comfortable overstuffed cream-colored sofa, a tan leather armchair, smaller, rose-colored upholstered chair, green marble-top coffee table, some oil paintings on the walls, bought more as decorative pieces than as art. Lani's touch. For that reason, maybe, Beam didn't want to settle down in the room with Corey and Looper.

He used both hands to lift the rose-colored chair—Lani's chair—and carried it down the hall and into his den.

The chair didn't go with the den's decor, but that was okay. Three of the den's walls were oak paneled, the fourth painted off-white and covered with framed photos or department commendations. A baseball trophy sat on a table with some other framed photos. Some of the photos were of Beam and Lani, sometimes with their son Bud, who'd played All American minor league ball in the Cincinnati farm system in Florida and been struck in the head by a pitched ball. He'd died the next day of massive subdural hematoma. Only nineteen years old, and his death had killed something in Beam and Lani, in their marriage. The pitcher who'd hit Bud, a retread player named Rowdy Logan, had also aimed for his head on the previous pitch, so it was a deliberate beaning. Logan had been demoted from the majors for similar headhunting, and this time charges were brought against him. Charges that were going nowhere. Murder on the baseball diamond was a difficult thing to prove.

That was something Beam owed da Vinci. Da Vinci said he had connections in Florida and could help to actually prosecute Logan. As it turned out, that wasn't necessary, as Logan was found a few days later full of barbiturates that had given him the courage to shoot himself in the head. The bullet had struck with the same effect that the ninety-mile-per-hour fastball had on young Bud Beam.

Justice, delivered not by the legal system but by the killer himself. Beam's faith in the system he served had been severely shaken. As had his faith in everything.

Seven years ago. First Bud gone, now Lani.

Beam placed the rose-colored chair at an angle facing his large mahogany desk. There was already a brown leather chair in a similar position at the other corner of the desk. Beam would have the two detectives sit in the chairs, facing him across the desk. They would talk. They would plan. They would take the first step in finding and stopping the maniac who was killing people in his city.

At first, hesitant to take on the case, Beam now was beginning to feel the old eagerness take hold. He was on the job again. He was a cop. He was a hunter set to stalk his prey.

Exactly what da Vinci wants.

"You home, Bev?" Floyd Baker called.

He stood just inside the apartment door, his golf club bag slung over his shoulder. Something about the place wasn't right. It wasn't just that it was twilight and the apartment was dim without a lamp on. Or that his wife Bev wasn't yet home from work. She often stayed late on the job.

It was something else making him uneasy.

It was the stillness.

Floyd Baker had been an Army Ranger in action with UN troops in Kosovo. He and another ranger had once come across a house with its front door hanging open, and investigated to find an entire family of five slaughtered inside.

The feeling, the stillness, the subtle scent he was experiencing now made Floyd think of that house, that day, what they'd found. *Jesus, what we found!* His heart clawed its way into his throat.

"Bev!" There was a note of desperation in his call.

He leaned his golf bag against the wall by the door and moved farther into the dim apartment, then switched on a floor lamp.

Still no sign of Bev, but there was her purse on the table near the door. He hadn't noticed it before. It meant she was probably home.

The sight of the purse filled Floyd with even more dread.

He made his way across the living room, down the hall, past the kitchen to the bedroom, and looked inside. He noticed immediately that, though the bedroom was dim, the bathroom light was on.

When he went to investigate he found his wife in the alcove between the bedroom and bathroom, where she had her mirrored vanity set up. She was sprawled on the floor, and at first he thought she'd possibly fainted. Prayed she'd fainted.

Then he saw the red letter *J* smeared on the vanity mirror with what looked like lipstick.

Nothing Bev would do.

He moved nearer, looked closer.

"Ah, Jesus! Bev!"

He leaned toward her to touch her, then realized he shouldn't. And his right foot was planted in blood. His wife's blood. He did lean forward slightly so he could see beneath her right arm that was raised so her hand was near her head. He could see darkness on her breasts, see the exit wound.

See into her!

Floyd stood up and staggered backward. He swallowed the bile that rose bitter in his throat, then wiped his sleeve across his mouth and chin. He realized his mouth was slightly open, his lips rigid. He licked his lips with a dry tongue and pressed them together.

Turning away from the horror, he made himself trudge back into the living room.

Must be a dream. Has to be . . .

He stood at the phone and slowly lifted the receiver.

The voice of the 911 operator from the outside world made it all real.

It wasn't a dream; it was real. It would stay real.

The buzzer sounded. Beam went to the intercom and called down for confirmation that Corey and Looper were downstairs, then buzzed the two detectives up.

Not knowing quite what to expect, he stood with the apartment door open so they wouldn't have to knock.

A short, slender woman wearing dark slacks and a rumpled gray blazer emerged from the elevator. She had dishwater blond hair combed back in a convenient rather than flattering hairdo. Her eyes were dark, her chin defiant. Her shoes were black and sensible, with low heels, and she walked with a slouchy kind of determination, as if with a certain slow eagerness she might be heading toward a fight.

She was followed by a tall, sallow man in a suit that didn't fit his angular body. Beam thought it was a fairly expensive and well cut suit—it was the body that was the problem. Looper was built like a mannequin assembled from spare parts. He looked a little like an awkward Fred Astaire, or maybe that was because Beam knew his first name was Fred.

They did the introductions. Both detectives looked Beam in the eye as they shook hands. He noticed that Nell Corey's hair had dark roots. Looper was holding the murder files tucked beneath his left arm, thick brown folders, each fastened with cord over a metal clasp.

"Want something to drink while we talk this over?" Beam asked.

Looper declined.

"Bottled water, if you've got some," Nell said.

Beam excused himself, got her a bottle of Zephyr Hills from the refrigerator, then returned to usher the two detectives into his den. One of them smelled strongly of peppermint—Looper, Beam thought. He wondered if the man was covering for a drinking habit.

When they were seated, he saw how Looper, in the leather chair, glanced around to see if there were any ashtrays. Then he noticed the detective's yellow-stained index and middle finger on his right hand. Not a drinker, a smoker. And if Beam was any judge, badly in need of a cigarette.

Beam, who enjoyed an occasional cigar, started to open a drawer to get out an ashtray, then paused. "Mind if we smoke?" he asked Nell.

"Tell you the truth, I do."

Looper shot her an annoyed look.

Beam smiled and pushed the drawer closed. "Okay. We can save it for outside."

Looper leaned forward and laid the murder files on Beam's desk. "Your copies," he said. "We each have ours."

"You've studied them?" Beam asked.

Both detectives nodded.

"And?"

Nell spoke up first. "Same gun, same letter *J*."

"An anti-Semite killer?" Beam asked.

She surprised him. "I don't think so. It's too much of a stretch."

"I agree," Beam said.

She swallowed, nervous, as if about to take a plunge. "I was up late working my computer," she said, "checking into various databases. There's something stronger linking these victims, something that can't be coincidental. At one time or other, they all served as jury forepersons in the city of New York." She glanced at her partner. "I already filled Loop in on this."

"There doesn't seem to be any other common denominator among the victims," Looper said, coming to her defense. "Different parts of town, different occupations, different circles of friends and acquaintances, different sexes."

"There's something the juries they presided over had in common, though," Nell said. "In all the cases, the defendants were almost certainly guilty but got off."

"Were any of the prosecutors or defense attorneys the same?" Beam asked.

"Nope," said the blond woman with dark roots, now with a certain confidence. Beam was taking her seriously, buying into her theory.

"Anybody Jewish in all this?"

"Not so's you'd notice," Nell said. "What you'd expect in New York, a royal mix. And some of the trials were years apart. The most recent was last year, the one longest ago happened . . ." She leaned forward to pick up one of the files and refresh her memory.

"Six years ago," Looper said.

Nell sat back and took a swig of Zephyr Hills.

Beam leaned back in his chair and laced his fingers behind his head. "So whaddya think?"

"Serial killer, obviously," Looper said. His hand went to his shirt pocket, then quickly withdrew. Smoker's arm. "He doesn't seem to have a hard-on about the defendants, though; it's the juries that set him off, especially the jury forepersons."

"The jurors are the ones responsible for the defendants going free," Nell pointed out. "And if you had to hang it on any one of them, it would be the foreperson."

"So it's the system our killer doesn't like," Beam said.

"You could say that," Nell told him, "unless there's a common thread we haven't discovered yet."

"What about a common thread connecting the freed defendants?"

Nell and Looper glanced at each other.

Looper emitted a volley of hoarse coughs, raising a yellowed finger to implore Nell and Beam to be patient. Each time he coughed, the scent of peppermint wafted across the desk.

Finally he stopped coughing, cleared his throat twice, and swallowed phlegm before trusting himself to speak. "The defendants: One wife killer; one gang member making his bones by shooting three people in a diner; one kidnapper-torturer who did a twenty-year-old NYU student."

"Female student?" Beam asked.

"Yeah. The victims are three females and two males. Females are the dead wife and dead student. And of the three victims in the diner shooting, one was a woman."

"So by way of defendants who got lucky and walked," Nell said, "we got a jealous husband killed his wife, a gang-banger trying to impress his peers, and a sex maniac who liked college girls. Not much in common among defendants."

"Except that they went free," Beam said.

"Not for the same reasons. The gangbanger had a phony alibi that couldn't be disproved, the sex maniac hadn't been sufficiently informed of his rights, the wife killer simply got off even though the evidence against him was overwhelming."

"So they all *should* have been convicted," Beam said.

Nell took another swig of bottled water. "Read the court transcripts and you'd have to say that."

Beam unlaced his fingers and sat forward, causing his swivel chair to squeak. "What we're gonna do," he said, "is pore over these murder files again—I haven't had a chance to read them yet. Then we'll revisit the crime scenes, talk again to witnesses, go over ground already covered, see if anybody's memory can be jogged." He looked at Looper. "You say it was the same gun used in all three murders, so what do we know about it?"

"Thirty-two caliber. That's about all they can tell about it so far, with just the slugs to work from. No ejected cartridges were found."

"So he cleans up after himself. What about the possibility of him being a professional?"

"Maybe," Nell said, "except for his choice of victims and that red letter *J* he always leaves at the scene. That's not very professional."

"*J* for *justice*?" Beam asked.

"That's what we both figure. Or maybe *Judgment.*"

"Most logical thing," Looper said. "We figure it's *Justice.*"

"Our guy hates the justice system," Nell said, "but loves justice too much."

"Yet he doesn't hit the obviously guilty defendants who got off," Looper said, playing with his shirt pocket again in search of phantom cigarettes.

"That would be the prosecutor's job," Beam said. "Retry them if possible. Nail them on a different charge. Don't let them walk."

"But they do walk. The cops, the prosecutors have moved on and are too busy worrying about the present and future to be able to reconstruct and repair the past. Crimes keep getting committed. Other assholes are moving through the system."

"It's the system that he hates," Nell reiterated.

"So?" Beam stared at her, smiling, waiting.

She began to squirm, then suddenly sat still and gave him a level, appraising look, appreciative of the fact that he'd gotten there ahead of her. "He's trying to change the system."

Nobody spoke for a few moments.

"Could be," Looper said finally. "Could very well be."

"We can't assume it yet," Beam said, "but—"

He was interrupted by the phone chirping on his desk.

When he lifted the receiver and identified himself, he was surprised to hear da Vinci's voice:

"Corey and Looper there yet?"

"Yeah. We were just discussing things."

"You've got another one to discuss, Beam. Upper West Side, not far from your place. The letter *J* is written in lipstick on a mirror this time."

"Shot to death?"

"That's the preliminary.

"Got an address?"

Da Vinci gave it to him, in an area of apartment buildings and townhouses about five blocks away. "Uniforms have got the scene frozen. CSI unit is on the way."

"So are we," Beam said.

9

"The victim, Beverly Baker, worked as sales manager at Light and Shade Lamp Emporium on the West Side, not far from her apartment on West Eighty-ninth Street. Hubby Floyd returned from a golf outing with his buddies about five thirty—forty-five minutes ago—and found her dead body."

So said the uniform guarding the Bakers' apartment door, a young guy named Mansolaro. He had an improbably long chin, would always need a shave, and looked vaguely familiar to Beam. Looper seemed to know him.

"That hubby in the living room?" Beam asked, noticing beyond Mansolaro, in the apartment, a smallish, plump man in plaid slacks and a white golf shirt, seated slumped forward on a maroon sofa.

Mansolaro nodded. "One Floyd Baker."

As if there were a two Floyd Baker, Beam thought. He'd been away from cop talk long enough that some of it struck his ear wrong.

"Floyd was gone all day," Mansolaro continued, "out on the links with his fellow hackers."

"With his alibi," Looper said.

"And not a bad one," Mansolaro said. "He came back, found his wife's body, and called 911. Me and my partner Al caught the complaint and got here almost immediately after the call."

"You go right in?" Beam asked.

"Floyd Baker met us at the door, looked like he'd been crying, and led us to the body. Swore he never touched anything, just like he learned on *Law and Order.* I saw the big letter *J* on the mirror near where the victim must have been sitting, so me and Al froze the scene immediately and called it in as an obvious homicide."

"Where's Al?"

"Downstairs manning the lobby. He told the doorman to stick around, we were gonna talk to him."

"Excellent," Beam said, and Mansolaro sort of puffed up. It impressed Nell, what some of her fellow cops obviously thought of Beam. Maybe this odd-ends investigative team would work out. Maybe something positive would come of it beyond capturing or killing whoever was murdering these people.

"Crime scene unit's inside, along with an assistant ME," Mansolaro said. He glanced at his watch, anticipating Beam's next question. "They been here about twenty minutes."

"Get the neighbors' statements," Beam said to Nell and Looper. "Somebody probably heard the shot, even if they thought the noise was something else. We might be able to determine time of death."

He patted Mansolaro gently on the shoulder in passing, a gesture of approval, as he moved into the apartment.

Another uniform was standing near a fake fireplace—the kind that had a red light in it that was supposed to look like glowing embers—with his arms crossed. Beam nodded to him, and nodded to the distraught man on the sofa. The man on the sofa didn't nod back, merely gave Beam a distracted, agonized glance.

Beam went into the bedroom, where most of the action

was taking place. Crime Scene personnel wearing plastic gloves were standing, bending, reaching, down on hands and knees, searching. They were examining, luminoling, placing minute objects in evidence bags as if they'd found rare and extravagantly expensive gems. And what they found could *be* extravagantly expensive. It could be life and death.

Beam noticed a high-heeled shoe, a woman's foot and ankle, and beyond it the open door to a tiled bathroom. When he moved forward a few careful steps, he saw that the victim's body was in an alcove between bedroom and bathroom.

There was a lot of blood on the carpeted floor. Beverly Baker was sprawled awkwardly on her back, and had apparently fallen from a small upholstered chair that had tipped over. The chair was covered with a cheery floral design that was a mismatch with the ugliness of the event, except for the hole in the material that was stretched across the curved back support.

A little man in a black suit was bending over the dead woman with an intensity that suggested he was making love to her. As soon as Beam saw his balding head, with the thatch of gray hair that stood almost straight up in front, he knew who he was. Assistant ME Irv Minskoff, one of the best at his job.

Minskoff sensed his presence and glanced up. His face had a fiercely gnarled look to it, softened somewhat by thick lensed glasses. "Ah, Beam. I heard you were on this one."

"Good to see you, Irv. What've we got so far?"

"Dead since morning, done sometime between seven and ten o'clock. Shot once. Bullet went in the right side of her back, probably angled in and caught her heart. I'll know a lot more when I get in there."

"Looks like a thirty-two caliber."

"Be my guess, too. Can't say for sure, since the slug they dug out of the wall's so misshapen. But before it went through the victim, the bullet went through the back of the chair, and the hole in the underlying wood looks like it was made by a thirty-two."

"Slug must have been misshapen before it hit her," Beam said, looking at the vast and ugly exit wound. He could imagine the kinetic force of the distorted bullet slamming through the woman's slender body. His gaze took in her exposed shapely legs, slender waist, strong features. She must have been vital and attractive before the bullet. He noticed her mouth was smeared red in an obscenely crooked grin despite her horrified eyes. The smear wasn't quite blood red. It was the same color as the letter *J* scrawled on the mirror of a small vanity cluttered with cosmetics.

"Nice legs," Minskoff said.

"Gonna mention that in the post-mortem?"

Minskoff gave him a gnarly look.

"Shot while putting on her lipstick?" Beam asked.

"Or surprised by whoever she must have seen in the mirror. Caused her hand to jerk, then she was shot."

And almost immediately, Beam thought. It appeared that Beverly Baker hadn't had time to stand up.

Minskoff must have known what he was thinking. "Entry wound is about where it would have been if she'd been sitting all the way down on her little tush in her little chair, so maybe she did die while applying her lipstick. Could be she was so shocked by seeing her assailant in the mirror, her body gave a little start, then she was paralyzed."

"As if maybe she saw somebody she trusted standing there with a gun pointed at her," Beam said. "Somebody like hubby."

"Hubby's always enticing in these kinds of cases," Minskoff agreed. "But then there's that letter lipsticked on the mirror. My guess is the lipstick tube won't reveal the fingerprints of the victim—or the killer, though I'm sure the killer wrote with it. This woman died instantly, but even if she had time to leave or begin a dying message, if it meant anything incriminating, the killer would have simply made it illegible or removed it from the mirror."

"So Detective Minskoff is sure it was the killer who wrote on the mirror."

Minskoff grinned, embarrassed. "Just trying to help, not play detective. But, yes, I am sure."

"Always the possibility of a copycat killer."

"I'll keep an eye out for hairballs," Minskoff said.

Beam figured it was time to stop speculating and talk to Floyd Baker.

10

While Nell and Looper made the rounds of neighbors and doorman, Beam sat on the living room sofa with Floyd.

At both ends of the sofa were low tables supporting ornate brass lamps with long, cream-colored fringed shades. While the rest of the furniture was unremarkable, the lamps looked like collectors' pieces.

"I know it's an awkward time to talk," Beam said to the slumping new widower who looked about to sob, "but the sooner we know some things, the better."

"I want the bastard who shot her caught," Floyd said. "I want you to give him to me."

"If only the law allowed."

Floyd gave Beam a slightly surprised look.

"Any idea who the bastard might be?" Beam asked.

"None whatsoever. We had the perfect marriage. I know that sounds corny, but you can ask anybody who knows—knew—either one of us. Everybody liked Bev. She was outgoing."

"I don't mean to be indelicate," Beam said, "but keep in mind these questions are standard ones that have to be asked.

And answered. Is it possible your wife was seeing someone else?"

Floyd raised his head and looked over at Beam with a combination of grief and rage. "There was none of that shit in our marriage. We were happy together."

"Did you spend a lot of time together?"

"Not as much as we would've liked, and that was my fault. Bev was a kind of golf widow. I mean, I retired and got interested in the game. Golf's like a drug to some people. I could cut my wrists for it now, but I spent too much time on golf courses and not enough with my wife."

"And you were golfing today?"

"Yesterday and today. Spent the night in Connecticut, in a motel near the Rolling Acres course. It's a terrific course, got these big lakes and tricky greens. You gotta watch for the water and sand on damn near every hole. Three of my golfing buddies were with me."

"All the time?"

"I don't need a damned alibi!"

"I'm sorry, but you do."

"Then I have one—them. We were on the course together, had our meals together."

"Separate motel rooms?"

"No. There were only three rooms available. I doubled up with Alan Jones. Glad I did now."

"This Jones would know if you slipped out at night?"

"And what? Drove or took a train into the city, killed my wife, then returned to bed at the Drowsy Ace motel?"

"Doesn't sound likely," Beam admitted with a smile.

"Way I snore, anyway, ask Alan Jones and he'll tell you I was there all night. Poor bastard probably didn't get a straight hour's sleep. Upset his game, too."

"At this point you're not really a suspect," Beam assured Floyd.

"Bullshit. Husband's always a suspect. Should be."

"Would be," Beam said honestly. "But I'm sure your alibi

will check out. And lucky for you, the times don't work out. Of course, you could always have hired someone to kill your wife." No smile with the words.

Floyd practically levitated with indignation, then he looked almost amused, so improbable was the notion. "Not my style, or my desire."

Beam believed him.

"I wouldn't even know how to get in touch with a hit man."

"Or hit woman. I asked about whether your wife might be having an extramarital affair. What about you, Mr. Baker?"

Floyd glared at him with a kind of hopeless rage. Beam, so nice for a while, had turned on him. "You're a cop I could learn to dislike."

"That'd be okay, if it would help me find your wife's killer."

Floyd's features danced with his inner conflict.

Bull's eye, Beam thought. "Time for the curtain to drop and all secrets to be revealed," he told Floyd.

"Poetic."

"Because it rings true. This is a homicide investigation, Mr. Baker. It's all going to be known in the end. That's my solemn pledge to you."

"Pledge?"

"Uh-huh."

Floyd let out a long breath. "A couple of times when we were on golf outings, there were some women. Two of them. We paid for it."

"Happen this time in Connecticut?"

"No! Hasn't happened for over a year. And none if meant anything, not to us, or to the women. Hell they were just . . ."

"Prostitutes."

"I guess you'd have to say that. We showed our gratitude with gifts or cash."

Beam, during his years in the NYPD, had become something of a human polygraph. He felt sure Floyd was telling the truth. He also was sure the man had loved and trusted his wife and was genuinely grief stricken. Add what would also doubtless turn out to be a tight alibi, and Floyd was pretty much out of the picture as a suspect.

"It appears your wife was dressing up when she was killed, putting on her lipstick, in fact."

"She had a responsible job. She couldn't go to work like some of these women do these days, no makeup, stringy hair. She was in sales, for Chrissakes!"

"Just one more question, Mr. Baker. Did your wife ever serve on a jury in New York?"

Floyd leaned far back as if to stare at the ceiling, but his eyes were closed.

"She sure did."

"The Adele Janson case," Beam told Nell and Looper, when they were seated in his Lincoln parked at the curb in front of a fire hydrant. He had his NYPD placard on the dash so no one would bother the car.

"About four years ago?" Nell said. "The woman who poisoned her husband with antifreeze?"

"Right," Beam said. "She got off because her expert witness convinced the jury there was a natural disease that showed the same symptoms as ethylene glycol poisoning."

"I remember now. The defendant had motive and opportunity, not to mention what was left in a gallon jug of antifreeze, but her lawyer maintained hubby just sickened and died."

"And two years later she was convicted of poisoning her daughter," Looper said. "After the trial, she confessed to both murders."

Beam lowered the power window on his side to cool down the big black car; the gleaming dark finish was starting to soak up more sun than it reflected. "Beverly Baker was foreperson on the first jury, the one that turned Janson loose after she'd done her husband."

"Which made the late Beverly a prime target for our guy," Nell said. "This one was his work without a doubt."

"So what have we got besides mutual certainty?" Beam said. "I mean, beyond the red letter *J*?"

Nell and Looper tried. They'd gotten nothing of significance from the Bakers' neighbors, or from the doorman. It wasn't the kind of building where security was tight, so it was no shock that a killer might have come and gone without being noticed. No one heard anything remotely like a gunshot, so a silencer was probably used to shoot Beverly Baker. No one had a word other than kind to say about the deceased: She was outgoing and friendly and a generous tipper. She gave neighbors discounts on lamps. The way she obviously enjoyed life, it was a shame—it was a crime—she was dead. It seemed the only notable thing about her was that she'd been foreperson on the Janson murder trial jury, though it had been long enough ago that none of the neighbors had mentioned it.

"What did they say about her husband?" Beam asked.

"Floyd?" Nell said. "He's just a guy. Got in an argument with the doorman about a month ago, when one of his golf clubs was missing after he'd left his bag in the lobby. But he found the club later and apologized. Other'n that, no problems with anybody in the building. But it was Bev, as they called her, who everyone really liked."

"And who somebody didn't," Beam said.

"We got the thirty-two caliber slug to help tie it in with the other murders," Looper said.

"If it is a thirty-two," Nell said.

"And no shell casing," Looper pointed out. "This shooter walked away from a clean crime scene—typical of our guy."

Beam stared out the windshield of the parked car for a moment, then said, "Looper, you talk to Floyd again, then drive the unmarked up to Connecticut and check out his alibi. Nell and I are gonna go to the lamp emporium or whatever, where Bev worked, and talk to her boss and coworkers."

Looper opened the Lincoln's right rear door and started to get out, then paused. "Anything I should know about Floyd?"

"He didn't murder his wife, but he's got a guilty conscience. You work him right, he'll tell you the truth."

Beam watched Looper walk away; he appeared to be absently feeling his pockets for cigarettes.

"He'll suck a cigarette before he goes back upstairs to talk with hubby," Nell said. "It's that way every day. He needs it to calm down."

"That's his business," Beam said, "as long as it doesn't kill him before something else does."

Or before this investigation's finished, Nell thought.

When the jittery Looper was out of sight, Beam opened the driver's side door and started to climb out from behind the steering wheel. The intensifying morning heat lowered itself like a weight onto his back.

"I thought we were going to the lamp emporium," Nell said.

Beam leaned farther down and looked across the car at her. "We are, but let's walk. That was how Beverly Baker usually went back and forth to work. Let's follow in her footsteps. Maybe, sometime or other, they took her past her killer."

After leaving Beverly Baker's building, Justice had strolled a few sunny blocks, then taken the Eighty-sixth Street entrance into the park. It was such a beautiful morning that people he didn't know nodded to him and said hello. He returned their friendliness with his own. The latex gloves he'd used to be sure he wouldn't leave fingerprints in Beverly Baker's apartment were neatly folded in his pocket, turned inside out just in case some of her blood might have gotten on them. Blood particles could be so minute the human eye wouldn't spot them, but a police laboratory might. He knew the police had tricks that were almost magic.

As he strolled along sun-dappled paths, he replayed the Beverly Baker murder in detail—*mind like a DVD*.

Good looking bitch, lots of leg, perched with her ass spread and her back arched the way women do when they're concentrating hard while sitting before a mirror and putting on lipstick. She'd seen him in the mirror, got the message, didn't want to believe it, been momentarily paralyzed by the realization of her impending death—as they all were. That moment was ice. It froze them.

Those crystallized seconds belonged to him. In that brief and vulnerable time, they comprehended the reason for their death at his hands. Surely they read the papers, watched television news, overheard conversations. The NYPD had of course long ago informed the media. The entire city knew why people were being killed, former jury forepersons whose hands were bloody, who'd been instruments of injustice. He assured himself that in their final, frozen moments of life, they understood that his was the final judgment and the hand of justice, righting the wrongs they'd perpetrated, the imbalance and pain they'd been so instrumental in causing. Always he read the cataclysmic knowledge in their eyes, but so there would be no misunderstanding, as the light died in them, he whispered the religion and the word that carried his victims to the other side: *Justice.*

They died knowing. He lived knowing. He was setting the universe right. On a day like this one, with the sun laughing through the high leaves and the birds telling tales, his mission was especially satisfying.

He still had work to do, but it was good work. It was *right* work. Not nearly finished.

"Bev," Mary Jean Maltz, assistant sales director at the Light and Shade Lamp Emporium, said to Beam and Nell.

She was a stolid woman with dark bangs, a white blouse, brown slacks, and extremely wide thighs and hips. "Everyone called her Bev, not Beverly." Mary Jean brushed a knuckle across a reddened eye; she'd obviously been crying. "She was a Bev."

Beam was prepared to believe it. He looked around at the sea of lamps and shades and dangling chandeliers. Almost everything was lighted. For display purposes, or in honor of Bev Baker.

"Everyone loved her," Mary Jane said.

Don Webb, an elderly, mustached man whose family had long ago founded the lamp emporium, and who was Bev Baker's supervisor, finished the phone call he'd been making when Beam and Nell arrived, and walked over to join the conversation. His long, lined face wore a somber expression, but his blue eyes were dry behind thick rimless glasses.

"It's a blow to all of us here," he said, "what happened to Bev." He fixed Beam with a steady, magnified gaze. "She was the best sales manager we ever had."

"Do you mean that literally?" Beam asked. "Forget for a moment about speaking well of the dead. We're here for the truth. We're trying to find out who murdered Beverly Baker."

"*One* of the best," Webb amended.

"An absolute peach to work for," Mary Jane added.

Webb looked at her. "Why don't you check that floor lamp shipment that came in yesterday, make sure none of the shades are bent."

She nodded, slightly embarrassed. With her hips cocked sideways so as not to bump anything, she hurried away in a little side shuffle through what seemed like acres of glowing table lamps, floor lamps, and light fixtures on chains. Beam thought the electric bill here must be phenomenal, but then, they were selling illumination.

Isn't that what we came for—illumination?

"I had no complaints about Bev," Webb said, when Mary Jane was out of earshot. "She really was damned likable, and she worked hard and got the job done. Sales increased every quarter in the four years she was sales manager." He gave Beam the same sincere expression he'd worn earlier. "It didn't hurt that she was attractive and knew how to treat customers, how to talk to them."

"How to bullshit them?"

"How to sell."

"Can you think of any enemies she might have had?"

"No. But then I wasn't privy to her personal life." Was there a note of regret in Don Webb's voice?

"Might she have been in debt?"

"I wouldn't know, but I doubt it. She was well paid and knew how to manage money. Smart woman. Take-charge type."

The sort who'd volunteer to be jury foreperson.

"Any changes in her behavior over the last six months or so?" Beam asked.

Here Webb hesitated. "A few months ago she began taking longer lunches, coming in late sometimes in the morning. I never complained. I mean, if she came in late, she tended to stay late."

"What were her reasons for being late?"

"Oh, one thing or another. Tell you the truth, I never asked her very often. I wasn't kidding when I said she was a valuable employee. You don't mess with people like that in this business or any other; you want to keep them."

A flurry of motion made them look to the side. A gray-haired woman who was apparently Webb's assistant stood just outside the door to his partitioned office, holding up a telephone receiver and motioning frantically to him with her free hand that he had a call.

"Must be important," Webb said.

"Go ahead and take it," Beam said. "Thanks for your help."

Webb nodded gratefully and hurried away.

As Beam and Nell moved toward the exit, Mary Jane,

who'd returned to the sales floor, tacked sideways through the sea of lamps toward them on a collision course. Beam liked that. She seemed to have more to say, and she hadn't wanted to say it in front of Webb.

Mary Jane was smiling as she intercepted them near a bamboo and wicker floor lamp that was part of the tropical line. "Was Mr. Webb any help to you?"

"Maybe," Nell said. "Time will tell."

"He mentioned that Bev was coming into work late the past several months," Beam said.

Nell decided to keep silent and let Beam handle this, watch him work and maybe learn something from the master.

Mary Jane didn't look surprised. "He say why?"

Beam shook his head no. "Said he didn't know why."

Mary Jane suddenly seemed hesitant, now that it was time to release the words she'd stored up for them. Nell had seen it before when people with something to say to the police also had something to lose: *Word jam.*

Beam reached out and gently touched the tropical lamp's glowing shade, as if caressing a work of art. "Beautiful piece of merchandise. Makes you think of the South Seas."

Mary Jane definitely didn't want to talk about lamps. "Did he mention Lenny Rodman?"

"No . . ." Beam seemed thoughtful. Nothing rough or threatening about him now; merely a benign if looming gentleman who happened to be a cop. He seemed just as interested in the lamp as in what Mary Jane had to say.

"Lenny's why," Mary Jane said in a near whisper.

"Who exactly is this Lenny?" Beam asked with a smile. Definitely on Mary Jane's side. "Other than Bev's reason for tardiness?"

"Fire extinguisher lamps."

"Ah!" As if Beam understood.

"Lenny wholesaled us grosses of the damned things and they haven't retailed for beans. Lamps made outta obsolete fire extinguishers. Can't give the things away. Lenny sold himself to Bev, though. He fed her a line and she took the bait along with the hook. Smart as she was, she couldn't control her heart, love being so blind. She thought she was using the guy, sneaking around with him, and he was using her."

"An old story but sad one," Beam said. Nell thought he might actually cluck his tongue. "Did her husband suspect?"

Mary Jane looked incredulous. "Are you kidding? That guy's so wrapped up in fairways and doglegs it's all he thinks about. He was ignoring Bev for a little white ball. That was part of the problem."

"Really? Did she confide this to you?" Beam leaning closer, intent with interest, making Mary Jane his coconspirator.

"Some of it, but not all. Didn't have to. Women can tell. You understand, I'm sure."

Beam did. He also understood that Mary Jane didn't like Lenny Rodman, or maybe liked him *too* much, or she wouldn't have made it a point to mention him.

Now she wanted to do more than merely mention. She was ripe.

Time to dish.

He aimed his kindly smile at Nell like a flashlight, then at Mary Jane. "So tell us about Lenny."

11

Beam and Nell were in Beam's Lincoln, on their way to Lenny Rodman's Brooklyn address, when Beam's cell phone vibrated in his pocket. Taking a corner with one hand on the steering wheel, he yanked out the phone, flipped up its lid, and glanced at the Caller ID. Looper.

"Beam, Loop."

They were breaking the law, using a hand-held phone in New York while driving, Nell thought. Felt good.

"I talked to Floyd Baker, then called two of his golf buddies," said Looper's voice on the phone, almost breaking up as the big Lincoln rounded the corner and rocked as it straightened out. Looks like his alibi is tight. In fact, he already seems to be getting over his grief at his wife's death. Once it was obvious he wasn't going to be a suspect, all he wanted to talk about was this eagle he made on the tenth hole. Popped the ball out of a sand trap, it bounced once and hit the pole, then dropped straight down into the cup. Says he shot two on a par four. You believe that?"

"I dunno," Beam said. "What do his golfing partners say?"

"I checked it out with them and they swear to it, too."

"Think you could get them to say it under oath?"

Nell was looking intently at Beam.

"Hah!" Looper said. "You a golfer?"

"Used to be. Get them to swear to it and we can believe it."

Beam broke the connection.

"What?" Nell said anxiously. "We catch a break?"

"Ever actually seen anyone use their sand wedge to clear a trap and eagle the hole?" Beam asked.

She stared at him, confused.

"Floyd Baker's not a suspect," Beam said. "His golfing buddies confirm his alibi."

"Golf," Nell said. "It's one of the few male diseases that don't infect women."

Beam thought about telling her that was because women couldn't drive the ball as far, then decided he'd better not. Besides, plenty of women liked golf.

The phone, still in his hand, vibrated again, startling him. He flipped the lid back up and said hello without taking his eyes off the traffic ahead.

"Da Vinci here, Beam. Get anything interesting on the Beverly Baker murder?"

"I just talked to Looper. Looks like Floyd Baker's in the clear. He was out on the links when his wife was killed."

"Links?"

"You don't golf?"

"Never."

"Floyd was playing golf in Connecticut at the time of his wife's murder, shot an eagle out of a sand trap, has witnesses."

Da Vinci was unmoved. "Ballistics says it was a steel-jacketed thirty-two caliber slug that killed Beverly Baker. It matches the others. Same gun that killed the previous victims."

"Killer doesn't seem to care that we're making a match," Beam said. He braked to a stop for a traffic jam as they neared the bridge. "I mean, he's careful enough he recovers his shell casings, and wears gloves so he doesn't leave prints, but using the same gun and knowing we can match it doesn't seem to concern him."

"Maybe he's only got one gun," da Vinci said.

"Could be that simple." Traffic was moving again, but barely; Beam's foot came off the brake and the long-hooded Lincoln crept forward like a dark, chrome-festooned predator. "But a guy like this, you'd think he'd know where to get his hands on more than one gun."

"He doesn't worry about getting caught," da Vinci said.

"None of them think they'll get caught. At least not until they're ready. They're all smarter than we are. I think he wants to be sure we match the murders, just in case one of the letter *J*s blows away or isn't noticed. The steel-jacketed slugs penetrate flesh and bone better and don't get too misshapen, so the lab can pick up marks on them and ID the gun. The bullets are part of his signature. He wants to be sure he gets the notch when each of his victims dies."

"Not just for us, though," da Vinci said. "The media's starting to heat up on this, just as I feared. They're zeroing in on the anti-Semitism angle."

"They're wrong," Beam said, and told da Vinci about Nell's theory, along with the fact that Beverly Baker once served as a jury foreperson.

"Impressive," da Vinci said. "You buy it?"

"Hard not to. The media'll like this angle, too."

"You bet they will. That's just what the asshole wants, I'm sure. You know how they are, in it for the notoriety, even if their name's not in the papers."

"Not in the papers at first, anyway," Beam said.

Traffic was moving rapidly now. He had to concentrate to steer one-handed while talking on the phone. Breaking the law. Well, not technically, since he was the law. "I think we oughta let everything hang out," Beam said. "Hold a press conference. Give the media what we know. The NYPD leaks anyway. You might as well get credit for being up front with the press, get them on our side. And the publicity might shake something loose."

"I was thinking we could hold back on the matching bullets, give them another red letter *J* to chew on."

"They'll find out about the bullets anyway, if they don't already know. And they're dead certain to stumble across the jury foreperson tie-in."

"You're right." Da Vinci obviously didn't like admitting it. "You're also beginning to break up."

"Nell and I are in my car, approaching the bridge; that's probably screwing up the signal. You want me with you for the press conference?"

"I don't know. We'll cross that bridge when we come to it, too."

The connection was broken. Beam flipped the phone closed and slid it back in his pocket so he could drive with both hands on the wheel.

"Pressure getting to da Vinci?" Nell asked.

"He's still got his sense of humor," Beam said. "So called."

12

Lenny Rodman's address belonged to a seriously rundown brick and stone building on Kloss Avenue in Brooklyn. The block was made up of almost identical buildings.

Cloning gone bad, Nell thought.

Except for a few that showed signs of being rehabbed, the buildings shared the same state of hopelessness. Small patches of grassless dirt on each side of the concrete stoops harbored only a hardy weed here and there, as well as rusted tricycles, empty soda bottles, and beer cans.

Beam parked the Lincoln two buildings down from Lenny's, placed the NYPD placard where it was visible on the dashboard, and hoped for the best. Under the casual scrutiny of half a dozen or so people sitting out on the stoops, he and Nell walked down the jaggedly sectioned, uneven sidewalk to Lenny's building.

There was a dirt-splattered red and yellow plastic car for a kid about five in the front yard, next to a leafless tree about three feet high that was surrounded by a low wire fence and supported by three pieces of twine wrapped round the spindly trunk and staked in a triangle. Nell stepped on an already shattered glass crack vial and thought the tree had about as much chance as a child born into this world on this block of Kloss Avenue. She knew that parts of Brooklyn were quite beautiful, desirable, and getting more expensive by the minute. This wasn't one of them.

No one sat on the steps of this stoop. And no one was in the small vestibule that reeked of stale urine. There were more crushed crack vials on the stained tile floor.

A faded card slipped into the slot above one of the mailboxes confirmed that Lenny was in 2D. There was an intercom that probably didn't work. Didn't matter to Beam or Nell, anyway, as they quickly climbed the wooden stairs to the second floor, located apartment 2D, and stood on either side of the door.

Beam rapped on the age-checkered door with his knuckles.

He and Nell were both surprised when a voice promptly said, "Who is it?"

Beam told himself to be careful. "Police. We'd like to talk to you, Mr. Rodman."

"Sure. Be right there." Rodman's voice exuded cheer and cooperation.

Beam knew what that meant. He motioned for Nell to go back downstairs and check around back. Rodman might at that moment be descending the fire escape, if there was one.

Nell ran down the stairs and outside, then headed for one of the narrow passageways that separated the buildings. It seemed there were more people on the sidewalks now or sitting outside their buildings, watching expectantly, as if there might be some entertainment in the offing.

Something's up, she thought, rounding the corner of the building.

Something—

The man running full tilt down the passageway slammed into her, but it was a glancing blow and he barely slowed down. She caught the reek of cheap cologne, a whiff of foul breath, and a lot of pain as the impact spun her and her shoulder bounced hard off a brick wall.

Reeling like a drunk, she almost fell, then managed to fix her gaze on a running man in tight, faded jeans and a black T-shirt. He was picking up speed, swinging his long arms wide. Not a trained runner, but he could outdistance her, Nell was sure.

Still disoriented, she tried to yell halt. Tried to yell police. But she couldn't find her breath as she staggered after the man.

Fumbling, she drew her weapon from its belt holster.

Warning shot?

What the hell was procedure?

She couldn't get her mind to work. Couldn't get her legs to work.

Tires screamed on concrete. At the corner she saw a small van skid past at an angle and bang over a mailbox. In the shadow beneath the van was a darker shadow shaped like a person tumbling, tumbling, arms and legs flailing in limited, crushing space. Nell caught a glimpse of light flesh for a moment before it was claimed again by the shadows beneath the van.

Barefoot!

He's barefoot. How he must have wanted to get away!

The van came to a rocking stop. Nothing in the shadow beneath it moved. People started to drift closer, then crowded in on the vehicle.

Nell began walking fast toward the corner. She realized she was carrying her gun at her side and slid it back into its holster, then made sure her blazer was buttoned to cover it.

"He broke out through a window and down the fire escape," a calm voice said beside her. Beam.

The nearness of him calmed her somewhat, but her heart was still pounding in her ears. "He decided to run. That van got him."

"I know, I know . . ."

They reached the corner and flashed their shields, telling people to stand back. Beam kneeled down to look under the van, then quickly stood up.

"There's a woman under there."

Nell saw that there were smears of blood on the pavement between the skid marks left by the tires and looked away. The van's driver must have been distracted by Rodman and struck the woman.

Knocked her out of her shoes.

Nell's stomach kicked and she swallowed brass.

A radio car arrived and blocked the street. Sirens whooped, and another car came in from the opposite direction, then braked and parked angled sideways. The uniforms piled out and hurried toward the van, moving swiftly, looking this way and that, sizing up the situation.

Beam identified himself and Nell to the nearest two uniforms and explained what must have happened. They all gazed up and down the street, as if Rodman might still be somewhere in sight.

The van driver was out of the vehicle now, leaning on a fender and yammering to one of the uniforms. He was a short, dark-complected man wearing gray work pants and a darker gray shirt. He looked as if he might vomit any second. He'd killed someone; one day it had been work as usual delivering packages, necessary and monotonous, the world in its revolutions, then he'd killed someone and everything was changed.

"Rodman didn't have a record, so why'd he run?" Beam asked.

Nell looked at him, rubbing her shoulder. "Because he's who we're looking for?"

Beam gave her a level, unreadable look. "You really think this guy's the killer?"

She shook her head no. "Not unless our guy establishes a romance with his victims before killing them."

Beam studied her as if wondering if she'd bumped her head as well as her shoulder on the bricks, then turned away, maybe giving her more time to recover. He spoke briefly to one of the uniforms, making sure the scene was secured, then returned to Nell. "Let's go back up to his apartment, see why he might have bolted."

"Drugs would be my bet," Nell said.

"Always the favorite," Beam said, walking beside her. "How's your shoulder?"

"Still attached."

"Wanna have it looked at?"

"Later, if it needs it."

In the corner of her vision, she might have seen Beam smile.

No one stopped them or spoke to them as they made their way to Lenny Rodman's building and up the stairs to his second floor apartment.

Beam must have realized along with Nell that Rodman had rabbitted, because the door was hanging open. Nell saw that the wooden frame was splintered around the latch from Beam kicking his way in.

They entered the apartment carefully, though they figured if anyone had been in there besides Rodman, he or she surely would have taken the opportunity to leave.

Nell said, "He must have had reason to want out of here fast."

She looked around. The place was a mess. It was an efficiency, and from where they stood just inside the door they could see all of it except into the closets and bathroom. There were heaps of clothes on the painted hardwood floor, and a sofa bed was open and unmade. Furniture had obviously been shifted around, and along one wall were stacks of large cardboard boxes.

Beam and Nell went to the apartment's two closets and made sure they concealed nothing human or dangerous. The first closet contained half a dozen dress shirts, a gray suit, and two blazers. There was a pair of black shoes on the floor, and a stack of yellowed pornographic magazines on the wooden shelf. The second closet contained nothing other than wire hangers on the rod and in a tangle on the floor, and two roaches that scurried beneath the baseboard to escape the sudden light. Nobody in the bathroom. The torn plastic shower curtain dangled from its rod on two hooks. The window near the tub was wide open. Rodman's access to the fire escape.

Beam opened the medicine cabinet. Arranged on sagging shelves were a disposable razor and aerosol can of shaving cream, toothpaste, a toothbrush, comb, deodorant, lemon-scented cologne. Nell remembered the sickening sweet scent of cologne when Rodman had shouldered her aside in his desperate flight.

"You think he lived here," she asked, "or used the place as a kind of combination office and hideout?"

"Maybe all of the above," Beam said. "Let's look into those cardboard boxes."

"If they contain drugs," Nell said, "we got us the mother lode."

Beam removed a small bone-handled folding knife from his pocket and began slicing the tape holding the boxes' flaps down. But the tape was so flimsy there was no need for the knife, and he and Nell began opening the boxes eagerly with only their hands, examining contents then pushing down the flaps and shoving the boxes aside.

They learned soon enough that the boxes contained sea shells.

"Conch shells," Beam said.

"They look like the kind of sea shell you might be able to blow like a horn," Nell said. "Or put to your ear and hear the ocean."

"They are," Beam said. "Down in Key West and other places they fry and eat what lives inside. Conch fritters."

"I've heard of them," Nell said. "I haven't spent my whole life in New York."

"There are plenty of these shells down there, but not a lot as perfect as these are. Notice they're all unbroken?"

"I did," Nell said. "What on earth was Rodman doing with sea shells?"

"He stole 'em," a voice said.

Beam and Nell turned to see a skinny African American girl about sixteen standing in the doorway. She was wearing baggy red shorts, rubber sandals, and a sleeveless white T-shirt lettered JUST VOTE. She would have been pretty if it weren't for severely crooked yellowed teeth.

"He tol' me he stole them shells," she said. "What you gonna do to him?"

"Try to catch him and find out why he stole them," Beam said.

"Oh, I know why. Lenny's kinda man like to brag on hisself. Like to play the lead role in his own movie. Need the audience. Need a leading lady. We close. He tol' me lotsa things. You know what I mean?"

Beam and Nell glanced at each other. They could imagine.

"We know," Beam said. "We don't want to hurt Lenny, but we do need to find him. You understand that?"

"Sure. I warned him more'n once. He jus' laugh the way he do."

"Where would he steal sea shells from?" Nell asked.

"Place in New Jersey buys shells and ships 'em up here from Florida, uses 'em to crush and pave things like driveways an' such for rich folks here an' down south. But the good shells that ain't broke, they set aside and sell 'em to souvenir shops and the like."

"Lenny told you this?"

"Sure. He trust me. Got his reasons."

"But now you're telling us about him," Nell said.

"Don' make me no difference now. He ain't comin' back, not ever. Ain't nobody standin' here don't know that."

"So Lenny just stole the unbroken shells," Beam said. "But why?"

"Telephones. He tol' me he's gon' make phones outta them shells—*de*signer phones, he called 'em—an' sell 'em all over the place. Make hisself some cash." The girl looked from Beam to Nell. "You know how people likes to hold them shells to their ears an' all."

"Mind telling us your name?" Beam asked.

The girl smiled with her horrible teeth. "Candy Ann."

"Last name?"

"Kane, thas' with a *K*. I lives right downstairs in 1D, me an' my kids. I knowed the kinda things goin' on up here even before Lenny tol' me. Man don't know how to keep a secret no how. Got hisself a tongue too big for his mouth."

"How old are you, Candy Ann?" Beam asked.

"Eighteen next month. Lenny was gonna give me one of them shell phones for my birthday. Promised me. I didn't pay him no mind."

"Got any idea where Lenny might have run to?" Nell asked.

"Not nothin' like an idea. Lenny the kinda man know how to hide."

Beam and Nell didn't doubt it.

"I'm going to have an officer come up here and seal this apartment," Beam said to Candy Ann. "It's going to be examined closer by the police. You'll stay out of it, won't you?"

"Sure. You got no worry over me. You wanna talk to me some more, I be right downstairs from here. I stay clean. Outta trouble with no law."

"Good." Beam smiled at her. Nell sensed that he genuinely liked the hapless young woman.

"You think it woulda worked?" Candy Ann asked as they were leaving and closing the damaged door.

"What's that?" Beam asked.

"Them *de*signer shell phones. You think people really woulda bought 'em?"

"No," Beam said.

Candy Ann smiled. "Tha's what I been thinkin'."

13

Nell sat hunched over her notebook computer at her kitchen table, scouring various data bases from around the country. Wind-driven rain peppered the window. At her right elbow was half a glass of diet root beer with ice in it. She'd gulped down the other half. Her upper lip, which she now and then unconsciously licked, was rimmed with foam from the root beer.

The tiny apartment was still warm from the heat of the day, and all the more humid from the rain. The window air conditioner in the living room had stopped working. She had a call in to a guy whose name a Manhattan South detective had given her, a repairman and sometimes actor who'd done work for some other cops and given them a break. The problem was, the guy—Terry Adams—was seemingly impossible to contact. No doubt he was enjoying his season of being much in demand, the man with a corner on cold air. The thought kind of pissed off Nell. After half a dozen calls, she'd left a curt message telling him she was about to perish and would he please call back, and soon.

On the floor next to her was a folded *New York Post*. The headline read JUSTICE KILLER JOLTS CITY. The *Times* and *Daily News* had similar headlines. Nell thought the killer would probably approve of the title the media had bestowed on him. It was probably exactly what he was seeking with his letter *J* calling cards.

She huddled closer to her glowing laptop. Though it was slightly cooler in the kitchen than the rest of the apartment, this was still painstaking work. She'd exhausted NYPD data bases, the federal National Crime Information Center bank, and was reduced to hooking into various obscure sites with no, or unofficial, affiliations with investigative agencies. These websites were mostly the work of skilled amateurs, and not all of them were reliable. But in conjunction with established data banks, they might prove useful. One didn't need to be a computer genius to do this, but one did need to be obsessive, relentless, and tireless. Right now, Nell was having difficulty with tireless.

It was almost midnight, and the summer storm blew more rain against the window and rattled the glass. Beneath the bottom of the old wooden frame, Nell saw moisture appear, build to form a small drop, then track down an ancient stain toward the baseboard. It made it about halfway before spending itself and disappearing. Another drop formed, wavered, then began its unsteady downward course. Nell watched it, hypnotized, her fingers stilled on the keyboard. Would it make it farther than the last drop?

Would it . . .

What the hell?

She was awake with a start, staring at the computer's small screen.

She realized she'd fallen asleep and her hand had slid from the keyboard into her lap.

Shoulda gone to bed a long time ago.

Nell tightened her hands into fists, threw her shoulders back, and stretched her aching spine. Her right shoulder was still sore from bumping the brick wall when Lenny Rodman brushed her aside in his flight to freedom. Though the shoulder was badly bruised and taking on a nasty purple and green coloration, she was sure it wasn't seriously injured. Nell had experienced debilitating damage and knew the difference.

The apartment was still a sauna. Perspiration was stinging the corners of her eyes. She rubbed them and looked more closely at the computer screen. The website that had been slowly loading when she fell asleep was now up all the way. *Dark Nor'easters.vis* was the name of the site, and it seemed to be made up of notable unsolved crimes committed in northeastern states.

Awake again, even feeling somewhat refreshed, Nell went through her search routine, specifying deliberate clues, single victims (in number, not marital status), shootings, stabbings, bludgeonings, strangulations, indoors, outdoors, men, women, days, nights, in vehicles, urban, suburban, exurban settings.

She was astounded when the screen flickered and came up with more than a dozen shootings, nights, indoors, deliberate clues left by killer.

She specified New York City.

No problem.

It didn't take her long to scan back year by year and find what she wanted. Four years ago a woman named Rachel Cohen had been discovered shot to death in her Village apartment. A red letter *J* had been drawn with red marking pen on her forehead.

Only two years ago a wealthy woman on the Upper East Side, Iris Selig, was discovered dead in the bathroom of her penthouse suite, also shot to death. A red *J* was scrawled with her lipstick on the mirror.

A further search of the victims list wasn't productive. It was then Nell realized that when she'd fallen asleep she'd accidentally clicked on the "Hate Crimes" section of the website.

It was assumed then, as it had been now, that the two victims were killed because they were Jewish. Nell even managed to call up some old *Village Voice* and *Times* articles decrying the rise in hate crimes and anti-Semitism in the city, after the Iris Selig murder.

Nell didn't think this changed anything. New York simply had a large Jewish population. In light of the later victims, there was still no consistent hate crime pattern. The killer seemed to be eclectic in his choices of victims.

Still, Selig and Cohen *were* Jewish names.

She bookmarked the website then returned to her more traditional data bases.

Nell was wide awake now.

The more pertinent question was . . .

She soon discovered that Selig and Cohen had served as forepersons on juries in New York criminal cases.

Hot damn!

Nell could hear her breath hissing as she worked her computer, wishing she had faster internet service.

But within half an hour she had the information she sought: both jury trials had been for charges of first degree homicide—and both defendants had gone free.

That did it—the letter *J*s in the Selig and Cohen murders really did stand for *Justice*—unless somebody came up with a more likely possibility.

Two additional victims. Jury forepersons. Trials gone sour. Consistency. Confirmation.

Nell braced herself with both palms on the table and stood up. Her body was stiff from sitting for hours, but she was so nervous she started to pace. Her blood might be half adrenaline. She was eager for action, any kind of action. She felt great. She'd never been more than merely competent with a computer, and now look what she'd done. You could never tell about yourself. This was something. She was a geek!

She took several long strides to reach the phone, then hesitated when she noticed the time on her watch.

Past midnight. Beam would be asleep. Looper, too, dozing blissfully next to his wife, unless the snoring that Nell had endured in the car during stakeouts hadn't driven Mrs. Looper to a separate room. Despite the unpleasant notion, Nell found herself wondering whimsically what it might be like to be married again, this time to someone who loved her and acted like it. She was finding being single more and more problematic. It was like drifting through life as a ghost.

Don't be an idiot. You've got your independence, and everything that means. And you've got your job. Your work. Maybe someday you'll even live down the trouble with the shooting and the missing knife, the shooting that was goddamned righteous.

Don't rake up the past.

Focusing on the computer monitor, she felt her adrenaline kick in again and quicken her pulse.

Nell took a deep breath, then released it slowly.

She was calmer now, and more objective. So she'd hit pay dirt with her computer research. What did it mean? There were certainly two more Justice Killer victims; he'd been killing in New York for the past four years, but now he was picking up the pace.

That was predictive in serial killers. Really not such a big surprise.

Maybe Beam and Looper wouldn't be so impressed. Maybe she was exhausted and making too much of her find. Possibly she'd make a fool of herself by not waiting till morning to share her success. After all, if you held it up and looked at it, there wasn't much there that couldn't wait till morning.

Nell thought about it and decided again not to call and share her information. Not at this hour.

She rethought.

She picked up the phone and punched out Beam's number hard enough to hurt her fingers.

14

Melanie Taylor was juror number five and would act as foreperson in the capital criminal trial of Richard Simms, the rapper known professionally as Cold Cat.

Melanie was thirty-nine, single, and office manager of Regal Trucking, a general hauling company with executive offices in lower Manhattan. She'd been married briefly, to a man who turned out not to love her when it was discovered she'd be unable to bear children. The divorce had been fifteen years ago, and she hadn't again considered marriage. It was, after all, about children.

Her heart-shaped face, radiant smile, and generous figure had garnered her more than a few proposals of marriage. Some of the proposals she'd accepted, but without the marriage part. She was living alone now, in a small apartment in Tribeca, and seeing no one romantically. After her last bitter parting, she'd decided to take time off from romance—maybe the rest of her life.

". . . can be no doubt that he dearly loved his wife, Edie Piaf," Robert Murray, Cold Cat's attorney was saying.

Melanie's gaze went from Murray to Richard Simms, whom she could think of by no name other than Cold Cat.

She'd heard some of his songs, violent, assaults on the ear, full of deprecating lyrics about society in general, and women in particular. He didn't look at all angry or menacing now, a rather placid seeming black man about thirty, with pleasant, even features and liquid dark eyes. His hair was cropped short, and he was wearing a well cut conservative gray suit, white shirt, blue tie. To Melanie, he appeared more the type to be selling insurance or continuing his education than the author and performer of his big hit "Do the Bitch Snitch!" As the prosecutor had pointed out, the song advocated using a knife in unpleasant ways on a woman who'd turned evidence over to the police. But Cold Cat wasn't on trial for cutting or stabbing his wife, the singer Edie Piaf. Allegedly, he'd shot her.

Murray, a smiling, calm man with rust-colored hair and a spade-shaped red beard, paced before the jury and talked soothingly of Cold Cat's many musical accomplishments, his generosity to artists less talented or fortunate than himself, his participation in charity performances for AIDS victims and starving children.

"I must object!" Nick Farrato, the lead prosecuting attorney, blurted out, standing up from his chair as if jerked by strings. "Mr. Murray seems to be nominating Cold Cat for sainthood rather than making an opening statement. This defendant is the man who writes songs about slaughtering women, and who took his own lyrics too seriously and willfully—"

"You shut your lyin' mouth!"

Astounded, Melanie and the rest of the jurors turned in their chairs and saw a heavyset black woman standing near the middle of the crowded courtroom. Farrato, a chesty little man in a dark blue suit, normally cocky as Napoleon, was momentarily nonplussed by the outburst.

"You know nothin' 'bout my boy, you fat-headed piece of shit. You gonna be sued yourself, you don't watch that ugly mouth of yours."

Laughter rippled through the courtroom, but it was nervous laughter.

Judge Ernestine Moody, a somber African American woman with gray hair and deeply seamed features, was the only one who seemed unsurprised and unshaken. Melanie figured Judge Moody had seen it all.

"I'm going to ask you once to sit down and be orderly, ma'am," she said to the woman making all the fuss.

"I sit *you* down, you keep messin' with my boy!" the woman said, bringing gasps this time rather than laughter.

And Melanie understood. This was Cold Cat's mother. Late forties, overweight, overdressed, overheated, mad as hell.

Still, the judge was unmoved. "Ma'am—"

"I ma'am you, the way you helping these *po*lice an' bald-faced lyin' lawyers tell what ain't true an' railroadin' my boy straight to jail. You think I'm gonna sit here an' watch that happen?"

"Ma'am—"

"That *ain't* gonna happen!"

Murray was sidling up the far aisle, a smile stuck on his face, motioning with his arms for his client's mother to sit down.

The judge simply sighed and nodded to the bailiff, a husky blond man, who in turn nodded to a uniformed patrolman on the other side of the courtroom. The one in uniform made a hand motion that stopped Murray, and he and the bailiff converged on Cold Cat's mother.

That was when Cold Cat leaped to his feet. "You best leave my mom alone. Lay a hand on her an' I'll buy your ass and sell it to somebody not gonna treat it kindly."

From somewhere behind the bench two more uniformed cops appeared, a beefy man and a small, determined looking woman. They grabbed Cold Cat and forced him back down in his chair. Farrato was dancing around now, waving his short, stocky arms and objecting to everything. He finally lapsed into simply yelling, "Outrage! Outrage!"

Cold Cat's mother calmed down immediately when the two men reached her, as if she'd suddenly been shot through with a mild anesthetic that allowed her enough consciousness to remain on her feet, but no more. Braced between the two men, she accompanied them from the courtroom without a struggle until they reached the doors behind the gallery. Then she turned suddenly, as if she'd experienced a brief last surge of energy.

"This here's a place of lies!"

She repeated herself loudly in the hall after she was led from the room.

"Everybody," Judge Moody said, holding out both palms toward the courtroom. "Everybody calm down, and sit down."

"Put-up deal for the media!" Farrato grumbled. "Cheap stunt by the defense!"

"You sit down too, Mr. Farrato. You too, Mr. Murray."

"Certainly, your honor." Murray seemed sobered and much concerned over what had occurred.

"We're going to continue these proceedings in an orderly fashion," the judge said.

"Thank you, your honor."

"Quiet, Mr. Murray."

"Your honor—"

"I will not entertain an objection during an opening statement, Mr. Farrato. And for purposes of this trial, you will refer to the defendant as Richard Simms, not Cold Cat. And of course the jury is to disregard this . . . disturbance." To the defendant: "When Mrs. Simms—the defendant's mother— agrees to behave herself, she will be allowed back in the courtroom."

Murray smiled beatifically, as if he'd just achieved a victory. "Thank you, your honor. Your demeanor and judicious temperament are commendable."

"I'd like to request a short recess," Farrato said.

"Not in the middle of an opening statement, Mr. Farrato."

The judge fixed her baleful stare on Murray. "You may continue, Mr. Murray."

"Despite attempts to silence those who know my client as a kind and generous man," Murray began, seizing on opportunity and making Farrato squirm, "the defense will prove to you that it was absolutely impossible for Richard Simms to have murdered Edie Piaf."

"Right on!" a Cold Cat supporter in the courtroom said softly.

Judge Moody silenced him with a laser-like glance.

Melanie knew the judge's instruction to ignore the disturbance was simply a matter of form. How on earth could a juror actually put such a thing out of his or her mind?

She knew she couldn't, and decided that if any relevant impression stayed with her from the recent outburst, it was that Cold Cat loved his mother.

Of course, it was possible to love your mother, hate women, and murder one.

Wasn't it?

15

"This is just terrific!" da Vinci said in disgust.

He hadn't taken the results of Nell's computer research quite as she anticipated. She and Beam, seated in da Vinci's sun-washed office, glanced at each other.

"Not only do we have two more Justice Killer murders, but they're old homicides we never connected with him."

"It's important information," Beam said. "It enlarges a pattern, and it indicates that the killer's increasing the rate of his murders."

"Yeah. Just what the media in this town will want to know. Do you realize what they're going to do to me? To *you*?"

"Stay ahead of the curve and notify the media," Beam said, ignoring da Vinci's questions. "Act as if the discovery of two earlier murders represents progress, which in fact it does. These victims didn't die again just because Nell discovered their connection to the Justice Killer. The more we know, the sooner we'll nail this asshole."

"Can I quote you?"

"I'd clean it up."

Da Vinci grinned. "Well, I'd be quoting *you*."

Nell was normally intimidated by these two, but she'd

had about enough. Besides, the office was too hot; a trickle of perspiration found its way out from beneath her bra and trickled down her ribs. "I don't get it. I find something useful and you act as if I did something wrong. Maybe I oughta talk to the media."

Da Vinci stood up behind his desk and Nell actually winced.

So did Beam. "She didn't mean that, Andy. Not the way it sounded."

"The politics of this business are delicate and complex. I'll concentrate on that part of our game while you concentrate on yours."

"That's what I was—"

"Nell." Beam reached over and rested a big hand on her knee. For an instant she thought inanely that he might squeeze just behind the kneecap, prove she was boy crazy. "This is one phase of the game you don't understand, Nell. You did nothing wrong and everything right—we all know that. It's just that we handed Andy something valuable, but hot enough to burn his hand."

We. Nell liked that. Beam and Nell together against the bureaucratic monster. "Okay," she said, "I'm sorry, Chief."

"Deputy Chief," da Vince corrected. He actually smiled. Nell had to admire him for it. "Keep unearthing whatever you can," da Vinci said. "And go wherever the investigation takes you. You're the one who's right, Nell, we've gotta have faith that the truth will bear us out. It's our job, finding the truth."

Nell thought he was getting a little sickening. Beam gave her a cautioning glance.

Beam stood up suddenly, surprising Nell.

"We'll get back to our end of the game while you take care of business on your end," Beam said to da Vinci. "All I'll say is that if I were you, I'd dump it all on the media before it leaks on them. You know how it works; there'll be less pressure on us that way in the long run."

"Yeah," da Vinci said, obviously pretending to become engrossed in some papers on his desk. "They'll think we're actually doing something."

Outside One Police Plaza, as they were walking toward Beam's car, Beam said, "da Vinci's right about this, in some ways."

"I thought you were on my side," Nell said.

Beam smiled. "I am. You're right about it in every way."

"Departmental politics are a pain in the ass," Nell said. "I'll never understand them."

"Probably not. Best thing." They crossed the street. "Know what would help?" Beam said,

"Tell me."

"If we solved one of these crimes."

"And then the others," Nell said, reaching for the Lincoln's sun-warmed door handle.

"And then the others."

16

Cold case files, suddenly hot.

Beam and his detectives studied the Rachel Cohen and Iris Selig murder files, then Beam sent Nell and Looper to snoop around the Selig crime scene. He took the Rachel Cohen murder, in the Village, himself.

Cohen had been single and a freelance journalist who hadn't sold much. She'd been supported by her lifetime partner, a woman named Angela Drake, who'd discovered Rachel's corpse in their apartment on MacDougal Street. Drake had long ago moved from the city. The people who lived in the apartment now, a young artist and his wife, consented to let Beam look around; but as Beam suspected, nothing much resembled the four-year-old police photographs of the murder scene. The furniture was different, and the papered walls with their *fleur-de-lis* pattern had been stripped and painted.

Beam was driving back uptown and turned onto Fourteenth Street when he noticed a small antique shop, Things Past, where he'd expected to see a jewelry store. His reaction was out of proportion to his surprise. A block away, he pulled to the curb and switched off the ignition.

Five years ago Things Past had been Precious Gems

Limited, and was owned and managed by a fence, Harry Lima, who was one of Beam's most valuable and reliable snitches. More than one burglary ring had been broken up after using Lima's services to handle stolen goods, without the arrested parties suspecting the reason for their downfall was their fence.

But Beam had pushed when he shouldn't have, and pressured Lima into informing on a jewel theft ring that was connected to organized crime and particularly dangerous. Despite Beam's promises of protection, Lima was killed. Most of his body was found in a dumpster; his severed right hand, wearing his gaudy trademark diamond ring and clutching a dollar bill, was discovered six blocks away and served as a ghoulish and striking message as to why he was murdered. Tabloid news photos of the hand and ring were viewed by others in Harry Lima's business who might be considering informing. It was more than a year before sources of information about jewel thefts in Manhattan began to open up again.

Beam was still haunted by the ghost of Harry Lima. Harry was one of the few major mistakes in his career, but more than that, he'd given his personal guarantee and let Lima down. Beam had been—and this is what Beam still came face to face with in his dreams—responsible for Harry Lima's death.

It wasn't only Harry Lima who haunted Beam. It was Harry's wife, Nola, who'd been skeptical from the beginning about her husband's safety, and who'd never completely believed Beam about anything. Nola had been a stunningly beautiful woman whose dark eyes and wide cheekbones suggested Native American ancestry. Harry had once caught Beam looking at his wife with more than professional interest, and it seemed to amuse him. He'd begun bragging about Nola's beauty and passion, more than Beam wanted to hear, and told Beam she was half Cherokee. Both men knew Nola was off limits to Beam, not only because of Harry, but because of Nola herself. This wasn't a woman to be used; she was the brains behind the legitimate retail jewelry business, and for all Beam knew, the brains behind the fencing operation.

Beam had found himself thinking more and more about Nola's calm beauty, her slender waist, ample breasts, and what he saw as her noble bearing. He was attracted to her and couldn't deny it. For a while, it even threatened his marriage to Lani. Not that Nola showed the slightest attraction to Beam. He knew that to her he was simply a danger to her husband, a cop, somebody on the other side, a liar. Nola had been right.

Beam's problem was that he'd genuinely liked Harry Lima, and he'd more than liked his wife. Nola hadn't known she'd been a threat to Beam's career and marriage. She was the one woman who might have derailed him, if she'd taken the time to notice him as anything other than rain in her life.

Without really thinking about what he was doing, Beam climbed out of the car, fed the parking meter all the change in his pocket, then began walking along the sidewalk toward Things Past.

The antique shop appeared smaller than when it was a jewelry store, because of the clutter of merchandise. Antique clocks were mounted on one wall. The other walls were lined with display cases. In the central part of the shop were shelves of glassware and pottery, along with various antiques or collectibles ranging from ancient oil lamps to postcards. And to furniture, on which some of the merchandise was displayed.

Beam stepped around an antique oak bureau on which sat a brush-and-comb set, an old wash bowl, and a two-tiered painted globed lamp of the sort he'd heard called "Gone with the Wind" lamps. When he moved to his left and looked beyond a brass coat rack on which were draped various period garments, he could see a woman seated behind a glass display case on which sat a cash register and charge card scanner. She momentarily took his breath away.

Except for the gray shot through her dark hair, Nola Lima didn't look any older than the last time Beam had seen her. She was sitting down and had been reading something, and when she glanced up to greet the customer she'd just heard enter her shop, her amiable smile faded and her dark eyes bore into him.

In a fog, Beam moved toward her. "I'm—"

"I know who you are." Her distinctive, surprisingly throaty voice took him back years. "Detective Beam."

"Not exactly."

"Exactly enough," she said. "I follow the news."

He said nothing. Could think of nothing to say.

"Are you here because you're interested in antiques?" she asked, her tone businesslike.

"I'm not here for the reason you might think."

She smiled. "I might think somebody's stolen some antiques and you're here to see if any of my stock matches their description."

"It isn't that at all."

She stood up slowly, letting whatever she was reading slip to the floor. Beam couldn't help but notice she still had her figure. There was still something about her that made you think of royalty—the kind that had nothing to do with titles. Harry Lima had never known how lucky he was before his luck ran out.

"Then what?" she asked.

"I heard you'd stayed with the shop," Beam said, "turned to antiques instead of jewelry. I was in the Village and noticed your sign and wanted to look in on you."

"And now you have."

"Why didn't you continue with jewelry, with what you knew?"

"After Harry died, I chose to surround myself with the past. It's already happened, so it provides the ultimate in predictability."

Beam smiled. "Does that make sense?"

No return smile. "To me it does."

He shifted his weight from one leg to the other, as if it might help him find some kind of equilibrium with this woman. It wasn't to be found. Not today in this musty, smothering little shop that smelled of the past. "I'm not welcome here," he said, stating the obvious.

"Why shouldn't you be welcome? You extorted cooperation from my husband, tricked him into informing on dangerous people, and are responsible for them killing him." There was nothing in her impassive, beautiful face he could read. "Do you intend to try the same thing with me?" she asked.

"For God's sake no!"

"You're here looking for a discount, then? A policeman's discount? Or something bad might happen to my shop?" She was coming out from behind the display case, approaching him unafraid, her broad, handsome features still oddly placid. It was as if they'd played this scene before, and she recalled it but Beam didn't. "Is that what you want, Detective Beam?"

"Stop it with that crap, Nola."

She moved closer, until they were only inches apart. Beam almost backed away, but stood his ground. She looked up at him impassively.

"Then what? Why are you here?"

"To say I'm sorry."

She stared into him for several seconds before answering. "What I said about you being responsible for Harry's death, it's true."

"Yes, it is."

He wished he could explain to her the relationship between a cop and his snitch, the relationship he'd had with her husband. He'd respected Harry Lima. You might even say they were friends. But they were opponents playing the same game, and Harry found himself at a disadvantage. It was Beam's job to press *his* advantage, to use Harry Lima, and he'd used him up.

"I don't forgive you," said Harry's widow.

"That's not what I'm expecting, or asking. I simply wanted you to know how I felt."

"Why should I care?"

"You shouldn't."

"I remember the way you used to look at me," she said, surprising him. Horrifying him. This wasn't why he'd come here.

"Look at you?" Beam automatically feigning ignorance.

"When Harry wasn't watching."

Christ! Where's she going with this?

She surprised him again by slapping him hard. The sharp impact was like a gunshot in the cluttered little shop.

Beam didn't move. The left side of his face stung as if bees had swarmed it. He couldn't feel anger. She seemed completely unafraid of him. He understood why. *I've already done my worst to her.*

"You came in here to make yourself feel better," she said.

His heart was hammering hard. "Yes."

"Do you?"

"No."

"Then leave."

They stared as if trying to see deep into each other, neither so much as blinking, until finally Beam nodded, turned, and moved toward the door.

"I miss Harry," she said behind him.

"So do I," Beam said, and pushed out into the heat.

He thought she might yell after him not to come back, perhaps that she hated him. But she held her silence. She wasn't the sort to yell anything after anyone.

Beam knew he would be back, because he understood that he needed this woman's absolution.

And that she knew it.

17

The court had been informed that the witness, the former William Tufts, had legally changed his name to Knee High and would be so addressed. The squat, frenetic little man with the screwed up features was, as far as Melanie could perceive, Cold Cat's factotum, though his job title was, as he described it, Assistant to the Man. Like Cold Cat, he was African American, but unlike Cold Cat, his demeanor was anything but cool; he seemed unable to sit still in the witness chair.

"Is it true you and the defendant shared lunch in your apartment on the day of Edie Piaf's murder?" asked Farrato the prosecutor, as if the very act of sharing lunch on that fateful day somehow suggested guilt or, at the least, dark secrets.

"We did lunch, yeah."

"*We* being . . . ?"

"Knee High an' Cold Cat. Had us some sushi an' beer an'—"

"Please confine your responses to answering the questions," Judge Moody wearily reminded Knee High. It was the fourth such warning since he'd been sworn in. "And try to refer to yourself in the first person rather than the third."

"Yeah. Yes, your honor. Knee—We had us some—" Knee High bit down on his words and was silent. The judge seemed pleased by this restraint.

"Was this lunch delivered to your apartment?" Farrato inquired.

"Naw, was leftover from the night before. We had us—" With a glance at Judge Moody, Knee High fell silent.

"Was anyone else present for this lunch of"—Farrato made an unpleasant face—"leftover sushi?"

"Jus' me an—No."

"Then you and the defendant were alone?"

"Yes."

Farrato smiled thinly. He would step by step reveal to the jury that no one, not the doorman, not any of Cold Cat's backup musicians, not Cold Cat's chauffeur—no one—could testify in court that Cold Cat was anywhere near Knee High's apartment at the time of Edie Piaf's murder.

He faced the toad-like witness, who seemed so guileless that he worried Farrato on that minor point. Knee High didn't look smart enough to lie to protect his friend, though that surely was what he was doing. "During what time did this lunch take place?"

"Cold Cat—"

"Richard Simms," Judge Moody reminded the witness.

"Mr. Richard Simms, he showed up all dressed real sharp—"

"Simply give us the times," said the Judge

"He showed up right at one o'clock, left right at two."

"Are you certain of the time?"

"I am 'cause I got this new Rolex." Knee High held up his left wrist. "Knee High been checkin' the time most every few minutes, make sure I'm with Greenwich Village, an' jus' to look at the watch."

Judge Moody let that one pass.

Farrato appeared pained, but continued. "Is there anyone who can corroborate your story that Richard Simms was with you between the hours of one and two o'clock on the date of Edie Piaf's death?"

Knee High appeared puzzled. "Collaborate?"

"Corroborate," Farrato repeated.

Knee High looked to the judge.

"Did anybody else see or talk to you there?"

Knee High bit his lower lip, thinking hard. "No. But we was there. Ain't no way Cold Cat coulda got to his an Edie's place an' killed her. Not if she died 'tween one an' two."

Which Edie had, Melanie knew, because before the trial the news media had revealed that Edie phoned a friend and left a message at 12:55, and her body was discovered five minutes after two o'clock, when her personal trainer arrived to find Edie's door unlocked and Edie dead.

"Is it not possible that the defendant left your apartment slightly *before* two o'clock?" Farrato asked.

"No—yes, it is not possible. Knee High looked at his— my—gold Rolex 'cause—"

"Mr . . . High," the Judge cautioned.

"No." Knee High crossed his arms and shook his head. "Knee High an' Cold Cat was there together till one minute past two. Knee High looked, 'cause a second hand on a Rolex move steady like, an' Knee High wanted to—"

"Mr. High!"

"No. Yes. Not possible."

Melanie stole a look over her shoulder and saw that Cold Cat's mother had been allowed back into the courtroom. She was smiling, knowing the innocent believability of Knee High. This attorney-witness exchange was good for her son, with whom she exchanged encouraging glances.

Farrato was unmoved by Knee High's act. He knew the little man was lying, and he knew that before the trial was over, he would remove Richard Simms, aka Cold Cat, from that meal of day-old sushi, and place him where he belonged, in Edie Piaf's apartment at the same time Edie Piaf died. Knee High was impressing the jury now, and no doubt he'd impress them when Murray presented the defense phase of the trial, but Farrato would slice Knee High to pieces on cross-exam. The stubborn gnome obviously worshiped Cold Cat, and was obviously—to Farrato, anyway—lying to protect him. Farrato smiled a quarter inch wider. A lecture on the consequences of perjury would do the trick with Knee High, at the opportune time.

Melanie saw Farrato smile and didn't like him. He seemed so arrogant, so unlike the defendant Cold Cat, who looked genuinely hurt and puzzled that he should be here. And he was suffering emotionally because of Edie Piaf's passing—you could read the grief on his face for his lost love.

Even as Melanie thought this, she watched Cold Cat glance at his mother, who was returning the look with an expression of mother's love that couldn't be faked.

Cold Cat's mother seemed to sense Melanie staring at her. She glanced Melanie's way, then lowered her gaze to her lap, as if embarrassed to be caught in a moment of tenderness.

Melanie looked down at her own lap, where her hands were folded, and tried to focus her attention on what Farrato was saying. Instead she found herself thinking of the defendant. Such an interesting man. His music was violent, but wasn't he a poet of the streets, reflecting, rather than helping to create, a violent culture? There were those who called Cold Cat a musical genius, and perhaps he was one. Melanie wouldn't know. But his music sold. He was worth millions. She'd never before seen anyone worth millions, and who'd been referred to as a musical genius. Now here she was sitting not twenty feet from one.

Farrato, and Judge Moody, had cautioned the jury about the power of celebrity. They were to regard Cold Cat as simply another defendant to be treated fairly and dispassionately. The facts of the case were what mattered here, not that the accused happened to be famous.

Melanie thought the warnings about the effects of celebrity were overblown. People were people. It was as simple as that.

Judge Moody had been right when she declared that inside the courtroom, the accused was in no way special.

Melanie raised her eyes and looked at the defendant, and found Cold Cat looking directly at *her*.

Melanie melted.

"This is approximately the number of days we might have before we lose our jobs," da Vinci said, holding up a digital photo he'd taken of an image on a TV screen, then enlarged.

They were in Central Park, where da Vinci requested the meeting with Beam. Which rather amused Beam. Had they reached the point where da Vinci didn't want to be seen with him?

Beam turned so the late afternoon sun wasn't glinting off the photo. "It looks like a big red number six."

"Know what it stands for?" da Vinci seemed agitated now. Where had the cool young bureaucratic climber gone. "That's the number of victims the Justice Killer's notched. That photo's of the news on Channel One a couple of hours ago. They were reporting on that press conference you advised me to hold."

Beam nodded and waited. He didn't see where da Vinci was going with this.

"The papers haven't had time to get it out yet," da Vinci said, "but do you know what tomorrow's gonna be like for me, Beam? The main media's gonna be all over me, wanting to know why we aren't closing in on this sicko. Why we didn't realize until recently that we had a serial killer operating in the city."

"Didn't they hit you with those kinds of questions at your press conference?"

Da Vinci glared up at a blue jay that was nattering at him from a nearby tree, as if the media had sent the bird to antagonize him. "I didn't take questions."

Beam was surprised. "I thought that was the idea of the press conference."

"No. My idea was to get the information out there, let the public know through the media what's going on."

"Do it that way, it just makes you look like you're trying to duck questions," Beam said.

"That's exactly what I was doing. Because I don't have answers. You and your detectives were supposed to supply me with answers."

Beam gave him a level look. "Is this supposed to be a chewing out?"

"Of course not. I know what you're up against."

"Then why'd you request this meeting?"

Da Vinci seemed at a loss for words. He gave a nervous, crooked grin like the kind Tony Curtis used to in the movies. Beam wondered if da Vinci was aware of his resemblance to the movie star and had studied those expressions. Maybe even practiced them in front of a mirror.

Beam said, "You asking my advice again?"

Da Vinci seemed suddenly calm. A pretty blond woman, perched high on in-line skates, glided past on the path behind him. The skate wheels made a rhythmic growling sound that became fainter with distance. "I guess maybe that's part of it," he admitted, glancing after the woman. "Isn't that some ass?"

"I noticed, even at my age. My advice is the same as before—get out ahead of it."

"*It* is the result of getting out ahead," da Vinci said. The blue jay fluttered to a lower limb, closer, and was definitely observing da Vinci.

"You should have fielded questions, told them anything." Beam thought that if they knew bird language, it would be clear that the jay was cursing at da Vinci.

"They don't settle for anything," da Vinci said, "and now I'm in a shit storm."

"You were gonna be anyway. If not today, tomorrow. Today woulda been better, cut down on media speculation. Not much better, but better."

"You know the kinda pressure goes with this? From the mayor on down to the commissioner, to the chief, then down to me, and then to you and your detectives." The blue jay flew at da Vinci's head and he slapped at it and missed. "The hell's wrong with that thing? Don't it like me?"

"Not so you could tell."

"Anyway, you heard what I said."

"You forgot somebody in that chain of increasing pressure," Beam said. "The killer. Sure, he's gotten some of the notoriety he wanted, but he knows now there's an army of cops searching for him. That brings about a certain amount of pressure."

"You said it yourself, though, he'll enjoy the publicity."

"He will. Like some of us enjoy walking the edge of a cliff. The publicity brings us closer to catching him."

The jay zoomed at da Vinci again. He swatted at it, then walked about twenty feet farther away from the tree. "Must have a nest in there."

"Must," Beam agreed.

"All the noise in the news might bring something else closer," da Vinci said. "Number seven."

Beam knew he was right. And in a perverse way, he was almost looking forward to victim number seven. Every murder was a tragedy, but it was also a card to play. It was all the more likely they'd be able to stop this killer if he did more of what they were trying to stop. Ironic.

Beam didn't like irony. He was a cop. He liked things to the point, black or white, right or wrong.

Alive or dead.

"I swear," da Vinci said, "if that friggin' bird flies at me again, I'm gonna blast it with my nine-millimeter."

The jay knew when to quit.

18

Tina Flitt and her husband, Martin Portelle, sat on the balcony of their twenty-first floor East Side apartment and watched dusk settle over New York. They felt fortunate.

Martin, a stocky, bald man with mild gray eyes and a scraggly beard grown to compensate for his lack of hair up top, had nothing about him in youth portending success. Yet here he was, a highly paid acquisition appraiser for a major holding company.

His wife, Tina, was a smallish woman in a way that suggested extreme dieting, and was pretty in an intense, dark-eyed fashion. She was a defense attorney. The two had met in court, when Martin was jury foreperson in the trial of the infamous Subway Killer, Dan Maddox. Tina had been one of the jurors. Maddox had been acquitted.

Martin used the remote to switch off the small Sony TV they used on the balcony. They'd been watching Channel One news. A special titled *Six and the City*. It was all about the victims whose deaths were attributed to the Justice Killer.

"Six so far," Tina said. "New Yorkers are getting frightened."

"Or the media wants us to see it that way." Martin sipped the vodka martini he'd brought with him out to the balcony.

The greed and paranoia of the media were subjects he could talk on for hours.

"Anybody who's served as jury foreperson in the past ten years has reason to worry," Tina told him.

"Only if the defendant got off in court, but was convicted in the media."

"That list of forepersons could include a lot of people."

Martin smiled. "It includes me, counselor."

"I don't find it particularly amusing," Tina said. She didn't like it when Martin called her counselor. It was as if he had little respect for her profession.

An emergency siren sounded far below, a police car or ambulance shrieking protest at the uncooperative traffic.

"You worry too much," Martin said, reaching across the glass-topped table and squeezing Tina's delicate hand. He was careful not to squeeze too hard; his wife was one of those women addicted to rings, and wore three on each hand.

"You haven't met some of my clients."

"You get them off," Martin said. "Sometimes when they don't deserve to walk."

"They all deserve legal representation." This was a discussion Tina and Martin had almost worn out.

Martin released Tina's hand and leaned back in his chair. He wished she'd practice some other form of law. Four months after his acquittal, ten years ago, the acquitted Maddox had pushed a woman into the path of an oncoming subway train. It had shaken Martin's faith in the legal system, his faith in the world. He'd felt responsible for the woman's death, and for six months he was clinically depressed. He was in analysis for years. Even as he and his fellow jurors had voted Maddox out of legal jeopardy and back onto the streets, they'd strongly suspected he was a killer.

But "suspected" wasn't enough. The defendant's confession had definitely been made under duress, and was disallowed by the judge, who'd had no choice. So the jurors voted to acquit, because they had no choice.

That was what his doctors had finally gotten Martin to realize: he'd had no choice. It was the system.

Martin brushed back the long hair over his ears as a high
breeze washed over the balcony. A week after the trial, he'd
phoned the tiny, dark-haired juror he'd so admired in the assembly room and asked her for a date. Their relationship had
developed into love, and she stayed at his side throughout his
troubles. She'd somehow realized in the beginning what it
had taken Martin over a year to understand.

Six years ago they were married. Tina had attended law
school and become an attorney, while Martin continued to
regain his mental equilibrium. It had been a step by step,
painful passage, but Martin made the journey. He had moved
on with his business career, with his life. Day by day, he'd
built a better world for himself.

Now old wounds were being probed, but he refused to acknowledge any pain. He really did understand that the system and not the jury had freed Maddox. Martin Portelle,
personally, was not responsible for Maddox after Maddox
walked free from the courtroom.

Martin had to smile again as he sipped his martini. Tina
had barely changed since he'd first laid eyes on her almost
ten years ago, and here they were, still thinking about discussing the late Dan Maddox. Like a time machine. Hell of a
world, Martin thought, but if you kept scrapping, you got
your reward. At least some people did.

"I think you might be in danger," Tina said.

"From who? Maddox? He's long gone."

"From somebody who loved his last victim."

"It's been almost ten years, Tina."

"That might not seem long if you've lost someone you
love. It might only seem like days, if you want vengeance."

"The killer we're talking about wants justice. Or his idea
of it."

Tina stroked her small, pointed chin, as she often did

when she thought. "Justice? Did we play our role in trying to see that Maddox got justice?"

"Yes. We did what we could."

"Does the Justice Killer know that?"

I'm glad you don't cross examine me in court. "I'm not sure. I'm not inside his mind, thank God. But I'll put my faith in percentages. You said it yourself, if I'm in trouble, so are lots of other people. Tells you something about our justice system, doesn't it?"

Tina knew that it did, but she didn't admit it.

Like a good attorney, she changed the subject. Outwardly, anyway.

If Martin only knew . . .

Number six had been fun.

The Justice Killer sat in a brown leather easy chair in his apartment, sipped Jack Daniels from the bottle, and looked at the window. It was nighttime and the window had become a mirror reflecting the room—an ordinary room, well decorated and well kept, with its traditional brown easy chair as the center of gravity.

The man in the chair was not ordinary, nor did he want to be. He had a cause. A cause had him. A just cause.

But now he also had doubts.

Not doubts, actually, but a niggling discomfort.

The unexpected had occurred. He couldn't deny he'd enjoyed killing Beverly Baker.

There had even been in the act an unanticipated sexual component. He recalled in vivid imagery her eyes when she'd noticed him in the mirror, the very instant when she understood that hope had run out and she was about to die. That was when her will turned to ice, when mind and body were frozen and there was no resistance.

His time.

Our time.

Something, an arc of cold emotion and sacred knowledge, had passed between Beverly and her killer, something as true and old as hunter and prey. As old as the human race.

You're drunk.

Am I?

Not that *drunk.*

He knew what his quest was also about, he begrudgingly admitted to himself. Not only life and death and retribution, not only justice—but power.

He took a sip of bourbon. *So what?* Were power and justice necessarily separate entities? Certainly they were all of a piece. Ask any helpless defendant in a courtroom. And if the Justice Killer found titillation in his revenge, what substantive difference did it make?

Why shouldn't I enjoy it?

He sipped his booze and let his mind chew on the question.

His mind extrapolated. Why must he be bound by the conventions of the archetype serial killer? He certainly wasn't typical.

The problem was the judicial system—the callous, damaging, arrogant, heartless system that did *not* work—that he was attempting to change. And there was more than one way to change it. There was no reason why he shouldn't expand his pool of potential victims beyond those who'd chaired juries. The ordinary jurors themselves were equally guilty of setting free the guilty. Their vote was their own. In a criminal trial, the guilty verdict had to be unanimous. But if the verdict was for acquittal, the jury was usually polled. How each juror voted was a matter of public record. For the purposes of the Justice Killer, simple jurors as well as forepersons were fair game. And the effects of such victims' deaths would be much the same—perhaps even more potent. Fear times twelve.

Many jurors, of course, were women.

The Justice Killer raised his glass in a silent toast to the seated figure reflected in the window, and the toast was acknowledged.

He was beginning to comprehend that in the world he lived in, on the far side of the law, beyond human abhorrence, he couldn't expect to be understood. So be it. What did it matter? No one *really* understood anyone else, anyway. And in the world he had chosen for himself, there were advantages. There were no taboos, no walls, roadblocks, fences, rules or limits, because *he* decided what was moral and permissible. More and more he was realizing he had every right to enjoy the power that was his, and that anything was possible

More and more.

He leaned back in the soft chair and closed his eyes.

And saw Beverly Baker's terrified, resigned, and understanding eyes. Heard her silent, pleading voice that he had never heard: *Get it over with! Do it! Do it!*

And smiled.

Why shouldn't I enjoy it?

19

St. Louis, 1988

Justice seldom slept. His life had become as fragmented as his thoughts. Even if he took a sleeping pill, within a few hours he was awake, his mind darting and exploring like that of an insect confined in a matchbox. During the day, exhausted, he found himself dozing off when he least expected. Not only was it embarrassing, but the increasing lack of control he had over his life was terrifying. Time lost all but its literal meaning. Day was like night to him. Night became his day.

He lay in the night beside April in the bedroom of their shabby south side apartment and wondered if they both might be better off dead. Overhead, a slow moving ceiling fan, almost invisible in shadow, ticked dreamily as it turned. His wife's breathing was shallow and labored, and he couldn't be sure what kind of drugs were in her body. She'd become devious in her addiction, lying to him skillfully, and artfully concealing her stash made up of old prescription vials and hoarded pills.

How did it come to this? How did it happen? Will . . .

Her breath caught like a blade in her throat and she woke

suddenly, staring over at him as if surprised to find him beside her. Seeming, in fact, not to recognize him at first.

"You okay?" he asked.

"Why are you awake?" Her hair was wild, her tone accusatory.

"Couldn't sleep."

"You were watching me."

He propped himself up on an elbow, leaned over, and kissed her forehead. "Because I love you." *What you were, what you are . . .*

"People don't spy on people they love."

"I wasn't spying." She'd lowered her head and he couldn't see her face clearly enough in the dim room to know its expression, but he imagined her heavy-lidded eyes, the dull, barely comprehending look of the seriously medicated, the genuinely hopeless. It was like his heart being cleaved sometimes, seeing that expression. "I was watching you, that's all. To make sure you were okay."

"Neither one of us is okay and we both know it."

He dropped his head back on his pillow, lying on his back and staring at the ceiling that was like a gray sky with no stars. The hate, the fear, the agony, combined to create a sour, distinctive odor that permeated the sheets and April's sweat-damp nightgown. Sometimes he could smell the odor briefly when she was near him during the day. He had smelled something like it in hospital wards for the dying.

"We can't go through the rest of our lives like this," he said.

"I've come to the same conclusion."

"We've got to change things."

"Things have changed us."

"I'm tired of these goddamned word games, April."

She laughed low in her throat in a way that horrified him—almost a death rattle. "I'm just goddamned tired," she said.

Justice lay still in the warm, humid bedroom that stank of mortality, hoping that if he said nothing she'd remain silent.

After a while her breathing evened out, then slipped into its familiar shallow rhythm. He was the only one awake and alone again in their dark world.

Their bright world had been shattered, but began its complete and irreparable disintegration when Elvis Davison, the rapist and killer of their son Will, walked smiling from the courtroom a free man, and soon dropped out of the news. The trial was over; he had his life back.

Justice and April would never have their lives back, because Davison had taken away their son.

"If someone killed Davison, we'd be the first people the police would suspect," April said.

It startled him that she was awake, and it frightened him. *Is she privy to my thoughts? My night thoughts?*

"I don't want to kill him," he lied.

"You do. We both do."

"It isn't Davison, anyway. It's the system."

"System?"

"Judicial. The judges, the juries—especially the juries. They didn't have to find him not guilty."

"They were following the letter of the law. Or thought they were."

"Juries *are* the law," Justice said. "They can do what they want. They had to know Davison, what he . . ." His voice failed him. Neither of them could speak directly about what Davison had done to Will. "They knew he was guilty."

"Reasonable doubt," April said wearily.

"Do *you* have any?"

"No."

"Then how could they?"

"I would like to kill each and every one of them," April said. "Only it wouldn't bring Will back, and it would put *us* at the mercy of juries."

"I simply don't understand their reasoning, their lack of understanding."

"They were led. They got into that damned jury room and somebody took charge and led them to their verdict."

"The jury foreman? You think he's responsible?"

"He was part of the system we know was responsible."

"The jury foreman . . ." Justice said. He remembered the man, a wiry redheaded CPA named Coburn. He'd always worn the same brown suit to court; probably had it cleaned and pressed on weekends. Maybe April had something. Maybe as jury foreperson, Coburn bore a disproportionate responsibility for the verdict. A disproportionate amount of guilt.

"If we killed Coburn," April said, "It'd be like we killed Davison. The police, the system, would know who did it. Then they'd kill us. I wouldn't care."

"I would. I don't want you to die. I don't want to be alone."

"Be honest."

"All right, I don't want to suffer alone. I don't think I could bear it."

"You're a coward," she said. "You'd be able to bear it if you weren't a coward."

"I'm hearing pills talking," Justice said, turning on his side to face away from her. There was a burning in his belly that drew up his knees. "I hear somebody who wants to pick a fight to rid herself of her rage. Pills talking."

"I'd like to pick a fight with the system that allows a monster to walk freely away from the pain he caused."

"We can't kill the monster without losing our own lives," Justice told her.

"I don't mean the monster Davison. He isn't part of the system."

"You mean Coburn? He's not much of a monster."

"Oh, he is. But we couldn't touch him or anybody else involved with Davison's trial without arousing suspicion. So I'm generalizing. Maybe I'll blow up the goddamn courthouse."

"Pills talking."

He hoped.

"Pills're going to sleep now," April said, and fluffed her pillow.

She would be asleep soon. She could find refuge in sleep for hours at a time and escape her agony. Sometimes he envied her, but the cost of her ability to escape was her addiction to her medication, and if she didn't get it under control, it would kill her.

Staring hard at the shadowed ceiling beyond the rotating fan blades, Justice knew April was right. If Davison were killed, they'd be prime suspects. But the truth was that Davison wasn't the problem—it was the system. April was right about that. The system didn't know how rotten it was, didn't seem to understand that an act like Davison's created poisonous ripples that seemed never to end and became all the more toxic as they spread. And if the perpetrator escaped justice, the ripples became wider and spread more destruction with each passing day, month, year.

The secondary victims, the survivors of the slain, simply died more slowly.

That was what April knew, and what Justice was learning.

"You awake?"

April, awake again herself.

"I'm asleep," Justice said.

He wondered how many other people were out there suffering the same way he and April suffered. The obviously guilty too often went free, but the families of their victims would never again be free.

The wrongness of it overwhelmed Justice, and he lay beside April and wept.

April heard him but didn't make a move to comfort him. He had to suffer so he would come to understand what she already knew.

It seemed he never would fully comprehend. There was only one way for April to make sure that he might.

One final duty.

20

Three days after Beverly Baker's death, the Justice Killer sent Beam a letter, care of the NYPD, copy to *The New York Times*.

There it was in da Vinci's sunny office, on da Vinci's desk. Everyone in the office had read the note but not touched it. The brief message was neatly printed in pencil:

> Hunter Beam:
> *I know about your exploits and what you have for breakfast and what you dream. It is my pleasure that you've been assigned to track me down. Great men are judged by the quality of their enemies. We need each other. God provides for the just.*
> *You can no longer screw your wife. Are you screwing Officer Nell?*
>
> JK

"At least there's one thing he doesn't know about you," Nell said.

Looper was sitting next to her, smiling. Beam was standing off to the side, his hands in his pockets. Da Vinci sat in his big black swivel chair behind his desk. The fifth person in the room was police profiler Helen Iman. She was a tall woman, athletically curvaceous and attractive, who would have looked right at home playing beach volleyball. She had slanted emerald eyes and the kind of bony, ageless features that would look the same at sixty. She was about twenty years shy of that now. She stood on the opposite side of the desk from Beam.

"We got us a madman for a perp," Looper said, sitting back after reading the note.

"I think we can all agree on that," da Vinci said.

"Techs looked at this yet?" Beam asked.

"Of course," da Vinci said. "It didn't take them long. There's nothing in the way of prints that might be brought out on either the envelope or paper, and both are from stock sold in office supply stores, drugstores, and even grocery stores."

"Any DNA?"

"No. Analysis of the envelope flap reveals no saliva. He didn't lick it. A few microscopic cotton fibers were found, indicating he dampened a cloth and ran it across the adhesive areas. But the fibers are so common they lead nowhere."

"What about the printing itself?" Beam asked.

"Handwriting analyst says it's so carefully drawn and proportioned, maybe using a ruler or some other straight-edged object to maintain evenness, that it doesn't reveal much. Certainly nothing that would bear meaningful comparison in court. Pencil's number two lead, like ninety-nine percent of the pencils sold. A wooden pencil, probably, not mechanical. Lab says it didn't wear down the same way as less tapered mechanical lead."

Da Vinci turned the note paper so it was angled Helen Iman's way. "Tell you anything about this guy?" he asked, "Like how tall he is, is he a Mets or Yankees fan, what's his favorite color?"

Helen Iman admirably ignored da Vinci's sarcasm. In her business it was the usual thing. Some cops, especially the older ones, or those in higher office like da Vinci, didn't have much faith in profiling.

Helen moved nearer to the desk and looked closely, the second time, at the printed note.

"She's gonna tell us everything about this guy," da Vinci said with mock confidence, "including whether he wears boxers or Jockey shorts."

Helen felt like telling da Vinci the killer wore shorts that were all twisted up like his own.

"He's psychic," she said. "He knows what Captain Beam dreams."

Da Vinci glared at her, waiting for her to smile. She didn't.

"What would be his reaction if I answered this note," Beam asked the profiler, "and we get my reply printed in the *Times*?"

"He'd probably love a public display of your reply to his letter. It would make it seem the two of you were a set, acting out a drama on a vast stage. You might see this investigation as a job, but he sees it as an epic."

"I'll tell him I'm simply doing my job," Beam said. "I've seen insane killers like him before and I will again. After he's lost his freedom or his life, I'll move on and he'll be forgotten."

Helen smiled. "He wouldn't like reading something like that. Especially the mention of insanity."

"Might it rattle him?"

"It might. I think he'll almost immediately write an answer. He'd love to carry on a public correspondence with you."

"I'll tell him this will be the only message he's going to get from me until I read him his rights."

"Tell him again he's a nutcase," Looper suggested.

"Once is enough," Helen said. She looked at da Vinci. "What do you think of the idea?"

"You're the profiler," he said. "What will it accomplish?"

"It'll anger him. Maybe to the extent that he'll make a mistake. And it will make him dislike Captain Beam all the more. And respect him all the more."

"Will he fear him all the more?"

"Yes, but remember, he chose him because he feared him."

"I'd like you to look over the letter before I send it," Beam said to Helen. "If you don't mind."

"I don't mind at all." Helen was gaining respect for Beam herself. If the Justice Killer had wanted a formidable opponent, he'd chosen well.

"Will it make him kill again?" Nell asked.

Helen shrugged. "It might make him kill sooner, but I doubt even that. He's going to kill again one way or the other. He's going to keep killing until he's stopped. And he knows it. A certain part of him even wants to be stopped, because he knows he can't stop himself. That's why he's happy to have Captain Beam in charge of the investigation. After six victims, the killer might be in the early stages of coming unraveled. He wants to be famous when he is caught or killed, and he knows he's working toward that moment. He's sure that in the end, Captain Beam won't let him down."

Da Vinci chortled and shook his head. "God! Is it really that complicated?"

Helen grinned as if she and da Vinci shared a secret. "Maybe not."

"Madmen can be complicated," Looper said.

"I'm not so sure he's mad," Helen said. "Not in the way we're talking about—uncontrolled, irrational. That's not what comes across to me in the note. He's more like someone pretending to be mad."

"Laying the basis for an insanity defense when he's caught?" Nell asked.

"Possibly. Or maybe he's simply playing for effect."

"Killer like that's already a leg up on an insanity plea," Looper said.

"*If* he's only pretending to be irrational," Beam said.

Helen looked at him and nodded. "It's true that at this point we can't know for sure, but my hunch is that he's feigning insanity."

"I know six people who'd disagree with you," da Vinci said, "if they could."

Martin Portelle liked to ride the subway to and from work. Not that he couldn't afford a cab. For that matter he might have twisted somebody's arm and gotten a company car to drive him back and forth. He was at that level, since the report he'd made on Sculler Steel, a small foundry in the Midwest that had the potential of increasing top line earnings by fifty percent with only a few minor operational changes.

He wished he were paid a commission on all the money he'd saved his company. He might be the firm's highest paid employee. Mr. Kravers had referred to him more than once as its most talented. Martin could spot, in corporate financial statements, anomalies that other analysts' attention glided over. It was as if they were half blind and he had perfect vision.

Besides knowing how to squeeze a dollar, that was Martin's great gift, perceiving anomalies however slight. Which was why over the past several days he'd become increasingly worried.

More than worried, actually—spooked.

"You mean afraid?" Tina asked, when he tried to explain. They were seated, each with a cool drink, on their high balcony, tiny creatures affixed to their building and waiting for the sunset.

Martin wasn't so sure now that he should have confided

in Tina. She was such a fearless, practical woman. Yet she'd been afraid for him; that was why he'd told her about what had been happening lately, how he felt.

"All right," Martin said, "I'm not too proud to admit it. I'm seeing . . . I don't know, pieces that don't quite fit."

"What's that mean—pieces?"

It was so difficult to explain this to someone else. "I might see someone in the corner of my vision, and when I turn around they're not there. Or a door might close, someone going out just as I enter a room."

"That happens to all of us."

"It's a small thing, but to me it's been happening too many times." He took a sip of his drink." I've seen the same man seated across from me on the subway three times in five days. What are the odds?"

"Slim," Tina sipped her Long Island iced tea. She could drink the lethal things without showing any signs of inebriation. Up to a point, of course. "What does he look like?"

"Average. Very average. He's always wearing sunglasses."

"Not unusual," Tina said. "Summer in New York. Are they always the same kind of sunglasses."

"Yes . . . Well, I don't know. They're always the most common kind. You know, like aviator's glasses. But I suppose they could be different ones."

"And he always sits directly across from you?"

"Not directly, no. But always on the opposite side of the car, facing me."

"You wouldn't notice such a man if he were sitting on the same side of the car, would you?"

"Of course not." Martin was getting irritated. Tina seemed to be suggesting that if he switched sides, he might very well see a similar man who'd draw his suspicion. "I also get the feeling someone's been following me as I walk the sidewalks. To and from my subways stops, and sometimes when I go out for lunch."

"Same man?"

Martin put down his drink on the glass-topped table and cradled his head in his hands. "I don't know. It isn't as if I've ever directly looked into the eyes of whoever might be tailing me. Maybe they're that skilled, or maybe I'm that paranoid. If you're telling me this might be my imagination, you could be right. But it's got me going. Yesterday, when I got this creepy, watched feeling, I even walked up to a cop that was handy and talked to him."

"Told him someone was following you?"

"No. I didn't want to open that can of worms."

"You should go to the police and request their protection."

"You're not saying they actually *could* protect me—or anyone else?"

"Theoretically they could," Tina said. "But in reality, no. Not with certainty. Yet, when you thought you might be in danger, you went to a cop."

"I just knew if somebody meant me harm they wouldn't try it with a uniformed cop next to me. Besides, this could all be my imagination. Maybe I'm paranoid. The calm and reasoning part of my mind thinks I'm spooked by shadows, but it gave me a sense of security, talking to that cop about the weather. One I've never needed before."

"I don't think you're paranoid," Tina said. "And I didn't marry you for your imagination."

Martin opened his eyes and peered at her through spread fingers. "Lawyers aren't supposed to be enigmatic. What does that mean?"

"That I think you might have real reason to fear. I've thought so ever since this Justice Killer psychopath started murdering former jury forepersons. In case you've forgotten, we acquitted Maddox. You were jury foreperson. He killed again, later."

Martin lowered his hands from his face, lifted his martini, and took a long sip. "Unfortunately, there are too many such cases, in New York and other cities, where the obviously guilty have to be set free because of trial irregularities or just plain dumb-ass prosecutors, judges, or juries. That's how the system works; there are Constitutional rights, and lots of guilty people take advantage of them and are walking around free even though they should be imprisoned or executed. Lots of them. What that means is, logically, I'm not much more likely to be this sicko's next victim than I am to win the lottery."

Tina stared at him over the rim of her glass. "Logically, *somebody* wins the lottery."

Martin gazed out over the darkening city, understanding why his wife was such a good trial lawyer. "I guess that's why I'm afraid."

"Then we're both afraid for you." She set the glass down and leaned toward him. "But Martin, we don't have to be afraid."

"Are we back to me leaving the city until this nut is caught?"

"It makes sense. At least you can get away for a while. You've got vacation time coming."

Martin smiled. "The kind of job I have, you retire with vacation time coming."

"It doesn't have to be that way. You could explain the situation to Mr. Kravers. He'd understand."

"He'd think more of me if I stayed in town."

Tina glared at him. "This isn't a pissing contest, Martin. The object is to see that you don't get killed. Kravers has the good sense to understand you're more valuable alive. Just as I do. You know who doesn't seem to have the good sense to realize that?"

"Don't tell me."

"You could visit your brother Irv in Chicago. Listen to him bitch about his divorce, go with him and take his kids to some Cubs games. A hit man's not likely to follow you there."

"Very few hits at a Cubs game," Martin said.

Tina grinned. "See! You're not so scared you've lost your sense of humor."

"I'm not really scared," Martin said. "I'm . . . uneasy. Like a part of me knows something bad's gonna happen."

"You won't be so uneasy in Chicago. And Irv and the kids'll love seeing you."

"Maybe, since I'm going someplace, I should go to Miami or Sarasota in Florida, eat lobsters, and walk the beach."

"I don't give a damn where you go, Martin, just that you go. If you're out of New York, *I* won't be so uneasy. You say somebody might be watching you, I believe it. Maybe more than you do. I love you, Martin. I don't want to lose you."

He couldn't hold back a smile. "Is that your second drink?"

"Damn it, Martin! I'm being serious."

"So am I," he said. "I love you too, Tina. I can clear it at work; I'll phone Irv and make sure it's okay if I stay with him a while."

"I'll call and make your flight reservation," Tina said. There was so much relief in her voice, he thought she might be about to stand up right then and head for a phone.

"I'll do it through work," Martin said. "That'll make it deductible."

When they finished their drinks and went inside, the sun had set.

The city was completely dark.

Beam awoke in the hot bedroom; he was cold but coated with sweat. He'd resisted taking a pill to help him sleep, and the dreams had been waiting.

His dreams.

It was like taking the lid off a jar and dumping out everything in his subconscious. Letting it all tumble this way and that. *Tumble and jumble.* None of it meant anything—though Cassie might disagree—but it was damned unpleasant if not horrifying.

Harry Lima and Nola, together, writhing, Harry grinning down at her, choking her while she stared up at him, not struggling, seeming almost bored by the notion of dying. Then was it Harry and Nola, or was it Beam?

Was it Nola?

Beam reached over and switched on the light. Shadows fled.

He lay back and ran his hand through his hair. It was soaked, like his pillow. A car or truck drove past slowly outside with deep, throbbing beats blasting from oversized speakers. Oddly, it had a calming effect. The normal, recognizable world was out there.

After a while, he got out of bed, stumbled into the bathroom, and took a pill.

21

Beam's reply to the Justice Killer's letter appeared in every New York newspaper. It was on the front page of the *Post*:

> JK:
>   *I've been busy and only just now have time to answer your letter. You are not my opponent, you are merely part of my job, as a roach would be part of an exterminator's job. Deranged killers are parasites and are dealt with routinely in the city. When you are gone, another psychotic killer will occupy the police. That will be soon.*
>
>   Capt. A. Beam

The Justice Killer set aside the *Post* on top of today's *Times* and *Daily News* on the seat of the cab he was in. He was smiling. The cab jounced over a pothole and the driver's eyes fixed momentarily on his passenger.

The Justice Killer's smile disappeared. "They oughta fix those things," he said of the pothole. "It's a wonder this city's cabs have got any suspension left at all."

"They'll fix 'em when we're both dead and gone," the driver said, eyes straight ahead now as he braked to turn the corner onto Park.

"I can hardly wait," the Justice Killer said, barely concentrating on the small talk he was dishing out, still thinking about Beam's letter.

Certainly the related news articles surrounding the letter were more frantic and hinted at more fear than the letter itself. Which, the Justice Killer knew, was how Beam had planned it. Beam was persuasively feigning nonchalance, pretending the Justice murders were nothing special and didn't occupy his every waking thought as well as his dreams.

So the veteran cop said publicly that the killer is deranged. Psychotic. The Justice Killer knew that nothing could be further from the truth. It was precisely what he wanted the police to believe, to announce; it was their unintentional way of saying they had no inkling of what was in his mind.

Of course you don't.

Of course you know I'm sane.

The seemingly dashed off reply to his letter was calculated to make the Justice Killer feel slighted. Angry.

But the tone of the letter was no surprise, and made the killer feel neither slighted nor angry. He felt gratified. Beam was living up to expectations. His reply was actually quite a good attempt, and it was a smart thing to release it to all the media.

But Beam and his detectives weren't smart enough to guess their quarry's next move. They thought in the usual channels and assumed he was a classic serial killer, that he was moved by compulsion and locked into patterns of thought and action.

Not at all. They didn't know, for instance, that his list of potential victims had increased eleven-fold.

He smiled again. He couldn't help it, and he'd scooted sideways on the seat so the cab driver couldn't see him now in the rear-view mirror. A part of the Justice Killer's mind was leisurely, almost lovingly, contemplating the identity of his next victim. A common juror rather than a foreperson. Which juror hadn't been decided yet. That was all within the power of the Justice Killer. *Only* the Justice Killer. He felt a tightening in his groin and was surprised to find that he had an erection.

That isn't what this is supposed to be about. Not primarily, anyway.

Think about baseball. He grinned inwardly. *Damned Steinbrenner. All the money in the world and can't buy a world championship. Now, the Mets . . .*

The baseball diversion actually worked pretty well. Within a few blocks the bulge beneath his fly was gone.

The designated hitter. What a dumb-ass move that turned out to be.

He casually scanned Beam's letter again beside him in the *Post.* It really was an admirable effort, deceptively simple.

It hadn't the desired effect, but of course Beam couldn't know that. He was probably reading all the papers, like his opponent, and smiling, like his opponent.

They were both pleased this morning. Beam would doubtless consider his published reply progress. And maybe it was, though in the wrong direction. Still, a move, progress.

Something, anyway. A countermove.

The Justice Killer had anticipated no less of Beam.

The Selig and Cohen cases were both colder than the victims, but Beam had manufactured an excuse to return by himself to the Village.

He stood perspiring in the doorway of a closed bookshop across the street and watched the entrance to Things Past. Nola was visible from time to time behind the collectibles and notices displayed in the window, a dark form beyond dark glass, moving gracefully. Or was Beam filling in the grace himself? Remembering? The truth was, it might even be another woman moving around inside the shop. A customer. Not Nola at all except in Beam's mind.

Making a fool of myself . . .

The temperature was almost ninety, and he was starting to suffer from the heat. His legs were heavy, and now and then he felt a slight dizziness.

Getting too old for this kind of thing. For lots of things.

It had been almost half an hour since he'd seen anyone enter or leave the shop. He wondered if Nola made enough profit to stay in business. Some of the tiny specialty shops in the Village weren't on solid financial ground in and of themselves. They were causes, or fixations, or playthings of the rich. Beam wondered if Nola had collected a lot of insurance money from Harry's death. If Harry had life insurance, it might have paid big. Death by misadventure made for immense settlements for the beneficiaries. Maybe Nola was getting by financially that way; it sure didn't look like the antique and collectible business was all that lucrative.

Finally Beam gave up. He had to talk to her.

He patted sweat from his face with a folded handkerchief, then stepped out from the doorway and crossed the street diagonally, drawing a horn blast and an angry shout from a guy in a black van.

When he entered the shop, she was alone. No surprise.

The door that had tinkled a bell when he came in swung closed, and there was a heavy silence in the shop. It wasn't much cooler inside, but for Beam the change in temperature felt drastic.

Nola was standing behind the counter near the register, staring at him. She had on a sleeveless red blouse. Her arms were tanned and smooth, like those of a much younger woman. Did she exercise regularly? Was she a jogger? Or was her physical beauty all hereditary? He wanted to know things about her. Everything. Harry had talked about her from time to time, but it was mostly sexual innuendo. Harry bragging, needling Beam.

"I was standing over there watching you," Beam said, trying honesty as an approach.

She didn't change expression. "I know. I saw you. Why did you come in?"

Not "Why were you watching me?"

She knows why.

She was staring at him unblinkingly, like an Indian princess misplaced in time in a Greenwich Village antique shop, waiting for an answer.

He gave her one, a peace offering: "I had to see you. I need for you to understand—to believe—I didn't suspect Harry might be killed. I didn't want him harmed."

"Of course you didn't. He was valuable to you. I understand that."

"That's true, about him being valuable. But it's also true I underestimated the danger."

"You risked my husband's life. Are you trying to tell me you didn't know that at the time?"

"Of course not. I mean, I knew there was risk. We all did. I didn't want him—I didn't think he'd be killed. It's important that you know that."

"You want forgiveness, you bastard."

The heavy heat from outside seemed to have invaded the shop now. The back of Beam's neck was perspiring.

"I want understanding," Beam said. "Harry was a fence, Nola, and the truth is, so were you. There was enough evidence to bring charges against both of you."

"Now you want thanks?"

"No. I want you to put away your grief and anger and live in the present." He waved his arms. "Not with all this stuff from a past that'll keep dragging you back."

"My. How concerned you are for me."

"Damn it, I am!"

"Why?"

"You're Harry's widow. And believe it or not, Harry was my friend."

"You're lying. Harry was your snitch. Friends and snitches are mutually exclusive."

That wasn't true, but in another way, it was. That was why Harry was dead.

Beam knew he'd feel at least somewhat better if she'd show some righteous rage, if she'd shout and throw something at him, instead of being so damned focused and reasonable. So damned . . . right.

"I want forgiveness," he admitted.

She didn't seem surprised that he'd blurted it out. Nothing would shake her composure. Warm as the stifling, cluttered shop full of yesterday was, she wasn't perspiring. "Do you think you deserve forgiveness?"

"Yes. Maybe we all do."

"This killer you're hunting—does he deserve forgiveness?"

"No," Beam said. "He's different."

"From you?"

Perspiration zigzagged down Beam's back beneath his damp shirt, a persistent tickle that stopped when it reached his belt. "Yes."

"So he doesn't deserve forgiveness and you do?"

"Yes. And you need to forgive."

Nola understood what he needed, and what she herself needed, but for now she wasn't capable of giving or receiving. He should be able to see that in her, to stay away. He was making things worse.

"Captain Beam, you go to hell."

In the face of her unwavering stare, he moved toward the front of the shop and opened the door. The bell above tinkled, as if announcing another round with the heat. Beam didn't say goodbye to Nola. He went outside.

It was something like hell.

*   *   *

Tina drove the white Saab sedan out of the apartment building's garage and stopped at the curb so Martin could get in on the passenger side. He'd been standing talking to Jerry the doorman about God knew what, and even before the car came to a complete stop, he was climbing in.

Taking it slow, not attracting attention, Tina leaned forward and waved to Jerry before pulling out into traffic. She'd wheeled Martin's large black suitcase into the elevator and across the garage's concrete floor, then wrestled it into the car's trunk. If anybody was watching the building, she didn't want them to know Martin was leaving for any extended time. They might be followed to the airport. The killer might want to strike before Martin could leave New York. The psycho might have some kind of fixation about that—about all his victims dying in New York. Serial killers were compulsive.

Yet in many ways they were unpredictable; their thought processes weren't like ours.

What Tina did know was that such killers were moved by forces even they might not understand, making them to do some things over and over and in the same way. Like killing the same type of victim. Like jury forepersons. Like Martin. Repetition was the narcotic that lulled and then tripped them up, and eventually it should lead to the capture of the Justice Killer. But maybe not in time, if he had his sights set on Martin as his next victim. The killer had the edge. It took the police a while to catch on to repetition.

Tina goosed the Saab to merge with heavier traffic and headed for the tunnel. It wasn't the only way to LaGuardia, but it was the route she always took without even thinking about it.

Repetition.

22

It was getting dark, and headlights and streetlamps were gradually joining the battle against the night, when the doorman gave Nell the okay, twisted his key in the elevator control panel, and she rose fifty-five stories, to the penthouse of J. K. Selig.

Amazingly, it seemed only a few seconds before the elevator adjusted itself smoothly to floor level and its door slid open to an anteroom of Selig's apartment.

The first thing she noticed was how refreshingly cool it was. Not like her crummy little apartment where she had to spend time in the bedroom because it was the only room with an air conditioner that worked. If that Terry guy didn't return her phone calls and repair the living room unit, she'd have to give up on him and pass the word that he wasn't as reliable as she'd heard.

No one seemed to be about. There was a comfortable-looking loveseat in the anteroom, a Persian carpet over gleaming hardwood floor, and a colorful tapestry on the north wall. Beyond the anteroom's ornately paneled arch was a vast room containing a long, L-shaped white leather sofa, flower patterned chairs, and glass-topped tables with bulky gray lamps with square shades. All on a stretch of pale blue carpet as vast as a sea gone flat. Nell saw no wall hangings; what she saw was the city laid out for miles and coming alive with light. The view was stunning.

She'd stopped two steps out of the elevator and was taking all this in with awe, when a tall, slender man with a lean face beneath a full head of coarse white hair approached. His features had an ax-like sharpness but were symmetrical and handsome. He was wearing a white shirt, gray slacks, black loafers, and a perfect tan. In his early or mid sixties, Nell thought, as he smiled at her with even white teeth. The smile creased his bold features as his blue eyes appraised Nell.

She was appraising him right back. Money. Lots of it. The East Side penthouse might be just the tip of his wealth.

He held out his right hand. "Jack Selig."

Nell shook the hand, noticing a diamond ring. "I'm Detective Nell Corey." She reached toward her blazer pocket for her shield.

Selig gave a dismissive, backhanded wave. "Don't bother. Eddie, downstairs in the lobby, checked you out." His inquisitive eyes very obviously continuing the checking out process.

Nell liked it. *Knock it off! This character's in his sixties. An old man.*

She flashed him the shield anyway before returning it to her pocket. Still with the smile, Selig motioned with his right hand for Nell to enter all the way. He invited her to sit on the leather sofa and asked if she wanted some water or a glass of wine. She accepted the sofa but declined the drink.

"I'm sorry about your wife," Nell began awkwardly. This guy threw her, old as he was. A rich widower. Vulnerable? Was she some kind of money grubber at heart?

Selig nodded. "It's been two years. I still miss her a great deal."

"You know why we're putting you through this again?"

Another nod. "I read in the papers that the police think Iris was an early victim of the Justice Killer."

"What do you think?" Nell asked.

"That she was. As soon as I became aware of the Justice Killer, I assumed the police saw her that way. Two years isn't that long ago, and this being the age of the computer, it was likely the circumstances of Iris's death would already have been linked with what was happening now . . . the other Justice Killer murders." He shook his head and frowned. "I don't understand this killer. Iris was only doing her duty. She didn't ask to serve on a jury. Why doesn't he go after defendants he thinks were mistakenly released back into society?"

"We think it's the system itself he's raging against," Nell said.

Selig considered, blue gaze turned momentarily inward. "I see."

"Unfortunately, your wife became an integral part of that system."

"She might have been foreperson of that jury, but she only had one vote. And why doesn't this maniac go after the prosecutors and judges? They're part of the system, too. Some of them *are* the system."

"When we catch him," Nell said, "we'll ask him, but we probably won't be satisfied with the answer."

Selig's expression hardened. Everything about him shouted that he'd been born rich and enjoyed all of life's advantages, Ivy League education, connections, soft safety net.

But *soft* wasn't the word for this guy. There was a surprising steeliness to him as he looked at Nell. "I'd like to be alone with him and ask him some questions before I wring his neck."

Nell smiled faintly. "I can't promise you that, but we're doing everything possible to put you in the same room with him—a courtroom."

Selig sighed. His hands were clenched tightly into fists.

Nell hated to ask him to relive the night of his wife's death, but she had no choice.

Selig didn't seem to mind. "I came home from the office at eight twenty, after working late, and called out Iris's name when I couldn't find her. When I looked into various rooms and got to the bathroom off the hall . . ." he swallowed hard; Nell could hear it ". . . I found her. She was lying on the floor in a pool of blood . . . so much blood. I could see the bullet hole in her chest, between her breasts. It was so small . . . It didn't look necessarily fatal, but later, when I saw photographs of the exit wound . . ." He bowed his head. "A large area of her back was missing. Her spine . . ." Selig stood up. "You mind if I have a drink myself?"

"Not at all," Nell said.

He started across the blue carpet, then he paused and turned back to her. "You sure you—"

"Nothing for me," Nell told him.

"Working girl."

"Working cop."

He looked at her closely then managed a thin smile. "I'm sorry."

"I won't tell the politically correct police." She waited, staring out at the galaxy of the city, until he returned carrying a glass of what looked like water with ice cubes.

"It's surprising to me how that night's coming back." He settled down again on the white sofa, on the leg of the *L,* seated at a slight angle so they were facing each other. He seemed calmer now, even relaxed. Nell had to admire the drape of his gray slacks as he crossed his legs.

She said, "After you found your wife's body . . ."

Selig took a sip of water. "I phoned the police, of course."

"911?"

"No. It didn't occur to me. But the police notified somebody, and an ambulance and paramedics arrived the same time they did."

"When you found Iris's body, did you notice the red letter *J* scrawled with lipstick on the bathroom mirror?"

"No. The police asked me about it later. I told them I knew nothing about it, but I—we—thought at the time that maybe Iris had been trying to write something to me, beginning to spell out *Jack* when she died. Later, they told me that wouldn't have been possible. She'd died instantly. There were no fingerprints on the lipstick tube. The killer had either wiped them off or worn gloves. The police said he wouldn't have bothered if he hadn't touched the lipstick, so they figured he was the one who wrote on the mirror."

Nell glanced around at all the opulence. "How did he get in here? I mean, you need to have the doorman use his key to get the elevator to go all the way to the penthouse. I'm assuming his key and yours are the same."

"As was Iris's key."

"According to the file, the killer might have come up here with Iris." Nell moderated her tone so Selig wouldn't get the wrong—or the obvious—idea. Had Iris brought home a lover?

"The doorman remembers her coming up alone," he said.

"Eddie?"

"A different doorman." Selig chewed the inside of his cheek for a few seconds, thinking, then said, "I do remember there'd been a series of burglaries in the building that same year. Some without signs of forced entry. The police checked all the keys, everyone's in the building. There weren't a lot of spare keys floating around after that. I'm sure there still aren't. It's still a mystery as to how the killer got in here."

"Have you changed the locks?"

"Of course."

"You were a suspect for a while," Nell said, not liking it but knowing she should push here.

No sign of guilt or uneasiness on Selig's face. "I know. That's natural, since I was the victim's husband. But my alibi, my presence at the office, was well established."

"They considered the possibility you might have hired someone to kill your wife, and provided him with a key."

"It's still a possibility," Selig said calmly. "But I didn't do that. I loved my wife. I wish she were still alive. I had no motive. Iris had money when I married her, and I made plenty of money in New York real estate. We had no children. Either of us could have walked away from the marriage clean. Neither of us dreamed of doing so."

Nell believed him. Not only that, she felt sorry for him. *Not very professional.* Her eyes threatened to tear up, so she pretended to concentrate on the notepad in her lap until she gained control. *Working girl. Not me!*

"The past two years have been lonely ones," Selig said. "I'd give every penny I have if there were some way to get Iris back." His chest heaved beneath the neatly pressed white shirt. "Impossible, and masochistic to keep thinking about it. And of course," he added, "I don't think about it all the time. Two years ago isn't yesterday."

Nell didn't know quite how to phrase this next question. "Is there anyone in your life now?"

"Another woman? No. There've been a few minor attachments, that's all." A shadow of sadness passed over his features, this handsome, mature man who looked as if he should be carefree on the bridge of his yacht, who for all Nell knew might very well own a yacht. "I've made my fortune. Fortune enough, anyway. Now I manage my investments out of my home office, take most meals alone, and travel by myself."

Minor attachments, Nell thought. Maybe for him, but she bet not for the women. This guy was quite a catch for an older woman. In fact . . .

"Have I been of any help?"

Nell refocused her attention. "I'm sorry?"

"I thought you were finished with the interview. You were quiet, and you closed your notepad."

Nell glanced down again at her lap. She had absently

closed the notepad. It didn't matter, as she hadn't taken any notes. What Selig had told her coincided precisely with what was in the two-year-old murder file.

"I was thinking," she said. "The doorman at the time of Iris's death, do you know where he might be found?"

"He was struck and killed by a bus a year ago," Selig said. "I sent flowers to his family where he was buried, somewhere in Louisiana."

Alexandria. Nell had already known the answer to her question. Selig had answered accurately again, volunteering information, not seeming in any way guilty of anything. Seeming, in fact, to be just as he described himself—rich and lonely. That could be a dangerous combination for a man. It would be terrible if some fortune-hunting bitch glommed onto this guy.

Of course, there were women other than fortune hunters who might be interested in him. Wealthy widows who frequented the same yacht club.

Nell stood up.

"Will there be more questions later?"

"I'm sure there will be," Nell said, though she could find no reason for more questions.

"Good," Selig said, smiling as he ushered her back to the elevator. He watched over her as if the thing might explode before it began its descent.

"Good," she heard him say again, as she dropped.

When Nell was gone, Selig went to his desk in the penthouse's den that had been converted to his office. He opened a drawer and withdrew several framed photographs and laid them out on the desk.

He hadn't looked at them in months. He'd tried, in fact, to forget they existed. But he could never have thrown them away.

For the next five minutes, in the hushed, lonely silence, he studied the photos.

It was amazing how much Nell the detective resembled the younger Iris Selig.

Tina left the car in short-term parking and went into the terminal with Martin. If it were possible, she would have accompanied him down the concourse and watched him board. She was becoming more and more uneasy about his safety and wanted him free and clear of the city as soon as possible. She needed reassurance.

Martin had forty minutes before his flight left, so he bought a *Newsweek* to read on the plane, and he and Tina sat and watched people stream past, some of whom would be Martin's fellow passengers. It was slight comfort for Tina to know that none of JK's victims had been killed on a plane. Silly, she knew, but she wondered if Martin also had considered it. Serial killers were supposedly programmed to follow certain patterns, so maybe you were safe on a plane.

"Once you're on board, we can breath easier," she said.

He glanced over at her and smiled. "I suppose you're right, but I still have my doubts about running away from what might only be my imagination."

Tina was a little irritated, especially since, as he spoke, Martin couldn't resist eyeing a long-legged blonde with exceptionally large breasts flounce past. *Machismo* kicking in, now that fear had partially retreated. "That's not how you were talking earlier."

"This is later," Martin said. "And I'm boarding the plane anyway, so relax."

"I'll relax when you're up, up, and away." She watched every male head along the concourse turn to observe the tall blonde. Pathetic, thought tiny Tina, then wondered if the tall blonde would be on Martin's flight.

"I much prefer you," Martin said, guessing what she was thinking.

Tina leaned toward him and pecked his cheek. "Bastard."

Grinning, he stood up and slung the strap of his carry-on over his shoulder. "They'll be boarding pretty soon."

Tina also stood. "I'll walk with you to security."

"You want to sit on my lap on the plane?"

"If I didn't have such a workload, maybe I would."

"You make me feel as if I don't have life insurance."

"Bad joke, baby."

He shrugged with his unburdened shoulder. "Yeah, I guess you're right." As they began walking toward the security check point, he said, "To tell you the truth, I wouldn't be turning tail if I didn't share your premonition of doom."

"You're not turning tail."

"Showing the white feather."

"You're showing good sense," Tina insisted.

As he joined the end of the security line, Martin kissed her goodbye on the lips. "That's what all us cowards say."

"Live cowards," Tina corrected.

She stood and watched the line move along. Martin had to remove his wristwatch and go through the metal detector twice. Good, Tina thought, Security has the device fine-tuned. Maybe there was some sort of terror alert. That would be ironic, if she talked Martin into leaving town so he'd be safe, and he boarded a plane that was commandeered by terrorists. Martin's black carry-on made its way along the conveyor belt and through the fluoroscope. No one opened it or had him remove his shoes.

He glanced back at her, smiled, and waved as he blended in with the other passengers beyond Security and moved along the concourse. *What if I'm seeing him for the last time?*

When he was out of sight, Tina felt unaccountably lonely as well as relieved. She was sure that, later, relief would win out. They were doing the right thing, whatever Martin's inner conflict. Men were bullheaded and carefully nurtured their egos, and he was no exception.

She returned to short-term parking and got into the Saab.

As she was about to fit the key into the ignition, the light seemed to flicker, for less than a second, almost beyond her notice. Though she did notice, she thought nothing of it. She didn't know the brief interference with her vision was the passing of an extremely fine, extremely strong wire before her face.

At each end of the wire were affixed four-inch wooden handles fashioned from a sawed-off broomstick, so the Justice Killer would have a firm grip with each and wouldn't suffer any cuts or scrapes. As he straightened up in the back seat of the Saab, he yanked hard on the wire then crossed and twisted it at the back of the front seat's headrest. Tina's head and neck were immediately pinned to the headrest. As the Justice Killer applied more strength, Tina's hands rose and flailed briefly. She tried to cry out but managed only a high, choking screech, almost exactly like the alarmed caw of a crow, before the wire sliced into her larynx, then her carotid arteries, and blood spurted forward onto the dash and windshield.

The Justice Killer left the wire embedded in Tina's neck—he wore gloves and didn't worry about fingerprints—then reached forward between the front seats and ran the tip of his forefinger in small circles through the blood covering Tina's right nipple. He glanced around to be sure no one was nearby, then he scrawled a red capital *J* on the inside of the car's left rear window. He opened the door, climbed out, and closed the door without slamming it.

Strolling away from the car, he quickly peeled off the gloves, leaving them inside out, and slipped them into a pocket. It took less than a minute for him to walk along the row of cars to where his own was parked, get in, and drive away.

He drove slowly, satisfied. *More than just an erection this time.*

Half an hour passed before a family with vacation tickets for Florida noticed the pale, horrified looking woman seated bolt upright behind the steering wheel of her parked car and gaping wide-eyed at nothing.

23

Beam, Nell, and Looper watched as Tina Flitt's body was removed from behind the steering wheel of the Saab. The medical examiner and crime scene unit had done their preliminary work, so Tina was no longer needed. One of the techs used tiny snips to sever the wire on both sides of her neck. They'd wait until the autopsy to remove the length of wire deeply imbedded in her throat. The ends of the wire, with their small wooden handles, were bagged as evidence. It had already been determined that there were no fingerprints on the handles.

"Our guy wore gloves again," Nell said. "There won't be any usable prints anywhere on or in the car, either."

"If he's our guy," Looper said. "Jeez, I wish I had a cigarette."

"This is the airport," Nell said. "They shoot you if you light a cigarette at the airport."

"The *J* written on the rear side window looks exactly like the others left by JK," Beam said.

"They've been all over the papers and TV," Nell pointed out. "Could be a copycat."

"Could be," Beam agreed, but didn't believe it. It wasn't what his gut was telling him.

Nell's cell phone chirped, and she walked away about twenty feet. Beam and Looper watched as she had a brief conversation, then returned, stuffing the phone back in her blazer pocket. "Computer check showed no Tina Flitt on our jury foreperson list," Nell said. "But a letter in her purse indicates she's an attorney."

"Part of the system," Looper said.

Beam rubbed his chin. "Different part, though. Different weapon, too."

"Same red letter *J*, though."

"Address on her driver's license has her on the Upper East Side," Nell said.

Beam made it a point not to look at Tina Flitt's small, still form as it was loaded into the ambulance. Her head had been almost severed, and he'd seen enough of death lately.

Irv Minskoff from the ME's office walked over. Beam saw that since the last murder he'd been attempting to grow a mustache. It was coming in gray and bushy, and along with his gnarly features and thick-lensed glasses, made him look like a country-town general practitioner who mostly gave flu shots and birthed babies. Didn't talk that way, though. "Poor bitch was damn near decapitated."

"What kind of wire was it?" Beam asked.

"Hard to say. Very thin but with lots of tensile strength, like dental floss or fishing line leader."

"But it wasn't either of those?"

"No, it was wire. Maybe piano wire. She died quickly, probably didn't make much noise." Minskoff used a forefinger to smooth both sides of his mustache. "Nice car, but it's not gonna be worth anything after this, what with all the blood and what came out when her sphincter relaxed. Smell just about knocks you out when you stick your head in there." He turned to watch the silent ambulance pull away. "Probably a looker when she was alive. Slender body, good enough rack. Not much tit but terrific nipples. Killer noticed that, too. Looks like he ran whatever he wrote with—his finger, probably—over her right nipple to get his blood ink." He shook his head. "I see a waste like that, it saddens me. Know anything about her?"

"I thought you might tell me," Beam said.

"I make her out to be in her mid-forties. Fashion label clothes to go with the new car. Married."

"How do you know she was married?" Beam asked, almost dreading the answer from the callous little medical examiner.

"Wedding ring," Minskoff said with a smile. "Looks reasonably expensive. More to the point, she's been dead less than an hour. So if she came here to catch a plane, it either left not long ago or it's still here. You might wanna hurry."

"Maybe she just flew in and was about to drive away when she was killed."

"Yeah, I suppose that's possible."

"She didn't come here to catch a plane," Beam said, "and she didn't just arrive. No luggage in the car. No airline ticket. And she's in short term parking."

Minskoff looked slightly embarrassed. "I guess that's why I do my job and you do yours. Need anything else on prelim? Like cause of death?"

Beam thought Minskoff was probably joking, but he simply shook his head no. About ten years ago he'd investigated to see if someone had been pushed out a high window, and an autopsy revealed a bullet in the mess the victim had become.

"Safety belt wouldn't have saved her," Minskoff said, with a glance at the Saab behind the yellow tape. He gave Beam a little half salute, then walked away toward the city car he drove.

Beam figured the last word must be important to Minskoff in crime scene humor, so he let him have it.

Beam beckoned Nell and Looper over. He told Looper to

go into the terminal and start a check on passenger lists to see if anyone named Flitt was booked out of the airport for that evening.

Then he walked over to the car that was surrounded by crime scene tape. Three techs from the crime scene unit remained. "Check the car out all the way," Beam said. "Photograph it, check for prints, black light it, vacuum it, then have it towed in so it can be gone over again. The bastard we're looking for was in the backseat, probably waiting for the victim to get in. He must have left something. A bloody footprint, maybe a hair. We get a hair, we got a DNA sample."

"You don't have to tell me," the tech said, sounding miffed. Beam didn't care.

"You want the whole purse bagged for evidence?" one of the other techs asked.

"The purse and everything in it. And make sure you bag the set of keys on the floor by the accelerator."

Tina Flitt not only hadn't had time to fasten her safety belt, she hadn't even gotten the car key in the ignition before the killer had struck. He'd been ready for her. Eager for her.

Beam glanced around, noticed a small object affixed to a nearby post, and smiled.

Security camera.

24

The next morning, da Vinci's office: Hot. Stuffy. It smelled as if someone had recently smoked a cigar in there.

The scene on the TV looked like one of those slow dissolves that French directors love to use.

"He stood out of sight and squirted wasp killer on the security camera," Beam said. "Stuff sprays a stream about twenty feet so you can get outta the way and not get stung when the wasps get pissed off."

"Hell of a way to take out a camera," da Vinci said.

"Attracts less attention than shinning up a pole with a can of spray paint. It messed up the lens, but not all the way, so we got some images on tape."

"Anything that'll help?"

"It's doubtful," Beam said. "Security guy inside the terminal didn't notice right away that the picture was blurred on his monitor, and when he did, he assumed it was equipment failure."

"Naturally," da Vinci said. "Much easier to deal with than vandals or serial killers."

Both men were silent, staring at the screen.

As Beam had said, the insecticide didn't do a perfect job.

Blurred human figures came and went on the black and white tape, but not many. The light was dim in the parking garage, and the airport hadn't been busy at that time, so traffic was at a minimum. The upper right part of the screen was where things were less blurred.

"What was that?" da Vinci asked, pointing as a dark, uniformed figure briefly appeared on the screen.

"Airport security," Beam said. "They patrol the area. Unfortunately, they weren't at the right place at the right time. Fact is, there aren't enough of them." Beam fast forwarded the tape, then slowed it to normal speed. "This is the approximate time of the murder."

Da Vinci sat forward. "Hell, you can't even see the car."

"There!" Beam said. He stopped the tape, backed it up, slow motioned forward, stopped it again. "That's it." Beam pointed to a light-colored sedan halfway down a row of parked cars. A figure behind the steering wheel was definitely visible, and so was a dark form in the back seat. The picture blurred again into meaningless patterns like paint splashed on a window.

"That was him?" da Vinci asked. He sounded awed, but also disappointed.

"We think so. He was visible, so he musta been raising up from where he was crouched behind the driver's seat. And the victim was in the car. This had to be seconds before he looped the wire around her neck. As you can see, the time marked on the tape is eight sixteen. Her ticket's got her in the lot at seven forty."

"Thirty-six minutes in the airport," da Vinci said. "She musta been dropping off someone. Or picking them up."

"What we managed to piece together, from witnesses and airline records, is she dropped off her husband for a flight to Chicago. Flitt used her maiden name. He's Martin Portelle."

"And she musta gone inside the terminal with him," da Vinci said, "since she was in the short-term garage." Da Vinci looked thoughtful. "Wait a minute!"

He moved aside the scale model sculpture of the motorcycle he'd ridden as a young cop, then rooted through some papers on his desk. Beam saw on the wall behind the desk a framed photo of an even more youthful da Vinci posed seated in full uniform on an identical cycle.

"Ah!" Da Vinci had found a computer printout. "These are the jury forepersons from ten years of the trials we think might get the killer's blood up." He ran down the page with his forefinger, then slapped the desk with the flat of his hand. "I thought it sounded familiar. Here it is—Martin Portelle was the foreman of the jury that let Dan Maddox, the subway killer, walk six years ago." Da Vinci flipped the paper in reverse across the desk so Beam could read it. "We were concentrating on the victim, not her husband."

"It looks like our sicko's changed tactics and is killing family members of forepersons," Beam said. He not only didn't like this development, it didn't make any kind of sense to him, not even twisted sense.

"Not exactly," da Vinci said. "Read on and you'll find that Tina Flitt was one of the jurors in the Maddox trial. That's where she and her future hubby met."

"So she was an ordinary juror?"

"Uh-huh. Which means our killer's broken the mold."

"Only cracked it," Beam said. "He's still killing within the justice system. But he's changed his pattern. It's happened before. Some serial killers are damned smart, and they read the literature. They know their vulnerabilities, and what the police are looking for, so they deliberately vary their behavior."

"They can't vary everything," da Vinci said. "Not according to our police profiler and psychiatrists."

"They're right, generally," Beam said, "but sometimes picking up the thread isn't so easy if the killer's a smart one. And this one is."

"I don't wanna make you blush," da Vinci said, "but you're smart, too. That's why I wanted you for the job."

"There's something else about the Flitt murder I don't like," Beam said, not blushing. "Another reason JK might have varied his method. It seems to me he's beginning to enjoy what he's doing."

"Like he never did."

"I mean, whatever his original motive is or was, killing's providing sexual pleasure for him. He took the time to diddle with Flitt's nipple while dipping for blood to write with."

"Sexual . . . I'm not so sure about that. It doesn't seem to be what motivates this puppy."

"One way or another, it motivates all of them. Or that's the way it turns."

"Sexual is just what the media loves."

"It motivates them," Beam said.

Da Vinci thought about it, looked stricken, and spun 360 degrees in his swivel chair so he was facing Beam again. "This is a bunch of shit we don't need."

"The possible upside is, he'll start enjoying killing so much that in his excitement, he'll make a mistake and we'll nail him."

Da Vinci didn't seem interested just then in the upside. "I don't mean only his sick enjoyment is a bunch of shit. I mean everything he's doing different, assuming he's the one that did Tina Flitt. You understand how this complicates things?"

"Sure," Beam said.

"I mean the politics of the case?"

"I'm not thinking about politics, just my job."

"And I'm thinking about my job. Which I might not have if this case goes sour. This city's justice system's gonna go bonkers when it finds out all twelve of the jurors might be targets. Nobody'll wanna do jury duty."

"Nobody wants to now," Beam said. "Nobody ever did."

Da Vinci stared across the desk as if Beam were responsible for everything that had happened. "Have you, for Chrissakes, got any *good* news?"

"Lab got six human hairs from the back of Tina Flitt's car," Beam said. "We're waiting now for possible DNA matches."

"That'd be too simple," da Vinci said, but not without hope in his voice.

"Handles on the garrote he made were probably sections of a wooden broom handle. They're manufactured in China and sold by the tens of thousands. After looping the wire around Tina's neck, he used the handles to gain leverage so he could twist harder."

"I know the method," da Vinci said, raising his hand in a motion for Beam not to explain further.

"Looks like he got the handles from a broomstick using a fine-toothed saw."

"Also sold by the tens of thousands. Any fingerprints?"

"No. He wore gloves again."

"You're really sure it was our guy?"

"I'm trying to make sure," Beam said, "but we can't rule out copycat. We *can* rule out the husband. Portelle did board the plane, and security cameras did record him and his wife inside the terminal at the passenger checkpoint. And according to the time stamp on this tape, the plane was taxiing for takeoff at the time of the murder."

"Is he back in town?"

"Flew back from Chicago a few hours ago. Nell and Looper are interviewing him. I talked to Nell. She says he's an emotional mess."

The desk phone rang. Da Vinci picked it up, then said, "Put him on." He covered the mouthpiece with his hand and dropped it below chin level. "It's the commissioner. Anything more?"

"No You want me to leave the security tape?"

Da Vinci shook his head no. "Put it in the murder file."

As Beam was removing the tape from the machine and leaving the office, he heard da Vinci behind him: "Yes, *sir*. How are *you*, sir?"

Practicing the politics of the case.

* * *

The Justice Killer had ordered lunch at Admiral Nelson's, a new restaurant in lower Manhattan with an improbable sailing ship theme, and was seated in a booth resembling a cutaway lifeboat, waiting for his food to arrive. He sipped his gin martini and wondered what the police laboratory would make of the wire he'd used to kill Tina Flitt. He'd seen it protruding from an old lamp shade at an outdoor flea market in SoHo, glinting in the sun. The wire had been part of a beading design at the base of the shade, running its entire circumference.

Why the glint of sunlight at the base of the drab yellowed shade had given him the idea, he wasn't sure. But he realized he'd been considering a different way to kill Tina, a way more . . . personal than a bullet from ten feet away, or simply fired into her head or the base of her spine from the backseat of her car. After the moment of ice, when she was paralyzed by what was about to happen, he wanted her literally to die at his hands. He wanted to feel her death like a message in the wire.

That was it; he wanted to experience the vibrations of her death, and of his vengeance.

He sipped his drink.

More than vengeance.

So he'd bought the old brass and ceramic lamp for twelve dollars, and a block away deposited it in with some trash at the curb, and kept only the shade. It had been easy, that evening, to cut away part of the shade's fabric and beading and remove the wire.

The garrote he'd fashioned had worked more efficiently than he'd anticipated. Too efficiently, perhaps. Tina Flitt had died within seconds, and the wire had been so deeply imbedded in her neck that he hadn't even attempted to remove it.

Still, he'd felt her die, heard her die, even heard the rush of her blood as it spilled from her.

It was like nothing so much as sex.

He pushed away the thought .

Yes, he was enjoying his mission now, but that made it no less a mission. He'd joined the fraternity of serial killers that murdered women for sexual thrall. But it was a fraternity he'd long misunderstood, and one whose members were distinguishable from each other.

He had reasons beyond the thrill of the hunt and the primal satisfaction of the kill. He was meting out justice to a system that had failed and was failing and must be changed. And of course he didn't always kill women. Jurors were his target, not women, though every jury included women. He didn't fall into the classic serial killer pattern he'd read and heard so much about. He wasn't like the rest of them. Not at all.

He had his reasons to kill, and they were good ones.

His thoughts were interrupted by the arrival of his food, brought by an attractive young woman wearing some kind of nautical outfit. Her blond hair was chopped short and she wore one gold hoop earring, pirate style. Her top was horizontally striped red and white and had a square, low-cut neckline.

As she smiled and bent low to place his dishes on the table, the Justice Killer was aware of a nearby booth full of businessmen observing her generous breasts.

He couldn't stop looking at her neck.

25

Melanie couldn't look away.

Cold Cat smiled. Or almost smiled. She couldn't really be sure. He had this way of slightly curling his upper lip so he *might* be smiling. But whatever message his lips were sending, the look in his eye was for her.

It took real force of will for her finally to avert her gaze.

Every day in court, since the outburst from the defendant's mother, Cold Cat and Melanie had made some sort of contact she was sure no one else in the crowded courtroom noticed. And often she'd seen him exchange looks with his mother, who was always present. But they weren't the same kind of looks.

The defense was presenting its case, and slick Bob Murray was standing directly in front of the table where Cold Cat sat, so both men were in the witness's line of sight. The witness was a man named Merv Clark, whose appearance in court was over the strenuous objection of the prosecution.

"Would you tell us where you were at approximately two fifteen on the afternoon of February the sixteenth?" Murray asked politely, as Clark was his witness.

"No approximate about it," Clark said. He was a well-groomed man in his thirties, with puggish features and slicked-back curly blond hair cut short on the sides and neatly parted in the middle. He'd said he was a cook but was presently between jobs. "I was out walking and happened to be passing the Velmont building on East Fifty-second Street. High-class apartments there, uniformed doorman, the whole bit. I know the time for sure because I'd told my wife I'd be back within an hour, and she's a stickler about that kind of thing. I didn't wanna be late, so I checked my watch a lot. I was checking it when I looked up and saw him."

"Who was it you saw?" Murray asked.

"That man. The defendant." Clark pointed. "Seen him coming out of the building."

"Let the record show that the Velmont Building is where Mr. Knee High lives."

Melanie sat forward in her chair so she had an unobstructed view of Clark. She was aware of some of the other jurors also leaning forward. Already the testimony of the funny little man Knee High made it unlikely that Cold Cat had the opportunity to murder Edie Piaf. If Merv Clark was telling the truth about seeing Cold Cat on the East Side at quarter past two, he corroborated Knee High's testimony. There was no way the defendant could have killed his wife on the West Side between two and two thirty, as the prosecution claimed.

Murray asked that the court record the fact that the witness had pointed to the defendant. Then, moving away from the table, he asked, "How did you know the man you saw emerging from the Velmont Arms was Richard Simms?"

"You mean Cold Cat? I recognized him right off. I know him, man, what he looks like. I buy his music. I'm a music fan, never miss the Grammys, all that stuff."

"And you're sure of the time?"

"Positive." Clark held up his left wrist so his suit coat sleeve slipped down to reveal a silver watch. "New watch.

Birthday gift from the wife. Keeps perfect time. So does the wife." The jury and courtroom onlookers rewarded Clark's humor with a ripple of laughter. That seemed to encourage him. "I knew if I was late she'd whap me upside the head with a skillet." Too far. No laughter this time.

In the silence, Judge Moody cleared her throat.

"What's a skillet?" a young woman in the gallery whispered.

Murray jumped in, addressing the witness. He didn't want his examination to become an unintentional comedy routine. "And did you attempt to approach Richard Simms in front of the Velmont Arms at the approximate time of his wife's murder?"

Farrato, the Napoleonic little prosecutor, rose from his chair, standing erectly with his chest thrust out. "Objection, your honor. Leading question."

Almost unnoticeably, Murray shrugged. "Mr. Clark, did you talk to—"

"Leading!" Farrato was still on his feet. "Leading, leading, leading!"

Judge Moody sighed. "Sustained."

No Murray shrug now. He was all business. "What happened after you saw the defendant?"

"I wanted to approach him. I was gonna ask for his autograph, but he turned and walked the other way on the sidewalk."

"Did you call out or follow?"

"No. I mean, I was so surprised to see him. I always admired him. And there he was right in front of me. I mean, he's a celebrity and a great artist. I guess I was kinda paralyzed. Then, before I got my wits about me again, he was gone, kinda lost in the crowd. There were lotsa people out walking that day, and the sidewalks were crowded. I missed my chance to talk to him, one of my idols."

"This occurred at approximately quarter past two?"

"Exactly quarter past two."

"Exactly," Murray repeated, almost absently.

At the defense table, Cold Cat was taking all this in with a stone face. His facade slipped only for a moment, when he glanced Melanie's way as he was shifting in his chair to make sure his mother was in the courtroom. Melanie glimpsed the vulnerability in him, the softness and the pain.

Murray thanked the witness and sat down, and Farrato stood up to cross examine. He adjusted his oversized tie knot and began to pace.

"Will you have time to finish your cross before we break for the day?" Judge Moody asked.

"Yes, Your Honor," Farrato replied immediately, talking on the move, four steps each way, leading to compact and surprisingly graceful turnarounds. "I'll be brief. There isn't any reason not to be." He stopped after two steps and did his tight little ballet turn toward the witness. "Mr. Clark, isn't it a fact that your apartment is ten blocks from the Velmont Arms?"

"It is. I like to—"

"A simple yes or no will do," Farrato said.

"Mr. Farrato," said Judge Moody in a tired tone, "I'm the one who gives witnesses instructions in this court."

"Of course, Judge. I was trying to be brief."

"Be so," said the judge.

Farrato raised his eyebrows and looked at Clark expectantly.

"Yes," said Clark

"Is it not also true that you are scheduled for a court appearance on a battery charge next month?"

"Yes, it's also true."

"For beating your wife so severely she almost lost an eye and will require reconstructive surgery on her left cheekbone?"

"Well . . . yes."

"What prompted you to volunteer your services as a witness?"

"I saw on the news about Cold Cat's case, then I read about it in the papers and realized that I had a duty to help to ascertain the truth."

That last suggested Murray had prepared his witness well, but Farrato seemed only momentarily angry. "Then you're here doing your civic duty?"

"Exactly. That and because I like Cold Cat's music. I think he's a poet of the streets."

"Mr. Clark, do you expect anything in return for testifying for the defense?"

"Return?"

Farrato nodded. "A *quid pro quo*. You said yourself Richard Simms is a celebrity. A rich one. And you're in need of good legal counsel. Perhaps Mr. Simms, or one of his *people,* will see that your legal fees are taken care of. Perhaps even Mr. Murray himself would be so kind—"

"Objection," Murray said, in the same weary tone the judge used when dealing with persistently pesky attorneys.

"Sustained."

"Were you promised anything in return for your testimony?" Farrato asked the witness again.

"No! Definitely no!"

"Does your wife love you?"

"Object!" Murray said.

"I'll rephrase," Farrato said, before the judge could sustain. "Mr. Clark, do you *believe* your wife loves you?"

Puzzled, Clark looked to the judge, who said nothing. "Yeah. Yes, I'm sure she does."

"Would she lie through her broken teeth to keep you out of prison despite the fact that you beat her almost to death?"

"Hey!"

"Object."

"Sustained," said the judge. To Farrato: "You know that kind of behavior is inexcusable, counselor."

"I'm finished, your honor."

"Not quite, but you're getting close. We'll adjourn until tomorrow."

As usual, everyone rose when the judge did, and waited for her to leave before making their own exits. Too much ceremony and tradition, as far as Melanie was concerned. The truth could get lost in all that following the rules.

The last question, about Clark's wife possibly lying for him, had been interesting to Melanie. She thought about it as she stood up and filed with the rest of the jurors from their chairs and toward the doors. Farrato had as much as told them Clark's wife would corroborate Clark's account of leaving their apartment to take a walk. If the jury believed her, Farrato knew they might very well believe Clark. Which is why he was trying to impugn her testimony, along with her husband's, even before she took the stand and testified.

Might Clark be lying? Melanie didn't think he looked like a perjurer. He wore a conservative suit, a maroon tie with a matching handkerchief peeking from its coat pocket. His blue eyes and pug face suggested no guile whatsoever; he looked *nice,* like a man who'd never entertained an evil thought.

But he *had* beaten his wife, according to Farrato.

So why would she lie for him? Her husband had hurt her, and she'd want to lie to hurt him back, not help him. If Clark was an opportunist committing perjury in the expectation that an acquitted Cold Cat would see that he received some money, there was no guarantee that he'd share it with his wife, the wife whose cheekbone he'd shattered.

Maybe she'd lie under oath because she was afraid of him.

Or maybe Clark's battered spouse would commit perjury simply because she loved him. Melanie didn't quite understand why a wife would do that, but she knew it happened frequently.

Some women would do the strangest things for love.

26

"It's not getting any easier," Looper said.

"Because you're getting older," Nell told him.

"You know what I mean."

They were standing with Beam at Rockefeller Center, near where the row of colorful flags waved in the breeze above the sunken level where there was a restaurant and, in the winter, an ice skating rink. Business people in suits and ties scurried past, dodging the slower moving and more casually dressed tourists, some of whom were gawking and photographing. A few people glanced at the shapely, elfin woman with the short and practical hairdo, wearing jeans and a black blazer, standing between the angular man in the cheap brown suit, and the tall, athletic older man who wore a well-tailored gray suit and might easily have been a banker or top CEO were it not for a certain set of his shoulders and roughness to his oversized hands. Maybe he was a former big-time football or baseball player the tourists should recognize. Unless they'd happened to catch him in a rare TV interview or seen his photo in the paper, they wouldn't guess he was a cop on the trail of a serial killer. So they didn't approach him or aim their cameras his way, even though he was the kind of man who looked like *somebody*.

"The techs haven't been able to do much with the security tape," Beam said. "Looks like the killer's at least average size, judging by the relative size of Tina Flitt's car, but they can't clean up the tape so any of his features are visible."

"What about race?" Nell asked.

"No way to know. On the tape, he's really not much more than a shadow." Beam knew Helen Iman, the case profiler, had the killer down as a white male, but that was because most serial killers were white males.

A man paused walking past and attempted to light a cigarette in the breeze with a book match, but gave up after three matches, flipped away the barely burned cigarette, and walked on. The cigarette bounced, rolled, and dropped through a sewer grate. Looper looked as if he were torn between springing toward the wisp of smoke carried on the wind, or the cigarette itself.

Beam noticed Nell give her partner a disdainful glance. This investigation was wearing on everyone. The killer might be starting to come unraveled. Nell and Looper were getting on each other's nerves. Da Vinci was starting to react to pressure from inside and outside the department. And of course there was the rest of the city, and all those former and prospective jurors—prospective victims. Beam found himself getting edgy, and thinking more and more about Nola Lima, so maybe he was coming unraveled like the killer he was pursuing.

The increasing pressures of the investigation—not unusual at this stage, when there's a growing number of pieces and none of them fit.

But that didn't explain Nola somehow becoming more and more confused with Lani in Beam's thoughts, in his dreams.

"So far nothing connects the Justice Killer with Tina

Flitt's murder," he said, "other than the letter *J* written in blood on her car window. I'm still thinking copycat."

"Now we're getting nowhere," Looper said with mock enthusiasm, taking a last, lingering look in the direction of the fast-dissipating smoke. "And that letter *J* is some connection," he added. It didn't pay to be too much of a smart-ass with Beam.

"There's no way to get much of a handwriting sample out of one letter," Nell said, "unless the killer writes in Gothic script or some such thing."

"Like a German?" Looper asked.

Nell didn't bother to answer, knowing he was being deliberately obtuse to get under her skin. Seeing the smoker trying to light a cigarette had set off Looper; it was making him irritable and irritating. Nell had been here before. "Different murder weapon," she said, "different kind of victim. A juror, not a jury foreperson. I'm with Beam. We could have a copycat killer."

"Using a different murder weapon on a different kind of victim." Looper said. "Some copycat."

"The bloody *J* could have been an afterthought, to throw us off the scent of the real killer."

"I don't remember any scent," Looper said. "And the victim was on a jury whose foreman was her husband. A jury that let a killer walk."

"That's why a copycat might think it would work if he killed Tina and wrote the *J* with her blood."

"I thought you said that was an afterthought," Looper said.

Beam decided he'd better stop this before his detective team got in a fistfight.

"We can't rule out a copycat killer on this one," he said. "And we're all feeling the pressure. That would include the killer."

"What about the human hairs found in Tina Flitt's car?" Looper asked, not looking at Nell.

Back on point, Beam thought with relief. "Lab said four of the hairs were hers. Two others, from the back of the car, were her husband's."

"Think hubby might be sticking it to somebody other than wifey in the car?" Looper asked.

Nell looked at him in disgust.

"Or maybe hubby and Tina got it on in the backseat." Looper still speculating, maybe to aggravate Nell. "Some couples get a sexual kick outta that. Takes 'em back to the first time, maybe."

Nell seemed about to say something, so Beam said. "There were no pubic hairs."

Looper looked disappointed.

"Lab said the breeze from an open window, or even the car's air conditioner, might have carried hairs shed by hubby back there. Hairs from his head. The point is, none of the hairs were the killer's."

"So maybe the killer did wear a hat that kept him from shedding any hairs," Looper said.

"Or he was—"

"I know," Beam interrupted Nell. "Bald. I've been through all this with da Vinci. Lab says it's possible a hat would have prevented normal hair shedding that you might otherwise expect under the circumstances. Everyone sheds about eighty individual hairs per day."

"*Every*one?" Looper brushed his fingers through his thinning hair mussed by the breeze.

"Everyone," Beam confirmed. "On average."

"Unless they're—"

"Bald." Looper finished Nell's sentence this time.

"Or recently combed their hair," Beam said. The breeze grew stronger, and the flags overhead cracked like sails and bounced steel pulleys noisily against steel poles. "Lab indicated something else: None of the hairs vacuumed or tweezered up at any of the crime scenes matches any of the hairs found at the other scenes."

No one spoke for a while as that information was processed.

"Different killers?" Looper suggested finally.

"Or one killer with a hat," Nell said.

"Or bald," Beam said.

As soon as Melanie pressed the button on her TV's remote control, Geraldo Rivera appeared on the screen and asked a panel of attorneys, whose staid images were arranged in a pattern of squares, what Merv Clark's testimony meant to the Cold Cat murder trial.

Melanie's instructions were to avoid reading, listening to, or watching any news of the Cold Cat murder trial, but she heard one of Geraldo's guest attorneys say, "Trouble for the prosecution. Col—" just before another channel came on.

"Clark testified—"

She pressed the button again to climb the channels, holding it down as they flickered past. Many of them featured something about the Cold Cat trial. She paused only to look for several seconds at a still shot of Cold Cat entering the courthouse with his entourage. He was stopped by the camera in full stride, glancing over at the lens and smiling sadly.

It was a sound bite, rather than an image, that caused her to pause at the next channel: ". . . says the judge is considering having the jury sequestered."

Melanie passed the channel, went back to it, and saw that a commercial featuring a talking duck was coming on.

She switched off the TV so she'd neither hear nor see it. And she'd stopped herself from buying a newspaper from the vending machine at the corner. But it seemed almost impossible to escape news about the trial.

Judge Moody had apparently come to the same conclusion. That must be why she was thinking about sequestering the jury.

Melanie didn't want that to happen, to be cooped up in a

hotel room somewhere in town, probably sharing it with another juror to save money for the city. And how difficult would it be for the jurors not to discuss the case with each other if they were held hostage in a hotel, probably taking their meals together, living under watch, and riding back and forth with each other every day in vans?

Of course, those weren't the only problems. The court paid a pittance to jurors, not nearly enough to make up for their stopped paychecks. Certainly not enough to slow Melanie's financial slide! Her bills kept coming, and seemed even to have stepped up their assault on her checking account.

Savings?

Forget savings. Melanie needed to get back on the job.

Regal Trucking had been long enough without her office management skills. Trucks would be loaded with the wrong cargo; bills of lading would be misplaced; cargo would arrive at the wrong destination. The place would be a mess and take her a month to set right.

Worse still, the office might be running smoothly and efficiently *without* her. Irma Frinkle, in Accounts Due, was interim manager in Melanie's absence and wouldn't mind so much stepping up to Melanie's job.

Plagued by the thought of demotion or even unemployment, Melanie *really* didn't want to be sequestered for the remaining days of the trial. Especially now, when she was beginning to believe Cold Cat—Richard—was innocent, and that his arrest was a horrible mistake, or he'd been set up. Celebrities were targets for that sort of thing. Especially celebrities like Richard, whose art was controversial as well as popular. Melanie had even heard a snatch of one of his recordings wafting from a car backed up in traffic as she was approaching her apartment: "Off the bitch what did the snitch!" Then the traffic light changed and the car with the loud radio moved on. Those were the sorts of lyrics that might prompt some nutcase to strike out at Richard by trying to frame him for Edie Piaf's murder.

Melanie thought the police should be paying more attention to real murderers, like the Justice Killer, who were going around doing actual damage to society. Soon no one would want to serve on a jury, if more forepersons were found slain. And the latest victim had simply been a juror, not a foreperson. No one on any jury was safe now. And why should they serve? Not only might they fall behind with their bills and lose their jobs to people like Irma Frinkle—"Off the bitch!"—but if they were assigned a serious criminal case, they might actually be killed themselves. Melanie, not a timid person, sometimes found herself afraid of the Justice Killer, and a verdict hadn't even been rendered in Cold Cat's—Richard's—trial. If the jury acquitted him, as she thought more and more that they might, how frightened would she be then?

It was a question she'd begun to ask herself every night before sleep came.

Da Vinci had taken a hell of a reaming and didn't like it. Some of the respect he'd long held for the chief was gone for good, dissipated in a storm of accusations and faulty blame. It wasn't that da Vinci didn't know how the game of buck passing was played; it was more that the chief had come down way too hard. *Feeling the pressure.* Da Vinci knew he was expected to come down equally hard on Beam.

Beam was a hard man to chew out. He sat in front of da Vinci's desk, meeting his superior officer's gaze calmly with eyes that had seen it all and left no doubt that he, too, knew how the game was played. Da Vinci had the distinct impression that Beam was right now viewing him as something not much more than a gathering storm that would blow over.

So what was the point? Da Vinci decided not to waste his energy. He said simply, "The chief gave me a hell of a going over about the Justice Killer investigation."

Beam said nothing. Might as well have died right there in the chair a few seconds ago.

"Damn it!" da Vinci spat out.

"Yeah, I go along with that." Beam might have smiled.

"He told me the commissioner wants this case broken yesterday. People are doing anything to avoid jury duty, and it's causing a backup in the judicial system you wouldn't believe."

"I believe," Beam said. He decided to give da Vinci something he, da Vinci, might give to the chief, and that the chief might pass on up the line of command, out of the NYPD and into the city's body politic. "We're thinking maybe copycat in the Tina Flitt murder."

"Not seriously?"

That shadowy smile again. "Seriously enough."

"You of all people know this sicko is willing to vary his method."

"I know it more than the chief or commissioner."

Da Vinci, with his usual mental alacrity, understood Beam's generosity but gave no sign of knowledge or gratitude. "It surely can't be ruled out," he admitted.

"You read the lab report?" da Vinci asked.

Beam nodded.

"There's nothing other than the bloody *J* to put the Justice Killer in that car when Flitt went out," da Vinci said. "No prints, hairs, smudges, footprints, DNA—how does this bastard come away so clean?"

"He's smart. He knows his craft. That's how he looks at it by now, a craft. An art. Each murder neater than the last."

Da Vinci swiped a hand down his face hard enough to hurt his nose and make his eyes water. "How are we ever gonna nail him?"

"We know our craft," Beam said calmly.

"To the chief and, I can tell you, the commissioner, you're still a cop even if you're not technically NYPD permanent ranks. The machine won't hesitate to make you the goat in this, Beam, screw you over."

"Or you."

"Goes without saying." Da Vinci's right hand went out as if of its own volition and caressed the polished brass motorcycle sculpture on his desk corner, reminiscent of his early days as a cop. "Much as I enjoyed it, Beam, I don't want to go back to riding a cycle. Just like you don't wanna go back to doing foot patrol." He patted the cycle sculpture as if it were a pet, then sat back in his chair "You understand what I'm saying?"

"Understood it when I walked in here," Beam said. "If it's gonna be me or you, you're gonna make it me."

"That's true. I wouldn't bullshit you. I'm sorry, Beam, it just works that way, dog eat dog eat dog. We've gotta leave it at that."

Beam stood up to leave the office. "I won't miss that part of it."

"Someday neither will I," da Vinci said.

"Now you're talking bullshit."

Da Vinci tried to keep his features stiff but he had to grin.

"Yeah, I am. Both of us are talking bullshit. In some ways, Beam, we're the same kind of animal."

"In some ways."

"Nell and Looper, I notice they're getting testy."

"We're all getting testy. Especially the killer."

"You really believe that?"

"Sure. That's how the game goes. Ask Helen Iman."

"Maybe I will."

Beam's presence was so dominant that when he left the office he seemed to take a lot of the oxygen with him. Da Vinci sat in the vacuum, beginning to perspire, and absently brushed the back of his right hand gently over the motorcycle sculpture again. His mind was turning over and over like a real cycle's roughly idling engine.

He felt unexpectedly sorry for his friend Beam. Honorable and tough old-school Beam, intrepid and smart in the bargain. Da Vinci thought he'd never known a better man or a finer cop.

The cruel tricks life played on people, the sadistic mazes that circumstances constructed, it was amazing.

27

Adelaide Starr sat in the back of the cab and watched First Avenue glide past on either side. She felt strong. She felt limber. She felt beautiful.

She felt ready.

Adelaide was all those things. Only five-foot one, she had a compact, muscular body, with legs and neck disproportionately long so that she appeared much taller when there was no one near her for comparison. She had a tumble of ginger colored hair, green eyes, a scattering of freckles across the bridge of her nose, and a carved, determined chin. Up close or from the last row in the theater, she was eye candy. Not to mention she could sing. Not the way she could dance, with a winning combination of pertness and elegance, but when it came to a show tune she could sing it and sell it and that's what was important.

So it was a cinch that sooner or later she was bound to make it out of the chorus line and into a larger, more demanding role that required voice as well as dance. Why not today? This morning? She was twenty-nine, talented and beautiful, so why *not* this morning?

"I've sure as hell paid my dues," she said out loud.

"Pardon, ma'am?" the cab driver asked, meeting her gaze in the rearview mirror and almost running up the back of the cab ahead. He was a swarthy man wearing a skillfully wound blue turban but had no discernible accent.

"Talking to myself." Adelaide smiled at the man in the mirror and watched the change in his dark eyes, a kind of melting. Yeah, she was feeling confident. She'd been told in confidence by another dancer already in the show that she had the inside track for the second lead in the developing Off-Broadway musical comedy *Peel the Onion*.

She'd just sat back in the seat and was looking out again at the sun-drenched morning when she felt rather than heard the vibration of her phone in her purse snugged up against her right hip. Careful not to break a nail, she adroitly plucked the phone from her purse, flipped it open and said hello.

"It's Barry, Ad."

Her manager, Barry Baxter. She knew by his tone that this wasn't going to be good. *Shouldn't have answered the phone.* "Shoot, Barry." She didn't like the tone of her own voice. The cabbie caught something in it, too. His eyes were wary in the mirror.

"It's not *that* serious, Ad. They don't use real bullets."

"Sometimes they do, Barry."

"You sitting down?"

"I better be. I'm in a cab, on the way to the theater for the audition."

"I'm afraid you can save the fare. I just got a call from Gerald. The role's been filled."

"How the hell did that happen?" She saw the cabby's eyes narrow.

"Some friend of the producer, actress out of Chicago name of Tiffany Taft. She's in some Off-Off-Broadway thing now that's about to fold. She blew them away, Gerald said, and she'd already played the part in local repertory theater. She did ten minutes onstage and that was that. Everybody wanted her."

"Screw Chicago, Barry. And screw Tiffany whatever."

"Yeah. Well." When she didn't say anything, he said, "I'm sorry, Ad. It looked like gold. They lie to you sometimes in this business, you ever notice?"

Adelaide took a deep breath. "I've noticed. Everybody's a shit but you, love. I'll get over it, Barry." *If I don't get fat, or pull a hamstring, or my skin doesn't go all pale and crinkly, like what happened to Erin McCain, another redhead who was now out of the business. God, I'm twenty-nine!*

"I know you will, Ad. Faster than me, probably. This is a lousy deal. I thought you had a real shot at it."

"So'd I."

"It's not that good a play."

"It's great, Barry."

"It would have been with you in it. Now I'm not so sure. I seriously doubt this Tiffany bitch can do cute like you can, and that's what the part calls for—cute with a big voice and a big kick. That's you, Ad."

Adelaide smiled. Seemed to cheer up the cabbie. "A few minutes ago I felt cute enough to gag," she said. "Now I'm semi-suicidal. Damned business can give you whiplash." *At twenty-nine, how much longer can I do cute?* "I think I'm gonna drown my sorrows in a latte."

"Too early for anything else."

"Signing off. If I do weaken and shoot myself, I'll leave you all my stuff." She snapped the phone closed and slid it back in her purse. "Pull over there," she said to the eyes in the mirror. "By that Starbucks." She pointed across the street.

The cab veered to the curb near the intersection. "Whatever you want, ma'am."

I wish. As she withdrew her hand from her purse, her knuckles brushed paper, the morning's meager mail she'd hurriedly grabbed from her box in the lobby when she left the building. She'd stuffed it unexamined into her purse and stepped outside in time to hail an unoccupied cab immediately, thinking it must be her lucky day.

Instead of withdrawing the mail, she reached back into her purse for her wallet to pay cab fare.

Adelaide hadn't been serious about drinking a latte, but when she climbed out of the cab, it seemed like a good idea. It wasn't as if she had anyplace else to go. With her purse slung by its strap over her shoulder, carrying her duffel bag with her dance equipment on the same side of her body, she strode with a graceful leftward list across the street toward Starbucks. The light flashed the signal not to walk, but the way Adelaide walked, traffic turning off Fifty-fourth Street onto First Avenue stopped for her.

The morning breakfast crowd had mostly cleared out of the place. She ordered a large latte and carried it to a booth, picking up a crookedly folded *Daily News* on the way. Sometimes when she was low she could lose herself in the news, in accounts of other people's misfortunes. What Adelaide absolutely and without exception refused to do was to feel sorry for herself. She'd always taken pride in her ability to get back on her feet after a knockdown, ready to fight on. Take the right attitude, be in your own private play, and good things tended to happen. Reality could conform. Besides, Barry might be right about *Onion* being a box office bomb.

Within half an hour she'd finished the paper—what parts she wanted to read, anyway—and was in a somewhat more tolerable mood. She sat for a while watching people hurry past outside the window. It seemed everyone had someplace they had to be. Everyone but Adelaide.

God! Stop it! Like there won't be other plays Off-Broadway. Off-Off-Broadway.

On *goddamned Broadway!*

Damned straight! There's always a demand for cute. Irrepressibly cute. And I can be a tsunami of cute.

She decided to read some more about the Justice Killer. That would cheer her up.

Then she remembered the mail in her purse. She got it out and spread it on the table like a hand of cards. Three envelopes. The first was an obvious advertisement for life insurance. The second was a chain letter from a college friend she hadn't talked to in six years, urging her to send copies of the letter to five people she knew and she could avoid contracting an infectious disease and in fact enjoy a run of good luck. Others who'd ignored the instruction to keep the chain growing had met terrible fates. A few had died. Adelaide read the enclosed letter. It explained how you could be healthier, happier, and live longer if you had sex in the presence of certain aromatic candles that were for sale. Not that you had to purchase any of the candles; sending along the letter to five friends was all that was really required of you. Yeah, sure.

Adelaide set the chain letter aside with the insurance ad to be dropped in the trash receptacle on the way out. Then she opened the third envelope, using a plastic knife, as she'd painfully bent back a fuchsia fingernail while opening the chain letter.

Holy bejibbers!

A jury summons.

28

Looper had taken the unmarked home and dropped Nell across town where she could get a subway. Trouble was, it had been a long day, the subway train had been stifling, and it was a long, hot walk from the stop to her apartment.

Nell's feet hurt enough that when she opened the door she limped over and slumped down on the sofa, even though she saw the red light blinking on her answering machine, signaling with urgency that she had messages. She used her feet to work off her sensible black shoes, stretched her legs almost straight out, and wriggled her toes.

I've got cop's feet, maybe getting flat. I'm getting to be a goddamned cliché.

She realized suddenly that something was wrong. The back of her neck was damp with perspiration. The air conditioner in the apartment's living room window was malfunctioning again. It had been doing that more and more lately. Where was this Terry Adams who'd done work for other cops and was supposed to give her a deal? She'd call someone else, except she needed a deal, and every air conditioner repairman would be running behind in this heat anyway and would put her off. She needed for Adams to show up, or at least call her back and lie about it being a heat wave so everybody's air conditioner was breaking down and he'd been hard at work since six this morning and she was the very next on his list. That was what Nell expected, anyway. She'd been told the guy was an actor doing home repair work between parts, so she was curious about how convincingly he'd lie.

It was still too early for the evening to be cooling off, so she decided she'd go out and get some supper at a nice, air-conditioned diner over on Seventh Avenue, then she'd come home and, if it was still too warm in the living room, switch on the window unit in the bedroom and read in bed.

As she was pushing herself up from the sofa, she noticed again the flashing red light on her answering machine. So maybe the air conditioner guy had left a recorded lie. Before going to the bedroom to get more comfortable shoes, she might as well listen to her messages.

One message, actually, from Jack Selig. Iris Selig's husband. The late Iris Selig.

According to the machine, Selig had phoned just twenty minutes ago. Nell lifted the receiver and punched out the number he'd left at the end of his message before she forgot it.

Selig picked up on the second ring.

"I was hoping it was you," he said, after Nell had identified herself.

"Have you thought of something?" Nell asked.

"Thought of . . . ? Oh, no. Well, yes." He sounded oddly ill at ease. "I've thought quite a bit about you, Miss Corey, so I decided I'd give you a call."

"About the investigation?"

"About us."

It took a few seconds for what was happening to sink in. This guy was coming on to her! Nell was speechless.

"I know it's out of the ordinary, but I thought, so what? It's been two years since . . . my wife died. I don't want you to think I'm callous, and I'll certainly understand if you say no. You are investigating a series of murders, one of which was that of my wife. But it was two years ago, and I thought it might not interfere in any way with the investigation if we saw each other socially. I don't know what the police department's regulations are in such matters—"

"Say no to what?" Nell interrupted.

"Dinner. Nothing more. I thought possibly you wanted to talk about something other than the investigation."

Nell conjured up a mental image of Selig, distinguished, handsome, obscenely wealthy. Old enough to be her . . . Well, old enough. Too old. She imagined him on the other end of the line, waiting like a nervous schoolboy for her reaction. It must have taken some guts, calling her.

"Mr. Selig—"

"Only dinner and talk," he assured her. "I know how old I must seem to you."

"I'm thirty-nine, Mr. Selig. Nobody seems old to me."

He laughed, surprising her. "Oh, you'll find out differently."

This wasn't a good idea, but something about his offer kept her from saying no. Was it his wealth? Maybe that was part of it. His looks? He was almost movie star handsome in a mature way, but Nell had never imagined herself with someone mature.

Maybe I'm getting ahead of myself. He said only dinner and conversation.

Hah!

"Can I think this over, Mr. Selig?"

"Of course. If you prefer, you might consider it part of your investigation. I don't mind the third degree, if that's what it takes to spend time with you."

She had to smile. "I wouldn't see dinner with you as part of an investigation."

"Then why not tonight, Miss Corey? You can check with your superior officer tomorrow and find out if you did something against the rules."

"You're a bit of a devil, aren't you, Mr. Selig." *And a charming one.*

"Only a bit, Miss Corey."

Part of Nell cautioned her against this. Another part thought of dinner in a cool restaurant with wine and actual tablecloths, unlike the moderately priced places where she usually ate. A restaurant without a counter might make for a nice change.

"What about Tavern on the Green?" Selig asked.

He somehow knew what I was thinking.

Nell had been to Tavern on the Green exactly once, ten years ago. She'd dumped bread pudding in her lap. This guy Selig probably ate at Tavern on the Green once or twice a week. Even more often, if he liked the bread pudding. All she had to do was say yes and—

"I got your address from the phone book. Give me an answer and I can pick you up within the hour. Are you there, Miss Corey? I have a long list of women to call if you refuse."

Nell laughed. It wasn't as if Selig was a suspect, not after two years. As far as Nell knew, he'd never served on a jury and wasn't part of the Justice Killer case at all. And what would it hurt if she had dinner with him? She could casually mention it to Beam afterward, keep everything above board. "This would be a date?"

"Make no mistake about it, Miss Corey, this would be a date."

"We seem to have moved away from just dinner and conversation."

"We move nowhere you don't want to go, Miss Corey. But keep in mind my advanced age."

She did feel it wouldn't be a good idea to give in easily. Her mother had long ago told her it was better to be gold than silver. Also, she didn't like the idea of Selig simply calling her on what might have been a whim. This was probably a multimillionaire, and certainly a wily negotiator, so it wasn't a good idea to give in and agree to anything easily. Nell didn't like being maneuvered and wanted to preserve her self respect.

"How about tomorrow night?" she said.

"Wonderful!"

There. She'd forced a compromise.

"Pick you up sevenish?"

Sevenish!

"That would be fine."

After hanging up, Nell wondered if she'd lost her mind. On the other hand, what the hell? Dinner and talk. She had to have a life outside the NYPD. Beam would understand. If she told him.

She thought about how she felt actually dating a man in his sixties who called her "Miss."

Pretty good, she decided.

Adelaide had dinner with three other dancers near the studio in the Village where they all trained. All through the meal and over coffee or additional wine, everyone sympathized with her for the way her good luck had suddenly turned bad, but all agreed it was part and parcel of the business they were in and that they all loved.

Everyone, including Adelaide, left the restaurant somewhat tipsy from too much wine.

By the end of the short subway ride to the stop near her apartment, she felt slightly better about losing the *Peel the Onion* role. Adelaide had found the company misery so loves, and it had elevated her mood. But now, as she made her way up the concrete steps to the surface world, she was sober and hungry again.

When she turned a corner, the dimly lighted sidewalk ahead was empty. She was vaguely aware of someone rounding the corner behind her. So quiet was this dark street that she could hear faint footfalls, but she didn't turn around.

The tip of her tongue worked on a morsel trapped between two of her molars, and her thoughts returned to the restaurant. She hadn't eaten much of the angel hair pasta she'd ordered, concentrating instead on conversation and her wine glass. As she walked the shadowed pavement, she wondered about her earlier lack of appetite. Definitely, worry had caused it. But what had she been attempting to put out of her mind, losing the Off-Broadway part, or gaining a jury summons?

Adelaide had served on a jury about six years ago, and she recalled that receiving the summons had been, more than anything, irritating. But after an initial attempt to get out of doing her civic duty, she resigned herself to serving and it hadn't been such an ordeal. It had been a two day trial about a stolen car, ending in the conviction of the thief. Much of the time had been taken by the prosecutor explaining how to hot wire a car and jump the ignition. She'd found it interesting, but not so much that she wanted to repeat the experience, and not at all useful. Adelaide didn't think she'd ever have to steal a car.

The sound of leather soles on concrete behind her was getting closer, but she didn't give it much thought. As she strode along the sidewalk with a dancer's elegance, she squeezed her purse, feeling the jury summons still inside it. She was annoyed now by the summons, and moving beyond sobriety toward a headache and the queasy feeling she always got after she drank too much.

Someone had told her that once the courts got you in their computer they never forgot you. That might be why so many people avoided jury duty—that the system kept drawing on lots of the same people over and over. Adelaide didn't want to be one of those people, but she was afraid that in the eyes of the court she had become one.

Afraid.

She hesitated before regaining her stride. Yes, she wasn't only irritated this time; she was afraid. The newspapers were full of stories about people doing bizarre things to get out of jury duty. They were afraid to serve, and why shouldn't they be, with a maniac waiting to kill them if they arrived at the wrong verdict? Adelaide was sure she wouldn't have been summoned at all if so many other prospective jurors hadn't shirked their duty. Most of the people she knew said they'd *never* served on a jury. Supposedly the city was programmed to call on you every ten years or so, not six.

Six years. Wasn't it also about six years ago when the Justice Killer's last victim, Tina something, had also been on a jury? She hadn't been a foreperson or anything, either, just a common juror—like they wanted Adelaide to be—and now she was dead. Adelaide shivered. Tina something hadn't exactly died a pleasant kind of death.

A turning car's headlights momentarily played down the block and the lengthened shadow of whoever was behind Adelaide almost reached the point where she might have glimpsed it in the corner of her vision. Then the street was dark again.

Damn it! If she'd landed the part in *Onion* she surely could have gotten out of jury duty, or at least had it postponed. She would have had to rehearse—the court would have understood that the play depended on her. That would have been enough to be excused from sitting in a stifling courtroom, listening to something that was bound to be unpleasant; enough to be excused from being afraid until Mr. Justice Killer was killed or captured.

One thing the experts seemed to agree on: the killer had widened his pool of potential victims. Adelaide knew she might be right at the edge of that pool, and she didn't want to so much as dip a cute and dainty toe in it.

The slight scuffing sound of footsteps behind her drew closer, and she sensed a presence very near. Not breaking stride, she saw a moving shadow merge with her own, almost completely devouring it.

"You shouldn't be out walking alone at night in this neighborhood, sweetheart. You want some company?"

Adelaide stopped and stood still, then turned and faced a large, bearded man wearing a dark turtleneck sweater and jeans. His beard was jet black and trimmed so it came to a point. He was carrying a white plastic bag by its loops, and the way the plastic was stretched indicated there was something heavy inside.

When he saw her face, his eyes changed in the way she expected. He gave her a smile surely meant to be disarming. "You are every kind of cute. I said—"

"Back off, asshole!" Adelaide told him.

He backed away a step, the smile freeze-framed in his beard, then spun on his heel and jogged across the street.

"You don't know what you're missing!" he yelled from the opposite sidewalk.

Adelaide didn't bother to answer. More important matters occupied her mind. She wasn't going to serve a single day of jury duty. First thing tomorrow she'd phone Barry. First thing!

She dug a pen out of her purse and wrote a little reminder on her left palm, as she often did: *Call Barry.*

Adelaide had an idea.

29

St. Louis, 1989

"I'm exhausted," April said, in the middle of putting away the groceries.

Justice wasn't surprised. April spent her days exhausted. Part of the reason was the depression, and part of it was the prescription medicine she was shoveling down. It seemed the proper cocktail of medications couldn't be found to bring her relief. She'd tried doctor after doctor. She was seeing a psychologist regularly now for analysis, and a psychiatrist who prescribed medicines. The one thing the medicines seemed to have in common was that they sapped her of energy. April slept around most of the clock, and seldom left the house. She'd accompanied him to the supermarket this time only so she could choose some of what she wanted to eat, in an effort to improve her appetite.

They could no longer afford to dine out, and they were living in a gray-shingled, rundown rental house in the wrong end of town. April's surroundings were hardly calculated to help her escape the depression that held her in a vise, but then neither was their dwindling bank account.

Justice opened the refrigerator and began putting perishables away. "Do you want me to fix you something to eat?"

April shook her head no. "I'm gonna take a pill."

Justice felt his stomach tighten. To April, taking a pill was synonymous with taking a nap. Unless she took wrong combinations or dosages, which happened frequently. Then she'd be manically active, desperate, and heart-breaking.

She'd once described her depression as falling down a slippery dark well that got more and more narrow and constricting. And as you fell, you knew with increasing certainty that you would never be able to climb back up to the light that now you could no longer even see.

As Justice finished putting away the groceries, he could hear April clattering around in the bathroom. The old house's pipes rattled briefly as she ran water to wash down whatever in her galaxy of medications she was taking.

Twice she'd mistakenly taken overdoses that would have proved fatal if she hadn't told Justice about them. Once in bed beside him in the middle of the night, and once by phone when he was working in a twenty-four-hour convenience store that had since closed. Both times he'd called 911 and they'd reached the emergency room in time, where April consumed what they'd both come to refer to as "the charcoal milkshake" that neutralized what was in her stomach, and was then pumped out.

After the second overdose, a doctor had told Justice that April might have taken an overdose deliberately in a suicide attempt, but Justice knew better. April wanted to live. She fed off his own determination that she should live, that everything should return to normal—but a different kind of normal, without their son, Will. It was possible. It must be. It seemed far away at times to Justice, but it was possible.

He went into the bedroom and found April lying fully clothed on the bed that hadn't been made for days. The old window air conditioner was humming and squealing away, not doing much about the humid St. Louis heat in high summer. The shades were pulled. Even if they didn't fit well and light leaked in all around them; at least the room was dim. At times April got headaches that were unbearable, and lying perfectly still on her back in the dimness seemed the only thing that might help.

Justice sat down on the bed beside her. "You doing okay?"

She squeezed his hand. "I hate to put you through this shit."

He smiled. "It won't be forever."

"It's already been forever."

He sat and was silent, looking at her closed eyes, watching her pupils move beneath the thin flesh of her eyelids, knowing she might be exhausted but she wasn't near sleep.

"Headache, too?" he asked.

"No. Just everything else." Her breasts rose, fell. "It's so goddamned hopeless."

He pressured her hand rhythmically with his own. "Don't say it's hopeless. It only seems that way sometimes."

"I know what I put you through," she said, still with her eyes closed. "It isn't fair."

"Maybe it'll even out."

Her pale lips arranged themselves in a tired smile. New deep lines at the corners of her mouth. "You mean someday you'll put me through the same thing?"

"You know what I meant. Our life together will be better someday."

"You believe that? With Will gone from us?"

"It won't be as good as with Will, but it can be better than it is now."

"Isn't that the truth."

She began to cry. He touched the backs of his knuckles gently to her cheek and she turned her head away.

"I'm afraid," she said. "I'm afraid all the time."

"Of what?"

"I don't know. The future. Nothing and everything. I'm tired of being afraid."

"You don't have to be."

"If I didn't—"

"What?" He could tell by the tightness around her mouth that she was getting frustrated. With him. With everything. He knew he should think more before he spoke. If she didn't have to be afraid, she sure as hell wouldn't be.

"Maybe you oughta take a drive," she said. It was what he did when they both knew an argument was building like a summer storm on the horizon. "Get some ice cream and bring it back here."

"You didn't want ice cream in the store."

"Go to Ted Drewes. Get me a chocolate chip concrete."

Ted Drewes was a frozen custard stand that was the most popular place in St. Louis when the temperature got over eighty. And it was over ninety today. "I'll be in line behind a hundred people," Justice said.

She opened her eyes, looked at him, and smiled, not the way she usually was with a fight coming on. "The lines there move fast, and only frozen custard can make me feel better."

"Or ice cream."

"Not the same."

Justice leaned down and kissed her cool forehead. "Frozen custard it is." He stood up, went into the bathroom, and splashed cold water on his face and wrists. When he came back in the bedroom, he was tucking in his shirt. "You said chocolate?"

"Chocolate chip," she said, with her eyes closed again. She seemed tired now. When he got back, she might be asleep. That would be okay; he'd put both frozen concoctions in the freezer and they could eat them later.

When he left the house, he locked the front door behind him, then drove their five-year-old Ford to the custard stand.

After maneuvering through traffic surrounding the tiny stand, he finally found a parking space in the rear of the lot, near an alley. The car's air conditioner didn't work worth a damn, and as soon as he turned off the engine the heat closed in.

He joined a long line at one of the serving windows and stood in the sun and sweated for about twenty minutes before he walked away with two frozen custard specialties in a white takeout bag.

The drive back took another twenty minutes

As soon as Justice entered the house, he made his way toward the bedroom, where he assumed April was asleep.

Peeking in, he saw her still in bed, lying on her side, turned away from him. He went into the kitchen, put her frozen custard in the freezer section of the fridge, then sat at the kitchen table and ate his own chocolate treat.

Something wasn't right. Something about the silence in the tiny, stifling house. He was finished with his frozen custard, so he dropped the cardboard container into the trash, then went to the bedroom to look in again on April.

She hadn't moved. He started to close the door so he could turn on the TV and not disturb her, when it struck him that she was lying *exactly* as before. On her right side, left shoulder slightly hunched, left hand turned palm out, the tips of her fingers just visible over the curve of her hip.

His heart went cold; his legs numb; even before he knew for sure.

He didn't want to walk over and examine his wife more closely, didn't want to step into a new and darker world. But he had to. He couldn't go back to the kitchen, sit at the table, and pretend it was five minutes ago. So he walked across the bedroom's threadbare carpet. On unfeeling legs of rubber, he walked. He leaned. He looked.

Her eyes were closed, but her skin didn't look quite right. Already it had begun to acquire a slight waxiness, and her perfect stillness was that of something inanimate. On the carpet on her side of the bed was a litter of vials and bottles—her stash of untaken prescription medicines the doctors had warned Justice that she might have hidden somewhere in the house. He stared at the lidless, capless empty containers, at the empty water glass on its side nearby. She'd taken everything, every kind of pill, every pill.

In her right hand was a crumpled scrap of paper, a message perhaps to him. But when he detached the object from her hand he saw that it was a photograph of Will, their lost son, taken on his fourth birthday, beaming behind a three-layer cake while a hand that had found its way into the frame—Justice's own hand—was about to hold a lighted match to four waiting candles. The photo was an instant caught in time that stabbed him like a blade through the heart.

He had just enough willpower to dial 911 and give them a brief explanation and an address. When the operator asked if he was sure April was dead, he said he wasn't, but in fact he was. He didn't want them to take their time, not for any reason.

After hanging up, he sat down on the bed next to April and stared at Will's photograph. His breathing quickened without him realizing it until he was short of breath, then he was sobbing, taking in great gulps of air.

When the paramedics arrived, he couldn't talk to them, couldn't even manage to stand up by himself so they had room to do their job.

He heard their instructions and conversation as if from a distance. They were going to transport April to the morgue, as they always did initially with suicides. It was the law. Taking one's own life was a crime—not as serious a crime as what Davison had done to Will, but still a crime.

Someone leaned over Justice, placed a hand on his shoulder, and asked him gently if he had any family or a priest or pastor. He told them no, he had no family and he had no religion. He no longer had a world to live in.

They discussed him in the third person, as if he weren't there, and decided he needed medical attention and counseling. He sat slumped on the sofa in deep shock and watched them remove April, the criminal. One of the paramedics hurried ahead to hold the screen door open.

It all seemed so *wrong*. It wasn't yet time. A mistake had been made and could be set right with a little reasonable discussion. Her frozen custard was still uneaten in the refrigerator.

They parted then forever, she to the morgue, he to hospital emergency.

Forever.

30

New York, the present

Beam settled into the soft gray leather chair in Cassie's living room. Her apartment was furnished in restful, muted tones like her office. But while the office was in shades of brown, the apartment was blues and grays.

Cassie's broad, sturdy figure appeared in the doorway from the kitchen. Not much was different about her shape and features from the time she was a child, one of those rare people who somehow mature without changing; you recognize them at sixty if you knew them when they were six. She was holding two martini glasses. She came over to the gray chair and handed one of the glasses to Beam.

"Gin," she said. "Mine's vodka."

He smiled and raised his glass in a toast. The gesture was returned, and brother and sister took ceremonial sips of their drinks.

"I know you didn't come to me for help," she said.

"Not professional help." Beam tried his martini again. His sister had a real talent for mixing these things. "Personal help. It's been almost a year now since Lani died. How should I . . . I don't know, how should I feel?"

He felt stupid even asking the question.

Cassie settled down on the pale blue sofa opposite Beam's chair and regarded him. "You're seeing another woman," she said.

"Huh?"

"Don't act surprised. Are you?"

"Surprised? Yes. I'm not exactly seeing another woman. Not in the way you mean."

Cassie grinned. "Ah, you equivocate."

"The woman hates my guts," Beam said. "And is it too early for me to be interested? I mean, since Lani?"

"Lani's dead, bro. It's rough, and I'm sorry. But that's the way it is. She's gone."

Beam took a sip of martini he didn't need. "I knew I could count on you to be blunt."

"Direct."

"Yeah, sorry. I asked the question."

"Different people see it different ways. There isn't any kind of timetable as to how long you should wait."

"I don't care what people think, Cass. I care what I think. What you think."

"Like I'm not people. Okay, I think you've waited long enough if your heart's told you so. Feel better?"

"Yes."

"Now we seem to be left with the problem of this woman hating you. What did you do to her?"

"Killed her husband," Beam said.

Between calming sips of martini, he explained the situation with Harry Lima and his widow Nola.

When he was finished, Cassie stood up and drifted over to the window to look out at Riverside Drive. "You might be screwed up, but you also must be one of the most interesting brothers in this diverse world."

"I need her to forgive me for what happened to Harry," Beam said.

"Oh, you figured that out, did you?" Cassie didn't turn around, continuing to gaze outside. "What do you want me to tell you, bro?"

"I guess I want you to say you understand, then tell me what I should do."

Cassie turned around and swirled what was left of her martini in its shallow-stemmed glass. "The first part's easy: I do understand. You were doing your job. Nobody does his job perfectly, not a job like yours, anyway. That's because no one can see into the future."

"You can, Cass."

She shot him her gap-toothed grin. "Maybe a glimpse now and then. Usually more disquieting than useful."

"You really do understand, then?"

"Yes, and I don't see how anybody can blame you for Harry Lima's death. This man chose his course, or at the least placed himself in a position where you had little choice but to steer him into possible harm's way. But he's the one who set sail in that sea. He could have been an honest jeweler. Of course, his widow might have difficulty being that objective."

"You don't know her."

"Not for sure," Cassie said, "but I think I know something about her."

"What's that?"

"She needs to forgive you."

Beam smiled. He believed his sister; she had a way about her. It had made her a success in her field. He also believed her when she admitted to a glimpse now and then into the future. Some people had the gift, Beam was sure. His own hunches sometimes proved predictive, but he'd always seen them as the subconscious instantaneously rummaging through mental files, shuffling index cards and coming up with the right one. Maybe that was how it was with Cassandra. Whatever the reason, she'd had the gift since they were kids and she repeatedly beat him at cards. She'd somehow known when their father was going to die; then, fifteen years ago, their mother. She'd phoned him the night before.

Now for the big question about Nola.

"So what do I do now, Cass?"

She shrugged in back-lit, bulky silhouette against the wide window.

"Hell, that's entirely up to you, bro."

Nell and Looper sat in the unmarked on West Eighty-third Street and checked Nell's list of families who'd lost someone to a killer—alleged killer—who had walked, either through a legal technicality or because the jurors behaved in a way incomprehensible to the public. Near the top of the list was the Dixon family.

Lloyd and Greta Dixon's teenage daughter Genelle was raped and murdered in Central Park four years ago. The alleged killer, Bradley Aimes, who hung out with Genelle's group of teenage friends, was from a wealthy family and had the advantage of high-priced legal counsel. They managed to quash the introduction of damning evidence. Though the jury wasn't allowed to consider this evidence, they certainly knew about it from wide media coverage, yet nevertheless chose to turn in a controversial not guilty verdict.

"You do this one," Looper said. "I'll observe."

That was the technique they used—one would be the interviewer, the other would simply interject something now and then, but was mainly there to observe the family. Sometimes faces revealed what words concealed.

Nell didn't argue. Not only was it her turn to be the interviewer, but she remembered the case. Bradley Aimes had been a handsome, smug twenty-something sadist who'd seemed to know from the start that his family's money and connections would enable him to walk away from a murder charge. He was right. The Dixon family was left to suffer the loss of their ravaged and murdered daughter. If one of them turned out to be the Justice Killer, Nell wondered if she'd have the professionalism to make an arrest.

The Dixons lived in a modest brick and brownstone building not in the best repair. Looper worked the intercom, identified himself and Nell, and they were buzzed up to a second floor apartment.

Mrs. Dixon, Greta, opened the door when they knocked. She was a medium-height, dark-haired woman who was attractive despite her worn down expression. Nell made the introductions, and after glancing at their shields, Greta let them in.

They were in a modestly furnished living room with a woven oval rug over hardwood flooring. A sofa that looked as if it had once been expensive and handsome now sagged in the middle. One wall was lined with a mix of books, paperback and hardcover, and some stacked magazines. Most of the books were novels. The top magazine was a *Time*.

Two matching green chairs were angled to the couch, and a TV was placed where it was visible to anyone seated in the room. On a far wall was a mahogany secretary that made everything else seem cheap and functional and looked as if it might be a family heirloom.

A thin, round-shouldered man wearing a white shirt with its sleeves rolled up, suspenders, and pleated slacks, came in from a doorway that led to a short hall and kitchen. The kind of guy who looked like he should be wearing sleeve garters and a green eye shade, and whose books never balanced. He was chewing. When he saw Nell and Looper, he quickly swallowed. There was a furtiveness about him, as if he'd been caught eating something forbidden.

"My husband Lloyd," Greta said.

"We interrupted your dinner," Nell said.

"Not at all," said Greta. "We were just finishing."

"You're police?" the man asked. He wore rimless glasses and had a narrow, pointed chin. He and Greta were in their early fifties, Nell guessed.

"'Fraid so," Looper said.

"We hate to disturb you," Nell said, "but it's part of our investigation."

"Investigation?" Lloyd Dixon seemed unfamiliar with the word.

"About the Justice Killer," said a voice from the doorway behind Lloyd.

A young woman entered the room. Nell was struck by her dark-haired beauty, so like her mother must have looked when younger. So like her newspaper photographs.

But Genelle Dixon is dead.

"You seem startled," Greta said with a slight smile. "This is Gina, Genelle's twin sister."

"She might be the one you want to talk to," Lloyd said. "Gina and Genelle were close."

"Twins are," Greta said. "Were."

"You knew Bradley Aimes?" Nell asked Gina.

"He was a bastard. I'm sure he still is."

"Why don't we all sit down?" Greta asked. The family peacemaker.

Lloyd sat first, in a corner of the sagging sofa. Nell and Looper took the green chairs, which meant that Greta and Gina sat side by side next to Lloyd. Mother and daughter looked like an aged and younger version of the same woman. In the apartment upstairs someone began playing a piano. Not loud enough to be a bother, but it was clearly audible. Nell thought she recognized the tune from her childhood's brief run of piano lessons; something by Beethoven, *Für Elise*. It was often used as a piano exercise.

"Did you two ever meet Aimes?" Nell asked Greta and Lloyd.

"Never laid eyes on him," Lloyd said.

Gina gave a slight smile like her mother's. "Genelle was too smart to bring him around."

"Why do you say that?" Nell asked.

"He was older than the rest of us. Twenty-six, as we

learned during the trial. But he looked younger. We thought he might be nineteen."

"Did he act nineteen?"

"He acted even younger. For us. Our crowd was fifteen and sixteen. He seemed like an older kid to us, but not that much older. I'm twenty-one now, and I realize how he was manipulating us."

"Did he hang with you because he didn't have friends his own age?"

"Exactly," Gina said. "He was too mixed up and too big a prick."

"Gina!" A cautioning word from her mother, who laid a hand on Gina's knee as she spoke.

"I'm only telling the truth, Mom."

"I know, dear."

The piano player upstairs reached the end of the piece. Something, maybe a bench leg, scraped over wood.

"Brad was useful to us," Gina said. "He bought us liquor, using what he said was fake ID. And a couple of times he got us weed or crack."

"Gina!"

"It was all in the trial, Mom."

"She's right," Nell said. "We read the transcript."

"Then why are you here?" Gina asked. "Do you think one of my parents is the Justice Killer?"

Nell smiled. "They have alibis. So have you, by the way."

Gina seemed taken aback. She hadn't considered herself a suspect in anything, much less a series of murders.

"We do preliminary work before interviews," Looper explained.

"The night your sister was killed," Nell said, "you were at a pajama party. How come Genelle wasn't there."

"She and the girl who gave the party had an argument the day before and hadn't made up. So instead of being at the party, she wound up in the park with that scum Bradley Aimes, and she wound up dead."

"You have a way of driving to the truth," Looper said. "You should be a cop."

"Never. They should have shot Bradley Aimes when they had the chance. Then they shouldn't have let him go free after he killed my sister."

"We're not going to argue those points," Nell said.

"You'd lose if you did. Genelle is dead. Bradley Aimes is still partying with his rich friends."

"Things have a way of leveling out," Looper said.

Gina laughed without humor. "I don't see much that's level in the world."

"What are you doing now?" Nell asked.

"You mean do I have a job? No, except for part-time work as a food server. I go to school at NYU. After . . . what happened, I went into a kind of bad period, then I got my GED and started my life again."

"Have any of the three of you noticed anything unusual lately in your lives?" Nell asked. "Anything worth remarking on? Don't hesitate or dismiss anything as too trivial. We never know what's going to be important."

All three seemed to think about it. Greta and Lloyd shook their heads no. Gina said, "The Justice Killer. I keep hoping he'll broaden his range of victims and get around to Bradley Aimes."

"I wouldn't wish that, Gina," Lloyd said wearily.

"I don't see why not."

"It wouldn't bring Genelle back."

"But we'd all be able to sleep better, wouldn't we?"

Lloyd sighed. "Yes, we would."

"Lloyd!" Greta said, in the same tone she'd used to admonish Gina. "Let's leave retribution up to God. Agreed? *Agreed?*"

"Agreed," Lloyd said. "I was only spouting off, getting rid of my anger. They—these detectives—brought it all back, the night we heard about Gina."

"I'm sorry," Nell said.

"We both are," Looper told the Dixons. "Sometimes our job isn't so pleasant."

"Thank you," Greta said. "We understand. Gina?"

"Yeah, sure, I understand."

"Gina?"

Gina looked at her mother. "*What?* I said I understood."

"About retribution being up to God," Greta said. "I didn't hear you agree."

"I agree," Gina said. But nothing in her expression suggested that she meant it.

The piano started up again. Same tune.

When the detectives were gone, Gina returned to her room, where she'd been playing Castle Strike on her computer, a game wherein a futuristic Delta Force patrol invades a medieval castle and slays various armored knights with high-tech weapons. Glittering pieces of polished steel and various body parts flew in all directions from fiery explosions. It was a colorful game.

After only about fifteen minutes, she left the computer and stretched out on the bed with her eyes closed.

The detectives' visit had opened wounds never fully healed, and triggered more and darker thoughts of Bradley Aimes. He was one of the evil knights—no, *every* knight—she'd slain in the castle. As insensitive and self-involved as a vicious animal, Aimes wouldn't be suffering as she and the rest of her family were right now. Probably he wouldn't be thinking of Genelle at all, since he'd been exonerated of her murder. People like Aimes lived in castles impossible to haunt.

But he'd murdered Genelle.

Like all those people who'd responded to endless media polls, Gina was positive of his guilt. Aimes had murdered her twin. Her other self.

And hadn't paid for it.

Gina had paid and was still paying, and what a dear price

it was. And Gina still hated Bradley Aimes. Not only was he the reason Genelle was dead, he was the reason for all of Gina's nightmares. Twins were not like other people. The pain of her sister's death was still a powerful force in Gina's life. What Aimes had done meant to Gina a grief that became part of a soul no longer whole, difficult sessions with an analyst, medication, and nights that presented horrible dreams of a dead Genelle who lingered like a specter in the daylight.

Gina knew a sad truth she'd heard from other unfortunate twins: when one twin dies, it's almost as if the other also dies, only without stoppage of breathing or heartbeat. Gina was left alive in the conversational sense of the word, but part of her was missing, glimpsed in agonized memory only in shadows or unexpected reflections in mirrors or shop windows.

The part of her that remained craved vengeance the way an addict craved a drug.

Her need to avenge her twin's death might have been the reason Gina read all the true crime literature she could find, and had followed the Justice Killer investigation so carefully in the news. She knew that a copycat killer was briefly suspected in the murder of one of JK's victims. The concept of a copycat killer more and more fascinated her. She'd researched such killers thoroughly, who they were, why they killed. It was surprising, in widely publicized cases, how often they killed. Surprising to most people, anyway, but not to the police.

Might a copycat killer murder the killer of her twin? Her other self? Fair and just. Double double.

There was no reason a copycat killer had to be motivated only by the unreasonable compulsions Gina read about in the crime literature she so tirelessly consumed. It wasn't as if there was a law. Injured ego, feelings of inferiority, and a powerful lust for attention didn't have to be the reasons a copycat killed.

Vengeance would do just fine.

As in most crimes of daring, an alibi would be necessary. Gina thought about Eunie Royce, her coworker and friend at the Middle World Restaurant in Tribeca, where Gina waited tables part time. Gina had lied for Eunie more than once, so Eunie wouldn't be caught cheating on her husband Ray. Gina had marked restaurant checks with Eunie's initials so she could prove to Ray she'd been working as she claimed.

If Gina asked, Eunie would forge *her* initials on some tabs, establishing Gina's presence at work at the time of . . . say, a murder. Eunie would never admit she'd done such a thing, mainly because she wouldn't believe for a moment that Gina had stalked and killed someone, even if the someone was Bradley Aimes. Not until it was too late and she couldn't admit to a lie without implicating herself.

If it ever came to that.

The Justice Killer was widening his qualifications for victims. Bradley Aimes would seem a logical choice. Especially if an exonerated guilty defendant like him were to be killed by the real Justice Killer.

Then a copycat killer would probably get away with claiming another JK victim. If the Justice Killer were killed rather than arrested, no one would ever know or even suspect. If the police arrested him and he stood trial, who would believe anything he said?

Gina opened her eyes and saw nothing but the swirling maelstrom of her own thoughts. Her own desires.

A copycat murdering the killer of a twin. Double double. Such an intriguing idea.

Mom and Dad would approve, though they surely wouldn't say so.

They didn't have to know. The secret would be forever held between Gina and Bradley Aimes, and Genelle.

Well, something to think about.

Gina scooted sideways on the bed, then stood up and returned to sit at her computer, where Castle Strike waited.

The battle was rejoined.

31

The crème brûlée was delicious.

Nell wore her good navy blue dress, pleased that it still fit so well, along with a cream-colored light jacket and navy high-heeled shoes. A string of white pearls completed the simple but—she thought with some surprise when she looked in her full-length mirror—fetching outfit.

Fetching. A strange description. Yet a man like Jack Selig probably could convince some women to fetch for him. He looked like something off the cover of a romance novel, with his chiseled good looks, his flawless grooming, his casual beige sport jacket with just the right amount of gold flashing when he raised an arm to expose a cufflink or wristwatch. This guy was every mother's dream, but not for her daughter.

"Did I mention that you look stunningly beautiful?" he asked.

"Not that I can recall," Nell lied, spooning in the last of her dessert. Outside the dark windows, topiary pinpointed with strings of tiny white lights looked like earthbound constellations. Inside, the light was soft and flattering, the food and service excellent. Nell could almost believe there was a world where this kind of ease and quality could be a daily occurrence.

And of course there was such a world. And Jack Selig could afford it.

"Consider yourself told for the first time tonight, then," he said.

The waiter arrived and topped off their coffee. Selig's gaze strayed for a moment away from Nell. She needed the break. It was a relief not to be regarded as an object of worship.

"Are we going to be honest with each other?" she asked.

He looked back at her, slightly surprised. "Or course. We've taken the oath."

Nell didn't recall any oath, but then he might have slipped it in somehow. "What were you thinking just a moment ago?" she asked.

"Of how much you resemble a younger Iris."

Jesus!

"I hope that doesn't upset you," he said.

"No. Well, yes . . . At the same time, I guess I'm flattered."

"You see my problem," he said.

"Yes. But I'm not sure I'm the solution."

"Oh, I know you're not. No one is. But believe me, I enjoy being with you not only because of your resemblance to my late wife, but because of who you are."

"But you don't know me that well."

"Maybe better than you think. I have connections, Nell, and I confess I used them to gather some information about you. I know that you're spirited, generous, smart, and ambitious."

And that I'm divorced and assumed by some to be a killer cop.

Nell wasn't sure just what to make of this. "That's all not very specific."

"I'm not that interested in specifics, more in who you are. I know you've had marital problems in the past, and some scraps. Some run-ins with superior officers. I don't care."

"Mr. Selig—"

"Jack."

"Jack, I'm not Iris."

"I don't expect you to be, wouldn't want you to be. Would never ask that you be." He sipped his coffee and smiled at her. "You look confused."

"Is it companionship you want, Jack?"

"More than that, Nell. But we pledged honesty—"

Did we?

"—and the pathetic truth is that I'll take what I can get."

"Don't expect—"

"—I would never expect. Anything."

Nell looked across the candle-lit table at him. "I don't think you could ever seem pathetic, Jack."

He was obviously greatly pleased. "Ah, what you can do for me. Do I sound selfish?"

"Sure. We're all selfish."

When they were finished with coffee, Selig paid the check, leaving an outsized tip, probably to show off.

Outside the restaurant, the evening had cooled and a breeze carried the fragrance of nearby flowerbeds. There was a bright half moon, with only a few clouds scudding across the night sky. It wasn't far to the edge of the park and the brighter lights of the city.

"I can dismiss the driver and we can walk," Selig suggested.

"Fine," Nell said. Though her feet might start to ache in the high heels, she was tired of sitting down.

She watched as Selig walked over and talked briefly with the driver behind the wheel of their waiting white stretch limo, paid him, no doubt with a generous tip, and returned to her. Two women entering the restaurant gave him more than a passing glance. He was trim and moved like a much younger man. Nell could believe he was interested in more than companionship.

"Sure you're not afraid strolling in the park at night?" he asked, taking her arm.

"It's not that far," she said, as they began to walk, "and usually there's a cop nearby."

32

It was too warm in the jury assembly room. Melanie thought that might be on purpose, so juries would come in sooner with their verdict. One of the jurors asked the bailiff, who was standing just outside the door, to kick up the air conditioning. He smiled and complied. It made no difference.

Light spilled in through grilled windows that didn't allow for much of a view. Heat seemed to rise from the humidity-damp wood table and chairs, along with a subtle scent of furniture polish and painful deliberations past. No one on the jury thought this was going to be brief.

Melanie was the foreperson, primarily because no one else wanted the job.

The eleven other jurors stared at her for guidance. Each had a legal-size pad in front of them on the table, on which to make notes, but after only a preliminary discussion, Melanie suggested they take an anonymous vote and find out where everyone stood. So pieces were torn from the top sheets of legal pads and used simply to write "guilty" or "not guilty" on, then folded and passed to Melanie.

She unfolded and tallied them on what was left of her top

yellow sheet. Three abstentions. Two not guilties. Seven for conviction.

"I'm a 'not guilty,'" she said.

"What's your reasoning?" asked Juror Number Three, a greengrocer from the Bronx named Delahey. With his rimless glasses, refined air, and conservative suit, he looked more like a college professor than anyone in the room.

His question was a good one, because Melanie simply *knew* that Richard Simms—Cold Cat—wasn't a killer. "The time element," she said. "If Simms was seen outside Knee High's apartment around the time Knee High said he was there, he wouldn't have had time to cross town on foot, or even by cab or subway, to his own apartment and murder his wife."

"Barely time enough," said Juror Number One, Mimi, a dance instructor who looked like, and in fact was, an aging ballerina and was always dressed in black.

"And for time to be a factor in the defendant's favor," said Number Eight, a portly, sweaty gentleman who was a financial analyst, "we would have to believe Merv Clark. And, frankly, I didn't find him credible. Nor did I find his wife credible when she testified as to what a sterling husband he was."

"She almost made you think her broken teeth were her fault," said the ballerina.

"Clark might be a wife beater, but he was slightly more credible than Knee High," said Number Two, a freelance writer named Wilma King who lived in the Village. "Why should anyone believe anything said by someone who's legally changed his name to Knee High?"

"Because he was under oath," said Melanie.

Several of the jurors laughed. Others looked at her as if they were having second thoughts about her being foreperson.

"If you believed Clark, you don't have to believe Knee High," Melanie pointed out to Wilma.

"I know. And I believed Clark's testimony."

"There's also the fact that Edie Piaf was shot," Melanie said, "and Simms didn't have any powder burns on his hands."

"He could have worn gloves, like the prosecution said." Delahey the greengrocer added.

"Knee High and Clark were both lying," Mimi said. "This seems to me like a slam dunk."

"I thought you were a dancer, not a basketball player," said a gray-haired man at the far end of the table. Number Twelve, Walter Smithers. No one laughed. A few of the jurors groaned.

"My preliminary vote was guilty," said Delahey, "but I'm not firm on it. I'm willing to listen to reason."

"I'm firm on my not guilty vote," said Number Four, an African American man named Harvey, who worked as a super in a midtown apartment building.

"Naturally," said Smithers, from the other end of the table.

"No, not *naturally*," Harvey said. "It's just that I've got plenty of reasonable doubt."

"Of course you do." Smithers was pushing it.

"I guess you don't," Harvey said.

"Not a particle."

"*Naturally* not. You probably thought Simms was guilty the moment you walked into court and saw him."

"Or heard his music," Mimi said with a laugh.

"Stuff you're too old to dance to," Harvey said.

Mimi merely smiled. "I was only joking. If we don't joke now and then, we'll go mad in this stifling little room that smells like Lemon Pledge."

Melanie hadn't counted on this. She took a quick count. Six of the jurors were Caucasian, one Asian, one Hispanic, and three African American. "I don't believe race enters into this," she said. "We all need to agree on that."

One of the other black jurors, a middle-aged nurse named

Pam, looked dubious and said, "You ain't noticed we're trying a black rap artist?"

"Doesn't matter," said Wilma. "The law's color blind."

"He might as well be a Martian," Mimi said.

"See what I'm sayin'?" Harvey said. "How many Martians been acquitted in New York courts?"

"I think you understand my meaning," Mimi said imperiously.

"You some kinda diva?" Harvey asked, obviously pleased to have gotten under Mimi's skin.

"What we want to make sure we do," said Wilma, "is not let the Justice Killer murders influence our judgment. If we really think we should acquit Richard Simms, we must do it."

"Maybe you don't think the Justice Killer's guilty," Pam said.

"I think he deserves all his constitutional rights and a fair trial even if he enjoys cutting people's throats."

"Nicely put," Smithers said. "What kind of writer are you?"

"Right now I'm doing book reviews."

"We're getting off point," Melanie said. "We're here to discuss a man's guilt or innocence. Race has nothing to do with it."

"Amen," said a lanky blond man with shoulder-length hair. Juror Number Two, Harold Evans. He was about forty, with narrow blue eyes, prominent cheekbones, and a long, pinched looking nose.

"You a preacher?" asked Harvey.

"Comedian."

"You shittin' me?"

"Nope. I play the clubs, had an HBO special. Stage name's Happy Evans. Hap, offstage."

"So say somethin' funny, Hap offstage."

"That's not bad, Harvey. But comedians aren't necessarily funny offstage."

"Robin Williams is."

"He's got a point," Pam said.

"Billy Crystal!" said Delahey. "I bet you could wake up that man at midnight and he'd tell you a joke."

"I thought your name was Hap," said Number Ten, a tax accountant named Hector Gomez. "So make us happy so we don't notice the Lemon Pledge."

Everyone was staring at Hap.

Melanie was afraid she was losing control. She was supposed to be setting the agenda here, and her jurors were turning on each other. Her throat was dry.

Hap shrugged. "A guy goes into an apartment and shoots his wife." He grinned. "That's it, folks."

The Asian woman, Number Six, Marie Kim, held her nose between thumb and forefinger.

"Not funny," Delahey said.

Hap shrugged again. "Then here's the punch line: he didn't do it."

No one said anything.

"I abstained, but I'm a firm not guilty man," Hap said. "I figure the more people I acquit, the better my chances if I ever get in trouble."

"That one I liked," Delahey said.

Melanie smiled, counting her allies. She'd need them if she was going to save Richard Simms from people like Walter Smithers.

Manfred Byrd told the woman from Detroit that what she needed was a patterned sofa that contained all the colors of the room.

The woman, whose name was Marge Caldwell, looked angry and waved her flabby arms about. She'd confided to Byrd that she'd been on a severe diet and had lost over fifty pounds. Byrd thought fifty more might be in order. "I paid a fortune to move all this stuff here from Michigan," she said.

"I was hoping you could tell me how to arrange it, not advise me to sell it."

"Keep all the stuff, dear. Only not the sofa. It's Early American. Nothing else is." *Except for you, dear.* "It's a solid drab brown. Everything else you have is solid colored like the sofa. The room is static. You need something, *one* thing, that is busy, busy, busy."

Marge looked around. The expensive Third Avenue apartment was a puzzle to her, as was how to spend her money. She didn't mind that Manfred Byrd was one of the most expensive interior decorators in the city, anymore than she minded the exorbitant rent she was going to pay. Marge, while in the middle of her divorce from a Detroit Dodge dealer, had won the state lottery and managed to come away with all the money. The Dodge dealer was angry and had run out of appeals. She didn't want the Dodge dealer to find her. She wanted to start a new life in a new city she could lose herself in. What better place than New York? And if the Dodge dealer did locate her, the doorman wouldn't let the bastard in the building. Manfred Byrd loved clients like this. She would put complete trust in him.

He knew how to dress for this sort of client, too. Clothes made the man, and sometimes made the deal. He was still young, only forty-two and a half, and he exercised regularly to keep his slender body youthful. His suits were tailored and he favored silk in blacks and grays. His regular features were the sort that would always be boyish—he'd heard that said about him more than once. And it showed that he used a variety of skin conditioners. His hair was buzz cut and he sported no facial hair other than a tiny dark beard on the very tip of his chin. He wore one conservative diamond stud earring, and a silver bracelet. Byrd was intentionally obviously gay, but not too gay for a straight woman from Michigan.

"I suppose you're right," Marge said.

"Of course I'm right, dear. I'd better be. You're paying me to be right." Byrd laughed. "I'm right all the time." He touched her flabby arm and smiled. "Sometimes I get so sick of myself."

Marge smiled along with him. "We lived in the suburbs in Detroit. This is so different. I'm not used to being so high."

"I won't get into your personal life, dear."

Marge laughed and waved a ring-laden hand. "I meant high above the street."

"I know, and it's good that you chose this place. High above the street is safer, even in a good part of town like this. You *are* an attractive woman alone."

Marge wasn't buying into that one, but she seemed to consider what he'd said about being safer on a high floor. "Is New York really that dangerous?"

"Not after you learn to take a few precautions. And not for someone from Detroit."

"The suburbs," she reminded him.

"Uh-huh. Where John Wayne Gacy murdered and buried all those boys."

"That was Chicago."

"Ah, you're right! Well, Chicago!"

"I get your point, though. New York's no more dangerous than anyplace else."

Huh? "Exactly, dear. Well, Mayberry perhaps."

Marge pressed a finger to her dimpled chin and looked around, a thinking pose to let him know she was weighing his advice. "Pattern . . ."

"Pattern, dear. Fewer solids and unbroken surfaces, less blah. More busy, busy." He raised a cautioning forefinger. "But not too much. Only the sofa. And with a throw in an accent color."

"Yes, I do think I see what you mean. I wouldn't have realized it myself."

Byrd sent an offhand wave the way of the drab sofa. "I'll

make arrangements for you to have *that* removed, then you and I will go shopping for a divine divan. It will be fun."

Marge put on another smile, waging the ongoing battle to push away her past and fit into her new life. "It *will* be," she agreed. "There's no reason for it *not* to be."

"What I like about you, dear," Byrd said, "is you got the spirit!"

As he left the apartment, he was already planning their shopping expedition, a series of specialty furniture stores that wouldn't have what they needed, then Niki's Nook on Second Avenue, where there was plenty of pattern and he received twenty percent of markup for furniture sold to his clients. Furniture was such fun merchandise. Even after Marge's special discount, Byrd's finder's fee would be considerable.

Down on the sidewalk, he was waiting while the doorman tried to hail a cab, when he glanced across the street and saw the same man—he was sure it was the same one—he'd noticed twice during the last few days watching him in the Village. He was wearing a blue or black T-shirt with an eagle on its chest, dark sunglasses, tight Levi's tucked into black boots. Going for the Harley Davidson look, not so noticeable in the Village, but here on this block of Third Avenue, he stood out the way Marge's old sofa would. Though his eyes were concealed behind the dark lenses, Byrd was certain the man was staring directly at him. He could *feel* it.

The Dodge dealer? Had the Dodge dealer found Marge? Byrd had been spending a great deal of time in her apartment; might the man think he was Marge's new lover, moving in on her money that her ex-husband believed should be half his?

Me and Marge? Hah!

But everybody loved somebody, if they were lucky, and Marge *had* been the Dodge dealer's wife.

Or maybe the Dodge dealer's interested in me!

Am I insane? Maybe it isn't even the same man.

"Heads up, sir!"

Brakes *eeped* and tires scraped on concrete. Byrd had to leap back from where he'd wandered off the curb while lost in thought. The vehicle's right front fender had barely missed him.

His heart hammering, Byrd tipped the doorman and hurriedly got into the cab and blurted out his destination. He was determined to get hold of his imagination. His analyst had cautioned him about flights of paranoia that could lead to panic attacks.

Think pattern, think pattern . . . something that will pop . . . something wild . . .

But as the cab accelerated away from the curb, Byrd craned his neck to peer out the rear window.

Everyone else on the busy street seemed to be facing any direction other than toward the cab, but Harley Davidson man was looking directly at Byrd.

33

Looper suggested they prioritize, and Looper was right. Beam should have thought of it first.

In Beam's comfortably messy den, they sat around his desk and looked over the list of controversial acquittals during the past ten years, supplied to them by da Vinci. The air conditioning was working well and the den was cool. One of the trees planted outside happened to be right in front of the window, providing a view of morning sunlight glancing off green maple leaves.

Beam sat in his leather desk chair, and Nell and Looper were in chairs pulled close to the other side of the desk, where the murder files were stacked. Beam wished he had a cigar. He didn't want to smoke one in front of Looper, who was trying hard to quit cigarettes, and he had a suspicion as to what Nell would say, or at least think, about what he could do with his cigar if he asked if she minded. The world was rapidly closing in on smokers.

"These three," Beam said. "Bradley Aimes, Sal Palmetto, and Irwin Breach. They seem to have had the most publicity, and all three defendants sure as hell looked guilty but were allowed to walk."

"At least that's what the public thought," Nell said.

"Still thinks," Beam added. "Which means murdering someone who had any part in their trials will only make the Justice Killer more . . . famous."

He'd almost said *popular.*

"Breach is dead," Looper said. "Hanged himself in a holding cell when he was arrested on a later burglary charge."

"And Palmetto's left the country," Nell said. "He lives someplace now in Spain or Italy."

"A perpetual vacation," Looper said in disgust.

"It's the jurors we're most interested in," Beam said. "And we can't rule out Aimes as a potential victim. Not with this killer." He laid the three files out side by side on the desk. "You take the Palmetto jury," he said to Looper. "Make sure they know the danger to them, and at the same time try to find out anything they might know that might help us." To Nell, "You get the folks who gave Breach a free pass." He tapped the remaining file with his forefinger. "I'll do the Bradley Aimes jury."

"Loop and I already talked to the Dixon family as potential suspects," Nell said.

"You wanna do that jury?" Beam asked.

"I don't see where it makes any difference. Not unless we seriously consider any of the Dixon family members suspects."

Looper gave her a look over the Palmetto file. "Do we?"

Nell shook her head. "Not a chance. All they are in my view are Bradley Aimes's secondary victims. Somebody kills Aimes, I guess we'd need to consider the Dixons, but it'd only be routine as far as I'm concerned. No more likely than Genelle Dixon returning from the dead to kill Aimes."

"I've never known that kind of thing to happen," Looper said. He sniffed the air. Beam wondered if he could smell the cigars sealed in their desktop humidor. Beam could.

"Okay, then," Beam said, standing up behind his desk. "I'll do Carl Dudman. He was foreman of the Aimes jury."

"I've seen his real estate agency ads in the papers," Looper said. "He sells high end property. Guy like that, he's probably too rich to be in much danger."

Nell and Beam looked at each other. Maybe Looper was right; neither could, offhand, think of a serial killer case where the victims were wealthy, their murders spread over a period of time and following a psychotic theme.

But then, the killer they were chasing had a nasty unpredictable streak in him.

Beam picked up the phone to dial information for a number for Dudman Properties.

He watched Nell and Looper leave the den, and as he was jotting down the phone number, heard them find their own way out.

It was surprisingly easy to see Carl Dudman. His offices were in Tribeca, in a tall, prewar building that covered half a block and contained three banks at street level. It was being remodeled, and while no one was visibly working at the moment, the main entrance was flanked by iron scaffolding painted a dull, flaking red. Pedestrians streamed over plywood that covered mud where the sidewalk had been torn up. The city was an organic being that changed constantly, and its citizens understood and accepted it.

The building's lobby was a symphony of oak paneling, polished brass, and dark-veined marble. Temporary but neatly painted signs directed visitors to the street-level bank entrances. A uniformed attendant behind a marble desk gave directions to Beam and had him sign in.

Dudman Properties occupied the building's entire ninth floor. Beam elevatored up in about a second and a half. A trim, efficient gray-haired woman, wearing a severe dark skirt and blazer with a white blouse and man's maroon tie, had him wait only a few minutes before ushering him into Dudman's office.

Dudman was standing behind his desk, smiling slightly and looking curious. He was about five-foot nine and broad shouldered, his chalk-stripe, double-breasted suit buttoned across a flat stomach. He had a broad, handsome face with a shiny, protruding forehead, and the over-groomed, rested look of a man who ate well, slept in pajamas, wore a robe to breakfast, and had just stepped from a shower into clothes that had been laid out by a valet. Beam thought all of that might be true.

He shook Beam's hand with a firm grip but didn't make it a contest. "Effie said you were police."

Beam smiled. "Effie was right. Detective Beam, Homicide, NYPD." He reached for his shield, but Dudman waved a hand to stay the effort. He trusted Beam. Or knew about him.

"Captain Artemis Beam. Retired. Sort of."

Beam almost winced. He didn't like people using his given name. Few knew it. He was sure Dudman was letting him know he was one of the few. "You're ahead of the game, Mr. Dudman."

"Only way to play," Dudman said. "It isn't difficult to learn about you, Detective Beam. You're getting a great deal of publicity right now because of the Justice Killer investigation."

"Unfortunately," Beam said. He was sure the name Artemis hadn't been printed or mentioned on TV news. Well, not *sure.* How could he be?

"Why unfortunate? I would think you'd enjoy being a celebrity."

"It can be inconvenient. I'd rather only the killer was a celebrity."

"Why so?"

"It can be convenient."

Dudman grinned. The guy was a game player who obviously relished verbal fencing.

"The investigation is what brings me here, Mr. Dudman."

"Carl, please. I hope I'm not a suspect."

"You know better, Carl."

Dudman's grin became a thin smile, letting Beam know their little joust was ended and it was time to get to the point, he was a busy man. "Yes. To the Justice Killer, I'm a prospective victim." He motioned for Beam to sit down in an overstuffed black leather chair facing the desk. "Maybe even a tempting one, as I've done quite well with my business since the Bradley Aimes trial. It's always more fun to kill somebody rich."

Beam sat. The chair hissed and enveloped him like a creature that might devour his body slowly and at will. But the damned thing was sure comfortable. "So far," he said, "the killer seems to be fairly democratic when it comes to victims. I wouldn't let your wealth bother you, sir. But that doesn't alter why I came here, which is to make certain you understand that you need to be cautious about your vulnerabilities."

"I've considered that, Detective Beam, and I have few vulnerabilities. I'm one of the lucky potential victims who can afford tight security."

"I got in easily to see you," Beam said.

Dudman gave him a smug look, then pressed a button behind his desk.

A door opened on Beam's left. A large man in a dark suit stepped into the office. He had a buzz cut but with a thatch of longer, gray-shot black hair in front, no nonsense brown eyes, a nose that had been broken a few times, and a balanced way of standing suggesting that despite his bulk he could be lightning in any direction.

"This is Chris Talbotson of Talbotson Security," Dudman said. "He's modest, so I'll tell you he's a former martial arts champion and Navy Seal, a decorated veteran. His two brothers are almost as qualified, as are all Talbotson employees."

Beam nodded at Talbotson. "I've heard of your firm. It's a good one."

Talbotson didn't smile, but said, "Thank you. Fifteen minutes after your phone call, we had you researched and entered in our data banks, sir. We have tape of you entering the building. Your identification was verified before you left the elevator. And I've been observing and listening to the conversation since you arrived."

"Impressive," Beam admitted. He looked at Dudman. "What about your family?"

"If I had one," Dudman said, "I'd be terrified for them. It didn't escape me that the late Tina Flitt was the wife of a jury foreman."

"There's no one?"

"A sister in England. Married to a poet, would you believe it?"

Beam smiled. "She should be safe, then. And the Justice Killer will likely confine his activities to New York. Of course, there's no guarantee. This killer doesn't necessarily run true to form."

"I think we're well prepared for anything he might attempt," Talbotson said.

Dudman looked at Beam as if to say, *There! See!* "I appreciate your concern, Detective Beam, but I do feel that all necessary precautions have been taken." He shifted his weight in his chair, not standing, but clearly signaling that Beam's time would be more productively spent elsewhere.

Beam remained seated. "Why did you find Aimes innocent?"

Dudman looked as if he might make a tent of his fingers, then laced them together and squeezed hard enough to whiten his knuckles. "Reasonable doubt. We were pledged to follow the letter of the law."

"Was it the letter of the law that got Aimes off?"

"Of course. Most of us thought he killed Genelle Dixon, but we weren't absolutely *sure*. Believe me, we didn't like him. And didn't like what we felt compelled to do."

"All of you?"

"As a matter of record, yes. As foreperson, and considering the gravity of what we were deliberating, I felt it incumbent upon us to talk everything out until our verdict was unanimous."

"Spreading around the guilt?"

"That was an unkind thing to say, Detective Beam, but accurate. Only it was more like spreading around the remorse we knew would follow. But perhaps less remorse than if it turned out we'd convicted an innocent man. It does happen."

"Just often enough," Beam admitted. He stood up from the chair, which hissed its relief and regret, and offered his hand across the desk.

Dudman stood and shook hands. "I hope you never get in the position we on the jury were in," he said. "Are you going to interview the other jurors?"

"Yes. You were the first."

"They must be very afraid. Give them my best. Tell them . . ."

Beam waited. Dudman hadn't released his hand.

"Tell them I still think we did the right thing," Dudman said.

"Right thing?"

"Only thing." Dudman released Beam's hand but remained standing. "Chris'll walk you out."

When Beam and Chris were at the office door, Dudman said, "You do understand, don't you, Detective Beam?"

"I do," Beam assured him. "I've had to do the only thing a few times myself."

Dudman seemed relieved as he sat down and the two much larger men left his office.

Chris rode the elevator down with Beam and walked with him through the lobby and out to the sunny sidewalk. Beam considered warning him about the Justice Killer's cold-bloodedness and capabilities, then decided it wasn't necessary. Talbotson, like Beam, was a professional. He might know more about cold-blooded killers than Beam, even if they weren't the serial kind.

"Take care of yourself and Dudman," he said, shaking hands with Chris.

He thought Talbotson would assure him he would. Instead the younger man surprised him by saying, "I've published a few poems myself."

Beam almost told him that was about the only way to get them published, then decided Talbotson wouldn't think it was funny. He was nothing if not the serious type. "What about?"

"The things I've seen, what people can do to each other."

"Good poems, I'll bet," Beam said, and patted the man's bulky shoulder as they parted.

Back by his car, he unfolded the sheet of paper he'd brought and checked the other Aimes trial jurors' last known addresses. His plan had been to save time and work his way uptown. Right now he was south. Not far from the Village.

From Nola Lima.

What people can do to each other.

34

"Cool enough for you?" he asked.

"For now," Nell said. She took a sip of cold Budweiser from the can. Terry Adams, the air-conditioner repairman, had finally gotten back to her on her cell phone number, and told her he could work her into his schedule. The problem was it had to be this afternoon. Could Nell have the super let him in? He understood why she wouldn't want somebody she'd never met left alone in her apartment to repair her air conditioner. Could she get a friend or relative to be there while he worked? Maybe the super would stay. Terry wouldn't be insulted, he said; he didn't want to be responsible if, after he left, something seemed to be broken or missing.

Nell didn't have a friend or relative who'd sit in her sweltering apartment and watch this guy work. And her building's super wasn't even on the premises most of the time. She'd been considering reporting him to Missing Persons. She was driving when she got Terry's call, on her way to interview another of the Palmetto case jurors. She really didn't want to go. The juror would be like the last three, deficient in any fresh knowledge of the Justice Killer investigation, and already sufficiently frightened by what they did know. If JK's goal was to scare hell out of the city, he was doing a good job.

"I'll meet you there in half an hour and let you in," she said to Terry.

"That'll work. I'll probably need only a couple of hours at most."

So here sat Nell on her living room sofa, observing her window air conditioner being operated on instead of pursuing a serial killer.

Terry had the unit on a blue tarp he'd spread on the floor so as not to dirty the carpet. He wasn't the repairman of TV sitcoms, overweight with low-slung work pants. He was slim and muscular, wearing a tight black T-shirt, jeans and moccasins. His hair was a curly brown and slightly mussed above a high forehead and symmetrical features. He had brown eyes with laugh crinkles at their corners, and was clean shaven, with a chiseled jaw and cleft chin. Quite the package. It figured he was an actor as well as an air conditioner repairman—or was it the other way around?

She'd given him a can of beer, too, and watched as he put down a crescent wrench for a moment and took a sip, then wiped his lips with the back of his hand. Nell found herself wishing she were wearing something other than her shapeless blue skirt and blazer and thick-soled black cop shoes. She knew she had nicely turned ankles, but not in these clodhoppers.

She scooted to the corner of the sofa, so she could see over Terry's shoulder, and crossed her legs. "How's it look?"

He didn't glance back at her. The hair at the nape of his neck was curling and wet with perspiration in a way she liked. She was sweating herself.

"Not bad," he said, exchanging beer can for wrench. "This brass tube"—he tapped a curved, rusty tube with the wrench—"is leaking coolant, needs to be replaced. You got a couple of leaky connections, too."

"I didn't notice anything dripping."

"The coolant evaporated before it ran over. But your filter needs changing. Condensation was building in your drip pan and running down the outside of the building."

"Sounds serious." Nell had no idea what the hell he was talking about.

He turned and smiled at her. The way his lips curled made him look kind of sardonic, like a fifties movie matinee idol who could rape his way through a movie and everybody liked it. "It isn't. I'll only be here about an hour."

He'd set up a paint-splattered old box fan he no doubt used to cool himself on the job, but he'd angled it to blow not on him but on Nell. It hummed steadily, with a faint clinking sound, sending a slight breeze over her.

"Want me to turn that to a higher speed?" he asked, pointing at the fan with his wrench.

"It's fine the way it is, thanks. Are you really an actor?"

"Don't I seem like one?"

"You seem like a man who knows a lot about air conditioners."

Again the smile. Right at her heart. "Got you fooled." He bent back to his task, gave the wrench a turn, and removed the rusty curved piece of brass tubing. "I've been in some plays, done a few commercials. Way I met cops, I co-starred a couple of years ago in *Safe and Loft.*"

"I remember it. Didn't see it, though. It was on Broadway."

"Well, close to Broadway. It was a genuine hit, though. Ran for over a year. I played a cop, and I did my research by riding in radio cars with some of the cops in the Two-Oh Precinct. I learned about folks like you, and about breaking and entering, too. The professional burglars. I was a cop in the play, but I was also the stand-in for the actor who played the burglar. I take my research seriously, so I got to be pretty good with a lock pick. Got to know a lot of cops, and made contacts for my sideline, which is repairing household appliances."

"That's how I got your name. You must do a lot of work for cops."

"Yeah. This time of year, mostly air conditioners."

"Maybe you should join the NYPD," Nell said.

"I thought about it." He sounded serious. "But after getting a taste of the job, I realized how difficult it is. And dangerous. Theater critics are tough, but none of them has ever taken a shot at me." He stopped work for a few seconds and gave her an appraising look that raised goose bumps on her arms. "I appreciate what you do."

Could you ever, Nell found herself thinking. "Acting's gotta be hard on the ego, though, right? I mean, the competition must be tremendous. There aren't millions of kids all over the world dreaming of being cops the way they dream of being movie stars."

"I work," Terry said, "even if I have to repair appliances between what I consider my real occupation. Yeah, it's a struggle, and you get kicked in the teeth regularly, but then, every now and then, you know it's worth it. Probably not so unlike being a cop."

"I don't recall ever getting any applause for being a cop," Nell said. "Not the way you must have."

He laughed. "I got some at that. Hated to turn in the uniform when the show closed."

He tightened some joints with the wrench, then let it clatter back into his toolbox and withdrew a small acetylene torch. "Gotta heat something up," he said, "do some soldering. Then I'll recharge the unit, change the filter, and be out of here. I'll be able to make an audition, and you can return to chasing the bad guys."

"No rush," Nell said. "At the moment, no bad guys close enough to chase."

He gave her a sideways glance as the torch popped and its nozzle emitted a narrow, hot flame. Another grin came her way. Then he adjusted the blue flame and began soldering. "Your name, Nell, is it short for Nelly?"

"It is, but nobody's called me Nelly in years." She waited for him to comment that it was a nice name, but he didn't. The only sound was the humming and clinking of the old box fan, the hissing of the torch. The torch reminded her of the one the Tavern on the Green waiter had used to scorch the crème brûlée, which brought to mind a comparison between Jack Selig and Terry Adams. Nell wasn't sure she was ready for a sixtyish lover. It might be too much like being in her sixties herself, rushing the season. Selig was certainly sophisticated and handsome—and rich. Terry was certainly sensual and handsome—and still relatively poor. Maybe Terry was Selig twenty years ago.

Nell was Nell now, and now wasn't twenty years ago.

Terry had finished with the blow torch and was fitting a new filter into place. When he straightened up, he wiped his hands on the outer thighs of his Levi's so they'd be dry, getting ready to hoist the air conditioner back into the window frame. He was going to get away.

Unless Nell's refrigerator needed repair. It didn't seem to be keeping the milk as cold as it used to.

She watched silently as he slid the heavy unit back into the window, muscles flexing in his corded arms. He began to anchor it to the frame with a screwdriver.

"Aren't you going to try it first?" she asked.

"It'll work," he said. "I knew exactly what it needed."

When he was finished, he switched the air conditioner on and turned it to high. It ran quietly and more powerfully than it ever had. Nell could see the brass pull chain on the nearby table lamp swaying in the artificial breeze.

Terry unplugged the old box fan and wound the cord. Then he replaced his tools in their box, and carefully refolded the tarp so nothing would get on the carpet. He stooped gracefully for his Budweiser can, which he'd placed on his clipboard, tilted back his head, and finished his beer.

"Mind if I wash my hands?" he asked.

"Bathroom's down the hall, first door on your right."

He placed the empty beer can on the smoothly running air conditioner, then made his way past her and down the hall. Nell knew he'd see her makeup, her toothbrush, intimate things. Maybe he'd sneak a look in the medicine cabinet and see the Midol. Maybe he'd look in the bottom vanity drawer and see her hair drier and her vibrator.

Can't get much more intimate than that.

For some reason, she didn't care.

"I bet you made a good cop," she said, when he returned with freshly scrubbed, almost clean hands. "Got great reviews."

"They said I was convincing."

"I can imagine."

"You should catch me when I perform sometime."

"I'd like that."

He crossed the room and picked up his clipboard and toolbox. Then he tucked the folded tarp beneath his arm. With his free hand, he picked up the box fan. Fully laden, he glanced at the empty beer can, then at her.

"I'll get it later," she said. "Want me to write you a check?"

"Not necessary. I'll bill you."

He started toward the door, then turned as if he'd forgotten something. But he didn't look anywhere other than at Nell. She hadn't risen from the sofa.

"Anything else you need?" he asked.

"Need? Maybe the refrigerator. You do refrigerators?"

"I do whatever needs doing."

"Mine's been heating up lately."

"Your refrigerator?"

"No"

He carefully placed the fan, his toolbox, tarp, and clipboard on the floor and moved toward her.

"Everything in the damned place is overheated," she said. "I guess I need a Mr. Fixit."

He sat down next to her on the sofa.

"We'll fix that."

35

Beam parked his Lincoln in a patch of shade across the street from Things Past. The space was available because it was a loading zone, complete with signs that threatened potential parkers with everything from arrest to castration. Nola knew the car and sooner or later would see it out the shop's window. He didn't care if she knew he was there. Maybe she'd think he was harassing her, and she'd come outside and walk over and complain. He wouldn't mind; he wanted very much to have any kind of communication with her.

Christ! I am harassing her. Just like one of those stalkers women phone the police about.

There was always the possibility Nola would call the police, and they'd send a car to investigate her complaint. That would be, among other things, embarrassing.

And there was always the possibility that she'd simply ignore him.

Beam's injured leg was starting to ache and stiffen up from sitting in one position for so long. It didn't do that often; maybe it was trying to tell him something.

He propped the NYPD placard on the dashboard where it

was visible, then he opened the door and used it to brace himself as he climbed out of the Lincoln. After waiting for a string of cars to pass, he crossed the street to the antique shop. He'd been parked there for twenty minutes and hadn't seen anyone come or go. *Does she ever sell anything?*

By the time he'd crossed the street, he was no longer limping. The warm sun felt good on his back and leg. At the shop's door, with its OPEN sign dangling crookedly in its window, he hesitated.

Then he remembered what Cassie had told him: *". . . she needs to forgive you."*

He wasn't sure precisely why his sister had come to that conclusion, but she was right enough often enough to give him confidence now. He opened the door and went inside. The muted little bell above his head sounded the customer alarm.

He seemed to be the only one in the shop.

Finally, alerted by the bell, Nola came in through an open door behind the counter. Her hair was pulled back, emphasizing her wide cheekbones and large dark eyes. The simple blue dress she had on wasn't meant to be sexy, but on her it was. Something about the way her body moved beneath the loosely draped material, what was and wasn't apparent. She was a woman with a subtle rhythm all her own. The thing about women that attracted and seduced was individual and rhythmic, Beam thought. Maybe it was a subtle synthesis of rhythms. He didn't understand it, but he sensed it was true.

Nola didn't look surprised to see him. "You get overheated sitting out there in your car?"

"It isn't much cooler in here," Beam said, aware not only of the warmth, but of the musty scent of the surrounding objects, the past.

"I'll complain to the landlord." She didn't seem angry that he'd turned up again. She didn't seem pleased. "What do you want, Beam?"

"I think we need to talk."

"*You* need to talk."

"We both do," Beam said. "To each other."

She rested her hand on an old black rotary phone on the counter. "I should pick up the phone, call the precinct, tell them I'm being threatened and I'm afraid."

"You're not being threatened and you're not afraid."

"But I could pick up the phone and call."

"Go ahead."

He waited, but she didn't move. Didn't look away from him. Nothing in the world was darker than the very center of her eyes. "I know you've asked people in the neighborhood about me, Beam. You wanted to know if I was married, if I was involved with anyone."

"I did that, yes."

Her hand didn't move off the phone. "What is this we need to talk about?" she asked.

There was a good question. But the answer came to him immediately. "Harry."

"He was my husband."

"He was my friend."

"Did he trust you? His friend? The cop who owned him and was bending his arm?"

"Yes. And he trusted you. He was right to trust us both. I don't deny I wanted you. But I never moved on it. Never touched you. I was married. And you were Harry's wife."

"I'm still Harry's wife."

"Not any longer."

"Your wife is dead now."

The simple statement, coming from her, didn't carry the weight and pain it might have. He was appalled, and then relieved, that he could hear it and not be pierced by grief and loneliness.

"You're right, she's dead," he said. "And so is Harry."

"You want to screw me. You want me to forgive you."

"Yes."

"One doesn't necessarily follow the other."

"I know. But we both need the same thing."

"Oh? And what's that?"

"To be free of the past without losing it."

She continued to stare at him. He couldn't decipher what was in her eyes.

"I'm being honest with you," he said.

"You sure as hell are. You think I'm stuck here in some kind of cobwebby, self-imposed purgatory on earth because of what happened to Harry."

"Yeah, I think that.

"And you think I can somehow ease the loss you feel for your wife."

She's right!

The knowledge, its clarity, so bluntly stated, struck Beam like a bullet.

"And you have the formula that will help us both," she said.

"It isn't a formula."

"Then what is it?"

"A plea."

"You don't sound so sure of yourself now."

"I'm not."

"What I said, do I have it right, Beam?"

"As far as it goes."

"It goes farther?"

"You know it does."

"I know I want you to leave."

"Question is, do you want me to come back?"

Her gaze locked with his own. "I want you to leave."

Finally she removed her hand from the phone.

He could feel her watching as he let himself out, the bell above the door tinkling a message in a code he didn't know.

He did know she hadn't told him not to return, and she'd hesitated a beat before telling him again that she wanted him to leave.

A beat. An infinitesimal fraction of time.
A change in the rhythm.

Adelaide understood that publicity was the oxygen of her business. Not that she wasn't sincere, but why not make her plight known? Why not speak for the other poor people in the same predicament as hers, being pushed around by the system? This was her opportunity, and in a way her responsibility.

Responsibility. That's the word Barry used when finally he'd warmed to her idea, and even sort of adopted it as his own. "We average citizens can't let ourselves be pushed around by the system," he'd said. "Somebody has to speak up, even if it means falling on his or her sword."

"Like a real sword?" Adelaide had asked.

"Like a book contract," Barry told her. "And talk shows and acting jobs."

So here she was on the steps of City Hall, with maybe a hundred people gathered beyond the dozens of TV cameras and smaller camcorders directed toward her. One of the TV people had given her a tiny mike to clip to her lapel, with a wire running down inside her blouse to a small black power pack they'd attached to her belt at the small of her back.

Adelaide looked young and beautiful in her tight jeans and her yellow blouse, tailored to emphasize her breasts and tiny waist. Her blond hair was piled high and with seeming recklessness on her head, with a few loose strands left to dangle strategically over her right cheek and left eye. Her tiny figure made even more diminutive by the solemn stone of City Hall, Adelaide looked soft and vulnerable. Adelaide looked cute.

In her right hand, she held a sheet of crumpled white paper. She raised it high and told the assembled what they already knew: it was a jury summons.

"It's unfair!" she said in her high stage voice that would

have carried even without a microphone. "I'd be eager to serve on a jury if the city could guarantee my safety. And your safety. They cannot. It's asking citizens to perform much more than their civic duty when they're asked to risk their lives." She waved the summons in her tight little fist. "This isn't a draft notice! We're not at war. I don't feel I should have to pay a price because the city can't perform it's first duty to us, its citizens, and that is to protect us!"

The crowd beyond the media had grown to almost two hundred now, and they began to cheer. Some of the cameras swiveled away from Adelaide and toward the mass of on-lookers.

"I'm not a criminal," Adelaide continued. "And I shouldn't be asked to pay for someone else's crime. But that's exactly what might happen, because the police aren't doing their job. They haven't done it well enough so far, anyway. Maybe it is a tough job. And I'm sure they're doing the best they can. But it isn't my fault—it isn't *our* fault—that it isn't good enough!"

Another loud cheer. Some in the crowd began waving the ADELAIDE'S RIGHT signs that looked homemade, but that Barry had had printed up yesterday by a friend of his who had a graphics art business in the Village. ADELAIDE'S ARMY and FREE ADELAIDE signs were already printed and being held in reserve.

"I have no choice but to announce publicly that until the Justice Killer is apprehended and the city is no longer in the control of a madman—"

"You mean the mayor?" a man shouted from the crowd.

"I mean the Justice Killer." Adelaide began waving both arms now, palms out in an appeal for a moment's silence so she could be heard. "Until the city's safe again, I will not obey this jury summons. I will *not* serve. I will *not* be a sacrifice."

The crowd was getting ever larger, and uniformed cops were having difficulty keeping it contained. A tall, skinny cop near the front used his nightstick as a probe to move a man back, but the man brushed it aside and pushed forward.

"I will go to jail first!" Adelaide screamed. "I mean it! I pledge that I will go to jail!"

"We got rights!" a woman in the crowd screamed.

"And sometimes we have to fight for them!" Adelaide responded. The crowd roared its agreement. She set her jaw and gave them her left profile. Cute as a feisty twelve-year-old, only with a grown woman's sexuality. "This is one of those times." She raised her dainty fist high above her head, as she had when she auditioned for *Les Miz.*

The half dozen men Barry had hired began chanting, "Adelaide! Adelaide! Adelaide!" The crowd joined in, many of them pumping their fists in the air. At a subtle signal from Barry, his hirelings pushed forward, knocking over a police barricade. The crowd followed, surging toward City Hall.

The cops moved fast, but they'd been taken by surprise and there weren't enough of them. A line had been crossed, an invisible switch thrown. Suddenly the crowd became a mob. It was held back only a few seconds before it surged forward, knocking over some of the media, sending equipment smashing to the ground.

"Holy shit!" Adelaide thought.

"Barry!" She began calling for Barry, but in the maelstrom of motion and shouting no one heard her. "Barry!"

Adelaide could count crowds, and she estimated that at least five hundred frenetic people were charging toward her. A uniformed cop was on the ground and couldn't climb back to his feet. He scooted backward, his soles scraping on the pavement, then he was lost from sight in the rush of humanity. That really scared her.

"Barry!"

She saw Barry emerge from the left side of the crowd and start toward her. His face was flushed an improbably bright red and he looked out of breath. He staggered, went down, and disappeared.

God! Barry, don't have a heart attack, please!

Adelaide began backing up the steps, afraid to turn away from the crowd, almost falling as her heel caught. She realized her face was frozen in a meaningless smile that masked near panic.

The blue of a police uniform appeared in the corner of her vision, then another. More and more cops were on the steps. Some of them had long, curved shields as well as nightsticks and were forming a kind of line that was meant to hold back the crowd.

Adelaide turned and saw uniformed cops streaming out of City Hall and down the steps. It was like the cavalry coming to her rescue in an old Technicolor western. And she was overjoyed to see them. She whirled and ran toward her rescuers with her arms spread wide, dropping her crumpled jury summons. A big cop who looked like a young Gary Cooper was gazing deadpan at her. She veered toward him.

She fell sobbing into his arms.

"Arrest me!" she gasped. "Arrest me, please!"

They didn't arrest Adelaide, didn't charge her for inciting a riot, maybe because Barry and his—her—lawyers almost came right out and dared them to. Or maybe she was simply too cute to arrest.

But they did take her into protective custody, and she spent the night by herself in a tiny, smelly holding cell. The bed was hard as a plank, and it was impossible for her to sleep. The place was noisy, too. There were voices she couldn't understand because of the way they echoed, and someone was snoring not far away. Now and then people came by to look in at her. Most of them were in uniform. They didn't say anything, only looked.

But there was something in their expressions that Adelaide recognized, a kind of reserved awe. Only a few other times had people looked at her that way, the way they looked at real celebrities they knew were beyond their reach and envied. At stars.

In the morning, they drove her home under police escort. Some of the people on the sidewalk seemed to recognize Adelaide and waved. As the lead cruiser she was in slowed to take a corner, a woman began hopping up and down, mouthing her name. *Ad-e-laide, Ad e laide.* Three of the cops asked for her autograph, and she smilingly obliged and asked how the siren worked.

Her attorneys told her that next week, when she was due to appear in court in answer to her jury summons and wouldn't be present, the police would issue a warrant for her arrest. She shouldn't be alarmed. It was according to plan.

Scared as she was, she was also excited. She was sure, as she had been all along, that Barry was an absolute genius and one of the truly sweet men in her life.

Marge trusted Manfred Byrd enough to lend him a key to her apartment. That always seemed to Manfred to be the Rubicon, marking a client's complete faith in him, the equating of decorator talent with honesty. A man less honest would take advantage of Marge.

She was having lunch with a friend, she'd told him, to discuss some sort of charitable contribution, and would meet him immediately afterward. Manfred thought it interesting that a woman could become suddenly very rich and give some of it away to those less fortunate. He didn't completely understand the impulse, but he found it commendable.

Apparently her lunch had run later than anticipated. It was past two o'clock and he was alone in the unfurnished living room of her apartment. No matter. He could take the measurements he needed without her. He'd already decided that the sofa she chose would go well with the slightly burnt umber tint to the previously dead white walls. When he was finished, the room would be much warmer, and with a sense of order and stability, which was what Marge wanted.

Manfred took off his gray silk sport jacket, carefully folded it lining out, and laid it on the carpet. Then he removed his tape measure from his briefcase on the floor and prepared to go to work.

He was headed for the corner where the tall étagère was going to be, when a slight sound made him turn.

And there was a man with a gun.

Guns were not part of Manfred's universe. All he could manage to say was, "Huh?"

There was something bulky on the gun's barrel, and while Manfred knew next to nothing about firearms, he recognized it as a silencer. It was all he could stare at as the man moved toward him.

The gun didn't waver as the man said, "Slip your jacket back on."

Manfred quickly did as he was told, so hurriedly he might have heard a seam rip in the silk fabric. *Dreadful sound.*

"Now go out on the balcony," said the very calm voice behind the gun. It might have been an invitation to step outside and admire the breathtaking view.

"No. You're—"

"Outside!"

Manfred turned his back on the gunman, opened the French doors to the balcony, and reluctantly stepped outside. Though the day was calm, at this height there was a steady breeze. He couldn't help but notice that fear was making his movements stiff. At the same time, there was an unreality about all of this.

He was shoved roughly from behind, stumbled forward, and caught himself on the waist-high iron railing just in time to keep from tumbling out into space. He gasped and began to turn around. He was dizzy, terrified.

The rudeness! This really shouldn't be happening!

He was only halfway around when he was shoved again. This time he felt his right ankle grasped and lifted, and his perspiring hand slipped off the railing.

Along with the momentum of the shove, it was enough to tip the balance.

Manfred Byrd was airborne and for several seconds too astounded to be simultaneously frightened.

It's all so fast!

Ten floors down he began to scream.

36

"Who the hell is she?" da Vinci asked.

Beam was standing. Nell and Looper were seated before da Vinci's desk. Helen Iman, the profiler, was sprawled in a chair over by the computer. The usually organized office was more cluttered than Beam had ever seen it. Papers were scattered over da Vinci's desk, a stack of file folders leaned precariously on top of the computer monitor. A crumpled yellow slip of some sort had missed the wastebasket. It was almost as if the job were getting away from da Vinci. The Adelaide effect, Beam thought.

He said, "She's an actress who lives in the Village."

Da Vinci raised his eyebrows in that way that made him look more than ever like young Tony Curtis. "Successful?"

"Not unsuccessful," Beam said. "Sings, dances, acts . . . the whole package."

"And cute enough to top a dessert," Looper said.

The others stared at him and he nervously tapped his breast pocket where he used to carry his cigarettes.

"She certainly stirred up some shit," da Vinci said.

"The kind she wanted," Beam said, standing with his arms crossed. "She's front page and leads the news all over town.

And out of town. The rest of the country's getting more and more interested in our predicament, thinking it might happen to them."

"Do you think she's the sort who could start a popular movement?" Nell asked.

All three men looked at her disbelievingly.

"She could start things moving that have never moved before," Looper said.

Da Vinci looked over at Helen. "What do you think of our Adelaide?"

"Not exactly my department," she said. Her voice was throaty and, in a quiet way, commanded attention. "But I'll try. She's self-involved, narrowly focused, clever, and not as dumb as she looks. Or at least she's got somebody with brains directing her. Don't let the cute act fool you. Could she start a movement? Think Joan of Arc."

Da Vinci looked disgusted. This was a turn in the case he hadn't counted on.

"This city's gonna have an even tougher time getting anyone to serve on a jury," Beam said, "unless we get ahead of the curve on this."

"I've heard that advice somewhere before," da Vinci said. "It seems to have more to do with surfing than homicide investigations."

"It's more or less worked."

"Mostly less. But what do you suggest this time?"

"When she doesn't report for jury duty," Beam said, "don't charge her."

Da Vinci shook his head. "We can't let her get away with it and set an example, or nobody will even open their mail from the city unless they need something to wipe their ass."

"Issue a statement saying she's being excused because she's a hardship case."

"She's an out-of-work actress," Nell said. "She's got nothing else to do, and the city does pay jurors a stipend."

"Only a stipend," Looper said. "When last I checked, it was forty dollars a day. That doesn't take you far in New York."

"She was in a show until six weeks ago," Beam said, "a musical called *Nuts and Bolts* at the Herald Squared Theatre, Off-Off-Broadway. It was panned by the critics, but it ran for almost three months."

Da Vinci moved an elbow that had been resting on his desk, almost sending a sheet of paper onto the floor. He absently weighted one corner of the paper under one of the wheels of his brass motorcycle sculpture. "And?"

"She's almost certainly collecting unemployment. It's a fact of life and a mainstay for most actors. And her jury pay would be deducted from what she draws, at least on a weekly basis. That means she wouldn't actually be collecting anything for serving as a juror. Her jury service would mean she wouldn't have time to look for work. We can call her, and theater people like her who are temporarily out of work, hardship cases and excuse them all from jury duty. The media would love it. New York's supposed to be a friendly town for theatrical performers."

Da Vinci leaned back in his desk chair. "You're a devious bastard, Beam."

Helen dug in a heel and began swiveling an inch back and forth in the swivel chair by the computer. "He really is," she said, looking at Beam appraisingly.

"Do you think it'd work?" da Vinci asked her.

"Might."

"Think it'd shut the little pest up?"

"Slow her down, at least."

Da Vinci smiled. "I gotta say I like it."

He was still smiling when his phone buzzed, but as he listened to what the caller had to say, the smile faded. His knuckles whitened on the receiver, and he looked at Beam. Away from Beam. Beam didn't like it.

"Wait here just a minute," da Vinci said when he hung up.

He rose from his desk and left the office before anyone could reply.

"What the hell?" Nell said.

"Looks like it could be bad news," Looper said, giving his shirt pocket a tap. When a minute or so passed and no one else commented on the obvious, he said, "You ever get your air conditioner fixed, Nell?"

Nell blushed.

She was about to stammer a reply when the door opened and da Vinci blustered back in. He went back behind his desk, sat down, and dropped a piece of red material on his green desk pad.

When he smoothed and straightened out the material, it was about five inches long and cut in the shape of a capital *J*.

"I wanted to make sure this was like the others," da Vinci said. "We've got another JK victim, over on Third Avenue."

"Shot?" Looper asked.

"No. Died on the street. Apparently he was made to jump or was pushed from a thirty-first floor balcony. He was an interior decorator who let himself into his client's apartment and was waiting for her. It looked like it could be a simple accident or suicide until the CSU found the cloth letter tucked into one of his sport coat pockets."

"Has anyone checked to see if he ever served on a jury?" Nell asked.

"He has," da Vinci said. "Five years ago. A rape trial. The defendant walked on a technicality."

"Not the jury's fault," Looper pointed out.

"Makes no difference," da Vinci said. "The jury still could have found him guilty. In our system, a jury can do just about what it damn well pleases."

"Was he foreman?" Nell asked.

"No, just one of the jurors."

"Like Tina Flitt," Nell said.

"We have another change of MO," Beam said. "Death by falling."

"A familiar one, though," da Vinci said, looking at Beam the way he had when he was on the phone. "I think our killer might be trying to tell us something."

Beam suddenly understood. He felt a chill. "You mean the way Lani died? You can't think—"

"That he killed your wife to motivate you to become his opponent?" da Vinci said. "I'm afraid it's possible."

"But not likely," Nell said. "If that were true, the killer would have made sure there was a letter *J* involved. Or he would have made sure some other way that Beam knew who was responsible."

Da Vinci glanced over at Helen.

"I think she's right," Helen said.

"He could still be sending a message, though," Looper said. "Taunting Beam."

"Showing us he can get by with anything," Nell said.

"Sounds more plausible," Helen said.

Beam slipped his fingertips into his rear pants pockets and paced a few steps toward the file cabinets, then back. He was trying to figure out how he felt about this, sort through grief and anger, reason it out.

Finally he said, "I think Nell's right. He couldn't have had anything to do with Lani. And Loop's right, too. The sick asshole deliberately mimicked Lani's death to send a message, a taunt."

Instead of turning to Helen this time, da Vinci seemed to think about it, then nodded. "Yeah, probably a taunt. The apartment with the balcony is a condo unit owned by a woman named Marge Caldwell. Crime scene unit's over there now getting what they can, but the place got too contaminated when we thought it was accidental death or suicide to give up much in the way of admissible evidence. You can start there on this one. But it looks like our killer got away clean again."

"The time's coming when he won't," Helen said. "He'll make a mistake because unconsciously he wants to. He wanted to play his game in the first place with Beam because he knew he'd eventually be nailed."

"That last one's hard to believe," da Vinci said. Now he did look over at Helen.

Helen shrugged.

"If it's true, he'll get his wish." Beam said. He'd sorted through his emotions and knew now how he felt—angry. Even if the killer had nothing to do with Lani's death, it was as if he'd somehow defiled her. "He's going to get a return message he isn't going to like."

Helen smiled like something carnivorous about to take a bite. Beam still didn't have much confidence in her, but he was beginning to like her.

37

"You really wanna score some coke?" Vanessa Asarian asked Gina.

They were in Häagen-Dazs near where Vanessa shared an apartment with two other NYU students. There were only a few places to sit after buying your ice cream or drinks at the counter. Gina and Vanessa were at a table near the back of the long ice cream shop. The only other occupied table was up front, where three preppy types Gina thought looked like future asshole attorneys were sitting spooning in ice cream.

Vanessa wasn't one of Gina's best friends at school, but she was a friend. While Gina had a reputation for being serious and studious to the point of being dull, Vanessa, beautiful, blond, and with improbably large brown eyes, had just the opposite reputation. Both reputations were pretty much on the money.

"I want you to put me in contact with this guy Reggie I always hear you and some of the others talk about," Gina said. She was trusted by those who knew her well, and they discussed matters involving lovers and drug suppliers in front of her without fear of betrayal. Or so Gina thought. Vanessa's reaction to her request surprised her.

"You haven't been talking to the police, have you, Gina?"

At first Gina thought she meant talking about the trial of Genelle's killer and the Justice Killer, and wondered how she could know. Then she realized what Vanessa meant.

"You're not really afraid of me snitching to the narcs, are you, Van?"

Not that it was narcotics Gina was interested in. She was more interested in Reggie. For a while he'd been away from the scene, and Gina had learned he was in prison, not for selling or possession of drugs, but because he'd been caught burglarizing a pawn shop in New Jersey.

Vanessa sipped her Diet Pepsi through her straw, making a show of it with her pouty lips for the three preppy types sitting up near the entrance. When she lowered the plastic cup there were lipstick smears the first inch of the straw. The preps didn't happen to be looking her way. Sometimes, Gina thought, Vanessa could be too much.

"Do you really think I'd turn snitch?" Gina asked again.

"No," Vanessa said. "But Reg has had problems lately. He was beat up a few nights ago and his merchandise was stolen."

"Coke?"

"Coke, grass, meth."

"I didn't know he dealt in all of that. I thought he was only a coke dealer."

Vanessa stared at her wide-eyed, with her jaw dropped as if in shock. It was known around school as the Vanessa look. "He's a businessman, Gina. Businessmen diversify."

"That's investors," Gina said.

"Same thing. Being smart. Branching out."

Gina studied her friend. She'd chosen Vanessa to ask about Reggie because she'd long suspected the two might be lovers. Or at least fornicators. The way Vanessa was defending her supplier seemed to underscore the notion. "The guy's a drug dealer, Van."

"So's your friendly pharmacist."

"I want to talk to Reggie in a friendly way."

"If you want to try coke, I can get you some."

"I want to talk to Reggie."

"You sure you two have *never* met?"

Gina smiled at her. "It's nothing like that."

The Vanessa look again. "Like what?"

"You know what. And you're making too big a deal out of it. I only want you to put me in touch with someone I don't know."

Vanessa looked away and took another sensuous sip through her straw. Distracted this time, though. Gina knew she was considering whether Reggie might be interested in Gina if they met. Gina doubted he would be, but then she didn't know much about Reggie other than that he dealt drugs and made a bad burglar. Gina knew she was the serious type. She couldn't picture a hedonist like Reggie being interested in her. But Vanessa might not see it that way.

"What do you want with him?" Vanessa asked around her straw, then did the pouty business with her lips again.

"Would Reggie want me to tell you?"

Vanessa's cheeks became concave as she sucked in soda. The preps up front were staring at her now, but she didn't seem to notice.

"I don't want to have sex with him," Gina said, "only talk to him."

Vanessa's eyes widened in genuine surprise this time. Gina didn't usually talk this way. "Gina—"

"Don't bother," Gina said. "It's none of my business who you or Reggie screw, and it's going to stay that way."

One of the preps, maybe a lip reader, looked as if he might get up and make his way back to them, but he didn't work up the nerve to rise from his little wrought iron chair.

"Okay," Vanessa said, "I'll set up a meeting with Reg. But tell no one."

"I don't intend to," Gina said.

"Whatever you wanna sniff or smoke, it's okay with me."

"I know that, Van, or I wouldn't have come to you."

"Done, then," Vanessa said. She glanced around as if she'd heard someone call her name, but only as an excuse to survey the front of the shop. "Those guys that look like potential lawyers and doctors been looking at us?"

"At you," Gina said.

38

"I hardly knew the man," Marge Caldwell said, obviously tired of Beam's questions after she'd already given a statement to the police—and less than an hour after Manfred Byrd had died.

"You knew him well enough that he died in your apartment," Beam said.

Except for Nell, they were seated in the unfurnished living room on imitation Chippendale chairs that Beam and Looper had dragged in from the dining room. Nell was out on the balcony, looking around again to see if the crime scene unit had missed anything, thinking this was an apartment most New Yorkers would die for.

"Well, not exactly *in* my apartment, thank God," Marge said. "He was a decorator who was recommended to me by my hair stylist."

"Who is?"

"Terra. I don't know her last name. She owns Terra's Do's and Don'ts, over on First Avenue."

"How long have you been going there?" Beam asked. Looper was silent; on the drive over, they'd agreed to let Beam do the questioning.

"I've been there exactly once," Marge said. "I've only been in New York a little over a month, and I wasn't crazy about Terra." She unconsciously raised a hand to touch her permed, graying hair. "She insisted on doing my hair her way. She's like a lot of hair stylists—she doesn't *listen*."

Beam had read the preliminary report on Marge; it briefly described a markedly ordinary woman except for one thing.

"You won the Michigan lottery?" he asked, making sure.

"Three point nine million dollars," Marge said, with an expression suggesting she'd answered the question many times before and it annoyed her.

"Congratulations," Looper said.

Marge looked over at him and smiled. He was a nice man, not like Beam.

"Why did you decide to move to New York?" Beam asked.

"To be somewhere my ex-husband isn't. We'd just been divorced when I was notified of my winnings. He's had a change of heart."

"I'll bet," Nell said, having just wandered back in from the balcony. She looked at Beam and Looper. "Nothing out there except for the fantastic view," she said. "Not so much as a scuff mark."

Beam wasn't surprised.

Marge's patience seemed to be wearing thin. "Look," she said, "it's not as if I don't want to help, but I really don't know anything. I talked to the police right after I came home and learned what happened. The officer took notes."

"I'm sorry to bother you again," Beam said, "but there've been developments that make it necessary we talk with you again."

"The Justice Killer?"

"He's the main development."

"Is the news right? Did the Justice Killer push Manfred off my balcony?"

"It looks that way."

"Then I can't see what you want with me. I was ten blocks

away when it happened." Marge seemed upset and was obviously getting uncomfortable in her chair. She didn't want to be unpleasant, but they were pressing her.

"We need to be thorough," Beam said, "so I'll have to ask your indulgence. Did anyone other than you and Byrd have a key to get in here?"

"No. Look, I hardly even know anyone in New York. Like a lot of other people, I came here for anonymity."

"Did you ever see Manfred Byrd socially?"

"Look," Marge said again, as if she actually had something to show Beam, "Manfred was simply somebody I hired to help me decorate this place. He was . . . flighty. We weren't about to see each other socially, but I think we liked each other okay. I could tell he was very good at what he did. And, I think if he was still alive, he'd say I was one of his clients that actually listened to him and took his advice."

"Did he complain about any other clients?"

"Not specifically. He only mentioned a few times that it was frustrating when people paid for his advice then refused to take it."

Like with Terra the beautician, Beam thought. He said, "Do you remember ever seeing Mr. Byrd in anyone else's company?"

"I only saw him when he came here," Marge said, "other than when we went shopping together for decorators' materials or furniture."

"And how often was that?"

"Three—no, four times. Once for paint and wallpaper, and three times for furniture."

"When was the last time?"

"Two days ago. We bought a sofa to go in this room. It will be the only furniture in here with a pattern."

"I don't see a sofa."

"We're—I'm still waiting for delivery, on the sofa and several other pieces of furniture. We didn't want any of it here until the painters were finished." Marge's body gave a quick little start, as if experiencing a tiny shock. "Look," she said, "I didn't lie to you, but I was wrong. I do think I remember something I haven't mentioned. Manfred told me once he kept getting the feeling he was being followed."

"Did he have any idea by whom?"

"No. He did think it was a man."

"Then he'd seen this person?"

"I don't know. If he did, I don't believe he described him." She clasped her hands in her lap and appeared pained, thinking. "His exact words—exact as I can recall them—were, 'This can be a dangerous city, Marge. Sometimes I think there's a man following me. But maybe I'm getting paranoid.'"

"He said that, about being paranoid?"

"Yes, I remember the conversation because I thought it was odd he'd be upset. I mean, a *man* following him. I should think he might have been pleased. You know, a *man . . .*"

"Got it," Beam said. "And when was this conversation about being followed?"

"Oh, three or four days ago, I believe. We were measuring for drapes."

"Was that the only time he mentioned this man?"

"Yes. And to tell you the truth he didn't seem *terrifically* upset about it. I mean, it was just idle conversation. That's why I didn't remember it before."

Looper and Nell were looking at Beam. Tina Flitt's husband had said the same thing not long before his wife was murdered; he had the feeling he was being followed. The Justice Killer stalking his prey while he was being stalked. The dangerous game he'd chosen to play.

Beam closed his notebook and stood up. His right leg felt weak and almost gave at the knee. Had it fallen asleep while he was perched uncomfortably on the hard chair, or was it suffering some sort of delayed reaction to his having been shot?

Whatever. The leg seemed to be regaining feeling and strength.

Beam made himself smile. "We appreciate your help, Ms. Caldwell, and we apologize for the inconvenience."

Marge stood also, a little stiffly like Beam. She smiled. "That's okay. You're only doing your job. And I like the way you don't call me missus. It makes me feel unmarried."

"No trouble at all. If you remember anything else, Ms. Caldwell . . ." He handed her a card.

"Of course." Marge slipped the card into a pocket of her skirt.

"Are you going to hire another decorator to complete the work?" Nell asked.

"No. Manfred and I were finished with the choices. Now it's only a matter of execution. I think I can handle that."

She showed them to the door like a dutiful hostess.

"Don't worry," Looper told her as they were leaving, "it's going to look great."

On the elevator ride down, Beam said, "Except for the remark about Byrd thinking he was being followed by a strange man, she knows just about zilch."

"Our killer works clean every time," Looper said.

"Byrd spotted him," Nell pointed out.

"Maybe you didn't notice," Looper said, "but Byrd had an eye."

Nell glanced at him from the corner of her own eye, marveling once again how the world was full of surprises large and small.

Reggie was a piece of work. He was only about five-foot six or seven, but the way he carried himself you just knew he was strong. When he approached Gina the next morning near the statue in Columbus Circle he was wearing baggy chinos, a tan shirt with lots of pockets, comfortable-looking brown hiking shoes, and a beat up gray backpack. His dark hair was long and greasy, and he wore a weathered slouch hat that had at one time been white. He was passably handsome, with a strong jaw, blue eyes, and a mouth that looked as if it smiled easily and often. All in all, he looked like an American student just back from bumming around a foreign land on the cheap. A youth hostel user and a drug user maybe, but not a dealer.

Gina pretended not to notice him. The morning was already too warm, and her palms were sweating.

"You Gina?" he asked. She could barely hear him over the noise of the traffic, and thought that might be why he chose this as a meeting place. Conversations here would be difficult to tape.

"I am if you're Reggie."

"I'm the Reggie you seek. Van didn't say you were so pretty." He did a little shuffle, as if her unexpected attractiveness made him nervous.

"She wouldn't."

"She did say I could trust you."

"Can *I* trust *you?*" Gina asked, not liking all the exhaust fumes she was breathing in.

"Hell, no. But you can always count on me to act in my self-interest."

"Are you in love with Vanessa?"

He laughed. "She thinks so. I like that."

"And you use it. Use her."

"Hey, I'm a user of people. I'd like to use you."

"It wouldn't be in your self-interest or mine. Do you confide in Vanessa?"

"Hah! I don't confide in no one." The shuffle again; he might have been shaking out a sudden cramp in one leg. He adjusted his soiled slouch hat so it sat far back on his head and made him look jaunty and younger. "You're certainly ballsy for one of Van's friends."

"Oh, maybe you don't know them well enough."

"I know 'em. They only act ballsy. You ain't acting." He smiled. He really wasn't a bad-looking guy. Gina could understand what Vanessa saw in him. But then sharks were, in their own way, beautiful. "We gonna get to the point?"

"Vanessa said you were a businessman."

"She's got that right."

"And you're a burglar."

He gave her a hard look that chilled. Now he wasn't so good looking. Momentarily, the shark had bared its teeth. "Van tell you that?"

"It isn't any secret," Gina said. "You did your time, and now you're out and a productive member of society."

"You must watch a lotta TV."

"Hardly any."

"The point," he reminded her. He actually glanced at his watch, letting her know he had more important things to do and didn't want to waste much more time here. "You wanna score some dope, right?"

"Wrong. I'm more interested in the burglary part."

He scratched his scalp beneath the greasy hair near his hat brim and grinned, showing he was learning to like her and was interested. "You want me to steal something?"

"Have you broken into any pawn shops since you got out of prison?"

"Since and before," Reggie said. "I like pawn shops. They got a lotta stuff in 'em I can turn into money." He did his little shuffle and glanced around at the ongoing maelstrom of traffic. Gina thought again he might have chosen this meeting place because the constant noise would make electronic eavesdropping on their conversation difficult, if not impossible.

She hesitated, wondering if she should simply call this off and walk away, if this was one of those crucial moments in life that would change everything that came after.

No, she decided, it didn't have to be. But hadn't somebody or other said the forks in life's road are usually only visible in the rearview mirror?

"You interested in something that might be in a pawn shop?" Reggie asked.

"A gun," Gina said.

39

"Can they do that to me?" Adelaide asked.

She was sitting, talking on the phone at the table in her tiny kitchen. In front of her was a plate with half a piece of buttered toast with a bite out of it, a tumbler with a residue of orange juice, and a full cup of decaffeinated coffee with cream added to it. She'd just poured the coffee—her third cup of the morning—from the Braun brewer that sat on the table near the wall and electrical socket. Alongside the cup was today's *Post*.

Adelaide was pleased with her photo on the front page. It was a shot of her standing on the City Hall steps with her fist raised, breasts thrust forward, a resolute expression on her face. The wind had for once cooperated and not done bad things to her hair. She looked like a stubborn child, but one to be reckoned with. She looked adorable.

What she didn't like was the story that went with the photo. New York City had decided not to summon her, or other temporarily unemployed show business people, for jury duty. They were classifying such citizens as hardship cases and rejects.

"They can do it to you," Barry confirmed on the phone.

"They can summon anyone they want for jury duty, and they can reject anyone."

"Reject," Adelaide said. "I don't like that word, Barry. I hear it too often."

"If you read further down," Barry said, "you'll find that the paper regards you as heroic. They say you made the city back down."

Adelaide paused in her one-handed attempt to spread more butter on her toast. "That's good, Barry."

"It would be, Ad, but it happened too soon. We want them to back down, but later, after you've had plenty of press. The bastards know that. They just want to fast shuffle you out of the news."

"The bastards," Adelaide said. She laid the butter knife aside and took another tiny bite of toast. Chewed. "Summoning me for jury duty was bad, but then canceling the summons like they say in the paper, that's a cruel trick."

"You could say that, Ad."

"I did say it." She washed down the bite of toast with a swallow of coffee. "Cruelty in others is something I cannot abide."

"Of course, what they'll say if we complain is that you're getting exactly what you've been demanding."

"I don't put that below them."

Adelaide turned to the next page. There were more photographs of her. Most of them were okay, but not as good as the one on the front page. One of them, taken at an upward angle from the base of the steps, made her nostrils look too large. Her nostrils did not look like *that*. She turned her attention away from the photos and began to read.

"Ad? Still with me?" Barry, ever patient with his client.

"My God! It says under my picture in the *Post* that I've won. How can they print that kinda stuff without getting sued?"

"You did win, Ad. That's the problem."

"This is outrageous. What are we gonna do, Barry?"

"I'll think of something."

"I hope so. I am really, totally, shit-kicking angry about this."

Beneath the table, her dainty foot began to tap.

Nell lay perspiring beside Terry in her bed and watched the morning light filter in through the cracks in the blinds. The air conditioner emitted a steady hum, providing white noise that seemed to isolate the room from the noisy city outside, still waking to a new and boisterous day.

Terry was an attentive, considerate lover, if sometimes a little rough. Nell wondered what kind of lover Jack Selig was. She wasn't going to find out now.

She was totally smitten by Terry Adams. Last night had been wonderful. She'd feared the bed would collapse as the headboard slammed over and over against the wall with each of Terry's thrusts into her. At first she'd been concerned about whether the proper Mr. Ramirez downstairs would hear the racket, but it wasn't long before she forgot about Mr. Ramirez altogether.

The longer she knew Terry, the more she was surprised by his many facets. He not only repaired appliances and was a struggling but respected actor, he'd yesterday mentioned that ten years ago he'd actually published a collection of short stories. He'd shown her a yellowing copy. The publisher was a small one Nell had never heard of. The stories were dark and lyrical, and, she thought, quite good. Of course, she was a cop, not a literary critic.

She did know that this far into their developing relationship, nothing about him had disappointed her.

Then why do I find myself thinking about Jack Selig? What does he represent to me? Safety? My father? Wealth?

She didn't like to think it might be wealth. But how well did people really know themselves?

Amazing! A few weeks ago I thought I'd never have a

relationship again, and now I'm trying to decide between two men.

No—I've decided!

But she knew better.

"You awake?"

Terry's voice beside her startled her and her body jerked. The iron headboard bounced off the wall and the bedsprings sang. The noise reminded her of last night and made her aware of the musty scent of sex that lingered in the room despite the flow of cool air from the window unit.

"Most of the way," she answered.

"What're you thinking?"

Better come up with something here.

"That actress who's got everybody stirred up about her jury duty," she said, remembering the conversation in da Vinci's office.

"Adelaide Starr?"

"Yeah. You know her?"

"I've met her. And I saw her in *Nuts and Bolts*. She's got talent, and she's cute as a bug's ear."

"You ever look close at a bug's ear?" Nell asked.

He laughed. "Don't be jealous."

"Don't be conceited. I was asking about Adelaide Starr professionally. Is she the type who'd be doing all this for publicity?"

"Since she's an actress, I don't have to know her well to answer that one. Yes, she would. Many, maybe most, of my fellow thespians would."

"Would you?"

"Maybe. This is a rough, competitive business in a tough city."

"Lots of businesses are. Even appliance repair."

"Refrigerators and air conditioners break and have to be fixed. Nobody has to put on a play. Adelaide Starr might come across as cute and naive onstage, but you better mark her down as shrewd and calculating. Being cute and innocent is her *shtick,* and she's good at it. Another actor can watch her and appreciate some of her techniques. And I know her manager, Barry Baxter, by reputation. He knows how to play the media like an orchestra."

"Is he honest?"

"Like everybody else."

"You think he's behind this?"

"Sure. He's trying to get publicity for his client."

"Simple as that?"

"Well, maybe not. Adelaide might be scared shitless. I'm sure she really doesn't want to serve on a jury in the city of New York. No one with good sense would."

"That's how the Justice Killer wants her to think. In a way, she's helping him."

"I doubt if they're friends," Terry said, and pulled down the elasticized neck of Nell's nightgown and kissed her left nipple. He used his tongue skillfully and she felt his hand move down her body and over the swell of her stomach.

"Again?" she asked, playing her fingertips over his ear, through his hair.

"Again and again and again," he said, and began working her nightgown up.

Nell dug her bare heels into the mattress and raised her buttocks to help him. He used his mouth on her until she was moist and ready, then mounted her.

The loosely connected iron headboard began its joyous clamor. Nell was lost again and didn't want to be found.

40

Beam, as always, showed up early for his weekly dinner with Cassie. Her high apartment was a comfortable enclave amidst the sheets of summer rain that were sweeping across the city. He sat and watched TV news while she carried things out from the kitchen to her elaborately set dining room table. Beam would have been glad to help, but he knew he'd get his hand slapped. Cassie liked to put on her dinners by herself. She liked to fuss.

She'd prepared almond-crusted trout this evening, along with green beans, and mashed potatoes with garlic in them. The meal was complemented by an Argentine white wine Beam had never heard of.

When Cassie was ready she called him, and Beam simply used the remote to switch off the TV, then went to the table and sat. Outside, thunder rumbled over New York.

The dishes were Haviland, with silver flatware and Waterford crystal. Cassie sat down opposite Beam, and dinner began with a silent toast with wine glasses, then with a salad of spinach leaves, scallops, and tomatoes, with an oil and vinegar dressing. Cassie had also prepared warm rolls.

Beam sometimes thought his sister would have made some man a good wife, but she never discussed her love life. He thought she might have a girlfriend down in Ohio. He'd even glimpsed them once on the street, holding hands, the hefty form of Cassie alongside a slim woman with long, straight hair, but had never mentioned it, didn't mind discussing woman since. However, Cassie didn't mind discussing Beam's love life. Ever the analyst, even when Lani was alive, his sister sometimes surprised him with her blunt and probing questions or observations about them.

Beam didn't mind. He and Cassie had learned to trust each other before they were ten years old. He usually answered her questions, and she his, though his were less personal.

"The profiler in the Justice Killer investigation thinks our man might be in the initial stages of coming unraveled," he said, and forked in a mouthful of spinach leaf.

Cassie sipped her wine. "I thought you didn't believe in profiling."

"Can't be dismissed completely," Beam said. "Like your predictions."

She understood he was joking. He knew better than to ignore his sister's predictions. They had a way of coming true, even if it happened to be in some manner that made you wish they hadn't.

"No predictions here, "Cassie said, "But the timing might be about right for the murderer to start coming unglued. Taking a human life is a destructive process for both parties. Is he killing more often and more brutally?"

"Yes, and varying his methods."

"Playing a game," Cassie said, and began moving her salad ingredients around with her fork, almost as if looking for something in the cut glass bowl.

"Very much like a game," Beam said.

"Like the ones the rest of us play."

Flashes of chain lightning illuminated the apartment. "The rest of us don't go around killing people."

"Oh, we do. In one way or another."

Beam finished his salad. People who'd never dealt with serial killers couldn't know how devoid of human empathy and conscience they were. They had a mission, a compulsion that, to them, was in and of itself enough justification for their actions. "It's not like you to get all cryptic and philosophical on me, Cass."

"Sorry. I'll revert to the prosaic. How's Fred Looper? He still off the cigarettes?"

"As far as we know. He still reaches for them."

"Nell okay, too?"

"Fine, I think."

"You only think?"

"She's a hell of a detective," Beam said. "She has insight and talent, and she's damned tenacious."

"But?"

"She tends to push things too far sometimes. Like when a security tape caught her beating up on a suspect."

"The one who tried to stab her?"

"That's her story. I've seen the tape and I believe her. But even if it's true, she seemed to like her job too much—the part of it where we take on the bad guys physically if they don't give up."

"Nobody hates the bad guys more than you do, Beam. And you've been in some scraps."

"Yeah. Can't deny it. But I've also learned how to hold myself back. It's part of professionalism."

"Would you be able to hold yourself back with the Justice Killer?"

Beam glared at Cassie. She did have an instinct for the Achilles' heel. "I would try to, Cass."

"Maybe Nell tries. She's not as experienced as you are. Give her a break. I've got a good feeling about her."

"Another thing I've noticed," Beam said. "Nell's been distracted the past few days."

"Maybe she's in love, or at least in sexual thrall. It happens. And she's still young and attractive."

"That could be the reason," Beam said. Actually, he was pretty sure of it. He'd seen the signs before, in cops of both sexes. It was the sort of thing that could make you careless and get you shot.

"Do you think it's interfering with her work?"

"I wouldn't say that." *Not yet.*

"So there's no problem."

"None," Beam said. "Except I get the feeling I don't know her as well as I used to."

"Do you still trust her?"

"All the way. But if she's in love . . ."

"She's vulnerable," Cassie finished for him. She pushed her half-eaten salad aside. "But from what you've told me, and what I've seen of her, I don't think you have to worry about Nell being vulnerable as a cop. She might be distracted now, but it's only temporary, while mind and body adjust. She takes her work seriously. We all have to take time off now and then for being human."

Some of us *from* being human, Beam thought.

"In my line of work," he said, "being human can be dangerous."

"In everybody's." Cassie stood up to go to the kitchen and get the main course.

She returned a minute later carrying two steaming plates. She set one down in front of Beam, the other on the side of the table where she would sit.

"Looks delicious," Beam said. He could smell the seasoning on the fish, the garlic in the mashed potatoes. And there were other, more delicate scents, herbs and melted butter. Cassie was one terrific cook.

Brother and sister picked up knife and fork, and for a few

minutes they sat silently and ate and sipped wine. The Argentine wine was perfect with the trout.

"It all tastes even better than it smells," Beam said. "If you ever give up psychoanalysis, you could have a career as a chef."

"Or a culinary psychiatrist." She took a bite of potato. "I have a theory that everything in life is connected in one way or another with food."

"Hmm. Didn't Freud think it was sex?"

Cassie lifted her square shoulders in a shrug. "That's Freud for you." She took a sip of wine and dabbed at her lips with her napkin. "Have you seen your friend Nola again?"

"I'm not sure I like the segue."

"Are you avoiding the question?"

"I suppose. And I shouldn't avoid it. Maybe you can tell me what's going on."

Ignoring his food—which to Cassie might be meaningful—Beam told her about sitting in his car across from Nola's antique shop, and what went on between them when finally he did go inside.

When he was finished, she said, "You went inside the shop. I congratulate you for acting on your fear."

"My nervousness, you mean."

"I mean your fear."

Beam knew she was right. He *had* been afraid. "I remembered what you told me," he said, "about her needing to forgive me."

"Do you agree now that's what she needs?"

"I told her it was what she needs."

"How'd she react?"

Beam told Cassie about Nola insisting that he leave, but not insisting that he not return. He was dismayed that in the telling, it seemed like wishful thinking on his part. It also sounded stilted and futile.

What had happened in the antique shop was beyond

words. Words simply weren't up to the task. They were as useful as paddles in mid ocean. Nola was beyond words.

"Do you think she'll want to see me again?" he asked Cassie.

"Was your account of what happened between you two accurate?"

"I'm a cop," Beam said. "I remember details. It was accurate."

Cassie finished her wine and grinned. "Then you can bet your sweet ass she wants to see you. Don't you understand, bro, you're her way out."

And she's mine.

When Beam left Cassie's apartment a few hours later, he drove past the antique shop even though he was sure Nola wouldn't be there.

The shop's windows were dark, like those in the rest of the businesses lining the block. Even the lettering on the glass was part of the night and unreadable. The windows reminded Beam of blank, uncomprehending eyes staring out at the street.

When he steered the Lincoln in a tire-squealing U-turn and drove for home, he didn't notice the car following him, as he hadn't noticed it when it fell in behind him as he'd pulled out of the parking garage half a block from Cassie's apartment.

In his business, distraction could be dangerous.

41

Fear, real fear, was one mean mother. You could put up a front and hold it off, but it wouldn't go away. It just backed up a step and stayed there, licking its chops, waiting.

Be a bitchin' song.

The commercial possibilities blew through his mind like an icy breeze. The fear came in its wake.

He wasn't Cold Cat now. He was Richard Simms, the defendant. He kept his fingertips touching the hard mahogany surface of the table so his hands wouldn't tremble. His knees were almost weak enough to give, and the same could be said of his bladder. His mouth was filled with cotton, and while he could keep his expression neutral, he couldn't keep the tears from welling in his eyes, which he kept fixed straight ahead at a picture of Justice Thurgood Marshall hanging on the wall behind the bench.

Cold Cat seemed to him more of an invention than ever, a hard structure to hide within, as Richard Simms stood in court and awaited the verdict in his trial for murder. Richard Simms knew he wasn't nearly as tough as Cold Cat, and the harsh world could be dealt with only if it were Cold Cat and not Richard trying to cope. Here in the emotionally charged, smothering heart of the racist bureaucracy, with a hostile world sitting in judgment, he found it impossible to be Cold Cat.

Richard Simms himself would have to face the system, would have to bear up, whatever the verdict.

It was the total silence that got to him more than anything. All his life Richard had hated silence. It made it difficult for him to breathe, to think. He felt as if he might pass out soon from lack of oxygen.

Richard felt ten years old standing there, the age he'd been the three times he'd attended church at St. Matthew's, at the insistence of a fiercely religious aunt who'd tried to force the spirit on him. Religion hadn't taken root in Richard; some of his lyrics, in fact, were virulently anti-faith—all faiths.

But he knew what a benediction was, and that was what he felt when the words were loosed in the stifling courtroom. They were only sounds with no meaning at first, and then, finally, they sank in. They bore in. They suffused apprehension and despondency with relief, and then incredible joy.

Not guilty.

If ever Cold Cat was going to be converted, to experience his epiphany, this was the moment. He almost collapsed with his newfound sense of freedom, sagging so that his attorney Murray had to stand up beside him and support him.

No more jailhouse food, no more god-awful threads, no more nights alone with those dreams.

There's never music in my dreams.

Then he and Murray were hugging, and the attorney whispered something in his ear that Cold Cat couldn't understand, because other voices were rising. His mother was screaming hallelujahs! over and over. Hands patted, pounded on his back. He was shaking hands. Everyone wanted to shake his hand, hug him, and hang on.

And the gavel *banged!* Again! Louder and louder, more and more insistent, until it overwhelmed every other sound in the courtroom and silence returned like a cool river.

At his lawyer's insistence, Cold Cat sat back down, with a backward glance at his mother, who was sobbing in her jubilation. He watched the judge as she dispassionately polled the jury, and he listened as each juror answered.

The verdict was unanimous. Cold Cat did not murder his wife.

He was *free!*

It was at that moment that the old rage, the furnace fire of his youth, still burning strong, began to take hold in him. The system had tried to get him but failed. He'd whipped its ass and he would again with his music. It was a scumbag society out to get him from the git-go and it couldn't shut him up, couldn't stop his message. He was better than the fools who'd tried to bring him down. Better in every way. He would tell them so. When the time was right, he'd let them know.

Unanimous. Try to reverse that one on appeal, Mr. Smart-ass prosecutor Farrato. Richard tried to catch the little prosecutor's eye, but Farrato, busy scooping up papers and stuffing them into his briefcase, wouldn't look in his direction.

Better not look my humpin' way!
Put ya way down
Ya don' see it my way
Make ya way pay
Turn ya way gray
Be yo one last *final day!*

Yes, there were definitely some lyrics here. Food for the beat. It was all material for Cold Cat, all part of his message.

As he stood up to leave the courtroom with his attorneys, he was full of the rage he'd turned to riches. He didn't glance at the jurors, wasn't going to mouth a "thank-you" like Simpson. The Melanie cunt that he'd got all wet between the legs in court and conned into helping him was of no use to him now. He knew how he affected some women, and she'd probably try making a pest of herself, but he wouldn't let her. Old bitch. Old*er*, anyway. Those were bones he didn't want to jump, so piss on her. He made a mental note to describe her to his security staff so they could keep her the hell away.

That Merv Clark, though, nervy guy that'd been around, had his own troubles, and lied his ass off to get a lighter sentence from the man, was a different matter. He'd have to see what he could do for that brother, maybe put him on his staff, loyal soldier like that.

Knee High was in the corner of his vision as two burly bailiffs cleared the way, and graceful Murray guided Cold Cat with a light touch to his elbow, nudging him toward the paneled door to freedom.

Murray, too. Man deserves a bonus. Smoother'n goose shit.

"Catch you later, man!" Knee High yelled.

Cold Cat glanced at him and raised a hand with thumb, forefinger, and pinky stiffly extended. Cameras hadn't been allowed in the courtroom, but the miniature lightning of flashes going off brightened everything, momentarily blinding Cold Cat.

"You'n me all the way now!" Knee High shouted, as the acquitted man and his entourage exited behind the bench. "You'n me all the way!"

"Goddamn believe it!" Richard Simms mumbled.

All the way.

Cold Cat was back.

Two days later New York Appeals Court Judge Roger Parker was found shot to death in his limo by his driver, who'd gone into a service station in Queens to buy a morning paper for the judge.

A slip of paper with a red capital letter *J* printed on it with felt tip pen was tucked beneath the limo's wiper blade on the passenger side, like a parking ticket.

The limo driver started to remove it, then thought he'd better leave it for the police.

42

When Beam, Nell, and Looper arrived an hour after the shooting, Beam knew almost immediately the crime scene wasn't going to give them much. The black Lincoln stretch limo was still parked at the pumps, being swarmed over by the crime scene unit. Judge Parker was slumped in the backseat, the tinted window down. In the harsh morning sunlight, he looked like a plump-faced, elderly man peacefully dozing in the middle of all the turmoil, but for the black round hole in the center of his forehead.

Minskoff, the little ME with the glasses and bushy mustache, was standing alongside the limo, near the dead judge, writing something with a blunt pencil in a small black notebook. He was concentrating on what he wrote, the tip of his tongue protruding slightly from the hairy corner of his mouth.

Beam approached him while Nell and Looper went to find the uniforms who'd taken the call and were first on the scene. Apparently the driver had gone into the station for the paper while the tank was still filling. The gas pump nozzle was still stuck in the limo; it and the hose reminded Beam of a snake that had sunk its fangs into the big car and wouldn't release it. Beam stood patiently, the sun starting to get hot on the back of his neck, until Minskoff finished writing and closed his notebook.

"What's the preliminary?" Beam asked.

"Looks like one gunshot wound, center of the forehead, bullet entered the frontal lobe of the brain at a slight leftward, downward angle. No exit wound. Death immediate."

"Thirty-two caliber?"

"Could be. We'll know when we remove the slug."

"Has the body been moved at all?"

"Lividity indicates not in the slightest."

"I mean since you arrived to make your preliminary examination?"

"The good judge is exactly as he was when I got here. I haven't even opened the car door. No need to, considering the location of the fatal wound."

Beam leaned down so he could peer into the car without touching anything. It appeared that the door where the judge sat was unlocked, as was the driver's door.

He straightened up, then walked alongside the car to the windshield, where the sheet of paper with the red *J* on it was still wedged beneath the wiper blade. He didn't have to remove the paper. The letter *J* was plainly visible, and looked like the others left by the Justice Killer.

Minskoff had walked along to join him. "Appears to be your man again."

"Hardly a man at all," Beam said. "Sick slugs like this killer have given up being part of humanity."

Minskoff shook his head. "Nobody resigns from the human race. But he's sure a part of us we don't like."

"When you arrived, was the rear door where the judge sat unlocked?"

"Yes. I saw that it was, but I didn't open the door. Didn't have to, so I tried to help keep the scene frozen."

"Window already down?"

"Yes, it was open just as it is now."

"The judge is facing forward," Beam said. "If someone

approached the car from the side and tapped on the window, and he opened it and turned his head to speak to whoever it was, then was shot, would his head turn to face forward again?"

"It very well could. Probably would, as his body slumped back. I don't rule out the possibility that he was shot by someone inside the car, but how we found him is consistent with what you just hypothesized, being shot by someone standing alongside the car. The apparent angle of the entry wound indicates that also." Minskoff looked mildly irritated, like a man who'd drawn a bad card at poker. "It'd all be easier to reconstruct if we had an exit wound and could examine blood splatters."

"Messier, though," Beam said.

"Oh, I don't mind that."

Beam left the M.E. as he saw Nell and Looper walking toward him. They stood out of earshot of the crime scene unit techs and watched the ambulance arrive to transport the body. It's flashing emergency lights were lost in the bright sunlight, like those of the police cars.

Too nice a day for a murder, Beam thought.

"A bigshot judge," Looper said, glancing over at the body in the limo. "Not good for our side. Da Vinci's liable to show up here with his nuts in a knot."

"Most likely," Beam said. "Maybe we can be gone. What's the story?"

"Uniforms got the call and arrived no more'n ten minutes after the shot was fired. Nobody heard the shot. Nobody saw anything."

"Busy intersection," Beam said, glancing around. "Where was the limo driver through all of this?"

Nell said, "He stopped here for gas, then while the tank was filling went inside to get a morning paper for the judge. It's the judge's regular limo service, and his regular driver. Since the tank had been almost empty, the driver chatted for a few minutes with the clerk. Then he paid for the paper and went outside. He thought at first the judge was dozing, then noticed the window was down and saw the hole in his fore-head. He said he opened the door, gonna try to help. Then he saw it was no use and shut the door, came back into the station, and called the police."

"You sure he said the window was down?" Beam asked.

Nell gave a little smile. "Yeah. I specifically asked. The chauffeur's a sharp guy. After phoning the police, he went back outside and stood by the car, made sure nobody touched anything. He paid by company credit card, but he still hasn't even touched the receipt sticking out of the pump."

"Did he see anybody leaving the scene?"

"No one. And he said he looked in all directions. Nobody saw anything. It's a slow morning, and the next people to arrive at the station were police."

"What about the clerk?"

"No help there," Looper said. "She didn't even know anything was wrong until the driver went outside with his paper and came running back in." He felt his shirt pocket. "Christ, I need a smoke."

"That'd be smart," Nell said. "Don't you smell the gas?"

"Yeah. It makes me want a smoke."

"You addicts."

"Any other customers inside the station?" Beam asked. "Somebody wanting coffee or shopping around for junk food?"

"No one," Looper said. "Just the driver and the clerk. It's quiet in there, but you can hear the traffic. Seems to me that if neither of them heard a shot, there was probably a sound suppresser on the piece. And I got a glimpse of the entry wound, most likely a thirty-two. Our guy."

Beam nodded. "That how you see it, Nell?"

"Unless that letter *J* is different from the rest."

"It isn't," Beam said.

"Then the shooter was our guy. This was a regular stop for the judge, usually just so the driver could buy a paper. But this time the limo needed gas, so opportunity presented itself. Way I see it, the killer musta moved fast when the driver went inside. Walked over to the limo and knocked on the window. The judge pressed the power button so the window'd glide down and he could talk to whoever'd knocked, and *pop!*"

"Sounds right," Looper said.

Beam looked again at the scene. There was another set of pumps beyond where the limo was parked, so visibility wasn't good from the street. Probably no one driving past would notice someone standing alongside a vehicle gassing up, or think anything about it if they did. As for the black limo, they were common as roaches in New York; it wouldn't have attracted any attention.

"A judge this time," Looper said, tapping his barren shirt pocket again. "Da Vinci's gonna shit a brick."

They stood silently for a few minutes, watching the ambulance pull away with the judge's body. A white and silver tow truck, belching noxious diesel exhaust, vibrant bass notes, and gleaming in the sun as if it had just been washed and waxed, arrived to transport the mayor's limo to the police garage. The limo would be dusted for prints, blacklighted, vacuumed, and partially disassembled.

Beam didn't think it was a waste of time. It was always possible the killer had left something, even if he hadn't gotten inside the limo. We all leave a wake as we move through life.

His cell phone vibrated in his pocket.

Da Vinci hadn't waited long to get into a frenzy. "You at the Parker scene?" he asked Beam, over the cell phone.

"We're here," Beam assured him. He filled in da Vinci on what little there was to know."

"So we've got the red letter *J* tucked under the wiper, and it looks like the judge was shot with a thirty-two caliber slug."

"Could be a thirty-two. We'll know soon as they do the postmortem, then ballistics can see if we've got a match with the other JK shootings."

"It'll match," da Vinci said glumly. "Remember Raymond Peevy?"

Beam didn't have to search his memory far. "The shitbird who shot up a van full of kids on the Verrazano Bridge about five years ago?"

"Yeah. It was six years. He lives in California now and grows grapes. The late Judge Parker refused a prosecutor's appeal on a verdict that set Peevy free on a technicality."

"Can't think of a better way to become the late Judge Parker."

"Why we've got us another JK killing, Beam. You and your team have gotta nail this bastard before the commissioner nails me. I'm the one talked you up, Beam, and I told it true. You're the best one to get inside this freak's mind, anticipate him, be where he is, and stop his evil heart. Are you working toward that goal?"

"You know damn well I am."

"Okay, okay. " Da Vinci seemed to calm down.

"Why do you think he uses a thirty-two?" Beam asked.

"It's what he has. Scumbags like JK usually don't go out and buy weapons. They use what's at hand."

"He doesn't use a twenty-two, like some pros," Beam said. "Three or four in the head at close range. A thirty-two's got more punch, but it isn't as sure as a thirty-eight, forty-five, or nine millimeter."

"It's had enough punch so far."

"True. But this is such a careful killer, you'd think he'd want to make sure his shots counted."

"They can count, with a thirty-two."

"If the shooter knows how to use one. Or increases the load."

"So you're saying he's a gun nut and a good shot, but not a pro?"

"Or he knows guns and is a good shot trying not to look like a pro."

"Hmm. Could be you're overthinking this."

"Could be," Beam admitted.

"And at this point I'm more interested in results than in theory."

"Understandable."

"I'm asking, Beam, please don't disappoint me." He sounded as if he thought Beam really had a choice.

"I'm trying not to disappoint anyone," Beam said.

"Aren't we all?" da Vinci said.

Sometimes Beam wondered.

He slid the phone back in his pocket and watched the glowing taillights of the truck towing the limo disappear around the corner like the watchful red eyes of some retreating animal.

The city was full of predators.

Gina had always thought Carl Dudman was the one most responsible for setting Genelle's killer free. It wasn't only that he was jury foreman. She'd watched him in TV interviews after the trial, a big man with sandy hair and an easy smile. He had charisma and confidence and it was obvious that things came easy to him. What would it be like to be a man like that in this world, instead of a helpless young girl like Genelle?

Gina had some idea, only she wasn't as helpless as Genelle had been. She was four years older than when her twin sister died, and she was wiser. She was also more determined. She'd always been more determined than Genelle, and obviously the stronger of the two. They'd both known it almost from infancy, and their parents had reinforced the knowledge. Their father had loved them both, but he was fond of saying Gina had self-confidence coming out of her pores. Of course, he was right. And now Gina had a mission. A celestial responsibility that only a surviving twin could understand. She had a duty to her dead twin.

With that duty had come sudden opportunity. Dudman

perfectly fit the profile of the Justice Killer's victims. All Gina would need to do after shooting him was leave the red letter *J* near his body. She'd seen reproductions of it in the press after the murders where the letter had been scrawled on paper, and once with lipstick on a bathroom mirror, and she'd practiced and could duplicate it precisely.

Could she do it? Actually squeeze a trigger and put a bullet in Dudman? There was no way anyone could know something like that for sure until the time came. She'd know it when she was looking down the barrel at him.

But she had confidence.

And in her purse she had the hard, cold thirty-eight caliber semiautomatic Reggie had sold her. He'd smiled as he counted her money, and he'd casually told her that if she did use the gun she should wear gloves and she could drop the weapon anywhere—and she should as soon as possible—because it couldn't be traced to her or to anyone else.

But she wasn't going to drop it anywhere. The Justice Killer didn't leave his gun where the police might find it.

She straightened up from where she'd been leaning against a building and eating a knish she'd bought from a street vendor at the corner. Her eyes narrowed against the sun reflecting off a windshield. There was Carl Dudman, emerging from the building across the street, where his real estate agency was located.

Gina hadn't seen him since the trial, and he looked slightly older and heavier. But he still made the hair stand up on the back of her neck. If she were a different sort of person, not as careful, less determined, she would have simply gone into the real estate agency offices and shot her way to where he was and then killed him. The way those people did on the news almost every week somewhere, and for less reason than Gina's. Newscasters often described them as "disgruntled." *Sure they were disgruntled.*

But Gina was more than disgruntled, and she knew that indiscriminate blasting away left too much to chance. Besides, she didn't plan on being apprehended or to kill innocent people.

There would be no direct and easy way to kill Dudman, not even one involving wholesale slaughter. Dudman was no fool. He must know he was in danger and was being careful. She'd have to bide her time.

A tall, hefty fellow, with a buzz cut only a little longer and gray in front, and wearing a tight blue suit, was right behind Dudman, looking this way and that. He strode with a step surprisingly light for such a big man. He reminded Gina of nothing so much as a bull getting a feel for the ring and a matador. A dangerous looking guy.

Gina took a bite of knish and smiled as she watched the giant usher Dudman through the orange scaffolding in front of the building, then into a waiting limo. As he moved, he let his gaze slide up and down the block, over her like cool water. Satisfied but obviously still wary, he lowered himself into the car after Dudman.

It wasn't surprising that a rich businessman like Dudman would have a security system, including bodyguards. That meant extra planning for Gina, and extra work and time.

Gina didn't mind putting in the hours, and she did have some advantages. A bodyguard with the Justice Killer on his mind wouldn't be suspicious of a pretty young woman with a smile just for him. Or a college student applying for an internship. Or a naive young girl new to the city and lost and needing directions.

The possibilities were almost endless, and one or more of them would work. The trick was in the choosing. Then in the execution.

Someone clever, patient, and determined, could breach any security system.

Gina truly believed that a genuinely determined person could do just about anything.

43

"You home, Beam?" Nell asked him on his cell phone.

Beam glanced at the luminous dial of his watch. Ten fifteen.

"Yeah, I'm home."

He tried to hide the thickness in his voice. He'd been sitting in the darkness of his den, sipping Glenlivet eighteen-year-old scotch to relax, letting his mind roam over the landscape of the investigation. He liked to do that, give his unconscious free reign from time to time. It had worked before, and he was willing to try anything to nail the Justice Killer.

Trouble was, he kept finding himself thinking about Nola. Nola cocking her head to the side the way she did when she listened to him. Nola standing behind the antique shop counter as if in judgment of him, her lingering look and the graceful line of her back and shoulder as she turned away from him in calm dismissal.

"Beam? You near a TV?"

"Not one that's on."

"Better turn it on to the Matt Black Show."

Beam knew who Black was, a young guy with a late-night local talk show on cable. He had tightly curly hair, wore snappy double-breasted suits, and had a space between his front teeth like Letterman. But there the resemblance ended. Black was lots of things, but funny wasn't one of them.

"Beam, you there?"

"Here and moving toward the television." *Feeling my way in the dark. Ouch! Stubbed toe. Teach me to sit around in my stocking feet.*

"You okay?"

"Okay, Nell."

"You won't be in a minute. Black's guest is Adelaide Starr."

Beam groaned as he found the remote and switched on the small-screen TV in the bookcase.

"I'm hanging up," Nell said. "I don't want to miss a cute word."

In the soft light from the TV, Beam carried the remote back to his desk, sat down, and sipped more scotch as he turned up the volume.

Adelaide Starr had on a lacy black and white low-cut dress and was wearing her blond hair in pigtails. She looked like Little Bo Peep, minus the sheep but with great bazooms.

"But we're *celebrities*," Black was saying through his gaping grin. "We *deserve* special treatment."

Studio laughter.

Adelaide was smiling innocently while leaning forward to display cleavage, pretending to be listening hard to her host. "If I really thought that," she said, "I'd move to France."

"You wouldn't have to do jury duty there," Black said. "They just *whoosh!*—off with your head."

"I'm being serious," Adelaide said. "I don't want to do jury duty."

"You've made that clear."

"But I don't want special treatment just because I'm an actress. And nobody I know in show business wants to be safe from this killer at someone else's expense."

Studio applause.

"Let me get this straight, Adelaide. You raised four kinds of hell because they were going to make you do jury duty. Now you're complaining because they're excusing you?"

"No! Well, no, yes! It's like a trick on their part. A gamwit."

Confusion on Black's face. "Gambit, you mean?"

"Gam something."

Black ogled her legs. "Gams! Yeah, sweetheart!"

"You know what I mean. Don't make fun of me, please!"

"I'm not, I'm not. So you think the authorities are simply trying to sidestep trouble by showing preference?"

"Of course I do! Don't you?"

"Well . . . yes. You're too much for them, sweetheart." Black grinned conspiratorially into the camera, then turned again toward Adelaide. Serious time. "So what, seriously, do you suggest?"

"A mora . . . whatchamacallit. Where somebody stops something?"

Black looked puzzled. Then he brightened. "A moratorium?"

"Exactly. Don't give celebrities special treatment. Give everyone equal treatment under the law. Let everyone be *safe!*"

"I like what you do with your lips when you say that, dear. *Saaafe!* And of course, you're *absolutely* right. On a serious note, you *are* right."

"We're supposed to be a country with equal opportunity and equal responsibilities, no matter what color we are or where we came from or any of that stuff. The city's giving show business people a free pass when it comes to jury duty. Until the Justice Killer is caught, they should give everyone a free pass. Everyone in New York who's legible for jury duty is an American!"

"If they leave out people whose handwriting you can't read, that'd include a lot of us."

Adelaide appeared puzzled and upset. "You know what I mean. We're all in the same boat, with the same rights as oars, and we can't sink together, and it's an American boat!" She rose to her full meager height and thrust out her breasts. "Maybe you're not supposed to stand up in a row boat, but I am! For myself and everyone else out there! In or *out* of show business!"

The applause was loud enough to make Beam ease back on the volume. The camera played over a standing ovation before returning to the set.

Black was on his feet, hands clapping. "Take it to 'em, dear!"

"We demand a moratorium!" Adelaide said. She bent over to smooth her skirt, flashing more cleavage, then began pumping her tiny right fist in the air as she had outside City Hall. "Moratorium! Moratorium!" The studio audience, still on its feet, joined in. Volume built. Larger fists pumped the air in unison, faster and faster.

Matt Black slumped down in his chair with an exaggerated look of wonder and helplessness. Never had he seen anything like this.

After letting the place cool down only slightly, Black pumped his own fist in the air. "Commercial! Commercial!" He grinned. "We'll be right back. Don't go away. Why *would* you go away?" Then, as the camera zoomed in for a close up, an aside to the TV audience: "Somehow I don't think she'll be moving to France."

Suddenly a sincere man in a leather jacket was trying to sell Beam a wristwatch that was an exact replica of the one worn by B-17 bomber crews in World War Two, only this one kept time with a battery and a chunk of quartz.

Beam's phone rang, the land line this time. He sat forward in his desk chair and lifted the receiver.

"Nell again, Beam," came the voice from across town. "Did you see it?"

"Saw it."

"Whaddya think?"

"Two things. I think she's way ahead of da Vinci. And I think I'm going to pour myself another two fingers of scotch."

"I just poured some bourbon in a glass."

"Raise your glass."

"'Kay."

"Up?"

"Yeah."

"Mine, too. A toast. To Adelaide."

"Adelaide," Nell said on the phone. "And France."

This morning Jack Selig was wearing gray flannel slacks, a navy blazer with big shiny brass buttons, and a white shirt open at the neck to reveal a red ascot. Nell thought he looked exactly like what he was—a rich guy who owned a yacht.

They were having breakfast in the grill of the Marimont Hotel in Midtown. The place was all red carpeting, red drapes, white tablecloths with folded red napkins, polished oak paneling, and subtle touches of gleaming brass. The china looked as if it might be rimmed with real gold. Nell was impressed, as she was sure Selig wanted her to be. The softening up period. Nell had seen and heard it all before and knew how it worked. But, damn, this guy was handsome despite his burden of years. And there was that yacht.

And there was Terry.

"Rough night?" Selig asked.

Mind reader. "Why?" Nell asked. "Do I look it?"

Selig smiled. "Instead of stunningly beautiful, you look stunningly beautiful and tired."

"It's this case."

"The investigation into the Justice Killer murders?"

"Yeah. The pressure to find this creep never lets up. I know when we're finished here"—she glanced at her watch—"which better be within an hour, I've gotta go join the battle again. And it's a hard one."

"It doesn't have to be your battle, Nell. You never have to go in to work again if you don't want to."

"Yes," Nell said, "I do. You need to understand that I do."

He looked puzzled behind his quiche. "But, why?"

"I suppose because we all have our roles to play in life. The ones we chose. I'm a cop. You're a . . ."

"What?"

"Wildly rich and successful."

"I wasn't always, and you weren't always a cop. Fate doesn't have to rule our lives. We choose, and we can unchoose. We can change roles when we get the opportunity, when we have the courage."

"That wasn't fair, Jack."

He smiled and dabbed at his lips with his napkin. "You're right, it wasn't. I apologize. Lord knows, I wouldn't question your courage."

They ate in silence for a few minutes. Nell could see outside a window, a double-decker bus full of tourists slowly driving past in the bright sunlight. New York pretending to be London.

"The point is, this killer doesn't have to be your personal responsibility," Selig said.

"He does, Jack. He is."

"What about your boss? Detective Beam? Seems to me the investigation is his responsibility."

"Not his alone. We're a team."

"Almost everyone's on some kind of team."

"Not where people are dying."

Selig forked in a bite of quiche, chewed, swallowed. "I wasn't thinking of it that way. You're right, of course."

"Not of course, but I'm right."

He smiled. "You getting your dander up, Nell?"

She made herself calm down. "No. Dander down."

But it wasn't. Not entirely.

Selig was looking at her as if she were something infinitely precious and available that was rapidly slipping away. "Is there someone else, Nell?"

Bastard! "Yes. No. Jesus! Yes, there is!"

He looked so injured she had to fight the instinct to reach across the table and squeeze his hands and apologize. He looked suddenly older. Helpless.

What have I done?

"Another, younger, man . . ." He said it as if he'd expected it to happen all along. Maybe he had. "Are you sure about him?"

"Oh, God, I'm not sure of anything, Jack! Honestly!"

"That's your problem, Nell, you can't be anything but honest."

Jack, if you only knew.

"Don't make a final decision until you're absolutely sure. That's all I ask of you. Okay?"

"Okay, Jack." She had to sip coffee and look away, afraid she'd goddamn start to cry!

She felt his cool fingers touch the back of her left hand then softly massage her ring finger. "You all right, Nell?"

She nodded, biting her lip. "Yeah, fine." She sat up straighter. "Let's have some more coffee, then I've gotta get to work."

Right now the red carpet, the red drapes, the red napkins, reminded her of blood.

Melanie stood on the sidewalk outside the entrance to Richard Simms's apartment building. The doorman wouldn't even let her stand in the lobby, where it was cool.

As he had all day yesterday and earlier today, he'd informed her that Simms wasn't home. This time she refused to believe him, and she'd raised enough hell that if she promised to wait outside, he'd call upstairs to make sure. Apparently others had suffered her fate, but for different reasons, because there was a litter of cigarette butts around where she stood.

The afternoon was heating up in earnest, and the hairdo she'd gotten yesterday and was nursing along was a tangled mess in the humidity. A bead of perspiration broke from her hairline and trickled along the side of her forehead. As she raised a wrist to look at her watch, she felt the tug of her clothes sticking to her and got the faintest whiff of her deodorant.

When Melanie was almost to the point of giving up hope and going back into the lobby to give the doorman one more blast of insults before storming away, the tinted glass door swung open wide, held by the doorman. He gazed blankly at her, unassailable in his position and uniform, as an African American man the size of a locomotive pushed past him and outside and looked down at Melanie. His straightened hair was gelled and combed sleekly back, and his eyes were tilted down at the outside corners to give him a permanent pained expression. He had on a flowered shirt and muted plaid pants held up by broad red suspenders, an obvious color and design mismatch to attract attention. Combined with his size, it worked. People hurrying past on the sidewalk couldn't resist glancing his way, and the somewhat startled looks they gave him lingered and suggested trepidation.

"I'm Lenny," he said to Melanie in a surprisingly high voice. "I work for Mr. Simms."

Melanie struggled to find her voice. "I'm—"

"I know who you are," Lenny interrupted. "Seen you in court."

Melanie tried again. Her throat seemed to be blocked. "I—"

"You wanna see Mr. Simms. That's unfortunate, 'cause Mr. Simms, he ain't seein' nobody today."

"What about yesterday and tomorrow?" Melanie asked, feeling less intimidated and more angry.

"You'd have to ask Mr. Simms 'bout that."

"But I can't get in to see Mr. Simms."

Lenny shrugged massive shoulders. "Way the world works."

Melanie fought to remain calm, but her hands were trembling. She knew her lower lip was, too. She tried to choose her words carefully, but they were slippery and kept whirling around in her mind and were difficult to grasp and match with her intent. "I want you to take—I want you to deliver a message."

"I can do that."

"You tell Cold Cat—Mr. Simms—that there's a madman in this city killing people for doing what I did for Mr. Simms. What I did was save Mr. Simms's life. The least he could do is see me, talk to me. He doesn't answer my phone calls and he doesn't invite me up when I come here personally. That isn't right."

"Maybe his lawyers have advised him not to talk to you," Lenny said. Was he smiling? Ever so slightly?

Despite herself, Melanie felt her heart leap with hope. "Is that true? Have they told him that?"

Now Lenny was most definitely smiling, and there was cruelty in those dark, angled eyes. "You'd have to ask Mr. Simms."

That goddamned smile!

"The Mr. Simms I can't get in to see so I can ask him?"

"Uh-huh. Same Mr. Simms."

"You tell Mr. Simms I feel *used!*" Melanie was aware she was out of control but couldn't help herself. Her rage, her shame, were in charge. Spittle flew as she spoke, catching the sunlight and adding to her humiliation. "You tell him I risked my shitting *life* for him, and I feel *used!*"

The big man gazed calmly down at her with disinterest. The smile only a shadow now. "That it?"

Melanie glared fiercely at him. "That is goddamned *it!*"

Lenny simply turned his huge bulk away from her and opened the tinted glass door to enter the lobby. He was part of Cold Cat's security, probably his personal bodyguard, or one of them. His business with Melanie was finished.

"Woman got a mouth on her," she heard him remark to the doorman as the door swung closed.

Melanie thought of making further trouble for the doorman but decided against it. She'd made enough of a fool of herself for one day—enough for the rest of her life.

She stalked along the crowded sidewalk, gripping her purse tightly and swinging it almost as a weapon to clear a path for herself. She knew one thing—she would never again play the fool for any man. She hated all men, every single one of them. They were the enemy.

And one in particular terrified her.

Beam set aside his coffee cup after finishing a lunch of angel hair pasta in an Italian restaurant on Second Avenue. He glanced again at the forensics report on Judge Parker. The bullet wound to the head was the only injury to the judge and had proved instantly fatal. The bullet, still intact after penetrating the skull, was indeed a thirty-two caliber, and it matched the others that had been used in the Justice Killer murders. There wasn't the slightest doubt that it was fired from the same gun.

He doesn't care if they match. He wants them to match. Likes to taunt. Helen the profiler is so right about that one.

Beam's mobile phone buzzed. He set aside the lab report and dug the phone from his pocket. Probably Nell or Loop; he'd assigned them to interview people close to the late Judge Parker. Drone work that would probably lead nowhere, but it had to be done. Every side road along the way had to be explored, because any one of them just might lead to a six-lane highway.

But it was neither Nell nor Looper on the phone.

At first Beam didn't recognize the voice. Nola.

"Beam, I need for you to come to the shop as soon as possible." Her voice, always so level and without emotion, had a slight quaver in it.

Fear?

"You alone, Nola?"

"Yes."

"Are you all right?"

"No. As soon as possible."

"I can get a radio car to you within minutes."

"No, I want you."

"I'm on my way." Beam signaled for the waiter.

"The closed sign will be up," Nola said, "but the door's unlocked."

She broke the connection.

On the wild drive to Things Past, Beam worked the phone's keypad with one hand and called to talk to her again. He got only her machine with its recorded message. Nola but not Nola.

44

They were moving rapidly through the lobby. Carl Dudman couldn't have felt better. He could see that it was a wonderful afternoon outside, with sunlight brightening his side of the street. He'd been on the phone most of the morning, and now it seemed as if his efforts were going to pay off and the agency would represent sales of a projected new West Side condominium tower.

What real estate bubble?

Dudman patted Mark the doorman on the shoulder as he passed. The considerable bulk of Chris Talbotson, his bodyguard, was in front of him. As soon as he'd cleared the door Mark was holding open, Chris's head began to swivel. Dudman followed him outside into the clear, sun-washed air. The orange scaffolding was still up in front of the building, but new sidewalk had been poured and the fresh concrete looked pale and unspoiled.

Chris had impressed upon Dudman that timing was important. Chris would precede Dudman, open the waiting limo's right rear door, and without hesitation Dudman would follow and duck as he approached the big car, then remain low and lean forward as he entered. Chris would quickly follow. All within seconds. All carefully choreographed.

Gripping his black leather attaché case, Dudman lowered his head and made for the inviting dark sanctuary of the limo beyond its open door. He edged past Chris, placed one foot off the curb in the street, and began to duck into the limo. The traffic signal had changed up the street; he was vaguely aware of a string of cars rushing past, the smell of exhaust fumes that would dissipate as soon as he was inside the limo.

It was the exact time that his foot touched the street and he was beginning his forward lean that he felt the sharp pain high on the right side of his chest.

What?

He was sitting awkwardly, one leg in the street extended beneath the limo, the other bent beneath his body. His attaché case had come open and papers were scattered all over the sidewalk.

Did I fall? Slip off the curb?

He knew Chris was trying to help him up, looming over and gripping him, but he couldn't *feel* anything from the neck down.

My suit . . . Ruined . . .

Chris was talking, his face contorted, but Dudman heard nothing.

"Chris, my papers . . ."

No one reacted. He hadn't made a sound.

Then the pain in his chest was back, blossoming, *exploding!*

And suddenly it wasn't afternoon. It was dusk. Dark. Nighttime.

The pain faded with the light.

As it turned out, the shot had actually been a simple one. The street Dudman's agency was on ran one way, so the limo had been on Justice's left, the driver's side of the car. The angle and opportunity were brief, but there, for just a few seconds, diagonally above the trunk of the limo, a shooting line straight to the target. Dudman. *Deadman*.

Justice had time to lead Dudman crossing the wide sidewalk. The target paused as the limo door was opened. Dudman actually seemed to pose as he ducked his head preparing to enter the vehicle.

Almost simultaneous to the shot, Justice managed to take his left hand from the wheel long enough to drop the plastic vial out the window into the street near the limo.

That was important.

They would know he was the one. The bullet, the letter, the hammer of fairness and fate and balance, balance . . .

After the shot, he'd turned the corner and was gone. He was positive no one even knew for sure the shot had come from a passing car—any passing car.

Driving legally at the speed limit, blending with the thousands, millions of vehicles in New York, he had to giggle at how easy it had been. How easy it would be to execute anyone in the city.

He missed the moment of ice, but that couldn't be helped. And Dudman *did* seem to hesitate getting into the limo, as if somehow he knew. Perhaps the cold moment of knowledge had frozen him, presented him to the bullet that would deliver him. Either way, this one had been warranted.

It had been righteous. He would do it again.

He *would* do it again.

Brake lights flared ahead. Horns honked. His foot darted from accelerator to brake and he brought the car to a halt with a brief skid and squeal of tires. Vehicles around him also slowed and stopped. All of them lined up neatly, drivers patiently staring at the traffic signal.

Red light. Had to stop. The law.

* * *

Da Vinci was a little out of breath from hurrying when he entered his office, and what he saw actually made him gasp.

The police commissioner was seated in one of the brown upholstered chairs angled toward the desk.

Da Vinci smiled, stammered, and absently smoothed back his slightly mussed hair.

"Startle you?" the commissioner asked. He'd moved the chair slightly so he had a better view of the door. Its legs had left deep depressions in the carpet, marking its previous position.

"Well . . . yes, sir, you did. It's just that I'm not used to anyone being here when I come in after lunch."

"Natural," said the commissioner. "It's *your* office."

Da Vinci didn't know quite what to say to that.

"I thought we needed to talk," the commissioner said.

That the commissioner had come to da Vinci's office, rather than the other way around, seemed to da Vinci to be meaningful. This meeting wasn't for public consumption.

It was also meaningful that the chief wasn't here. Trouble at the top? The kind of pressure the press and pols were applying could cause all sorts of dissent and ruptured relationships. But da Vinci had no doubt that the chief was, or would be, fully informed at some point by the commissioner. Timing could be everything.

Heavy, brooding, and intense, the commissioner was in civilian clothes, a chalk-stripe gray suit, white shirt, and blue silk tie. In his younger days, his knowing, solemn expression had spooked many a tough suspect into deciding to cooperate with the law. Whether you were a creep or a cop, *gravitas* was *gravitas*. He sat at ease and gazed balefully as da Vinci walked around to sit behind the desk.

"Adelaide Starr," the commissioner said. "She's getting to be a hell of a problem, Andy."

The commissioner was one of the few people who called Deputy Chief Andrew Da Vinci *Andy*. Da Vinci didn't correct him. "I take it we both saw her performance last night on the Matt Black show, sir."

The commissioner nodded.

Da Vinci cleared his throat. "We're still deliberating on what to do about it," he said.

The commissioner raised his eyebrows. "We?"

"Captain Beam and his team, and myself, sir."

"What are the ideas offered?"

Shit! Da Vinci hadn't yet talked to Beam about Adelaide Starr's latest stunt. "Obviously it's a play for publicity on her part, sir. She thinks by casting the city as elitist, even un-American, she's placed herself in the role of hero. Or heroine."

"I know you're sitting down, but I hear tap dancing, Andy."

"We've decided we can't possibly declare a moratorium on jury duty, sir. It would shut down the legal system. The problems it would cause are—"

"Unacceptable," the commissioner finished for da Vinci. "So what's your plan?"

"Still formative, sir."

"You don't have a plan?"

"Yet."

"You've been outwitted by a clever young woman."

"So far." Da Vinci felt himself beginning to perspire.

The commissioner looked cool as ice cream. "Here's what I want you to do, Andy. Issue a statement for the media, saying you're aware of Adelaide Starr's position and you're taking it under advisement. But make it clear that as of now there are no plans to declare a moratorium on juries and, subsequently, trials by jury. That, you will point out, would be disastrous for the city, and a boon for criminals. It would be unfair to the very people Adelaide Starr is trying to protect. Lean on that final point: it would be unfair to all the honest New York citizens who would be the victims of emboldened criminals."

Da Vinci smiled. "That makes good sense, sir." *And takes the load off me.* "And it buys us time."

The commissioner returned the smile and rose from his chair. "Tap dance, Andy. You're good at it, and I mean that as a compliment."

"Yes, sir. Er, thank you."

"You need to dance more in public, Andy, if you get my meaning. This killer's becoming too much of a hero. Or an anti-hero. You ever go to movies, Andy?"

"Sometimes. I'm awfully busy these days."

"Anti-heroes are very popular. People transfer that to real life. Count the newspaper and TV features favorable to the police, and those favorable to the Justice Killer, and I don't have to tell you who wins."

"No, sir."

The commissioner shook his head. "They don't see the blood."

The phone on da Vinci's desk began to buzz.

"Go ahead and answer," the commissioner said. "There's something else I want to talk to you about before I go, regarding the progress of the investigation."

"Yes, sir." Da Vinci picked up the phone.

The commissioner seemed to sense bad news on the line. Bad news da Vinci would have no choice but to relate to him immediately, without having time to figure out how best to present it. *Why did this call have to come in now and not five minutes later?* Da Vinci silently asked himself that question over and over as he listened to one of his trusted lieutenants on the other end of the connection.

When he'd thanked the lieutenant and hung up, the commissioner said, "Trouble, Andy?"

"Carl Dudman was killed while getting into his limo in front of his apartment building. Apparently someone shot him from a passing car, using a silencer."

The commissioner was very still, thinking. "Dudman . . . The real estate Dudman?"

"Yes, sir. He was also jury foreman in the Genelle Dixon Central Park slaying trial six years ago."

"The defendant walked," the commissioner said, rubbing his clean-shaven chin and recollecting. "Guilty bastard, too. We messed up with the evidence. Unlawful search, as I recall."

"Yes, sir. Dudman's security guard was nearby at the time of the shooting. He didn't have time to react to the gunman, didn't even see him, but when he realized Dudman was shot he helped him all the way into the limo then got in and instructed the driver to go like hell to the nearest hospital. Dudman was dead by the time they arrived."

Da Vinci was getting more and more uneasy, with the commissioner standing there staring down at him.

"Something else, Andy?"

"Yes, sir. After the limo pulled away, we found a brown-tinted plastic pharmaceutical vial, the kind prescription medicine comes in. We think it was tossed from the car as it drove past and the shot was fired."

"Tell me it has the names of the killer and his doctor on it," the commissioner said.

"It was unlabeled, sir. And empty except for a rolled up slip of paper with a red letter *J* printed on it in felt tip pen."

The commissioner stood quietly, and when he spoke it was calmly and softly. "The Justice Killer, Adelaide Starr, the media wolves, they're all making goddamned fools of us, Andy."

Without bothering to look at da Vinci or say goodbye, he turned slowly and left the office.

Da Vinci thought it had been nice of the commissioner to say *us*.

Beam double parked his Lincoln in front of Things Past, not bothering to put up the NYPD placard. He ignored the closed sign hanging in the shop window and pushed in through the door. Lucky it was unlocked, as Nola had said, or he might have punched out the glass with his shoulder, so eager was he to get inside the shop.

He didn't know what to expect, but he saw that there was no one behind the counter. The shop was empty.

Damn it!

He was headed toward the back room when he noticed Nola. She was standing to his left and slightly behind him, staring at him with wide dark eyes.

"What is it?" Beam asked, moving toward her sideways so he wouldn't knock anything breakable off the shelves. "What's wrong?"

"That." Nola's gaze lowered to fix on something on one of the shelves, and she pointed.

Beam sidestepped around a mannequin wearing a fake fur jacket and twenties feathered hat, and saw where Nola was pointing.

On the shelf before her was a man's ring. It drew Beam's attention, as it had drawn Nola's, because the shop's jewelry, the good stuff, was all displayed in a glass case near the register to prevent shoplifting. A key, held by Nola, was needed to get into the case.

At first Beam didn't understand the significance of the ring. Then, when he did, his blood went cold.

It was Harry Lima's trademark ring. No mistaking it. Large, gold, gaudy, a dusting of diamonds in the shape of a dollar sign, flanked by rubies and Harry's initials.

The ring Harry was wearing when he was buried.

45

The air was warm and reeked of fried onions. Seated in the diner down the street from Things Past, Beam said nothing until Nola had a cup of coffee and a glass of ice water in front of her. They were in a back booth near a door to the kitchen. They wouldn't be overheard here by the dozen other customers at tables or seated at the counter.

Nola took a sip of water, then looked at Beam as she never had before—as if she trusted him—or had to trust him because they were in something together. Something that scared the hell out of her.

"How could it get there?" Nola asked

Beam didn't have to ask her what *it* was. Ten years ago, the ring had been found six blocks away from where the rest of Harry's dead body lay wrapped in black plastic in a dumpster. It was on the ring finger of Harry's severed right hand. The dead hand was clutching a dollar bill, a clear message as to why Harry was killed: he'd talked for money. To stay out of prison, too, but mainly for money. Harry had always done everything mainly for money. The news photos served as a ghoulish and striking warning to others in his business who might inform.

The warning had worked. Information on the streets in that part of the city became almost nonexistent. No new snitches could be cultivated, and regular snitches disappeared. Either they left town voluntarily, or they had help along the way and would never return.

"I was about to ask you how it could have found its way into your shop," Beam said. "It was buried with Harry."

"Of *course* it was."

"The mortuary," Beam suggested. "Robbing the dead."

Nola was shaking her head. "It was on Harry's finger when the coffin lid was closed, then the coffin was transported directly to the cemetery. I rode in the hearse with it. The coffin never left my sight until it was in the grave."

"You saw it lowered into the grave?"

"No, they never do that. They wait until the funeral service is over and the mourners have left. To spare everyone the pain."

"Maybe—"

"Are you telling me Harry's coffin was opened?" Nola asked.

"I'm telling you I don't know. When did you first notice the ring?"

"Right before I phoned you. I even checked to make sure it wasn't listed as part of the shop's inventory. Someone must have planted it there within the past week. I don't think it could have been there more than a day or two, though, or I would have noticed it." Tears welled in her dark eyes. "Looking at the damned thing nearly stopped my heart."

"Someone must have put the ring there. One of your customers. Do you remember anyone suspicious?"

"No. Customers come and go. They browse, sometimes buy something. Most of the time they leave empty-handed."

"This time one of them left something behind," Beam said.

Nola was staring hard at him. "Beam, do you know anything about this you're not telling me?"

"For God's sake, no, Nola!"

The horrified tone of his voice must have impressed her. She nodded and sat back, sipping hot coffee. Maybe burning her tongue and not noticing.

"Why would anyone plant Harry's ring in the shop?" she asked, lowering her cup.

A part of Beam's mind had been sorting through the possibilities.

"After all these years . . ." Nola said. "Why now? What's different?"

"It might be my fault," Beam said. "What's different is I'm back in your life, and I'm hunting a killer. He might have followed me to the shop, figured out how I felt about you. Then he could have done some research, read old news accounts and learned about the past, with Harry, with you and me, what happened. It was all in the news, complete with names and photographs."

"Years ago."

"It wasn't years ago I started visiting Things Past."

"You think the killer you're stalking has begun stalking you?"

"It wouldn't be unusual. Serial killers are often interested in the person assigned to catch them. They see what they're doing as a game. This one certainly does, with his signature."

"Signature . . . ? Oh, the letter *J*, in red."

"Mean anything to you?" Beam asked.

"I only know what I read in the papers, Beam."

"TV news?"

"I don't watch television."

"This wouldn't be inconsistent with the Justice Killer's actions. He'd do this to taunt me. He enjoys taunting people."

The two guys sitting nearest them at the counter had gotten into an argument and were talking louder, yelling at each other with their mouths full of sandwich, something about Italian women. They were young, and both had on Yankees caps, and the caps' bills started bumping as the discussion became more heated. One of the caps was knocked crooked. Beam wished they'd shut up.

Nola didn't seem to hear them. "Your killer's taunting the entire city."

"I think he's our best bet as to how the ring got there," Beam said.

"But how would *he* get the ring?"

"It has to be a duplicate. He saw the photos in old papers or news magazines. The media made a big deal out of the ring, especially where it was found. As I recall, there were some pretty detailed descriptions and photographs. It was probably in the news somewhere that the ring was buried with Harry. Maybe that's what gave the Justice Killer his idea—he knew the ring would spook you, and of course he's throwing in my face the fact that I'm helpless to protect you or anyone else. He can do whatever he pleases, including having a duplicate ring made using a newspaper photograph and descriptions as a model."

"It doesn't look like a duplicate ring."

"Were the stones real?"

"Not as real as they looked. The diamonds were industrial grade, the rubies glass. The gold was fourteen-karat. This ring has the same makeup."

"How much would it cost to duplicate it?"

"Around a thousand dollars, maybe less. It was more flashy than expensive." She gazed down at the table, frowning.

"Okay, It might not be a duplicate." Beam rested his fingertips on the back of Nola's cool wrist. "There's a way to find out."

She didn't understand at first, then it hit her like a hammer.

"Oh, Jesus, Beam! We can't do that!"

"We have to if we're going to know for sure," Beam said.

Probably just what the Justice Killer asshole wants. "We have to exhume the body."

Nola sat staring into her coffee cup. More than a minute passed before she nodded. "You're right. It's ghastly, but you're right. "

"I'll arrange for a court order."

"The past never goes away, does it?"

"Never entirely," Beam said.

Nola sat forward and hunched her shoulders, as if whatever had been holding her erect had suddenly given. She began to sob. The two guys with baseball caps at the counter heard, fell silent, and looked at Nola and Beam, then in the other direction. The one with the crooked cap hadn't straightened it, and the bill was cocked crazily at an upward angle.

The sobs kept coming.

The past had suddenly and horribly caught up with Nola, and she allowed Beam to comfort her.

The mobile phone in his pocket began to vibrate. He waited for whoever was calling to give up, but they didn't. He finally removed his right hand from Nola's quaking shoulder, shifted his weight to the side, and worked the phone out of his pocket. Though it wasn't logical, he was a little angry, wondering who might be calling him at a time like this.

Da Vinci.

Gina was reading Kafka for pleasure. She had become hooked on the writer during sophomore year Russian Literature. When she glanced up, she saw on TV that Carl Dudman had been shot. Her mother was in the kitchen. Gina tried to call her but found that her voice wouldn't comply. Her throat was constricted.

Dudman dead. Incredible! Someone had figured out a way before Gina. The real Justice Killer.

Dudman dead.

It was real. It was true. It was on TV.

Gina stood up from the sofa and was about to go into the kitchen when a newscaster, standing in front of Dudman's apartment building, began explaining what the police theorized about the murder after piecing together accounts from witnesses.

It had been simple and effective, catching the overmuscled bodyguard flatfooted. *The one with the buzz cut with the little tuft of gray hair in front?*

The newsman held up a plastic vial like the one that had contained a rolled slip of paper with the Justice Killer's signature red *J* on it that was tossed from the shooter's car.

Dudman had dropped instantly. The bodyguard said he at first thought his boss had simply tripped. He'd hurried to help him up, but Dudman didn't respond. By the time the bodyguard noticed the blood on his hand, and on Dudman, the traffic had moved on. The bodyguard pushed the unconscious Dudman into the limo and instructed the driver to speed to the nearest hospital. Dudman was dead on arrival. None of the stunned witnesses could offer any description of any particular vehicle that was passing at the time of the shot.

The building's uniformed doorman was being interviewed now by another newscaster, a blond woman who seemed overly concerned with what the breeze was doing with her hair.

Gina continued her route to the kitchen and stood in the doorway until her mother, salting something in a large skillet, noticed her.

"*Mom . . .*"

In the living room, both of them stood staring at the TV, crying silently as the story continued to unfold on the screen.

Gina wasn't sure what exactly was going on in her mother's mind, but she knew what *she* was thinking. She was glad Dudman was dead—*satisfied,* actually—but it was Bradley

Aimes who'd killed Genelle. Bradley Aimes who, even more than Dudman, deserved death.

As these thoughts took form in her mind, Gina was somewhat disturbed by the fact that Dudman's death seemed to have whetted her appetite. For death? For vengeance?

For justice!

That the notion had come unbidden made it seem all the more natural, all the more logical. Yes, Aimes deserved to die for what he did to Genelle. His death would be justice. It would be *right*.

What didn't seem right was that someone else, not Gina, had killed Dudman and at least partially avenged Genelle's death. Executing Dudman had been Gina's responsibility, but she'd let Genelle down. Failed her. What didn't seem right was that her gun was in her bedroom, in her purse, in a bureau drawer, unfired except for target practice. It lay unused, cold, heavy, forged for a destiny not yet fulfilled. Her gun.

"Gina," her mother said beside her, "I'm going to phone your father."

Her gun . . .

46

"Dudman was a major player in this town," da Vinci said to Beam. They were in da Vinci's office. The blinds were closed and a couple of lamps were on. The atmosphere was almost cozy. Da Vinci had carefully returned the chair the commissioner had sat in to its original location, matching its legs with the depressions in the carpet. Beam sat in the chair now, and in his own way he was as intimidating as the commissioner. Those damned, flat blue eyes. Da Vinci was increasingly fighting the feeling that he was losing control of the investigation. "That's why I gave you all those uniforms to canvass the neighborhood where Dudman was shot."

"They're hard at work," Beam said. "Nell and Looper are correlating the information."

"They in charge?"

"In the case of Dudman, right now, yes."

"You should be in charge and up front," da Vinci said. "Instead you come here and want to talk. It better be important, because Carl Dudman sure was."

"It's because Dudman was important that I'm here. We both know his murder was pretty much a simple and clean operation done by a pro."

"We thought before that the Justice Killer might be a pro," da Vinci said. But he seemed interested now. Beam had something in mind.

"And a pro would find it easy to obtain all the information he needed on a rich and semi-famous target like Dudman," Beam said. "Once he'd done that, all the security in the world wouldn't have made much difference."

"You're saying our killer is a *real* pro—a hit man, or maybe ex-Special Forces or Delta Force."

"Maybe. But it's the victims I think we should be concentrating on now, and not the ones like Dudman. More like Manfred Byrd."

"The decorator? There are thousands of them in this town. It's not as if he had his own TV show or wrote a book on how to decorate on a dime. He was a nobody except for the Draco case."

"Which occurred almost ten years ago. Even Byrd had pretty much put it out of his mind. His friends and acquaintances said he never mentioned it. He wasn't like Dudman. To find out about Byrd, the killer had to dig deeper. Unlike with Dudman, for instance, he'd have to *find* Byrd. Simply locating him wouldn't be all that simple. Then what? Is he married?"

"Hardly," da Vinci said.

"The killer wouldn't have known. And he wouldn't have known what Byrd did for a living, where he did his shopping, drank, dated. Did he go to movies? What kind? Was he an early riser? Maybe a jogger? How old was he? When was his birthday? What was his credit rating? Did he have a car? Did he take cabs or subways or both? Did he drink to excess? Do drugs? Have a steady lover? Own a gun? Use the library? The Internet? Have a safety deposit box? All the kinds of things a pro would want to know in order to have a full picture."

"All or most of it, easy enough to find out," da Vinci said. "Much easier with Dudman than with Byrd, because

Byrd required more digging into public records. Court records, deeds, newspaper items, credit records."

"We talked about this," da Vinci reminded Beam. "We start digging to find out who's seen people's personal records, medical, the kinds of books they read, their Internet habits, employment history, what have you, and the civil libertarians are all over our asses."

"That isn't going to change," Beam said. "What is legal is to set up surveillance cameras in or outside libraries, newspaper morgues, courthouses, wherever public records are stored. We might just capture an image, then be able to capture the real thing."

Da Vinci sat back in his desk chair, thinking about it. He rubbed his chin as he'd seen the commissioner do. "It'd sure as hell save department hours. Manpower. Womanpower."

"It'd be legal, too," Beam said. "People can't claim the expectation of privacy in public places. I don't think the ACLU would object."

"Some of those places already have taping systems. Part of Homeland Security."

"True," Beam said, "but I'm talking about even more cameras, more angles, more coverage. I'd rather have cops poring over those kinds of tapes, trying to spot something to grab onto, than using their time covering ground we know from experience with this killer probably isn't going to give us anything."

Da Vinci was quiet, pondering, then he sat forward and grinned widely. "Okay. Makes sense. I'll see that more cameras are installed wherever pubic records are kept. We got people who can sit and view security tapes, maybe spot somebody doing nothing suspicious, but doing it where the records of more than one victim were stored. That kinda thing." In the still, warm office, he rubbed his hands together as if he were cold and trying to warm up. "This is the sorta suggestion I expected you to come up with, Beam. I'll notify the chief what we have in mind; I'm sure he'll approve it."

"Tell him it's your idea, if you want," Beam said. "I'm retired anyway, or will be again soon, I hope."

Da Vinci flashed his Tony Curtis grin. "That's awful generous of you, Beam."

"I don't mind seeing you get ahead."

Da Vinci understood. "We're the same kind of cop. That's why I brought you back for this investigation."

"That's why I came back," Beam said. "That, and I was having trouble being someone I wasn't."

Da Vinci stood up behind his desk. Busy man. Lots to do. "Anything else, Beam?"

"Adelaide Starr," Beam said.

Da Vinci made a face like a kid who'd expected chocolate and gotten broccoli. "Hey, I'm open to any ideas on that one."

"Send her another jury summons. Make her serve. She says she wants you to change your mind, so change it."

"We've been there," da Vinci said.

"I bet she doesn't want to go back," Beam said.

"She won't serve."

"Then arrest her. Put her in custody. Make an example of her. She's been shooting off her mouth on talk shows, asking for equal treatment. So give it to her. It's exactly what she doesn't want."

Da Vinci did his chin rubbing thing again. "I'm not saying it wouldn't be fun."

"That's not what we're talking about."

"I like it, Beam. I tell you what, I'll run it past the chief." *Or the commissioner.*

"Fine," Beam said, but didn't leave. "That one gonna be your idea, too?"

"Depends on the reaction."

Beam had to smile. "You're an honest man."

"Honest cop, anyway."

"One more thing," Beam said.

Da Vinci had started to sit, but straightened up. "My, my, we are fruitful."

"I want a court order," Beam said. "Soon as possible."

"For what?"

"We need to exhume a body."

Beam double-parked the Lincoln beside the unmarked, across the street from where Carl Dudman had been shot. He climbed out of the cool air from the dashboard vents into heat, humidity, exhaust fumes, and traffic noise.

A cable TV truck was parked down the block. Closer to Dudman's building, a guy in a sharp suit was standing in front of a shoulder-held TV camera, taping a spot for one of the local news programs.

When there was a break in traffic, Beam jogged across the street. The leg that had been shot ached with every other stride, but only slightly. *Old man can still run.*

The area in front of Dudman's building was guarded by a single uniform, standing with his back against the wall to one side of the entrance. He was a paunchy, graying guy, but he had the kind of heavy-lidded pale eyes that seemed to notice everything. Where Dudman had fallen, a small square of new looking sidewalk and curb was cordoned off with yellow crime scene tape. It looked more like a Con Ed work site than a murder scene.

Beam flashed his shield at the uniform, who nodded but didn't move other than raising one arm a few inches to the side and rapping his nightstick on the glass door. The door immediately opened and was held for Beam by a uniformed doorman who'd been invisible behind the dark, reflecting tinting. It seemed to be a routine the cop and doorman had down pat.

Nell and Looper were waiting for Beam where they'd said they'd be, seated in a grouping of furniture near the center of the cool, spacious lobby. Light poured in from high windows and reflected off rich paneling and gray marble flooring. The marble had a brownish vein running through it that matched exactly the color of the leather chairs and a long sofa arranged around a rectangular glass coffee table. Magazines and newspapers were neatly fanned out on the table like an oversized hand of cards.

The two detectives stood up when they saw Beam. After hellos, all three sat down, Nell and Looper in chairs, Beam in a corner of the brown leather sofa. In the hushed lobby, the furniture hissed like punctured tires beneath their settling weight.

"Got anything?" Beam asked, not expecting much.

Looper gave a low chuckle. "About what you'd expect from witnesses to any drive-by shooting."

"The killer kept it simple," Nell said, "but I doubt if it was haphazard. More like the result of careful planning. We went over Dudman's daily routine with his security. Those few seconds outside the building, when he was getting into his limo, represented about the only time in his busy days when he was vulnerable."

"Witnesses giving up anything at all?" Beam asked.

"What you'd expect," Nell said. "They saw a red car, a white van, a blue car, a cab, drive past about the time Dudman was shot by a blond man, a bald man, a dark-haired man with a Jesus cut. They heard a shot, two shots, no shots. Heard a shout, heard a laugh, heard a car backfire. The other witnesses saw and heard nothing."

"Those are the ones telling the truth," Nell said. "Being factual, anyway."

"Guy was a pro," Looper said. "He left us zilch. Dudman was alive. Killer drove past. Dudman was dead. We got a corpse, a thirty-two slug, and a slip of paper with a letter on it. That's all, and that's what it adds up to—*nada*."

There was a tone of admiration in his voice that annoyed Beam. "You starting to see the killer as a hero, Loop?"

"You know better," Looper said. He glanced around, licking his lips. "I wish it was legal to smoke in this expensive mausoleum."

"You quit," Nell reminded him..

"I wasn't thinking just of myself, Nell."

"What we all need to be thinking about," Beam said, "is running this sick freak to ground and bringing him in."

"We'll do that," Looper said. "It'll be the bullet or the needle. His choice."

Not ours, Beam thought. *We don't get to choose. Not unless it's close.*

He told them about what had happened at the antique shop with Nola, then about his meeting with da Vinci.

"So we're soon gonna be spending our time studying security tapes?

Nell asked.

"Eventually, maybe. If we can get camcorders set up where we want them."

She'd been studying him as he'd told them about his day so far. "Mind if I ask a question, Beam?"

"Probably."

"This woman, Nola Lima, do you and her have a history?"

"I told you about our history, how her husband was one of my snitches and got killed."

"Wanna tell us more?"

"No. You know enough."

Nobody spoke for a few minutes. They all watched a woman in a fur boa, despite the heat, enter the lobby, cross to the elevators, and ascend.

"When do you think we'll get the court order for the exhumation?" Nell asked.

"I hope tomorrow. Da Vinci's working on rushing it through. He's got some judges by the balls. Meantime, you keep everything going here, talking to people who don't know anything, looking good for the media."

"It's bullshit," Nell said.

"It's part of the job."

"Still bullshit."

"I didn't say it wasn't."

"I wish to Christ I had a cigarette," Looper said.

Nell said, "You might as well go ahead and smoke one as die sooner at my hands for continuing to harp on it."

"The bullet, the needle, or the filter tip," Beam said, and stood up and left them.

Outside, as the tinted glass door swung closed, he caught sight of the reflection of a man standing across the street staring at him. Beam wouldn't have noticed him except that he jogged his memory. He was sure he'd seen the man somewhere before, and recently. Not necessarily his face, which he couldn't make out, but his proportions and posture, the set of his head, neck, and shoulders.

When he turned around, the man wasn't there.

No matter. Silhouette and profile registered strongly in an old cop's mind.

Beam was sure he was being followed.

Terry Adams reached over from where he lay on his back on Nell's bed, felt around, then found his cold can of Budweiser and took a swig. It was difficult to drink lying down, and he felt a trickle of cold beer run down his cheek and neck toward the pillow. "So they're gonna dig up this guy's grave and see if he's still wearing his ring?"

"That's the idea," Nell said. She knew she probably shouldn't be talking to Terry about this, but it wasn't exactly an integral part of the Justice Killer case. That was what kind of bothered her. Beam seemed to want it to be part of the case. She wondered why. What was there between Beam and this woman, Nola?

"Sounds like something out of a play," Terry said. "Maybe a movie. Make a great scene."

Nell laughed. "You ready to play a cop again?"

"If I could get the part, sure. The real job—yours—no way. Just portraying a cop, getting inside his skin, was enough."

"You must have done it well."

"There was talk of a Tony."

Nell propped her head on her elbow. "Really?"

"Well . . . most of the talk was by me."

Nell laughed and let her head fall back on her wadded pillow. It was pleasant, the way the room was cooling down but still smelled like sex, the way the breeze from the ceiling fan played over her bare right leg that was extended from beneath the white sheet. Terry was an insightful and wonderful lover. He could sense when she didn't want him to be so gentle, and he accommodated, but always she was in control. And he was tireless. His sexual drive, his energy, captivated her.

Then why was she thinking about Jack Selig? This wasn't some sexual contest the three of them were engaged in. And if it were, the considerate and subtle Selig would finish a close second to Terry.

Nell admonished herself, feeling ashamed. These were not the sorts of comparisons that led to wise decisions.

What decisions? Hadn't she already made up her mind?

"You're pensive," Terry said. "What're you thinking about?"

"Would you believe baseball?"

"No. I don't think you're that big a fan."

"The Mets are playing the Cardinals tonight on TV."

"You're a Mets fan?"

"Just a baseball fan. Isn't it legal for women to be baseball fans?"

"Sure," Terry said. "He set his beer can back on the magazine on the bedside table, then turned toward her. He kissed her on the ear, flicking with his tongue. "I'll show you what's illegal," he whispered. "At least in certain states."

Nell forgot about baseball.

She forgot about Jack Selig.

The exhumation order was in da Vinci's hands the next day, but they waited for nightfall before executing it. That was da Vinci's decision. It wasn't that he wanted to heighten the mood. Harry Lima was buried toward the center of a century-old cemetery that covered acres bordering a New Jersey highway, so lights and activity wouldn't be noticeable from outside the premises. At night, when the cemetery was closed, there would be no one unauthorized inside the fenced and gated grounds to witness or disturb the exhumation.

Nola, whose signature had helped to authorize the exhumation, had decided not to attend. Beam was there, along with da Vinci. No need for Nell or Looper.

Beam stood in the night with da Vinci and a tall African American man named Dan Jackson from the Medical Examiner's office. Jackson stood off to the side, smoking a cigar. They were in soft light that seeped through a canvas tent that had been pitched around Harry's grave. A small bulldozer had unearthed most of the grave before the tent was pitched. Now, inside the tent, cemetery workers, watched over by a uniformed officer, worked with shovels and an electric winch.

"They sound busy in there," da Vinci said.

"It won't be long now," Jackson assured him.

"I can hardly wait," da Vinci said under his breath. He gave Beam an annoyed look in the moonlight.

"Having second thoughts?" Beam asked.

"I'm not allowed those." A strong smell of Jackson's cigar smoke came their way on the breeze. "Adelaide Starr was scheduled to report for jury duty today."

"She show up?" Beam asked.

"No."

"Gonna issue a warning?"

"No. We're going to bring her in tomorrow, if we can find her."

"You'll find her," Beam said. "It's what she wants. She's probably already got her toothbrush packed."

"If it's what she wants, why are we doing it?"

"Not much choice. And it sends the right signal."

"She won't shut up in jail," da Vinci said. "She'll find a way to send her own signals to her adoring public." He jumped and batted something away from his face. "Friggin' moths!"

"I saw it," Jackson said. "It was a bat."

"Jesus H. Christ!"

"I'm mostly interested in signaling one member of her public," Beam said. "The Justice Killer."

Light spilled out of the tent as the uniform held the flap open. "We're ready, sir," he said to da Vinci.

Beam led the way inside. His show.

The illumination from the portable lights inside the tent was almost blinding and left no place for shadows to hide. It was hot in there. There was no strong odor, only a faint musty scent.

Harry's casket was made out of some kind of smooth, light colored metal that looked as if it might have been buried yesterday. It sat on a couple of four-by-fours that had been laid across the open grave. It was open. The cemetery workers, the uniform, Jackson, all stood back away from the casket. Beam and da Vinci edged forward to look.

Harry hadn't held up as well as the casket. One glance at what was left of his face, and Beam looked away. It wasn't Harry's face he was interested in, anyway.

There was Harry's reattached right hand, awkwardly extending from his faded blue suit coat sleeve.

The gaudy ring was still there—much too large for Harry now—on the withered, leathery hand. *Hand that had touched Nola.* Beam swallowed and turned away.

"That it?" da Vinci asked.

"It," Beam said.

Jackson moved in with a camera and began photographing. With any luck, Harry could now rest beneath the earth forever.

"So the ring in the shop is a duplicate," da Vinci said. "But why is it there?"

"Not for Nola," Beam said. "For me. To taunt me. To let me know he's aware of my relationship with Nola and can do something about it any time he chooses."

Da Vinci squinted at him in the blinding light. "You got a relationship with Nola Lima?"

"Something like," Beam said.

"I don't care for this, Beam."

"It's what moved our freak friend to go to a lot of trouble."

"And expense."

Da Vinci went back out into the night, and Beam followed.

"Helen was right about him wanting to taunt you," da Vinci said, standing with his hands in his pockets. "One for the profiler."

"The ring borders on a threat," Beam said. "To me and to Nola. And there's something else in it for JK—misdirection. We're doing this instead of breathing down his neck."

"He had to have the duplicate ring made somewhere," da Vinci said. "The jeweler will remember working off the photographs and ring descriptions that were in the news. We can find him."

Beam stood gazing around the cemetery, at the silent, leafy trees black against the dark sky, at the tombstones and statuary pale in the moonlight. It didn't seem peaceful to him. He had the eerie feeling that everyone buried there was aware of what had been done tonight to one of their own, and was dismayed by it. Blamed Beam for it.

He shuddered and began walking toward where the cars were parked near a stone angel on a narrow, winding road. "I'm getting out of here," he said over his shoulder. "You gonna hang around a while?"

"Not friggin' likely," da Vinci said, and hurried to catch up with him.

Maybe he felt what Beam did.

Rest in peace, Harry. It's easier down there than up here.

47

"I didn't know you were a lawyer," Adelaide said.

"In a previous life," Barry told her, "and not actually a criminal lawyer, but I'm still a member of the bar. They had no choice but to let me in to see you."

They were talking on phones, separated by a thick sheet of Plexiglas. Three chairs down, another detainee was talking to his lawyer. With the phones, it was impossible to eavesdrop.

"So you're my lawyer as well as my agent."

"I'm your agent, Ad. We'll get you the real thing when it comes to trial attorneys. Are they treating you okay?"

"I don't like it in here, Barry. It smells like that pine stuff they use to clean restrooms. Smells that way all the time."

"Other than that."

"Nobody's hit me with a rubber hose."

"They better not. Half the people in this city would run over this place." Barry leaned closer, as if it made a difference over the phone. "We're going to get you out of here, Ad, but not too soon. The media are all over this now, but wait till they see some Free Adelaide demonstrations. I've got three spontaneous ones all planned. Big one in Central Park."

"Wow! I wish I could be there, Barry."

"For a while, it's better that you're not." He looked closely at her through the clear divider, as if assessing damage. "If they mistreated you in some way . . ." He was looking expectantly at her now.

"I'll tell you one thing, Barry, all the jump suits aren't this bright orange."

"Yeah?" He sat back.

"I've seen prisoners in some darker colored ones. More neutrals."

"I guess they have more than one color, Ad."

"I'm a natural redhead, Barry. Do you know what this goddamned color does to my complexion?"

"Ad—"

"I know how it must make me look—just hideous!"

"It's okay, Ad, you look your beautiful self. Cute, the way the suit's too big for you. The cuddly look."

"If looking flushed all the time is cuddly."

"On you it's cuddly, Ad." Barry stood up. "I've gotta go now. I'll think of something."

"I know you will, Barry."

He smiled at her, and when he left, Adelaide began to cry. Really.

Three of them. It would take a while, but they could cover most of the places in New York to see if anyone sold the duplicate ring lately, or created it using old newspaper photographs. They divided the list of shops and wholesalers, then split up. Sometimes Beam carried the duplicate ring to show jewelers, sometimes Nell or Looper had the ring.

By the end of the second day, no one had recognized the ring, or the hallmarks or characteristics of whoever had created it. Beam did learn, on his first stop at a small shop in the diamond district, that Nola had it wrong—the ring was worth about two thousand dollars. It was fourteen-karat gold, and the rubies were glass. The diamonds were real, but of low quality. All as Nola had said. Still, two thousand dollars. Because of the gold and the workmanship. That would be wholesale, the jeweler had said. Insure it for three thousand.

So they did learn one thing: The Justice Killer probably wasn't poor, though maybe not particularly rich.

Another odd thing: Harry's unearthing seemed to draw Beam and Nola closer together. There the past had been, lying in a casket, and they'd survived the encounter and reburied it. It no longer conveyed ambiguous obligation, and it wasn't nearly as threatening as the present.

No longer were they haunted.

Later that evening, but well before dusk, Beam was walking with Nola in Central Park. The heat had let up, and there was a nice breeze rattling the leaves overhead. Nola had briefly held hands with Beam, then gently withdrew her hand. They were strolling side by side, but close together. Beam was coming to realize that trust and forgiveness didn't come overnight.

Nola said, "Some cop's been hanging around the neighborhood near the antique shop."

"I know," Beam said. "I arranged for you to have protection."

"I don't think I need it. There's no reason the Justice Killer would be interested in me."

"He left that ring in your shop. And he knows how I'd feel if anything happened to you."

"He's also scaring away some of my customers."

"They're not selling you hot Chippendale and Limoges, are they?"

"I don't know, Beam. And I don't ask." She glanced over at him and smiled. "I'm glad to know you're learning something about the merchandise."

"Learning about you," he said.

They slowed, then stopped, in the shadow of a large elm. No one else seemed to be around. The wind kicked up, bending the tall grass in a field that stretched away toward a low stone wall and Central Park West, stirring the leaves over their heads so they alternated dappled light and darkness like a dancehall's reflecting mirrored ball. Beam leaned down and kissed Nola on the lips, and she kissed him back, slowly, letting it linger. Thinking about it.

No words afterward. Beam thought, Lani. Almost, I'm sorry.

Almost.

They continued walking along the path. Nola had his arm now, leaning her head lightly against his shoulder. Beam wondered what she was thinking. Was it about Harry? He hoped it wasn't about the past. They should be thinking about the present and future. They could do that now.

"What's that?" Nola asked, pointing ahead and off to the left.

Beam looked, squinting into the lowering sun. There were trees there. Movement that suggested people. A park entrance.

"I don't know," he said. "Looks like some kind of demonstration.

Even as he said it, he understood what he had loosed.

Melanie settled in before a large tuna melt with fries and a chocolate milkshake. Food comforted her, especially here, in her favorite diner on First Avenue. There was always a pleasant scent of simmering spices here. The help was friendly. There were signed and framed black-and-white photographs of celebrities hanging on the wall behind the counter. Real celebrities. Frank Sinatra, Lani Kazan, Miles Davis. People who created real music.

The tuna was warm, and the milkshake was almost cold enough to give Melanie a headache. She felt better. Some of her anger at again trying futilely to see Richard Simms fell away. At least now, and for the next fifteen minutes, she'd have exactly what she wanted.

The door opened and a man wearing badly wrinkled khakis, a T-shirt lettered FREE ADELAIDE, and worn jogging shoes entered and sat at the table directly across from hers. Melanie's annoyance meter climbed. There were plenty of other places in the diner to sit, so why did he have to crowd her? She doubted it was her looks—not right now, anyway. Her hair was mussed, she'd been perspiring heavily, and irritation must show on her face.

She glanced again at the lettering on his T-shirt.

"Adelaide Starr," he explained.

"Ah, the woman who refuses to serve as a juror."

"She's my hero," the man said. He was in his mid-thirties, well proportioned if slightly pudgy, and had his own hair and regular features. Worth talking to, Melanie decided, then reminded herself she'd sworn a private oath to hate all men.

Of course all men weren't like Cold Cat. They couldn't be.

"She's my hero, too," Melanie said. "I don't think anybody should have to serve on any jury. I think we should just electrocute people like Richard Simms."

"Forgive my asking," said the man across the aisle, "but who's Richard Simms?"

"Cold Cat, the rap art-singer."

"That guy who killed his wife and walked. Yeah. I don't dig his music. Sounds like somebody banging his head and scraping his nails on a blackboard at the same time." The man ordered, only coffee, then turned his attention again to Melanie. "So what do you care about Cold Cat? You glad he's free to make more noise?"

"Hardly. I think he killed his wife."

"You and lots of other people. I followed the trial in the papers. Witnesses had him someplace else when she was killed. That didn't leave the jury much choice but to acquit. Personally, I think if he didn't do it himself, he hired it done."

Talking about the trial was bringing back Melanie's anger. She'd saved Cold Cat's life, and now he refused even to be in her company. "One witness was currying favor from the police," Melanie said. "The other hero-worshipped Cold Cat."

"You think they were lying?"

"Of course they were lying."

"So how come the jury didn't see it that way?"

"Why do sheep cross the road?"

"Maybe they wanted to show they weren't afraid of the Justice Killer," the man suggested. He accepted a mug of coffee from the waiter, sipped it, then decided it needed cream and poured some in from the small white pitcher on the table. He stirred noisily with his spoon. "Human nature."

"That kind of false bravado might have helped to get him off," Melanie agreed. She finished half her tuna melt and sipped at her milkshake. The ice cream in the shake made the roof of her mouth ache so the pain spread higher in her head, behind her eyes. Does everything good in the world have to bring pain?

"I personally think all that legal stuff comes down to who has the best lawyer," the man said. "That's the way this country works."

"Oh, Simms had a good lawyer. He could afford the best."

"You seem to know a lot about the trial. You manage to get into the courtroom and actually see any of it?"

"No," Melanie said, "just followed it in the papers and on TV. I don't think you had to be there to know Cold Cat killed his wife."

Suddenly her appetite left her. She managed to finish her milkshake, then she asked for a take-out box for the other half of her tuna melt and most of her fries. Tomorrow's lunch.

"When I finish this coffee," the man said, "I'm gonna take a cab over to the park. There's gonna be a Free Adelaide demonstration. The bastards threw the poor little thing in jail."

"I didn't know that." *Too wrapped up in my own problems.*

"You wanna join me?"

"Thanks, but I'm too tired. Way too tired."

The waiter came with the take-out box, and Melanie carefully transferred her half sandwich and fries.

"Nice talking to you, Melanie," the man said, as she headed toward the cash register near the door.

"Same here."

"Have a nice evening."

It wasn't until she'd walked several blocks and was descending the steps to a subway stop that she realized something was bothering her.

"Nice talking to you, Melanie."

Try as she might to reconstruct their conversation, she couldn't remember telling the man in the diner her name.

48

"It's a mob," Nola said.

Beam said, "Not quite yet."

He estimated there were about a hundred people. They streamed silently into the park from Central Park West. They were flanked and followed by news vans and media types on foot, some of them lugging cameras. Many in the crowd were carrying signs, but from this distance, and in the failing light, Beam couldn't make out what the lettering said. A few had flashlights, even what looked like lighted candles, which they waved around or held high.

The crowd was led by a man and a woman who strode out about twenty feet ahead of everyone, maintaining their distance. There was a businesslike eagerness about these people. Beam thought that if everyone had rifles and uniforms, they would have looked like those Civil War reenactors who replicate famous battles—the advance and silence before the shouting and shooting. They seemed to know exactly where they were going.

Their destination was the wide area of windblown grass Beam had been admiring. In the approximate center of the field, the two leaders stopped and waved their arms, gathering people closer together, bringing in stragglers. The media vans and personnel took up position, quickly set up equipment, and suddenly the area was brighter than noon. So much for flashlights and candles.

The crowd began to chant. Beam and Nola couldn't make out what they were saying, so they moved in closer.

Beam wasn't surprised that the chant repeated what most of the signs said: "Free Adelaide!" Other signs declared that the city didn't care about its citizens, and that cops were the tools of fascists. The lettering was neat and all of the same type; obviously the placards had been turned out by a sign shop or similar printing facility. Of course, computers these days . . .

"Are you really a tool of fascists?" Nola asked.

"Have been for years," Beam said.

The chants were getting louder, the crowd more raucous. Television cameras did that to people.

Someone had clued in the police. Two radio cars arrived, their flashing roof-bar lights creating red and blue ghosts everywhere. Beam heard sirens in the distance, getting closer.

"Time for us to leave," Beam said. "I don't want any media to recognize me."

They wandered into the gathering dusk, an anonymous couple in the most anonymous of cities. The chanting had grown in volume and intensity: *"Free Adelaide! Free Adelaide!"* Beam tried to block it out as he and Nola angled toward the low stone wall running along Central Park West.

He climbed over the wide stones, then helped Nola.

They were out of the park now, suddenly among tall buildings, and bright, heavy traffic flowing along a busy avenue. Most of the vehicles had their lights on. The scent of leaves and grass had given way to that of exhaust fumes.

A bus rumbled past, accelerating to beat the traffic signal. When the sound of its engine had faded, Beam and Nola could still hear the chanting wafting from the park.

"A hundred or so people," Beam said, "but on cable news tonight they'll look like a thousand."

"That young woman's got this city under her thumb," Nola said. She sounded secretly pleased.

Maybe not so secretly.

They crossed the street, moving away from the park, and strolled toward the corner. A man and woman holding hands walked toward them. He was wearing jeans and a black T-shirt; she had on red shorts, a white blouse, and sandals. They walked as if they were in no kind of hurry. The woman smiled and nodded as they passed. Beam thought the man looked a little like Harry Lima, but he didn't mention it.

Without breaking stride, Nola moved closer to Beam.

"I think it's time," she said.

Her tone was matter of fact, but that was Nola.

He knew what she meant and didn't ask if she was sure.

They made love in Nola's apartment, in Nola's bed beneath a cracked ceiling and the creaking sounds of the upstairs tenant pacing. Nola was tentative at first, but when he entered her she moaned and bucked upward and upward beneath him. Then she met his gaze and very calmly dug her nails into his back, marking him, making him hers alone. And she gave herself back to him in ways that made it clear she was his.

They lay quietly together afterward, each aware that the world had changed. Both hoped the change was for the better. Both knew that now what they thought made little difference; there was no going back for either of them.

A powerful current held them and would keep them. The fascist tool and his lover.

49

"Did you anticipate this?" da Vinci asked.

"Not so soon," Beam admitted, "and not so many."

They were in da Vinci's stifling office, looking at tapes of the Free Adelaide demonstrations that had occurred throughout the city last night. The overhead fixture was off, as was da Vinci's desk lamp. The office door was closed, and the blinds were adjusted tight to admit as little light as possible. It was as if da Vinci had prepared the office for a movie screening. Beam noticed that the small TV that usually sat on top of the DVD player on one of the file cabinets had been replaced by a much larger one; which came in handy, because several demonstrations were being shown simultaneously in split screen shots. As it turned out, the demonstration in Central Park had been the smallest.

"So what's your advice now?" da Vinci asked, using the remote to switch off the TV just as a camera zoomed in on a demonstrator frantically waving a FREE ADELAIDE! sign.

"Sit tight," Beam said.

"Where I'm sitting," da Vinci said, "it's getting tighter and tighter." As if moved by his words, he stood up and opened the blinds. Light reclaimed the office, accompanied by harsh reality.

"The Adelaide fuss might blow over."

"Yeah. Like a tornado."

Beam took another tack. "We're canvassing all the jewelry stores and custom manufacturers. The Justice Killer might have made a mistake with that ring."

"I suspect it's pretty much a waste of time," da Vinci said, sitting back down behind his desk. "I think this business with the ring is just another diversion. Our killer's too smart to have dropped such a big shiny clue into your lap unless he thought it might send you off in the wrong direction."

"He did it because he hates me," Beam said. "We're getting close to him, and he knows it. It's tight where he's sitting, too."

Da Vinci gave a humorless chuckle. "I talked to Helen the profiler about that. She doesn't think he hates you. Says he hates himself, knows he's sabotaging himself because subconsciously he yearns to be caught. It's like a disease that grows in most serial killers, she says. The killing he's done is beginning to haunt him."

"What do you think?" Beam asked.

"I think she doesn't know diddly."

A uniformed assistant knocked, then entered the office with a tray on which was a glass coffeepot, two mugs, and a folded newspaper. A stolid, attractive woman devoid of makeup, she placed the tray near the motorcycle sculpture on the desk. Her unblinking eyes, the stiffness of her cheeks, suggested she wasn't crazy about this part of her job.

Da Vinci absently thanked her as she left and closed the door behind her. The inner sanctum was sealed and inviolate again.

Da Vinci laid the folded *Post* on his desk where Beam could reach it, then began pouring coffee into the mugs. Both men were prepared to drink their coffee black, which was fortunate, because there was no cream or sugar on the tray. Was their absence an expression of disdain from the annoyed assistant? Another rebellious woman in da Vinci's world?

"You seen the papers yet this morning?" da Vinci asked, as he poured.

Beam said he hadn't, then reached for the folded paper, as he was sure da Vinci intended.

"Page five," da Vinci said.

"I know," Beam said. "I see the teaser on the front page." He drew his reading glasses from his shirt pocket and put them on.

On page five of the paper there was a transcript of an exclusive interview with Melanie Taylor.

As Beam scanned it, da Vinci said, "She's changed her mind. Now she thinks Cold Cat killed his wife."

"I can believe it," Beam said, "but why was she dumb enough to say it?"

"You read between the lines, you can tell some asshole journalist conned her. She probably thought she was talking off the record, maybe not to a journalist at all."

"Still, she said it. She must not have realized what it meant. Maybe she doesn't yet. Though when she sees this she's gonna be mad as hell."

Da Vinci handed Beam his coffee. Beam accepted it with one hand, tossing the *Post* back on the desk with the other.

"Somebody else who's gonna be mad is the Justice Killer," da Vinci said. "He figures to go after her. Helen says its almost a cinch Melanie will be next. I have to concur."

"We've got to give Melanie protection."

"She's already got it, even though she might not have read the paper yet and know she needs it." Da Vinci sipped his coffee and made a face, as if he'd encountered something unexpectedly distasteful.

It made Beam hesitant to try his coffee.

"We've got Melanie's apartment staked out and there'll

be a tail on her," da Vinci continued. "We don't have unlimited resources, so it takes some police presence away from Cold Cat. Seems the move to make, though, since Melanie all but painted a target on her ass. But I've gotta tell you, if the Justice Killer could get to Dudman, with all his high-priced professional security, I've gotta bet on him to nail this airhead Melanie."

"Helen the profiler quote you any odds on that?" Beam asked, thinking da Vinci and Helen seemed to have been discussing things together a lot lately.

Da Vinci nodded. "She said it was about ninety percent he'd make the kill."

"You, I, and the profiler agree," Beam said. "What's the world coming to?"

"You don't want me to answer that," da Vinci said.

Beam forgot and sampled his coffee. It was bitter.

Melanie wasn't going in to work this morning. She simply couldn't. It was as if the throngs of people on the streets, the commuters packed into the subway, and her colleagues at work would all know, would somehow be able to see it on her like a telltale external bruise. The callousness of Richard's—Cold Cat's—continued refusal even to speak to her was like a slap in the face that wouldn't stop stinging.

Her bedroom smelled stale, and the sheet and pillow beneath her were damp with perspiration. Sleep had been impossible except in short stretches. She kept coming awake with her mind awhirl in a tempest of worries. Concerns that didn't seem so important in the morning light, but in her dark bedroom had seemed of crisis proportions. It was her loneliness turning mean on her, as it sometimes did in unguarded moments. Or possibly the sugar in that milkshake last night before bedtime had given her an energy surge that prevented sleep. And of course there was caffeine in chocolate.

She raised her head, prompting a stab of pain behind her eyes—the sugar again. The red numerals on her bedside clock read 8:02.

After finally dozing off around 6 a.m., she'd overslept and would have been late for work even if she were planning on going in.

It wasn't too late to call in sick, though.

She rolled onto her side and reached for the phone, then pecked out the familiar number of Regal Trucking. Waited while the phone rang on the other end of the connection.

A recording. Voice mail. Past eight o'clock and no one was in the office yet, readying the trucks for the day's run. Melanie was annoyed, then she almost smiled. They could hardly criticize her for being sick.

She left a brief message, unconsciously making her voice husky, as if her throat were sore, then hung up.

She replaced the receiver, then lay back and closed her eyes.

Opened them.

Now she was wide awake. She reached over for the remote, then plumped up her pillow and switched on the TV near the foot of the bed.

She was astounded to see herself exiting the diner on First Avenue where she'd had dinner last night.

She sat straight up in bed. The volume was set on mute, and she was too stunned to change it.

Print began to scroll over the frozen image on the screen. Print within quotation marks. Familiar words.

Her words.

Her eye blurred with tears so she could no longer read them. Didn't want to read them.

Who . . . ? How . . . ?

That bastard!

He must have been wired, recording our conversation I assumed was casual and private. A journalist! Goddamned sneaky, lying journalist, taking advantage of my distress. Another man deceiving me, using me.

Melanie hurled the remote at the TV and missed, but the impact when it bounced off the wall caused the volume to come on full blast. The bedroom vibrated under high-decibel assault.

Melanie placed her palms over her ears, as if to warm them, pressing hard enough that her head felt squeezed in a vise. She scrunched her eyes shut against the pain.

She felt like screaming.

She thought she might actually scream.

50

St. Louis, 1993

The roaring grew louder, time rushing past like wind.

Justice stood staring at the headstone, thinking it must be somebody else's name carved there, somebody with the same name as his wife's.

But he knew it wasn't. April was down there, in the grave, in the dark.

She needed him!

He rose from sleep, hearing his harsh, agonized gasp, as if from somewhere outside himself.

The bedroom was silent. His pillow was soaked with sweat. More awake now, more aware than he'd ever been, he felt his mind whirling out of control. He tried to steady it, tried to slow and organize his thoughts so they made sense. There was a bitterness at the back of his throat. He swallowed.

Didn't feel it.

Didn't hear it.

His heart was a stone in his chest.

He made himself open his eyes and turn his head on the pillow so he was looking at April.

Of course she wasn't there. She was still in his dream, in her grave.

She's succeeded.

Finally, she's ended it.

He began to breathe hard through his nose, and he lay listening to the relentless, labored hissing.

Air in, air out. Life.

She ended it. She was gone.

Nothing was the same. It would never be the same. Nothing.

His thoughts that had scattered like startled crows now settled down to roost in the familiar bleak landscape. The sadness that weighed like iron encompassed him.

And with the sadness came the rage. He blamed Davison, their son Will's rapist and killer, for what had dealt the crushing blow to their lives. But he blamed the justice system for April's depression and death, and for his own fury and misery.

The justice system had let their son's killer walk free. It had made it impossible for the bereaved parents to feel the finality of the book of justice closing, ending a sad chapter. They could never even begin the gradual ascent from a dark pit of grief and anger. The justice system had done nothing to keep them from sinking deeper and deeper into the pit, and finally April had reached the bottom, where the snakes waited.

He held the justice system responsible.

Feeling his head begin to pound, as if usually did when he awoke like this at—he looked at the clock—3 a.m., he sat up in bed.

For a while he sat motionless, listening to the mournful sounds of the house at night, of the night outside. Nothing around him but night.

He held the justice system responsible.

51

New York, the present

The Justice Killer sat at a table in the nave of a church of capitalism, the Citigroup Building, and sipped an egg cream as he watched people scurry past with their packages. Though he was indoors, the space was so vast it felt like outdoors.

Some of the other tables outside the shops were occupied. A tourist couple sat at one nearby, ignoring the doughnuts they'd bought and amusing themselves studying photographs stored on a digital camera. They laughed and chattered, their heads close together. At another table, two old men played chess and ate sandwiches they'd brought from home, or at least from somewhere else, because the sandwiches had been contained in clear plastic bags that were now tucked beneath a corner of the chessboard. The stratospheric ceilings and hard marble provided a spacious, brittle chamber of sharp but subtle noises—sounds of bustle, commerce, action, hope, and desperation—the background music of New York.

The Justice Killer sipped his egg cream through a straw and was amused. The news about Adelaide Starr was excellent, providing a young Joan of Arc to unknowingly champion his cause. And he was sure he'd tipped the odds more in his favor by increasingly observing his pursuers in their attempts to trace him. Always a good idea to keep close tabs on the enemy. It had even enabled him to go on the offensive.

He knew about the growing relationship between his nemesis Beam and the woman in the antique shop, Nola Lima. A lovely, strangely restful woman was Nola, with her natural stillness, prominent cheekbones, and dark, knowing eyes. So graceful, with a purpose and economy to her movements that fascinated. If ever he *did* decide to kill purely for pleasure . . .

Which of course he *would not* do.

His research had given him the idea for the ring. Harry Lima's gaudy, tasteless ring. He was sure the small, independent jeweler who made the duplicate ring in Canada wouldn't be discovered by the police. The jeweler was, in fact, a former fence and wanted nothing to do with the law in any capacity. He'd found anonymity and refuge in the arms of our neighbor to the north. Real names hadn't been exchanged. Even if the police did happen to locate the jeweler, he wouldn't be able to recall exactly what his customer looked like. And it had been a cash deal—no paper trail.

Beam was becoming even more involved with the woman, which was fine with the Justice Killer. Perhaps, at some point, he would teach Beam a lesson. But as of right now, things were going well. The idiot police profiler thought he was becoming unraveled, that the executions had taken their toll on him, but in truth he was in firmer control of himself and the situation than ever. He'd become a folk hero in New York, meting out justice to the system that denied it to the masses. The city was a safer place because of the Justice Killer. Adelaide Starr's followers were telling anyone who'd listen.

The police, Beam and his detectives, he'd sent on fools'

errands, such as the diversion of the ring. They were still wasting their valuable time with that. And they'd stepped up protection of Melanie Taylor. They'd be observing her constantly, waiting for an attempt on her life. She was, after all, the logical next victim.

So let them utilize their resources to protect her. Let her live through her nights and be afraid during her days, even though protectors were massed around her. In the case of Cold Cat, JK would for the first time execute the acquitted but guilty defendant himself. Then, later, he might focus his attention on Melanie.

It was a move Beam wouldn't expect. That was the idea. It was Beam and the idiot profiler who thought there were overarching rules to be followed, a cosmic design they could discern and predict. Though he altered victims and methods, they thought the killer's compulsion drove him to repeat, repeat, repeat, even if he couldn't see the pattern.

Not so!

It would be the defendant, the murderer himself, the dangerous detritus of the system, who would die this time.

The Justice Killer raised his cup of egg cream a few inches off the table and silently toasted himself.

He and not Beam or the NYPD controlled the game.

It wasn't only a matter of strategy, or of pride.

A free Cold Cat he could not abide.

Or neglect.

It was a matter of respect.

It wouldn't make a bad rap song.

As he coaxed the big Lincoln through noisy and maddening Manhattan traffic, Beam wished the car were equipped with an emergency light and siren. Maybe he should put in a request to da Vinci, really get him ticked off.

Instead of double-parking near the antique shop, he saw a space about a block away from Things Past and impulsively swung the big car into it. He locked the car, then began walking along the rain-puddled sidewalk toward the shop.

Beam didn't have a jacket or umbrella. After an initial downpour, the rain had decreased to a soft drizzle and mere inconvenience. Everything smelled fresh. Even the trash at the curb, with rainwater pooled in the creases and folds of black plastic bags, smelled okay. Or maybe it was all due to Nola's increasing presence in Beam's life.

He glanced at his watch. Almost six o'clock. She'd be closing the shop now, checking the bolt on the back door, getting the Closed sign to hang on the front. Or maybe an uncertain customer would be delaying her, pondering whether to buy some treasure that might be underpriced, or some overpriced junk that evoked some memory of childhood.

Beam was half a block from the shop when he noticed the man in a gray slouch hat and long, pale green raincoat standing in the doorway of the locksmith's shop across the street. The man seemed to notice him at the same time, then turned and moved to enter the shop. Beam knew the locksmith closed at five.

As he got closer, he gained the angle to see that the man had simply retreated deeper into the doorway and was standing motionless. Though he couldn't make out his face, Beam was sure he'd seen him before in the area of Things Past. And seen him somewhere else recently. An old cop's mind shuffles through memory, makes connections. It might have been in the subway, or on a crowded sidewalk, or in some restaurant, but the way the guy stood, maybe the ankle-length raincoat . . . something, the total package, struck a chord.

There was one way to find out if he'd been following Beam: ask him.

Beam began crossing the street at an angle, obviously moving toward the man in the doorway.

That's when the man surprised him. Emerged from the doorway then bolted and ran without a backward glance.

Shot away like a scalded animal and gained ground before Beam could grasp the fact he was fleeing.

Has reason to run.

Beam took up the chase, doing a neat half turn and barely avoiding a car that slid on wet pavement. Up on the sidewalk, he hit his stride. He bumped people, sploshed through puddles, and felt his right sock become saturated, but he kept the man in the long coat in sight.

Feeling it. Getting rough now. Beam's breath was becoming ragged, but his bad leg felt okay. He was keeping pace with the man. The Justice Killer.

Must be. Who else?

The man ahead raised an arm bent at the elbow and held his gray slouch cap on so it wouldn't fly off as he rounded the corner onto Sixth Avenue. Busier there. He was out of sight.

Beam lengthened his stride and ran for the corner, ignoring the swish of tires on wet pavement and the horn blasts he left in his wake. His right leg was beginning to ache now. Serious pain.

Hell with it!

He almost fell as he slid and stumbled around the corner. Lots of people on the sidewalk, but the man in the long coat had disa –

No! There, crossing against the light at the next corner!

Beam gathered his strength and began running again. He was sure he'd gained some ground. If he could keep him in sight, he'd catch this bastard. He knew it!

It began raining harder again, a steady drizzle. Umbrellas blossomed, obstructing Beam's view up the block. An umbrella spoke jabbed his cheek beneath his right eye as he veered around a woman who herself was striding fast in the opposite direction.

The eye began to tear up, causing everything to blur, but there was the man in the long coat, farther away.

Beam sucked in more breath, wincing at the sharp tightness in his chest, and ran harder. The leg was hurting badly now, beginning to pulse with pain. Ahead of him, the long pale coat moved like a graceful ghost along the crowded sidewalk, seeming to pick up speed as it passed people.

Damn, he can run!

So can this old bastard!

Beam stretched out his stride, feeling it in his groin as his muscles strained for distance. He was picking up speed. He was goddamned flying. Whatever he chased, he'd catch.

The clunky soles of his black regulation shoes beat a regular, sloshy rhythm on the wet pavement. He was running like a machine.

Then the machine began to malfunction. The rhythm of his footfalls broke, and one of his leather soles dragged on the sidewalk.

Beam was wobbling now, unable to suck in enough oxygen. His chest hurt and felt constricted. He couldn't control his aching leg. His right knee went rubbery, and he almost fell.

He staggered to a stop, then leaned his back against the side of a parked car, knowing one foot was in the gutter and getting wet.

A fat man carrying an umbrella at a low angle stopped and stared at him. "You okay?"

"I'll live," Beam gasped.

"You sure?"

"Who the hell is?"

The man walked on. But several more people had stopped now and were staring at Beam. An old woman with scraggly gray hair sticking out from beneath a plastic rain cap was studying him with an expression of infinite pity.

Beam placed his palms against the cool wet steel of the car and pushed away.

There. He was standing up straight, his foot out of the gutter.

"Somebody chasing you, buddy?" a man in a hooded

sweatshirt asked. He was jogging in place as he spoke, as if one word from Beam and he'd take off after whoever was bothering him.

"You want a cop?" the gray-haired woman asked.

Beam made a conscious effort to even out his breathing. "It's okay," he said, "I'm a cop."

No one seemed to believe him. He thought about flashing his shield, then decided what the hell? He fastened the buttons of his suit coat, turned up its collar to keep the rain from trickling down his neck, and started walking. He was limping, but the leg felt better.

He made his way to the next intersection and looked both ways. There was plenty of pedestrian traffic, but no long green raincoat among it. And people on the sidewalks gave no indication that someone had just rushed through them, rudely and roughly elbowing them aside. At the end of the block to Beam's right, a cop was calmly directing traffic in the middle of the intersection.

Beam turned around and walked back the way he'd come, but hadn't gone far when he noticed that, as when he'd passed, there were no empty parking spaces on the street— except for one. And the pavement beneath the car that had obviously parked there for some time was barely marked by the steady drizzle. It must have driven away recently, minutes, even seconds ago.

The rain had started before Beam parked, spotted the Justice Killer, and began the chase. Then it had become a bare drizzle, almost a mist. It became a steadier, more persistent drizzle about ten minutes ago.

Beam stood staring at the speckled pavement. For the Justice Killer, the chase might have ended right here, where he'd scrambled into his car, hunkered down and waited for Beam to pass, then driven away.

Of course, this was busy Manhattan; somebody else— anybody—might have gotten into a car here and driven off just after Beam limped past.

But something inside Beam believed otherwise. It was the man he'd been chasing.

As he watched, the dry rectangle of pavement turned as wet and dark as the concrete around it. A dented Pontiac with a NO RADIO sign in its side window braked to a halt in the street and backed into the parking space, the driver no doubt thankful for his luck.

Beam stood and stared. This wasn't a section of street that would be covered by security cameras. *All the more reason JK might park here.* There was nothing he could do now. He jammed his fists in his suit coat pockets and continued walking.

He was breathing regularly, and he noticed that the pain in his chest was gone. Actually, he felt as if he could start running again. He berated himself for giving up the chase.

Twenty years ago . . .

Even ten . . .

But not today.

52

By the time he reached Things Past, Beam's leg felt okay. He dabbed at his eye. It was sore, but not bleeding. He was wet, and somehow or other had torn the knee of his pants.

When he entered the shop and the little bell tinkled above his head, Nola looked at him from where she was standing behind the counter. He watched her deadpan glance travel up and down. He might have to bleed from every artery and pore to impress this woman. With a slight surprise, he realized that might be one of the things that so attracted him to her.

"What happened, Beam?"

He told her about his futile pursuit of the man in the long raincoat.

"And you've seen him before?" she asked.

"I think so. Somewhere."

She disappeared for a moment from behind the counter, then reappeared with a folded white towel. She tossed the towel to him, and he caught it and began rubbing his hair dry.

"He's been following us?" Beam heard her ask, his head beneath the towel.

"I think so. That's no surprise." He rubbed harder with the towel. "Twenty years ago—ten—I could have nailed the bastard."

"It's not ten years ago."

"No." He raked back his wet hair with his fingers, then used the towel to dry his hands.

"You saw him watching us," she said, as if trying to fix the notion in her mind.

He tossed the towel back to her. She caught it absently and dropped it on the floor behind the counter. "Watching you," he said.

Her dark eyes didn't change expression. She didn't seem at all frightened or even perturbed.

Beam thought that someday he might be so accepting and unafraid. It seemed a long way off.

It was a small thing, but it was *something*.

Street sounds found their way into Nell's bedroom. She'd just arrived home, just turned on the window air conditioner, and the stillness and stuffiness hadn't been chased. It smelled almost as if someone had been smoking in the bedroom, but that couldn't be.

She opened her dresser's second drawer to see if she had clean panties or would have to do a wash before Terry picked her up.

Nell stood before the drawer and studied its contents. Her panties and bras seemed to have been rearranged, but only slightly. And the nine-millimeter Glock handgun she kept there unloaded seemed to be pointed more toward the window rather than the wall. *Seemed*.

A faint scent, a subtle shifting of symmetry. Of course, it could always be her imagination. Probably *was* her imagination. She knew that lately she'd been irritable, uneasy, perhaps looking for something to spoil what was otherwise beautiful. Her mother had told her some people refused to be happy, and if they didn't learn to change, they'd be unhappy all through life. The message was clear. If only her mother had told her *how* to change, life to this point would have been a lot easier.

Nell knew that two things kept her from trusting someone enough to fall completely and unreservedly in love—her job, and her recent divorce. Those were the reasons she was standing here sweaty, skeptical, and maybe paranoid, trying to find a reason to distrust Terry and tell him to return the key to her apartment.

The truth was, she hadn't felt completely at ease since she'd given him the key. It was supposed to be an act symbolizing her love and the seriousness of their relationship. If a guy had your key, he had it all.

What had also come with Nell's key was her subtle distrust.

Terry deserved better. She understood that now. She told herself she understood.

The person Nell distrusted was herself.

She shut the dresser drawer and pressed it firm. Then she drew a deep breath and made herself smile.

Terry had her key. He had her. It was going to stay that way.

Jack Selig did not have her key.

Of course, he could always buy the building.

53

Time had healed nothing.

A brisk wind whipped across the cemetery, shaking the leafless trees and causing a lone crow to flap sideways into the gray sky and veer toward the shelter of the mausoleum that stood like a small Greek temple on the hill. The gusting wind drove particles of sleet that stung the eyes and anywhere skin was exposed.

Justice was wearing jeans, thick leather boots, a sweatshirt, fur-lined gloves, and a green parka with the hood up, but he was still cold. He bowed his head, staring at the dates on the modest tombstones. *Seventeen years since Will died. Thirteen since April died.*

The pain was unabated.

There had been no escape from it. The doctors hadn't helped, the pretending to be other people hadn't helped, the fierce dedication to his perishable work, the drinking, the medication, the soul-searching, the loss of soul, it all seemed to feed rather than subdue the monster in the basement of his mind. He could restrain the monster no longer.

He'd become obsessed with those who killed, who placed no value on human life other than on their own destructive lives. Over the years he'd seen too many of them go free, or serve brief sentences only to return to the streets to murder again. Killers like the one who murdered Will. Killers who, in their own evil and indirect way, also killed people like April.

April herself. It had taken time, but finally they'd killed her, even if her death had been by her own hand.

There must be a reckoning.

Always one to plan carefully, he knew that if harm came to his son's killer, or to anyone connected with his acquittal, he, Justice, would be the prime suspect. So he'd decided to exact his revenge by executing those who were involved in the acquittals of other violent criminals who were obviously guilty—starting with the forepersons of the juries that set them free. It was the system that had failed and continued to fail, that bore responsibility, that would be the target of his revenge.

There would be nothing to connect him to those cases or to those victims. And there would be a wide pool of potential victims, making it impossible for the police to protect them all. He would be performing a public service. And because of him, April's death, and the death of their son, would mean something in the chaos that he now knew life to be.

There would be meaning and purpose to the rest of his own life.

Justice and balance and purpose.

He had access to a gun, and to a silencer, and he'd obtained both. What he needed now, *all* he needed now, was April's understanding, her approval.

The wind kicked up again, moaning through the columns of the mausoleum and driving the distant crow back up into the roiling gray sky. Justice was unmoving, his feet spread wide, his head bowed, staring steadily at his wife's tombstone.

And from the grave she gave him her blessing.

54

New York, the present

Not right . . . Not right . . .

Cold Cat sat hunched over the control panel, toying with the equalizer, raising the volume of the second track. He was in his home studio on the Upper East Side. Self-contained in a corner of the vast living room, it was a small room with sound baffles all around to appease complaining neighbors. The apartment was violently furnished, with Chinese red carpet, thick green drapes that puddled on the floor, orange leather chairs, and a fifteen-foot leopard-skin sofa. The walls were festooned with gold-framed oils of nude women in various lewd positions. Such bad taste had to be deliberate. Cold Cat called it In-Your-Face decorating, and had threatened to open a chain of shops. When Edie had been alive, she didn't like to spend time here.

Cold Cat had both tracks going now. He leaned toward the microphone and jumped in on the one beat:

I be on the hunt.
Gonna waste that cunt.

She say no, no more.
I say hit the floor.

Something still wasn't right. He rewound and sat back, removing his earphones. Needed something *tight*.

He licked his lips. Composing was hard work, and he'd been at it more than two hours. What he needed was a beer. Something. He'd made it a rule: no liquid in the studio. There was too much sensitive electronic crap in there to run the risk of something spilling and shorting the shit out of it.

He looked through the thick, soundproof glass to where his bodyguard Lenny was sitting in an orange easy chair, reading some tit-and-ass magazine or other. Lenny had an opened Miller can on the table beside him. Cold Cat regarded his bodyguard. Fat Lenny. He oughta be told not to put on any more weight. It wasn't like he was all muscle, the way he'd been when Cold Cat hired him. Lenny looked like he could walk through a wall then. Now he looked like the wall.

Cold Cat contemplated leaving the studio for a few minutes to finish whatever beer was left in Lenny's Miller can. Show the potato brain who was boss.

But the beer can had given Cold Cat an idea. *Taste.*

Yeah, that'd work better. He put his ear phones back on and edged his chair up closer to the control panel.

Lenny must have sensed he was being stared at. He looked up from the magazine and glanced toward the studio's thick rectangular window.

But Cold Cat was already hard at work.

He ran the tape again, this time jumping in over the last lyric line:

I say taste the floor.

Much better.

The phone must have been ringing. He saw through the thick window that Lenny had put down his magazine and was standing near the desk, the receiver pressed to his fat head.

He hung up the phone, looking like something had scared him shitless, the whites showing all around his dark eyes. Then he marched right over and yanked open the studio door.

"What the shit you doin'?" Cold Cat said, peeling off the earphones. "Can't you see I'm workin'?"

"Building's on fire, Cold." Lenny was puffing with excitement, making his cheeks flutter. "Fire down in the garage."

"Parking garage is concrete," Cold Cat said. "Whole goddamn building is. There's a fire way down in the garage, fire department'll put it out. I hope whoever called you wasn't dumb-ass enough not to call the fire department first."

But even as Cold Cat finished talking, he could hear sirens below in the street. Some of them had to be right outside.

"Cold, listen—"

"You listen, Lenny. The brave firemen and women are on top of the situation. Fire's way below us, don't matter a bit 'less they tell us to evacuate. Which they ain't gonna do, because the garage is concrete and concrete don't burn. Meantime, shut the damned door so I can get back to work."

"You don't understand, Cold." Lenny was bobbing, waving his arms. "The super called here 'cause it's *my* car that's on fire! My brand new BMW!"

Cold Cat shrugged. "Ain't brand new, Lenny. Last year's model."

"I love that car, Cold!"

"So go to it. Help 'em put out the fire. Just don't bother me 'less we get the order to go. Fire's forty stories down in a concrete garage. BMW probably got some kinda self-fire-extinguishing feature, anyway."

Lenny looked thoughtful. "Maybe it does, Cold."

Cold Cat shook his head. "So get your ass down there and

see to it. What I'd be doin' if it was my car. Fire Department's here, so are the police. I can spare you for a while, so go tend to your wheels."

"Thanks, Cold. I mean, really!"

"Shut the door," Cold Cat said, and settled down again behind the microphone and sound controls.

Lenny complied, and Cold Cat was sealed in and sound-proofed again. Cold Cat was pleased to note that even the piercing sirens below were completely inaudible once the padded studio door was closed.

He didn't bother watching Lenny sprint from the apartment and almost yank the door off its hinges opening and closing it. Cold Cat was unconcerned. He didn't see how a fire could spread in the concrete parking garage; no way it could get to the upper floors. And all the civil servants in uniform were down there with hoses and axes and whatever the hell else they used to put out car fires. Can openers, maybe.

A lyric in that?

No. Let it go. Not easy to rhyme "opener."

Hey, wait a minute—"open-her."

He put his earphones back on and skillfully worked the control board again. Maybe he could add a line:

I say taste the floor.

Gonna open her.

No, no . . .

Gonna open whore.

Yeah! Gettin' it on!

It was glorious when the creative juices were flowing.

Now if he could get the blend down, raise the volume on "whore." Uh-*huh!* This one was going to work. He could *feel* it.

He manipulated the control board and ran though the number again, then played it back, all the tracks.

Needed more drum, be okay. Better'n okay.

In the isolation of his soundproof room, with his earphones on, his head bowed, and concentrating so intensely, Cold Cat didn't notice the figure, armed with a handgun and bulky sound suppressor, enter the apartment beyond the studio's window.

His first and only view of the intruder was when he glanced up an instant before the first bullet shattered the thick glass, and the second slammed through his right eye and into his brain.

When Lenny returned to tell Cold Cat the fire had totaled the BMW and had been deliberately set, he immediately saw the damaged studio window and stood still in the center of the living room.

Holy shit!

The glass in the window had gone milky. There were two jagged holes in it, close together, spiderwebbed. He was pretty sure what had made them.

"Cold? Cold? You in there?"

Foolish to call. The studio door was closed. Lenny rushed over and yanked at the door, but it was locked. He hadn't locked it when he'd run out to get to the basement garage. But it locked automatically sometimes. Or maybe Cold had locked it.

He knew he'd better force the door open, but he shouldn't touch anything other than his cell phone, and use it to call the police.

Other hand, Cold might be in there bleeding to death.

Lenny went to the ruined window and peered in through one of what he was certain now were bullet holes.

Cold was slumped over the control panel, his head turned to the side. He was looking back at Lenny with an empty eye socket. Lying flat in the center of his back was a red letter *J* cut from some kind of cloth.

Lenny reeled backward.

Justice Killer!

He found himself sitting on top of his magazine in the orange easy chair. It was difficult for him to breathe. He was squeezing the chair's arms hard enough to leave permanent indentations. This was badder'n bad.

Bodyguard career's all over. Nobody gonna hire me now.

In a dark dream, he fumbled with his cell phone and called the police.

It didn't take them long to get there.

They were right downstairs.

55

Beam stood next to da Vinci as they watched Richard Simms's body being removed, Cold Cat leaving his expensive, tastelessly furnished Manhattan apartment for the last time. The paramedics tending the gurney craned their necks, taking a final, lasting look around, as they guided their burden through the door. They knew they'd never see anything like this again.

"Dizzy modern," one of them said.

"Martha Stewart's nightmare," said the other.

"We've been had," da Vinci said.

Beam couldn't disagree, so he said nothing.

Nell was sitting over on the leopard-skin sofa, running Lenny the bodyguard through his story again. Beam knew it would be essentially the same as the first time. Lenny was telling the truth, just not adding that there would have been more police nearby, outside and in the building, if they hadn't been redeployed to protect Melanie Taylor. Everyone had assumed she would be the Justice Killer's next target.

Looper entered the crowded apartment, sidestepped some busy crime scene unit techs, and made his way over to where Beam and da Vinci stood. He'd been talking to neighbors and double-checking what the doorman had told the uniforms who'd been first to arrive on the scene.

"Nobody saw or heard anything unusual," Looper said. "The doorman noticed no one suspicious entering or leaving the building either before or after Cold Cat's death."

"The usual professional, clean job," Beam said.

"And the public'll be delighted this piece of shit was flushed away."

"He was shot from outside his recording room," da Vinci said. "So if the killer didn't use a sound suppressor, folks in the next unit might have heard."

"He used one," Looper said. "Nobody heard a thing. And the medical examiner says it looks like a .32 slug did the work."

"We'll know soon enough if it's a match with the other slugs fired by the Justice Killer," Beam said.

"Do you really have any doubt?" da Vinci asked.

"No." Beam looked at Looper. "You check out the parking garage, Loop?"

"Yes, sir." Very formal in front of da Vinci. "Tenants drive in and out with a plastic card they insert in a machine that raises and lowers a gate. Code's changed once a month."

"The kind of gate somebody can walk around?" Beam asked.

"No, a genuine gate. All fancy iron or steel. Like a see-through overhead door."

Beam looked thoughtful. Somebody had sure as hell gotten into the parking garage. "They set the bodyguard's BMW on fire, took the elevator up, and shot Cold Cat."

"You make it sound simpler than it must have been," da Vinci said. "This had to be carefully planned." He looked at Looper. "Did anyone in the building notice somebody slip into the parking garage when they drove in or out?"

"We've checked just about everyone who has an entry card. Nobody saw anyone on foot coming or going as they used the gate."

"We've diverted a lot of human assets to protect the Taylor woman," da Vinci said, "but this building was still pretty much crawling with cops. You'd think at least one of them would have noticed something worth mentioning."

"Two, sir," Beam said.

"What's that?"

"There were only two undercovers in the building at the time of the shooting. Two more outside."

"Okay," da Vinci said, "not exactly crawling. Our killer still ran a hell of a risk, getting in here and taking down Cold Cat. How'd he even know the apartment door would be unlocked?"

"It wasn't unlocked. Latches automatically when it closes. He either picked the lock or slipped it. Wouldn't have been much of a problem, since it wasn't dead bolted or chained from the inside, after the bodyguard shagged ass outta here to try to save his car."

"Any doubt the car was deliberately set on fire?"

"Arson investigator says there's no doubt about it. Somebody shoved some rags under it and put a match or lighter to them."

"Then waited for all the action that would eliminate the bodyguard and serve as a distraction, so he could make his way upstairs and do his thing."

"Why'd he risk the car fire business?" Looper asked. "Why didn't he just shoot the bodyguard, then go on in and take out Cold Cat?"

"He has ethics," da Vinci said. "Morals. He doesn't want to harm innocent people."

"He's a goddamn psycho," Looper said.

Da Vinci looked as if he might want to argue, then seemed to relax. "I'm only going by what Helen the profiler says. This is a basically moral man."

"For a nut case."

"For a nut case," da Vinci agreed. He looked over at Beam. "Too bad you didn't get a better look at this sicko when you were chasing him the other night. If it was really him."

"It was," Beam said.

"Then one thing we learned," da Vinci said, "is he can run like a striped ape."

Beam wandered over and looked into the recording room through the open padded door. There was blood on the control panel, the chair, the floor. While the rest of the apartment was extravagantly decorated, the recording room looked high tech and all business. Cold Cat, with his backup, could spend a few hours in here and make a million dollars. Beam thought it was amazing.

He saw that Nell was finished with Lenny the bodyguard. She was slipping her notepad into her purse, coming over to join him. Behind her, Lenny was sitting with his bowed head in his hands, staring through spread fingers at the floor.

"Some bodyguard," Nell said.

"Probably not very experienced," Beam told her. "Cold Cat must've seen all the bulk and figured Lenny was a tough guy."

"Tough he might be. Smart he's not."

"A man who loved his car too much."

"There you go," Nell said.

"Aw, *damn!*"

Everyone looked to see who'd spoken.

They saw an African American man about five feet tall who would have looked even more diminutive if it weren't for his built-up boots. He was wearing an electric blue suit that was tailored tight at the waist and had exaggerated shoulders. His drastically upcombed hairdo was probably supposed to make him appear taller but simply made it look as if his head were exploding. He'd ignored the yellow crime scene tape across the door and plowed on in.

"Aw, damn!" he said again, grinding the heel of his hand into his right temple. "Damn, damn, damn!"

"Who the hell are you?" da Vinci asked.

The little man looked astounded that da Vinci would ask. "I be Knee High."

"To what?" Looper asked.

"That's my name, man!"

"We want your *real* name," da Vinci insisted.

"That be it! I had it legally changed. You all can check, you wanna take this farther. I'm—I was—Cold Cat's right hand."

Beam saw that Lenny had his head up and was staring glumly at the little man.

"You know this guy?" Beam asked.

Lenny waited a while before answering, as if still numbed by shock and grief. "He's Knee High. He hangs around Cold Cat all the time."

"Hung around," Looper corrected.

Lenny buried his face in his hands again.

"Okay, Knee High," da Vinci said. "What is it you want?"

"Knee High wants to confess."

Everyone, even the remaining techs, stopped what they were doing and stared at him.

"This all Knee High's fault," Knee High said. Then he began wailing again. "Damn, damn, damn!"

"You're saying you killed Cold Cat?" Beam asked.

Knee High's eyes widened and he wore his astounded look again. "Cold Cat? Naw, Knee High loved that man. But this still all Knee High's fault. Knee High killed Edie."

It took Beam a few seconds to realize what the little man was saying, and not just because he was one of those people who referred to himself in the third person. "Edie Piaf? Cold Cat's wife?"

"She weren't no kinda decent wife," Knee High said. "Knee High did just what the jury said Cold Cat didn't have no time to do, left my apartment a minute after him and got a cab 'cross town, killed Edie, then ran most of the way back. Couldn't get no cab. Didn't matter then, anyways, 'cause Edie was dead. Knee High never thought you guys'd nail Cold Cat for it. Then, when you did, it figured he'd get off, him bein' innocent. Knee High was gonna say something if he didn't. That Merv Clark gave testimony got him off. Me, Clark, we both lied our asses off on the stand. Clark was our insurance. Cold Cat was gonna get some green to him. Don't know if he ever did." Knee High looked from da Vinci to Beam with anguished eyes. "One thing's sure, though. Knee High killed Edie cause she an' Knee High were gettin' it on behind Cold Cat's back. We was at each other for a while. She was gonna tell Cold. Imagine that cunt! It ain't that Knee High was scared of Cold if he found out, but it woulda killed Cold. Cold, he loved that bitch, but she took no notice of him 'cept he could help her career. Knee High had to kill her so she wouldn't talk and ruin ever'thing." He began to cry. "Ever'thing ruined now anyways. It all Knee High's fault."

There was a roar from the other side of the room that startled everyone, and the huge form of Lenny came rocketing at Knee High.

Looper and Beam intercepted him but could only slow him down. Looper had him around the waist. Beam caught an elbow in the stomach and sank to the floor. He could only hang on to one of Lenny's ankles. Da Vinci jumped in and wrapped an arm around Lenny's bull neck.

Lenny wouldn't be deterred. Dragging the three men, he continued to move toward the cornered, terrified Knee High. Nell hurled herself on the slowly moving pile of humanity but was brushed aside. She rushed to the door and summoned one of the uniforms on duty in the hall.

He was a man almost as large as Lenny, and he had a weighted baton, which he brought down over and over on Lenny's head. Hard wood bouncing off Lenny's skull made a hollow, thumping sound, as if a melon were being struck.

It seemed to dawn on Lenny only gradually that he was being clubbed. He finally slowed and stopped his forward motion, but he didn't go down, merely slouched. The uniform from the hall kept pounding him, as if angry at Lenny's lack of reaction.

Beam reached out a hand and caught the uniform's wrist. "Okay, okay, he's gonna cooperate."

The uniform nodded and moved away, still gripping the baton in his right hand, tapping it in the palm of his left. His chest was heaving and his adrenaline was pumping. He still saw Lenny as unfinished business.

Lenny stood with his head bowed, seeming to have suffered nothing other than a change of attitude.

Looper and Nell led him back to the sofa, where he sat morosely and gave no indication that he knew his head was beginning to bleed.

Knee High was still squatting in the corner, back on his heels, trembling. "You shoulda let him kill Knee High! You shoulda!"

"We can leave you two alone," da Vinci offered.

Lenny shook his head violently from side to side. "No, no! I jus' wanna do what I gots to do. Thas' all what's left for me. I jus' wanna—"

"We know," da Vinci said. He trudged over and sat down hard in an orange armchair. Beam was already sitting in the matching chair. Looper was standing bent over with his hands on his knees. The uniform was leaning back against a wall. Down from his adrenaline high, he'd stopped tapping his baton in the palm of his hand.

Nell read Knee High his rights. She was the only one in the room not out of breath.

56

Dust motes rioted silently in a shaft of morning sunlight lancing in between the drapes and casting a Picasso-like symmetry over the wall and bureau.

Nell's bedroom was cool. The air conditioner had cycled off, and only the blower was on. It was barely light outside the closed drapes, and the morning rush hadn't yet developed. The city was quiet except for the occasional swish of traffic, and distant shouting and metal clanging somewhere blocks away. A bird chirped determinedly nearby, maybe on the sill.

Nell lay beside the sleeping Terry, listening to the even rhythm of his breathing, and wondered if she'd mentioned to him that the police were pulling protection away from Cold Cat and assigning it to Melanie Taylor? The question nagged her more than it should. She couldn't remember doing so, but it *was* possible. Just as it was surely possible that whoever had shot Cold Cat knew with certainty about his reduced protection. The killer had created a diversion, then slipped like grease through the police and the building's security.

At the precise time when Cold Cat had been killed yesterday, Terry was alone in his apartment, scanning scripts for parts he thought he might have a shot at if he auditioned. Nell thought it odd that Terry seemed almost to make it a point to mention his whereabouts to her.

At about that same time, Nell had been talking with Jack Selig over drinks in the softly lighted lounge at Keys, a new four-star restaurant over on Third Avenue. Her watch at Melanie Taylor's had ended, and this was, in a way, she told herself, a continuation of the investigation. It had been a few drinks and conversation, nothing more; a gentleman always, Selig had kept his word about that.

But Nell, having been with another man, didn't think it was a good idea to press Terry about his whereabouts. That would be edging too close to the kind of pot-and-kettle argument that could end a relationship Nell desperately wanted to continue.

She recalled that Terry hadn't really much of an alibi for the time of Carl Dudman's death, either.

But Terry lived alone. And she was a cop; she knew how seldom people who lived alone, with no one to witness their lives, had firm alibis.

Terry's arm was suddenly across her chest, just beneath her breasts, startling her. His big hand closed on her bare upper arm.

"I thought you were asleep," she said.

"Been lying here looking at you," he said. "Not much I'd rather do."

She laughed. "Oh? Is there *something* you'd rather do?"

He raised his head and kissed her. Bad breath. She didn't mind.

"There is something I'd rather do," he said, "but we did it only a few hours ago."

Another light kiss, and he scooted away from her, sat on the edge of the mattress for a few seconds, then stood up. Nude and without the slightest self-consciousness, he yawned, stretched, then swaggered toward the bathroom.

"Gonna shower?" Nell asked.

"Gotta. And I don't have time for breakfast this morning. Woman on the East Side needs her oven fixed. It overheats, and she's desperate for relief." He winked.

Nell sat up in bed. "Damn you, Terry!" She threw his pillow at him and missed.

In the bedroom doorway, he paused and glanced back at her, smiling. "It's her ice-maker, actually."

He continued his nude stroll to the bathroom, and a few minutes later pipes clanked in the wall and she heard the shower begin to hiss. It was an oddly reassuring sound.

Nell lay back and stared up at the slowly revolving ceiling fan, as she'd stared up at it last night during and after sex. As she'd done before. The rhythms and cycles of life. There was something so *right* about it all. She smiled.

Too much paranoia in the world.

She decided she didn't really distrust Terry.

She couldn't.

But if she did distrust him, who would she confide in? Beam? Looper? Hardly. Simply on mere suspicion, they'd be all over Terry. Then the media might find out. They'd swarm. They'd discover one of the investigating officers was sleeping with a suspect.

Nell shuddered. *Jesus!*

Nobody to confide in there.

She felt a dark contempt for herself. The problem was her disease. Cop's disease. The creeping cynicism that ruined every relationship, personal or otherwise.

The disease that left you, finally, lonely and alone.

Or was the disease New York? The city was in its own way insular, and everything seemed faster and somehow enhanced. Just the place to lose your perspective, to begin to doubt yourself.

Lonely and alone.

Nell didn't want that ever to happen to her. Not on a permanent basis. She was still young enough to prevent it. And there was Terry.

Terry.
Selig.
She did love Terry.
But the one person she felt confident to confide in, she realized, was Jack Selig.

Melanie lay in bed alone with her eyes clenched shut.
Cold Cat dead! Richard!
Her avowed hatred for the rap artist melted away. It was, after all, her fault that he was killed. She recalled those moments during the trial when their gazes had met and they'd looked into each other's souls. Those were moments suspended in amber, moments that would last a lifetime.
Richard.
The man she loved. One of the few men she'd ever loved. Dead.
The thought was so burning that she couldn't lie still. Finally, she got up and plodded into the kitchen. The tile floor was cool on her bare feet, and cold air spilled out on her when she opened the refrigerator to get the carton of orange juice.
She sat at the table, her feet up on the chair's rungs to keep them off the tiles, and sipped juice from the carton. It helped, but not much. Made her feel a little steadier.
Then she looked over at the sink, with its empty beer can, and last night's takeout pizza box propped on the drain board. Tonight's supper might be exactly the same.
Lonely damned life. Miserable life.
She thought morosely that if anybody should have been killed, it was that coward Knee High. Maybe he'd get the death penalty for murdering Edie Piaf. He certainly hadn't been Richard's friend, sleeping with his wife, killing her, then sitting in court knowing Richard was innocent and watching him suffer, his very life in the balance. Edie Piaf. She'd deserved to die for betraying Richard. What fools

some women were! She, Melanie, would never have betrayed such a man, a poet of the streets, a major figure in modern music.

Melanie realized that tears were tracking down her cheeks. She wiped them away with the backs of her fingers and took another sip of cold juice. The refrigerator clicked and its motor began to run, making something glass inside vibrate shrilly with a regular rise and fall, as if taunting her.

A cruel trick had been played on her. She'd been Richard's fierce and persuasive advocate on the jury and actually *believed* in his innocence. The jury foreperson who instinctively *knew* he was too good a man to be a murderer. Now, ironically, she was the one who'd set him free only to be killed by a fool who'd shared most of the other jurors' misimpressions.

Melanie pushed the juice carton away and rested her cheek on the cool, hard Formica table. "Life is so unfair and unpredictable," she said in a choked voice. But no one was there to hear.

So goddamned cruel!

So this is how it feels to have a broken heart.

"The word is you're in love," Beam said to Nell.

They were walking along First Avenue, sipping lattes from Starbucks, on their way to meet Looper near Cold Cat's apartment building so they could do follow up interviews and double-check some facts—the kind of drudge police work you don't read about in mystery novels.

Nell sidestepped a frail, gray woman walking a dog that might have been a horse except for the fangs. Protection. "Whose word would that be?" Nell asked. "Looper's?"

"Among others. He's close enough to you to notice."

Is it that noticeable? "The word could be wrong, otherwise there wouldn't be much use for our kind of work."

Beam grinned. "*Is* the word wrong?"

"Gossip doesn't become you, Beam."

"Becomes no one," he said. "But you didn't answer my question."

"Why do you have to know if I'm in love?"

"I like you. I want to know so I can feel good about it."

"You're so full of bullshit, Beam."

"Sure. Otherwise I wouldn't be of much use in our kind of work."

They waited for the traffic signal at Fifty-sixth and First, not speaking.

"Okay," Nell said, as they were crossing the intersection. "I guess there's no point in trying to keep a secret from you. Answer's yes. I'm in love. Now what? Do I get flowers?"

"Not from me. I respect you too much to love you. So who's the lucky guy?"

"Terry Adams."

"Don't know him," Beam said, after a pause.

"That's because he's not a cop."

"Good."

"He's an actor."

"My, my."

"And he repairs appliances."

Beam broke stride, then took a sip of latte. "Your air conditioner. It's working now."

"Same guy," Nell said.

"Didn't he ride with some of the cops in the Two-Oh a while back, doing research so he could play a cop on Broadway?"

"Near Broadway. Said that's as close as he wants to get."

"To Broadway?"

"To being a cop."

"Smart fella. You and an actor. I can see it. He treat you okay?"

"Wouldn't put up with him if he didn't."

They walked for a few minutes without speaking. "You're right," Beam said.

"About not putting up with him if he acts up?"

"No. Well, yes. Also right about something you thought but didn't mention."

"Ah!"

"That your love life is none of my business."

They'd reached Cold Cat's building. A uniform was still standing outside, helping the doorman shoo away curious fans.

"Here we are," Nell said.

"Exactly where JK wants us." Beam glanced around. "He might even be here with us."

"I wouldn't disagree with you," Nell said. "You're on a roll."

57

"You on your way to talk to my mom and dad?" Gina asked.

She was wearing blue shorts, a ragged gray sweatshirt cut off at the armpits, and white jogging shoes that could use a turn in the washer. Her body was slim and lithe and well toned, Nell noted with a twinge of jealousy. *Youth.*

"Not really," Nell said. "They told me on the phone you weren't home. Said you'd gone running. I've been waiting around out here for you to turn up."

Sunlight illuminated a low haze hanging in the warm air, either the result of exhaust fumes, or dust from construction in the next block. Every few minutes distant jackhammers beat out the frantic clatter of machine guns. Traffic was streaming past, and Gina, with her shorts and casual hip-shot pose, attracted a few horn blasts, a male shout of . . . what? Admiration? More like verbalized testosterone.

"Why me?"

"So we can talk more freely."

That seemed to pique Gina's interest. She shifted her weight to the other slim, tanned leg.

"I wanted to talk to you about Carl Dudman's death," Nell said.

"My family's already talked about that. I'd think you'd be more interested in that rap star getting killed."

"No, it's Dudman I'm interested in. And I want to know how you feel."

Gina shrugged. "I'm glad he's dead. He was the person most responsible for Bradley Aimes walking out of the courtroom a free man even though he murdered my sister. It isn't any secret. We've told the police and the media as much."

"Do you see the Justice Killer as some kind of hero?"

"I wouldn't say that." Gina frowned and gnawed on her lower lip. "I would admit I'm grateful for what he did."

"Do you know a man named Terry Adams?"

"Not that I can recall."

"Did Genelle ever mention him?"

This time Gina thought a long while before answering. "If she did, I don't remember. It's possible that she knew him, whoever he is. We didn't have all the same friends."

"But would it be safe to say most of your friends knew both you and Genelle?"

"Most, yes." Gina cupped her waist with her hands and began jogging in place, causing some bouncing action beneath the baggy sweatshirt. "Whoo! Whoo!" yelled a guy from a passing car.

"What's this all about?" Gina asked, ignoring her motorized admirer. "You suspect this Terry guy?"

"No," Nell said, maybe too quickly, judging by the way Gina was staring at her. "We just want to make sure there was no connection between him and Genelle. Or between him and you, for that matter."

"I'm sure I don't know him, and I don't think Genelle did. But we can never be sure about Genelle. The only thing I know about her for sure is that I miss her. You know how people say they become sad because after a while they can't recall precisely what the people they grieve looked like?"

Nell didn't know, but she nodded.

"That doesn't happen with me and Gina. I see her complete every day in the mirror." Gina glanced up at the sky, then back down, her Adam's apple working. "That's about all I can tell you."

"I guess it is," Nell said. She smiled. "Thanks, Gina. Say hello to your mom and dad."

"Sure," Gina said. She returned the smile and jogged away toward her apartment building half a block down. She drew more admiring looks, a pretty girl catching the sunlight, hair flouncing with each stride. The young in New York. Nell knew they weren't as enviable as they appeared. Gina, who certainly had her problems, was an example.

Nell stood and watched her until she started up the steps to her building entrance, thinking about what had died along with Gina's sister. Thinking about the Justice Killer, how he was killing victims, and killing her trust in Terry. Evil really was like a rock thrown in a pond; the ripples eventually reached every part of it.

Well, she refused to let the ripples destroy her trust. Apparently there'd been no connection between Gina or Genelle and Terry. So there was a crime, Genelle's murder, that he had no alibi for, and it might as well have happened in another galaxy. Absence of alibi didn't mean likelihood of guilt.

Suspicion could eat like acid. Like guilt itself. The best way to face it was head on. Find out. Shine the truth on it.

Nell felt better after talking with Gina.

Gina felt better after talking with Nell.

She entered the lobby of her apartment building, stood hands on hips and let her breathing even out, then pushed the up button for the elevator. While she waited, she thought back on her conversation with Nell.

The detective didn't seem to consider that Gina or her mother or father might have murdered Dudman, a copycat crime.

If Gina *had* gone beyond simply stalking Dudman as a kind of cathartic exercise, and actually used her gun, she might well have gotten away with it. After all, Dudman had simply been shot from a passing car. The police had nothing to go on. Gina had read that the most difficult crimes to solve were the simple ones. Criminals tended to outsmart themselves.

The elevator arrived. Mrs. Grubman, from the apartment above the Dixon's, appeared when the door slid open. She smiled and nodded to Gina. She had her feisty and odorous little dog Worry on a leash. Gina nodded back and stood aside, giving Worry plenty of room to get past. The animal had a habit of snapping at people.

After suffering only a growl, Gina entered the elevator and pressed the button for her floor. She leaned back with her eyes closed. As the elevator ascended, she enjoyed the sensation; when she was younger she used to think she might rise all the way to heaven. Today she thought the elevator smelled like dog.

Nell, the detective, had for some reason been interested in the Carl Dudman murder, rather than the more recent murder of Cold Cat the rap star. Gina was more interested in Cold Cat's sudden and violent death, and not only because it screamed daily from every news source, along with that idiot woman's campaign to stop conducting trials. What interested Gina was that Cold Cat, Richard Simms, hadn't been a member of a jury, or any other part of the judicial system. He'd been the defendant.

It wasn't credible to Gina that the little man, Knee High, had killed Cold Cat's wife. Or if he had, it was a scheme of some kind and the husband was involved. The husband was always involved. Cold Cat had been the guilty defendant who'd gone free. Simms was the first of such monsters to be murdered by the Justice Killer. The police must be trying hard to figure out what that might mean.

Gina knew one thing it meant. Richard Simms's murder signaled open season on Bradley Aimes.

The elevator stopped, bobbed slightly to adjust itself, then dinged, and the door glided open.

Gina had reached her destination.

Homicide.
Murder.

Was there any difference now between him and the vicious killers the police hunted down and killed or placed in the hands of the bumbling, bureaucratic, and sometimes even kindly judicial system?

Not enough difference.

Not anymore.

Not after the murder of Richard Simms, an innocent man.

The scales of justice seemed wildly out of kilter, and the sureness and clarity they offered no longer applied. Suddenly nothing seemed concrete and certain. Nothing offered support or reason. Change could occur instantly, and not for the better.

It was unsettling.

The Justice Killer had been getting headaches lately, and right now he had a brutal one. A migraine?

He'd heard the term but really didn't know what it meant. If it didn't mean what he had, it should. He might as well have an axe buried in his skull.

Deep.

A guilt headache. That was how he actually thought of the pain behind his eyes.

But did he deserve it?

Was he a murderer?

He'd been afraid to go to a doctor; the fewer medical records—or any kind of records—he created, the better for him and more problematic for his pursuers. So he was limited to over-the-counter pain remedies and switched from brand to brand.

None of them seemed to help. He lay suffering in his bed and continued to ponder the question of his guilt.

A murderer?

No, not yet, he finally assured himself, a cold washcloth pressed to his forehead and covering his eyes. He was still an executioner. A force for justice. In a larger sense, genuine crime, genuine guilt, even murder, was in the intent, and his intent had been pure.

He'd been tricked into executing Richard Simms. The real killer had been sitting right in the courtroom during Simms's trial, had even been one of the key witnesses. That Knee High creature. The jurors hadn't taken him seriously enough to think he might be lying, deceiving, committing perjury.

But the little man with the big lie was being taken seriously enough now, by the police, by the system.

By the Justice Killer.

Whose headache raged like a fire behind his eyes.

58

When Beam entered da Vinci's office, he found the deputy chief seated behind his desk, watching a DVD recording of the latest Free Adelaide demonstration on his new TV. The blinds were half open this morning, admitting bright sunlight over a narrow area. Dust motes played everywhere, threatening to make Beam sneeze. The television's screen was a little difficult to see unless you found the right angle.

This demonstration had tied up traffic in Times Square for over two hours. The volume was barely audible on the TV. There was no sound in the office that wasn't muted almost to nonexistence. A faint, acrid odor hung in the still air, like that of burning electrical insulation, as if the subject matter being shown were too hot for the television perched on top of the file cabinet.

Da Vinci glanced over at Beam. "Isn't this a crock?" He motioned with his head toward the television.

"Crock and a half," Beam said. "Console yourself with the fact that Adelaide doesn't have TV in her cell."

"She knows what goes on," da Vinci said. "That lawyer-manager of hers, press agent—whatever the hell he is—tells her." He pointed at the TV, muted mayhem on a small screen.

"Look at the *Free Adelaide* signs! I count over a dozen. Free her to do what? I hear she's already got a schedule of talk show appearances lined up, and a goddamned book contract. She's writing the opening chapters in her cell."

"Industrious," Beam said, "but she never struck me as the writer type."

"Got some uppity little editor who visits and tells her the difference between who and whom," da Vinci said in disgust. "Or is it *whom* comes to visit her?"

"I'm not sure," Beam said. "We could ask Adelaide."

Da Vinci scowled and threw a paper clip at him. "I got more DVDs," he said. "You should see the one of the Cold Cat memorial service held in Riverside Park last night."

"It features some of the same faces that are in the Adelaide demonstrations, I'll bet."

"Yeah, but made saintly by candlelight. And maybe one of them is the Justice Killer. Helen said he might be compelled to attend some of these mob scenes. After all, he caused them."

"Like a pyromaniac hangs around the fire he's set," Beam said.

"Exactly. That's what Helen said."

Beam wondered about da Vinci's relationship with Helen. He was single, but still, an affair with a police profiler could squelch his NYPD career. Something like it had happened in recent memory.

"This shit has got to be stopped," da Vinci said, "before the Justice Killer's a bigger hero than Superman, leaving you, me, and the rest of the NYPD about as popular as kryptonite." He used the remote to switch off the DVD, then the TV. Tiny green lights dimmed, as did the TV screen. Hot plastic popped faintly, and the acrid scent in the office seemed to lessen. Da Vinci looked hard at Beam. "So you're the idea man, the cop who's supposed to be able to think like the killer. What's he thinking now, besides how much fun he's having at various demonstrations that make us look like monkeys and tie up traffic?"

"He's thinking about Knee High," Beam said.

Da Vinci began running his fingertips lightly over the motorcycle sculpture on his desk, as if the feel of cool metal reassured him. "Say again?"

"Cold Cat's death and the news of his innocence mean Melanie Taylor is probably no longer in danger."

"One victim for each trial."

"You noticed."

"Yes, but what's it got to do with Knee High?"

"I think the Justice Killer's been thrown badly off his game by killing Cold Cat, an innocent man. That makes him no better—even a damned sight worse—than the people he's been going around despising and murdering. The person to blame for that is the defense's main witness, who lied on the stand and provided a false alibi—Knee High."

"Not to mention," da Vinci said, "Knee High going out and recruiting another witness to perjure himself and back up that lie."

Beam was surprised. "Knee High recruited Merv Clark?"

"That's what they're both saying now. But we know how credible they are. It's a good thing for Knee High he's safe in jail awaiting arraignment."

"Spring him," Beam said.

Da Vinci stopped caressing his motorcycle and stared at him. "You serious?"

"Yeah.

Reduce his bond and let him walk. He'll need the police to protect him from the Justice Killer, so he'll be even more cooperative. More credible."

Da Vinci went into his chin-rubbing routine, thinking hard. "What if Knee High cuts and runs?"

"He won't. Too many cops will be protecting him for somebody not to notice him leaving. And where's he gonna go where Cold Cat's fans won't tear him apart, even if the Justice Killer doesn't find him?"

"You're right," da Vinci said. "And after a few days, he'd feel awfully naked without that police protection." He leaned back in his chair so he was looking up quizzically at Beam. "So we get Knee High back out in the world, then what's our next move?"

"We let it leak that we made a mistake. It's been decided he's too likely a flight possibility, and his bond reduction's going to be rescinded. Knee High will soon be going back to jail to await trial."

"We change our minds? Just like that?"

"Uh-huh. We say so, anyway."

"Which accomplishes?"

"The Justice Killer will know that if he wants to kill Knee High, the clock is ticking. His opportunity is limited to the time until Knee High's taken back into custody."

Da Vinci rubbed his chin a while longer, then smiled. "A rattrap with a timer, and Knee High will be the very nervous cheese."

"Run it by Helen and see what she thinks of the idea," Beam suggested.

Da Vinci reacted as Beam thought he would. "I don't have to run it by anyone. You're the one I put in charge of the investigation, and you ran it by me. I like it. We'll do it. But keep in mind, it's your ass if it goes wrong."

"Always," Beam said.

Da Vinci seemed mollified. He sat back and appeared to be more relaxed. "You're an even more devious bastard than I thought."

"Thanks."

"I'll run it by Helen anyway."

"I don't look outside without seeing a cop," Nola told Beam that afternoon in Things Past. The shop seemed brighter than usual. The display window had been washed, and the stock was less layered with dust and more neatly arranged. Beam could actually walk along the aisles without brushing something a hundred years old and sending it plummeting to the floor.

He glanced out beyond the display of antiques, through the window and across the street. "I don't see anyone out there now."

Nola looked exasperated, for her. "Of course not. There's a cop in here with me."

"Are you sorry about that?"

She leaned forward and kissed him on the chin. "Not really." She walked around behind the counter and began sorting through some papers. It occurred to him for the first time that she didn't need glasses for reading. He was pretty sure she didn't have contact lenses.

Aging well . . .

Despite her initial reticence, once they'd become lovers, her sexuality amazed him. Made him amaze himself.

"Ever think about sex in the back room?" he asked.

"These days, I think about sex now and then whichever room I'm in."

Beam grinned.

Nola tapped the edges of whatever it was she was sorting through and laid the neatened papers aside. "This is a place of business," she said. "Besides, we're both a little old for the kind of thing you have in mind."

"You're only as old as—"

"—you are," she finished for him. "Any progress in tracing where the duplicate ring came from?"

"Not yet." He didn't tell her that NYPD personnel had already been diverted from the task of finding the ring's origin to protecting the soon-to-be-released Knee High. The ring itself wasn't in its usual spot on a shelf next to a rose-colored vase. "Did you put the ring in your safe?"

"In a drawer. I'm hoping somebody will steal it."

"You should give it to me. It might become evidence."

She moved to the far end of the counter, reached down and opened an out-of-sight drawer, and tossed him the ring.

Beam caught it and stuck it in his pocket. "Do you want a receipt?"

"You're my receipt." Nola looked at him in a way that made him uncomfortable. "When this business with the ring, the Justice Killer, is over, Beam . . ."

"What?"

"I guess that's what I'm asking."

"I haven't gotten that far yet," Beam said honestly. "I'd like to think it's happily ever after for us."

"Such bullshit, Beam."

"Well, maybe tolerably ever after."

Nola smiled. "That's more like it."

The bell above the door tinkled, and a short, middle-aged woman in jeans and a T-shirt lettered NO FEAR entered the shop. She gave Beam and Nola a blue stare through rimless glasses and smiled. Beam pretended to be interested in a shelf lined with cut-glass vases that all looked pretty much alike.

Nola asked the woman if she was looking for anything in particular and the woman said she was just browsing. Which she did for about five minutes before buying a beat-to-hell looking antique doll and leaving.

Beam had heard the conversation before the sale. "She really pay two hundred dollars for that?" he asked.

Nola nodded. "It's nineteenth century, and it's eyes close when you lay it on its back. It's worth three hundred."

"What did you pay for it?"

"Ten."

Beam glanced around the shop. "Maybe there's more to this antique business than I thought."

"Oh, there is," Nola said. She walked over and turned the deadbolt on the door, then put up the Closed sign.

"Lunch time?" Beam asked.

"Already had lunch."

"Back room?"

"Let's go see."

"He's coming undone," the police profiler, Helen, was saying in a television interview done outside One Police Plaza. "He's finding more and more pleasure in his murders, and more and more hell."

"He's conflicted?" asked the interviewer, a man six inches shorter than the statuesque Helen.

"I thought I made that clear," Helen said. "Inner conflict is what started his string of increasingly brutal murders, and inner conflict will destroy him. That's the way it works with serial killers. The process is already well underway. It's like acid produced by the soul it's destroying."

"That's very poetic."

Helen smiled grimly. "I guess it is. What it means is that the killer's thought process is breaking down. It will eventually lead to his arrest or suicide."

"He'll get careless?"

"He'll take larger and larger risks," Helen said. "He won't be able to stop himself."

"You're saying he's going mad?"

"Oh, he's already quite mad."

The taped interview with the police profiler was too much to bear. The Justice Killer felt like throwing the remote at the TV. Instead he merely switched channels.

And there was another interview. This time with the intrepid Beam, saying something about Knee High.

Justice listened, turning up the volume.

A few minutes later he sat back, shaking his head.

Released on his own recognizance!

Goddamned judges!

A commercial came on the cable news channel he was watching. A duck, or some other kind of fowl, talking about term insurance. He used the remote to switch to another channel.

There was a photograph of Knee High, a mug shot taken shortly after his arrest. The hash marks and numerals behind him indicated he was five-foot one with his hair combed almost straight up. He wore a cocky, nervous smile, as if made apprehensive yet enjoying his notoriety.

"—released this afternoon," the newscaster was saying. He was a full-faced man in a gray suit with some kind of pin on the lapel. "The court ruled that it didn't consider the accused a risk to do public harm or to flee. He is *not* required to wear an electronic anklet." The anchorman turned to a guest. "Now, if Martha Stewart—"

Justice switched to another twenty-four-hour news channel. A female anchor with teased red hair was sharing a split screen with the same mug shot of Knee High. They were both smiling.

Why *was* Knee High smiling minutes after being booked? Advice of counsel? Was he already working toward an insanity plea?

Or perhaps the relief of confession had prompted Knee High's smile when the mug shot camera had captured his image. Or maybe even then Knee High had understood that not everything was lost. Like so many others before him, he could use the system to his advantage.

Justice full well knew how firmly fate was on his side, how Knee High was being delivered to him. Fate would side with the avenging angel of justice, the divinity of death. Because of Knee High, the Justice Killer had slain an innocent man. That was the very antithesis of what Justice was trying to do. It could undermine his mission.

"Oh, he's already quite mad."

What Knee High had done was an abomination. Justice

could not let the matter stand, and he would not. That wasn't madness; it was making a madness right.

The police would strive to protect Knee High, but even with the tightest security there would be lapses, vulnerable moments. Time would pass without incident, and even Knee High might consider himself in danger only from the usual justice delayed.

Delayed forever.

Not this time, little man. Justice hastened, Justice served, Justice pleasured.

Sooner or later, by breath, blade, or bullet, you belong, to me.

59

"This isn't the usual thing," Beam said, when Knee High approached him for their meeting in Grand Central Station.

The little man had phoned Beam personally and requested that they speak, and had chosen the place. The shuffling of hundreds of soles and heels was a constant echoing whisper, as if there were secrets in the stone and marble vastness.

"Knee High be short," Knee High said. He moved over toward a wall where they'd be more or less separated from the throngs of train passengers and tourists. "This the most public place in New York, lotsa people all the time. Hard for anyone to follow Knee High, 'cause he get in amongst the masses and everybody be taller, shield him from prying eyes."

"That makes sense," Beam said. "But what I meant is, it's unusual that a murder suspect who's out of jail would phone a police detective so they can meet someplace and he can complain about being free."

Knee High looked astounded. "Free? You call this free? Knee High got cops comin' out his ass, mornin' till night."

"All night, too," Beam said. "That's because they've been assigned to protect you."

"Protect Knee High, shit. What they're hanging around for is a shot at the Justice Killer. You think Knee High don't know how you guys set up Knee High? Knee High ain't no fool. Weren't born yesterday, nor at night, neither."

Beam wished Knee High weren't one of those people who habitually referred to themselves in the third person. It gave the impression there might be another Knee High here.

"You *want* that Justice Killer mother come after Knee High," said Knee High. "You tell Knee High that ain't the truth."

Beam felt no pity. "Whatever position you're in, you put yourself there," he said.

"*Po*-sition? Knee High's *po*-sition is bent over, tha's what."

"Why did you want to talk to me about it?"

"Knee High wanna be arrested. Then he want you to tell the media in this town, so the Justice mother know and won't be tryin' to shoot Knee High."

"I can't arrest you," Beam said. "The law doesn't work that way. You could sue me."

"Knee High don't sue people. Way the law works, it's s'pose to protect the citizens. Knee High a citizen."

"Edie Piaf was a citizen until you killed her."

"So why don't you arrest Knee High?" He held his hands out, wrists together, as if waiting to be cuffed. "C'mon, do your job an' put Knee High back where that Justice mother can't get to him."

"I can't do that unless there's a warrant out for you. You'll need to speak to a judge."

"Yeah. Knee High do that next time we be lunchin' at Four Seasons. Uh-huh. You see that?"

"See what?"

"That big guy in camouflage fatigues, carryin' an automatic rifle."

Beam peered across the teeming marble vastness to where Knee High was pointing. "He's in the military," Beam said, "part of Homeland Security. They're stationed throughout Grand Central."

"How you know what he is? What Knee High see's a man with a machine gun, might wanna shoot Knee High dead. You know tha's what he *ain't?* Anybody can go rent hisself a soldier suit, get hold of a gun, go walkin' 'round Grand Central, blast the damn eyeballs outta Knee High 'fore you can stop him."

Beam knew Knee High had a point, but he wasn't about to concede it. "I think Knee High's got a case of the nerves."

Knee High extended a stubby little leg and kicked the marble wall. Had to hurt his toes. "*Nerves?* Those cops you say s'pose to be protectin' Knee High—you know what their code name be for Knee High?"

"No."

"They call Knee High 'the cheese,' what they say to each other. Damn cop code."

"That wasn't my idea," Beam said, thinking da Vinci must have mentioned the cheese-in-rattrap analogy when assigning NYPD personnel to their tasks.

"Whoever's idea it be, Knee High don't like it even a little. What he wants is for you to use your considerable *in*-fluence and get Knee High back safe behind walls."

"Well, I guess that makes a certain kind of sense."

Knee High gave Beam a suspicious look. The cheese, Beam thought, wasn't very smart.

"And you'd like the media informed, so the Justice Killer will know you won't be available for . . . justice," Beam said.

"That be good. Knee High don't like bein' on that Justice mother's mind."

"Okay. I think I can get it done."

Knee High backed up a step. "Say what?"

"I'll see to it you get your wish: jail, and an informed news media." *Though not necessarily in that order.*

"Minute ago you be sayin' it was impossible."

Beam shrugged. "Things change."

Knee High was obviously amazed. What he'd considered a futile, desperate effort was about to bear fruit. "You shittin' Knee High?"

"Not in the slightest."

"Knee High be safe then." His relief was obvious.

"Knee High be safe then," Beam confirmed.

But not until then.

Nell awoke to Terry kissing her bare breasts. She smiled and pulled him to her, cradling his head with both arms, and felt his tongue explore her right nipple.

They were in Nell's bedroom, after late-night drinks, then a midnight tumble in her bed.

It was certainly bright in the bedroom. She noticed the clock—almost eight thirty—and was alarmed for a moment about being late for work. Then she relaxed, remembering the team had agreed to sleep in this morning after working late last night. Except for Beam, who had an early meeting at Grand Central with Knee High.

This might work out well.

"I happen to have some spare time this morning," she told Terry.

He answered unintelligibly, then kissed her left nipple, the hollow between her breasts, her stomach, lower.

And raised his head, then sat up.

"Something?" Nell asked.

"Yeah. 'Fraid I've got an early appointment. He smiled down at her. "Not that I wouldn't rather stay here for a while. It's been over eight hours since we've had sex."

"I don't like that to happen," Nell said, and gripped his arm to try pulling him back down on her.

Easily breaking her grasp, Terry stood up. "I really do

have to run. There's a restaurant over on Amsterdam that needs its fridge looked at before things go bad."

"I called you for days before you came over here to repair the air conditioner," Nell said. "Now you're mine for a while."

"More than awhile," Terry said. "But this morning I've gotta hurry, really. I promised. And you know me and promises."

"Do I ever."

She watched the athletic litheness of his muscular body as he moved toward the bathroom to shower. Nell loved to watch Terry walk. There was something catlike about him, as if he were unconsciously luxuriating in simple motion.

He was in the shower less than five minutes, then quickly dressed in short-sleeved shirt, Levi's, and jogging shoes.

"Gotta go by my place and pick up my tools," he said, then walked over to the bed, kissed her, and was gone, leaving behind his smile, a scent of soap, and a few drops of water from his wet hair on her pillow.

Here, then gone.

Men.

Nell lay in bed and closed her eyes, listening to the tick of the rotating ceiling fan. She moved her fingertips lightly over her nipples, then across her bare stomach. With a sigh, she rolled onto her side and found herself staring at the phone.

Alone in the silence, alone in her desire, she decided without really thinking about it to call Jack Selig.

He'd be glad to talk with her even if she woke him from a sound sleep. Jack would be up for phone sex, if she suggested it to him. Nell knew that despite his dominating personality, she could dominate him with his love for her. The thought was an aphrodisiac.

But what she got was Selig's machine, telling her to leave a message and he'd get back to her as soon as he returned home.

Nell didn't feel like leaving a message. Not now.

She replaced the receiver and fell back on the bed.

The hell with both of them, she thought, then set the alarm to sound in half an hour and went back to sleep.

60

"Cops everywhere," Knee High muttered to himself.

He was out on his balcony, thirty-five stories above the street, and could barely make out the blue uniformed figures; might not have noticed them at all, except by now he knew where to look. He knew there were also plainclothes cops down there, and undercovers in the building. Asshole detective Beam wasn't kidding when he said the law would be where Knee High was, but Knee High knew they were more interested in capturing who shot Knee High than in protecting Knee High.

He wished the wheels of bureaucracy would turn faster and he could be safe in jail. Damn paper pushers took forever to do everything.

His skin began to crawl. He didn't like being out on the balcony more than a few seconds, but he had to come out now and then so he could actually *see some* of his protectors—so-called, anyway—and know for a fact they were on duty. There was no denying the Justice mother psycho was coming after Knee High, and Knee High had a better chance of survival with the cops than without.

Justice mother might be sighting in on Knee High right now with a rifle, so Knee High hurried back inside and pulled the sliding glass door shut, then closed the drape.

Maybe he oughta call Beam, see if he could use his pull to hurry things along. Clerks and various ass kissers, even judges, take it seriously when a bad mother like Beam puts the eye on 'em and makes a suggestion.

But he'd already called Beam several times, and Beam either gave him a line of bullshit or didn't call back. Seemed nobody gave a shit about Knee High.

The apartment was cool and shaded by thick drapes, sparsely furnished except for black box speakers larger than most of the furniture. Alongside the door was the only wall hanging, a five-by-five blow up of Cold Cat, photographed from behind, performing at a jammed concert, people on their feet, yelling, Knee High down in the right-hand corner, waving his arms and urging them on. Knee High couldn't look at the poster without getting pissed at Edie Piaf.

Part of a kitchen was visible through a pass-through, white cabinets, refrigerator, a corner of a stove. On the pass-through's shelf sat several white foam takeout containers and some empty beer cans. Similar containers were stacked on a low coffee table with more empty cans. There were more containers and cans on the floor. Knee High hadn't left the apartment for days, and had all his food delivered from the Great Wall Restaurant over in the next block. Egg foo yung, usually beef, sometimes chicken or pork for variety, made up almost all of Knee High's diet. Sometimes he wished he had some cold or room-temperature pizza for breakfast, but for lunch or dinner he never chose it over egg foo yung. Knee High considered ordering a pizza this evening to go along with his regular order and not eating it, just putting it up someplace so he could have it cold tomorrow morning.

He looked at his watch, a TAG Heuer given to him a few years ago by Cold Cat. Food should be here soon. He'd phoned the order in twenty minutes ago. The restaurant always used the same delivery guy, Hispanic dude with tattoos all over him. The cops would recognize him and not get excited. Delivery guy didn't like all the cops around at first, maybe thinking they'd ask for his green card or something. But it wasn't him the cops were interested in, so by now he'd relaxed and enjoyed the fact that Knee High tipped tall.

"Notice the cops on your way up here?" Knee High would always ask him.

"Was nothing but," the guy would always answer with a smile. It made Knee High feel better, knowing his new friends in blue were present in such numbers.

Delivery guy would hand over the takeout, and Knee High would give him three ten-dollar bills even though the check was always for eighteen dollars. Guy would always tell him *gracias* and give him a big smile. Knee High would smile back, just for the human contact. He was a people person, had always loved being around people.

In anticipation, he pulled his wallet from his back pocket and got out three tens, slipped them folded over in his shirt pocket so he'd be ready for the delivery guy. Returned wallet to pocket.

His heart was hammering and he stood still, breathing deeply. This was getting to him, knowing the Justice mother was out there wanting to kill him. True, he had security, NYPD style, but security could only go so far. That Dudman guy, he'd had professional bodyguards, and Justice still got to him, shot him dead as John Lennon.

Dead as Cold Cat.

That whole thing was Edie's fault. Nobody should ever trust that kind of bitch. Knee High knew now, when it was too late, that he'd made a horrible mistake. But *damn!* she was fine-looking that day she'd come to him and lifted her blouse, gave him a wide smile, and asked if he'd help her with the clasp on her brassiere. When she'd turned around, he saw her brassiere was fastened and told her so. She said she wanted him to help her *un*fasten it, then leaned back against him and kind of rubbed herself against him, rotating that tight little rump.

That had been it for Knee High. *Whew!* Woman like that . . .

The intercom buzzed, jolting Knee High out of his thoughts.

He went over and pressed the button, asked who was downstairs.

"Great Wall," came the answer. Not the doorman, or the cop who was pretending to be the doorman, but a familiar voice. Hispanic guy.

Knee High buzzed him into the building.

In less than half a minute there was a knock on the door. Egg foo yung on his mind, Knee High absently reached into his pocket for the three tens as he worked the dead bolt then jingle-jangled the chain lock with his free hand and opened the door.

"You fast tonight," he said.

And was shot between his widening eyes.

61

"Who found him?" Beam asked.

"Delivery man with takeout from a restaurant a block over," said the uniform who'd been first on the scene. He was a tall, thin man with a weathered face and the long fingers of a concert pianist. Beam had seen him around; his name was Alfonse something.

"That what's all over the hall floor?" Beam asked.

"Yes, sir. Chinese."

That explained the peculiar, pungent scent in the hall that Beam had noticed when he stepped out of the elevator.

That, the aftermath of gunfire, and what was left of the back of Knee High's head.

Beam had almost stepped on the food mess when he'd first approached the apartment's open door. His gaze had been fixed on Knee High lying on his back just beyond the doorway, staring up at the ceiling in something like wonderment at having obtained a third round, dark eye just above the bridge of his nose. On his very still chest lay a neatly cut out red cloth letter *J.*

The crime scene unit had arrived shortly before Beam and was crawling all over the apartment beyond the body.

The halls were quiet, guarded now by men and women in blue and made off limits except for tenants. On a small, ornate iron bench halfway to the elevators, next to a brass ashtray and a stalwart looking uniform standing with his arms crossed, sat a glum Hispanic man in his thirties. He had on jeans and a white shirt, worn down Nikes, and was wearing a white baseball cap lettered GW. His arms were heavily tattooed.

"Delivery man?" Beam asked Alfonse.

"Him. Says his name's Raymond Carerra."

Beam walked toward the man, who kept his head bowed and refused to acknowledge that anyone was approaching. Beam saw that the tattoos were mostly of snakes and flowers. "Raymond?"

Carerra nodded without looking up at him. Beam thought he appeared a little sick to his stomach. He showed Carerra his shield and introduced himself as police.

"I already told what happened," Carerra said, with a slight Spanish accent.

"You watch TV, Raymond. You know I need to hear it again."

"I did nothing but come here as usual and deliver Mr. Knee High's egg foo yung."

"From?"

"Great Wall. Place where I work just a block away. Mr. Knee High's regular order."

"That all he ever orders, egg foo yung?"

"Always, that's all. Because ours is very good."

Beam didn't know whether Raymond was being a smart ass, so he let it pass. He got out his notepad and pen. "So tell me how it went, Raymond."

"I came to deliver the food, got off the elevator, walked down the hall to that apartment, and that's what I found. The door was open, and Mr. Knee High was laying there like that. I was so surprised I dropped my take-out boxes, then I got scared. At first I thought I might be in trouble and figured maybe I should get out fast. Then I remembered I was sent here by the restaurant, and I knew there were cops all over the building, guarding Mr. Knee High. Where was I gonna go?"

Raymond looked at Beam as if he might actually answer his question. Beam shrugged.

"I decided I'd go back downstairs," Raymond said, "and find a cop, tell him what I saw, then come back up here with him."

"Who'd you find?"

"That man." Raymond pointed to Alfonse.

"Was the letter *J* already on Mr. Knee High's chest?"

"Yes. Everything was just as it is now. Exactly."

"There are some ten-dollar bills in his right hand."

"They were there, to pay for the egg foo yung and my tip. Always the same amount. Mr. Knee High was a big tipper."

"You call upstairs on the intercom before entering the main lobby?"

"Yes, sir. I said hello to the doorman, too. He told me go ahead and use the intercom instead of calling up himself and announcing me, like they sometimes do."

Beam was surprised. The doorman was actually an undercover cop.

"Ever seen the doorman before?"

"Sure. Last three nights. Never before that. I been delivering to this building for two years. Doormen here, they come and go. Lots of picky tenants, I guess."

So he was familiar to the cop-doorman, deemed safe.

Beam pointed toward the mess on the floor down the hall. "I see the egg foo yung that spilled on the carpet when you dropped the order, but what's in that other, smaller box that didn't open when it was dropped?

"That's Mr. Knee High's fortune cookie," Raymond said. "I guess maybe I should have delivered that first, by itself."

Beam decided Raymond was okay, a guy with a sense of humor poking through his apprehension. "Did you see any-

one else down in the lobby, somebody who might have overheard what you were doing here, where you were going?"

"There was nobody else in the lobby. And I didn't say
into the intercom where I was going, just that I was here
from Great Wall."

"Was anyone else in the elevator?"

"No."

"See anyone else in the halls?"

"No one. And I saw no one after I got in the elevator until
I saw Mr. Knee High . . . like he is."

Beam scribbled, then put away his notepad and clipped
his pen back in his pocket.

"You guys aren't gonna take me in, are you?" Raymond
asked.

"Maybe, just to make a statement. Recorded, signed, that
kind of thing. To make it official." *See if there are any con-
tradictions.*

"You mean I'm gonna have to tell my story again?"
Raymond asked.

"No doubt about it."

"You mind if I borrow your notes?"

Beam smiled. Raymond was tuned in, all right.

So simple, the Justice Killer thought, sitting in the back
of the cab speeding through the neon and sodium-lit night.
He'd simply waited for the inevitable food delivery from the
Chinese restaurant, and made his way to Knee High's apartment just ahead of the deliveryman. Knee High, hungry for
his supper but not his death, had eagerly opened the door
and received death.

Justice.

It had gone precisely as planned. The police profiler, who
kept telling lies about him on TV and in the newspapers, was
proved wrong again. Justice wasn't coming unraveled. He

wasn't increasingly burdened by the deaths he'd caused—the executions. Why should he be? He was simply setting right what the city let go so very wrong.

Those who'd died by his hand deserved death.

Except for Richard Simms. Cold Cat. Pathetic sociopath who thought he had talent.

Who didn't deserve to die young.

Damn it! The crime is in the intent! And the intent remains pure.

It's Beam and his fellow hunters who are coming unraveled, not me. Surely public opinion must be convincing them they're wrong and I'm right. Look at the polls. They have only to look at the polls. The people want the city to be a place of peace and order and justice. Justice. The people—
The cab struck a series of jolting potholes and for a moment was airborne, landing with a thud that caused the driver's sun visor to flip down and jarred the Justice Killer's teeth.

He'd bitten his tongue and almost slid off the worn-smooth back seat.

Christ! Whoever's responsible for patching these potholes deserves to be shot!

62

Beam noticed movement down the hall and saw three figures approaching. Nell, Looper, da Vinci.

"I caught these two hard at work," da Vinci said.

When they'd arrived at Knee High's address, Beam had instructed Nell and Looper to talk to the doorman or any of the other cops stationed in or around the building, and find out if they saw anything suspicious in the time frame of the shooting.

"We came up together in the elevator," da Vinci explained. Beam figured Knee High's death had to have hit him hard. And he wouldn't be feeling kindly toward Beam, who'd talked him into using Knee High as "the cheese." He looked quietly angry, and frustrated. His usual smooth, tanned complexion was mottled and flushed.

Nell started to speak, but da Vinci held up a hand to quiet her.

"I wanna take a look at this debacle before I hear more about it," he said.

He walked to the door, careful to avoid the spilled egg foo yung, and looked down at the body, then peered into the apartment where the crime scene unit was working.

"Take-out food?" he asked Beam.

Beam nodded. "Chinese. Neighborhood restaurant. Delivery guy's over there." He motioned with his head toward the patient and stricken Raymond, still seated on the bench. "He made his usual delivery to Knee High, only difference was, when he got here the door was open and Knee High was the way you see him."

"He the one raised the alarm?"

"Yeah. Name's Raymond Carerra. He went down in the elevator and alerted a uniform. Alfonse, over there."

"Good man, Alfonse," da Vinci said. Ignoring Nell and Looper, he looked piercingly at Beam. "This wasn't supposed to happen, not unless there were two bodies—Knee High's, and the Justice Killer's."

Beam didn't have an answer, or offer one.

"There's a god-awful smell in here," Looper said. "Anybody mind if I smoke a cigarette?"

"Everybody in this city minds," da Vinci said. "From the mayor on down."

Nell gave Looper a cautioning look, tempered by a slight smile.

"How do you figure all this?" da Vinci asked Beam, making a swinging motion with his arm to take in the entire crime scene.

"The killer somehow found out Knee High was going to get take-out delivery," Beam said, "and either beat the delivery here or was already in the building. He knew Knee High was expecting dinner and would open the door because of the call-up on the intercom—then pop. Killer got here to knock on Knee High's door before the deliveryman. Must've used a silencer. Nobody else on this floor, or above or below, heard a gunshot."

"Looks like he used a thirty-two," da Vinci said, glancing over at Knee High.

"Could be," Beam agreed. "Once he shot Knee High, the killer must have moved fast to get away before word of the shooting spread. Probably he was going down on one elevator while the deliveryman was coming up on the other. He'd have no more than a few minutes to get clear of the building."

"Or get back inside an apartment on this floor, or maybe even one of the other floors."

"We're covering that," Beam said. "I have uniforms making inquiries. I think it's more likely the killer's miles away from here by now. That's been the pattern."

"You're probably right," da Vinci said. He looked at Nell and Looper, who'd been standing quietly by, respecting rank. "Let's hear what Frick an' Frack have to say."

Beam hoped one or the other would have something. So far, Knee High's death was simply another clean job by the Justice Killer. That he'd managed to outsmart and elude so much security, what amounted to a police trap, would make the bastard that much more of a hero. Odd how the public rooted for the underdog, even if it was a jackal.

"The doorman was one of ours, undercover," Nell said. "He'd seen Raymond the deliveryman here before, had checked him out, and knew he was genuine, so he told him to use the intercom and go on up with the take-out order."

"At this point the killer must've already been in the building," da Vinci said. "On his way to do Knee High."

"Question is," Beam said, "how did he know Knee High had a delivery coming?"

"Maybe found out at the restaurant," da Vinci said. "He knew Knee High got take-out from there, so he hung around the place till he heard a delivery was on the way. Got himself in gear and left the restaurant before Raymond."

"Except that no one entered the building for ten minutes or so before Raymond got here with the food," Looper said.

"Doorman tell you that?"

"Yeah. Our guy and the other one."

"Other one?" Beam asked.

"Working at the building across the street. Name's, believe it or not, Dorchester. He saw Raymond enter the building. Then he saw a uniformed cop leaving the building just after the time Knee High got shot."

Beam felt a twinge of uneasiness.

A homicide investigation goes where it goes.

"This Dorchester's a sharp guy," Looper continued. "He said he'd gotten used to seeing all the cops on the block the last several days and nights. He wouldn't have thought much of this cop, except at the time he was leaving, most of the other cops he saw were entering the building. Dorchester said cops were flooding in."

"That would've been right after Raymond raised the alarm," da Vinci said.

Beam looked at Looper. "You mean this cop stuck in Dorchester's mind just because he was leaving while other cops were going in?"

"No, something else. He said this cop wasn't dressed quite like the others. He couldn't put his finger on it at first, then he figured it out. It's a hot night, and the cop he saw was the only one wearing a jacket with his uniform, a kind of baggy blue or black jacket."

"One large enough to conceal a gun with a silencer," da Vinci said.

"Something else Dorchester said was the cop's uniform cap was a little different. He couldn't say why—like it didn't quite fit him right, maybe, was all I could get out of him."

"But he saw a uniformed cop?" da Vinci asked.

"Definitely," Looper said. "No doubt in Dorchester's mind about that."

"He mention this cop's description beyond the uniform?"

"Yes, sir. Average size, average weight."

Da Vinci snorted in disappointment, as if most killers were giants or midgets and they'd caught a bad break.

"That's it?" Beam asked.

"'Fraid so, sir."

"Sounds like the cop's uniform was a costume," Nell said.

"I sure as hell hope so," da Vinci said. He looked at Knee High's body, Knee High with a neat .32 caliber-size hole in his head, and shook his own head in frustration. "This psycho's so smooth at what he does, we never seem to get any kind of traction."

"I wouldn't say that," Beam told him. "We know how the Justice Killer managed to sidestep security to get to Knee High, and how he might have blended in to make his getaway. And maybe he also dressed as a cop to get to Cold Cat or some of the others."

"It's possible," da Vinci said. "But we've got just one eyeball account from across the street. We're not even sure he dressed as a cop at all."

"It's something, though," Beam said. "We'll canvass costume and used clothing stores in the city, find out who sold or rented a cop uniform during the last several months."

"What if he's a real cop?" Nell asked.

"We'll run through the costume and rental shops before going down that road," Beam said.

"She's right, though," da Vinci said. "It's a friggin' appalling possibility, but the Justice Killer might actually *be* a cop. We have to admit it makes a certain kind of sense. There's plenty of resentment in the department about the revolving-door nature of the city's judicial system."

"Ask Helen if she can think of a serial killer who was also a cop," Beam suggested.

"Point taken," da Vinci said.

Nell thought, *Ask Helen if there's ever a first time for everything.*

63

"He wants more than ever to be caught," Helen said.

She was standing near the photo of a discredited former police commissioner who'd displayed no such compulsion. But then, he hadn't been a mass murderer. Something of a hero, in fact. Justice did have a way of catching up with the most wily.

They were in da Vinci's office. It was too warm, and there was an unpleasant hint of stale sweat and desperation in the air, the kind of atmosphere Beam usually associated with interrogation rooms. Da Vinci was seated behind his desk. Beam and Nell were in the padded chairs angled toward the desk, Looper was standing near Helen, playing with the button on his shirt pocket that might have held a pack of cigarettes.

"You told us last week he was coming unraveled," da Vinci said to Helen, "yet he managed to outsmart us and get to Knee High."

"God rest his little soul," Nell said sarcastically.

Da Vinci glared at her. "Not friggin' funny, Nell."

Nell nodded. Da Vinci was right, even though he was the boss.

"He'll have to kill again soon," Helen said. "He's hooked on it. He'll need it more and more often."

Da Vinci wiped his face with an invisible rag and looked pained. "Coming undone, hooked on killing, feeling the pressure. You've been pretty much right all the way down the line, Helen, but that's not the picture I'm getting of this guy. He kills only those he considers to be the bad guys, who for one reason or another beat the system, or helped someone beat it."

"There's an endless supply of those," Beam pointed out.

"He can kill as often or seldom as he chooses," Helen said. "And he no longer feels he's simply meting out justice. Whether he knows it consciously or not, he kills to avenge imagined wrongs, but he also kills for pleasure."

"Sexual pleasure," Looper said. "Like all the rest of his kind."

"Uh-huh," Helen said. "It's a turn on for him, and he's reached the point where he has to admit it to himself."

"What we need from you," Beam told her, "is a good guess at who might be the next victim."

Helen looked thoughtful, crossing her arms beneath her tiny, tall-woman's breasts and staring at the floor. "The more unraveled our guy becomes, the more difficult it is to predict his next intended victim. Self-revelation can be an agonizing, ongoing event. He's in the stage where his own perverted logic is seriously breaking down as he's developing a different, undeniable concept of himself. One he doesn't like. That's why he might make a mistake."

"Do you figure him to go after a high-profile victim?" Looper asked.

"Could be," Helen said. "He thinks he has an adoring public to play to."

"He does," da Vinci said. "Read the editorial page in this morning's *Times*. Fifty-six percent of their readers view the Justice Killer as a hero. Seventy percent want Adelaide Starr released."

"Do they want more courts, better staffed, and with more judges?" Beam asked.

"Wasn't in the poll."

"What did they think of the NYPD?"

"Don't ask."

"It's a thankless job," Looper said.

Everyone stared at him.

"I wish I had a cigarette," he said.

"Another thing that's coming up empty," da Vinci said, "is trying to trace that cop costume."

"It's only been four days," Beam said. "We've covered most of the costume rental shops. Now we're checking S&M suppliers."

"Huh?"

"Sado-masochism," Looper explained, still playing with his pocket.

"Cop uniforms are sometimes used in . . . sexual psycho-dramas," Nell said.

Da Vinci stared at her. "How would you know this shit, Nell?"

"I read."

"We all read," Looper said.

Nell shot him a look. *Thanks.*

"The other possibility," Helen said, "is that the uniform's genuine, and the Justice Killer is a cop."

"Just what every cop on the force dreads," Beam said. He turned to Helen. "A bent cop? Does it fit your theory?"

"It could. Lots of frustration goes with the job."

"Tell me about it," Looper said.

"The revolving door of crime and courtroom," da Vinci said. "Sometimes it makes me wanna kill somebody myself, but I can't see a real cop doing this."

"It isn't likely," Beam said, "but eventually we might have to focus on the possibility."

"Hell to pay in the department," da Vinci said.

"Other things might turn up in that kind of internal investigation, derail a lot of promising careers."

"We've both seen it happen," da Vinci said. He sat forward in his chair. "But we're not to that stage yet, and we're gonna nail this Justice Killer prick before we start pointing fingers at each other. When that kinda thing starts happening, nobody wins."

"Adelaide Starr does," Helen said.

Da Vinci clutched his throat as if he might be having trouble breathing. "Stay on the costume thing," he said to Beam in a choked voice. "Make it a goddamned costume and not a real police uniform."

"We've still got plenty of places to check," Looper said.

Da Vinci nodded. "Yeah, I know. S&M suppliers."

Nell said. "There's another possibility." She found herself actually feeling sorry for da Vinci, who'd staked his career on this investigation. He was looking at her like a dog that had just been whipped and then offered a treat.

"There is?"

"Theatrical suppliers," Nell said.

Da Vinci had been expecting more. He slumped back in his chair, uncheered by Nell's note of hope.

"That it?" Beam asked da Vinci, wanting to get to work.

"It," da Vinci said. Under his breath, he muttered, "Theatrical suppliers . . ."

As they were filing out of his office, he added, "Break a leg."

"Those the only cop costumes?" Nell asked.

The man behind the counter in Ruff Play, in the East Village, said, "The ones for women come with high-heeled boots."

"Sure," Nell said. "I used to wear six-inch heels when I was in uniform."

"Now there's something to contemplate." He smiled at her. He'd said his name was "Erbal," like in the garden.

"Spelled with an aitch?" Nell had asked.

"Exactly, but pronounced the old-fashioned way."

He was in his thirties, about six feet tall but terribly thin. Even features, sharply defined cheekbones, dark chin stubble trying to be a goatee. Maybe good looking, if he filled out.

Nell pointed to the NYPD-like uniforms displayed on wooden hangers. "The swastika, that on all the shirts and caps?"

"We deal in fantasy here, Detective."

"I can see that." Nell let her gaze roam over the leather goods, vibrators, and shrink-wrapped dildos arranged on a pegboard behind the counter.

"If it means anything," Herbal said, "you don't look like a fascist to me."

"Nevertheless," Nell said, "I'm going to need the names of people who bought or rented cop costumes in the past few months."

"You can understand, a place like this, we don't like giving out our clientele's names."

"You can understand, a place like this, we can close it down in a wink."

"My, you *can* be dominating."

"Even arresting."

"We don't rent here, only sell. And to tell you the truth, Bad Cop has kind of gone out of style. Though you could certainly bring it off, if you're interested in buying a uniform. I'd alter it so it was skin tight."

"Thanks, but I see enough rough stuff in my work."

"It can be more a mental thing."

"Ain't that the truth."

Herbal excused himself and went behind a curtain that led to a space behind the pegboard. Nell tried to stop looking at some kind of electrified dildo that featured attached but independently movable rubber protrusions. The thing was seventy-five dollars. It must do something.

Herbal was back with a slip of paper, and a yellow stub of pencil that he tucked behind his ear as if he were playing a newspaperman in an old movie.

"Two sales of Bad Cop in the last three months," he said. "Two customers, a man and a woman. Here are their names and addresses. As you can see, they live in the neighborhood."

"Do you know them?"

"Not personally. I've seen the woman around. And the man comes in here now and then and buys something."

"What kind of something?"

"Magazines, usually. Sometimes a book." Herbal pointed to a rack of magazines and paperbacks.

"What's the subject, usually?"

"Bondage and discipline, S&M, that sort of thing."

"Male on female?"

"Yeah."

"And the woman?"

"I don't know her orientation. She bought the uniform, and that's the only time I've seen her in here. Other'n that, just passed her on the street." Herbal bit his lower lip. "Detective . . ."

Nell waited.

"I'd appreciate it if you didn't tell them where you got their names, or how you found out they bought the uniforms."

"I can try to keep that confidential, Herbal, depending on where the investigation leads."

He grinned, greatly relieved. "If there's anything you might need . . ." He made an encompassing gesture with his right arm.

"Maybe that electric dildo," Nell said. "The foot-long one that looks like it's grown warts. Is it waterproof?"

"Detective!"

Nell laughed, thanked Herbal for his cooperation, and headed for the door.

"Remember," said Herbal's voice behind her, "confidential."

"If I have to name my source," Nell said, "I'll tell them I tortured it out of you."

"Detective!"

Nell thought it was fun sometimes, being a cop in New York.

64

Looper figured he'd make one more call before lunch. Proper Woman was listed as a company that specialized in theatrical props and other supplies, and it was located in Tribeca, near a Greek restaurant that served great baklava, which to Looper was almost as satisfying as a cigarette after a meal.

The entrance to Proper Woman wasn't impressive. Nor was the building itself, an old brick and stone five-story structure a block off Broadway. The inside of the building was warmer than outside. In fact, the damned thing was a kiln. Looper wiped sweat from his face with a wadded handkerchief.

He had to trudge up a narrow flight of stairs to a converted freight elevator, which he rode to the top floor.

What he saw when he stepped out of the elevator was a vast, sunlit array of . . . everything. And it was cooler here. There was a system of shafts and vents suspended from the ceiling. Looper gazed out over sets of furniture, a suit of armor, long rows of ornate chandeliers, cases of paste jewelry, racks of firearms, medieval weapons, a rowboat, an antique car, staircases leading nowhere, a section of white

picket fence, and racks of clothing. Including various uniforms.

Looper had phoned ahead, but saw no one. Then a slim,
gray-haired woman appeared from behind some artificial
shrubbery and smiled, holding out her hand. "Detective
Looper?"

Looper shook her hand, careful not to squeeze. She was
in her seventies and obviously had once been beautiful. "I'm
Lavernc Blisner."

"Let me guess," Looper said, "you used to be an actress."

The smile brightened. "Close enough. I was a dancer.
Now I do this." She waved an arm gracefully—like a dance
movement. "My husband and I went into the theatrical
supply business twenty years ago. Now I and my daughters own and manage the company. We furnish play productions with just about anything, and if we don't have it,
we find it."

"I can't imagine you not having it," Looper said.

"Have you seen *Fiddler on the Roof*?"

"Several times," Looper lied.

"Our roof."

"Amazing."

"You mentioned uniforms when you called."

"Yes. New York Police uniforms."

"What period?"

"Present, or at least recent."

"Got 'em."

"No surprise, Laverne." Such an innately lovely woman,
he found himself wondering what her daughters looked like.

Laverne danced—or so Looper thought—over to a rack
of clothes that weren't uniforms, but Southern belle dresses
with lace-laden hoop skirts. "Let me explain that most of our
clothing is used. Those in charge of dressing a major play
have their designs, their costumes, tailor-made. We get them
after the plays close. Then, of course, smaller productions
come to us to rent in order to economize." Laverne obvi-

ously enjoyed explaining things, and might do so in detail for a long time.

"If you'd show me the NYPD costumes."

She smiled and led the way through more racks of clothing, past a genuine stuffed grizzly bear that gave Looper the creeps, then to more clothing, including a rack of blue uniforms. Looper saw what looked like nineteenth-century police uniforms, then later, nineteen-twenties stuff, with less defined shoulders and the standard eight-point caps that were still worn. Other time periods were covered. The uniforms seemed to be arranged in chronological order. The last two on the rack looked modern enough to pass.

Looper held them out separately from the other uniforms. "Have you rented either of these lately?"

"Not for months. Those are from an Off-Broadway production, *Rug Rats.*"

"Never heard of it," Looper said honestly.

"Well, it didn't last very long. But there was a bit part in it for a policeman who patrols a lovers' lane."

"*A* policeman? There are two uniforms."

"Everyone but the critics and the public expected the play to have a longer run," Laverne said. "And costumes have to be rotated so they can be cleaned, or the first several rows of the theater would notice. That distinctive dress you see in a play is actually at least two dresses."

"I get your drift," Looper said. He glanced around. "But lots of these clothes, you only have one of."

"Oh, maybe some are rented out, or maybe we only received one costume because its mate was damaged. And it isn't unusual for one or more of the actors to like an article of stage clothing and, after the play closes, keep it for personal use, or maybe as a souvenir. But if you're looking for a recent police uniform rental, I can't help you. I'm afraid cops aren't in great demand on Broadway."

"Except outside the theater, to control traffic when the shows let out."

Laverne smiled. "I get your drift."

They began walking idly back toward the freight elevator.

"We have all the decorations, patches, and badges to go with the uniforms," Laverne said. "I'm sure we have a badge exactly like yours."

"You're starting to make me uneasy, Laverne."

"I mention it because I'm assuming you suspect someone is impersonating a policeman and committing crimes."

"It's a theory," Looper said.

"The Justice Killer?"

Looper only smiled.

"He's the one on everybody's mind," Laverne said.

"Certainly our celebrity killer of the moment."

"I don't like what he's doing. I don't see him as a hero. And I think that Adelaide Starr bitch needs a good spanking."

Looper's smile turned to one of gratitude. "That's pretty much the way we see him. And her."

"I'm also letting you know it's possible he could be passing for a real policeman, right down to the details and identification. That kind of merchandise is available in this city."

Looper already knew that, but he said, "You're not making me feel any better."

"Well, that isn't why you came here."

She smiled at him and pushed the button that opened the elevator door.

Uptown, Bradley Aimes returned from a lunch with his accountant and jogged up the steps to the entrance to his apartment building. He was plenty worried. The IRS, those were people you didn't mess with. Harv, his accountant, kept telling him not to fret so much about the audit, or he'd get sick. But Harv didn't know that some of the receipts for business and travel expenses were copies of previous years' receipts, with the dates artfully altered. Harv was a stickler and would have been shocked to know. But hell, everybody did that kind of thing. It was a guy on a golf course in New Jersey who'd first given Aimes the idea, said he'd been doing it for years. You just had to be careful to use receipts that were more than three years old.

Well, the IRS agent hadn't figured that one out yet, and Aimes sure wasn't going to clue old Harv in. Harv was the kind of guy who spilled his guts about everything. Some of the things he'd said about his wife . . .

Ah! There was something showing through the vertical slots in Aimes's mailbox. Probably ads, or maybe something else from the Internal Revenue. Well, better check. Might *be* a check. Aimes had a fifty-dollar rebate check coming from when he'd bought some computer equipment last month.

He crossed the hexagonal-tiled lobby floor and fit his key in the brass mailbox with his name over it.

That's when the headache struck.

An explosion of pain.

A dizzy sensation. Everything moving, moving.

What? Stroke or something . . . ?

Too much strain because of the audit. Harv had warned him about worrying too much. He tried to take a step, but his foot moved through air. Odd. Harv had . . .

That's the ceiling, stairs leading up and up and up. How'd I get on the floor?

The wind . . . It's so cold . . . How'd I get in a boat?

I'm only five. I shouldn't be alone in a boat.

In the dark.

Looper had finished his Greek salad and was about to bite into his baklava, when his mobile phone buzzed.

He'd removed his suit coat and had the phone out of its pocket, lying next to the condiments on the table where he could get to it, so he answered after only two buzzes.

"Looper," he said simply, knowing from caller ID that it was Beam.

"It's Beam, Loop. We've got another Justice killing." He gave Looper a West Side address, while Looper used sticky fingers to grip a pencil and write on a napkin. "Victim's name is Bradley Aimes." He spelled it out for Looper.

"Isn't that—"

"Yeah," Beam said. "The asshole who killed Genelle Dixon."

"Allegedly." Looper licked his fingers.

"I'll meet you there," Beam said. "Nell's on the way."

Looper was already signaling for a take-out box for his baklava.

65

Murder was popular. The narrow vestibule of the brown-stone apartment building was so crowded that half a dozen cops and CSU personnel were standing outside. Tenants were directed to a basement entrance usually accessible only to the super. Several windows were open above, and people leaned out of them, silently watching what was going on below.

Beam flashed his shield but didn't go all the way into the vestibule, simply leaned in and saw Bradley Aimes's body on the bloody tile floor. Aimes was lying on his back, his eyes open and gazing up the stairwell but seeing nothing. Techs were tending to business with their tweezers and brushes and plastic bags. A photographer was sending brilliant flashes over the scene every ten or twelve seconds. The little mustachioed ME, Minskoff, was stooped next to the body. He glanced over and saw Beam.

"'Nother one," he said.

Beam looked and saw a bit of red cloth clutched in the dead man's right hand. "That what I think it is?"

"I'd say so," said the ME. "Haven't touched it yet."

"That a gunshot wound I see in his head?"

"Certainly is. Bullet went in just behind his right ear."

"Thirty-two caliber?"

"Could be. It's still in his head, so we'll know better after the postmortem."

On the floor, near the hand clutching the cloth *J*, was a small brass key. "Mailbox?" Beam asked, pointing to the key.

"Haven't touched that, either," Minskoff said, deftly using the back of his wrist to adjust his glasses. "But his mailbox is open. Looks like he came downstairs to get his mail, but never got a chance to read it. It's still in the box. Envelope I can see looks like it contains a rebate check. His lucky day."

"You notice a lot for an ME."

"Too many years hanging around guys like you. I learned to observe. Too much, I might add." He bent back to his task, signaling that he was now ignoring Beam.

"I'm observing blood getting on your shoes," Beam said, backing away from the doorway.

"Damn it!" he heard Minskoff say.

"Let's find the super," Beam said to Looper, "so we can have a look at Aimes's apartment while Nell keeps tabs on things here."

What they learned as soon as the super opened the door for them was that Aimes had bad taste and didn't bother keeping things neat.

Aimes had been a smoker. His apartment reeked of tobacco smoke, and there were ashtrays scattered around, most of them with ashes or filtered cigarette butts in them. Looper closed his eyes and took in a deep and blissful breath, like a man who'd stepped into a perfume factory. The blinds on one of the windows were broken and hanging crookedly. The furniture was a mishmash of styles, a couple of uncomfortable looking Danish chairs, a fat sofa with a rose and vine pattern, an Oriental rug that managed to avoid every color in the sofa. On one wall were some framed photos of a race-horse—"Secretariat," Looper announced, after closer inspection—and a blown-up color photo of a big sailboat, the racing kind, listing to starboard almost enough to capsize. There was a crew of about half a dozen in the boat. Beam looked closely and saw that one of them was a younger version of the dead man in the lobby.

"This prick used to have a lot of money," Looper said. "Did things like race sailboats and kill girls. After the trial, his family still thought he was guilty and disinherited him."

"Maybe played the horses, too," Beam said, looking again at Secretariat. "Trying to regain his lost wealth."

After putting on evidence gloves, they searched the apartment and found a sagging, unmade bed, a closet full of expensive but mostly out-of-style clothes. There was a desk drawer full of unpaid bills, past due notices, a checkbook that showed a balance of eighty-seven dollars and change. The checks were written for cash or to places like bars, restaurants, and shops.

Beam thumbed through the check pad. "Oh-ho! A ten-thousand-dollar deposit front end of every month." .

"Family buying his absence," Looper said. "Black sheep, wild goose."

"Probably." Beam glanced around. "Whatever the species, you'd think he could still live better than this on a hundred and twenty thousand a year."

"Gambled most of it away, would be my guess."

Beam opened the desk's shallow center drawer. There were some postage stamps in there, pens and pencils, a couple of race track stubs, Mets and Yankees schedules, a shabby deck of Bicycle playing cards. Beam thought Looper's guess was a good one.

Looper was looking over Beam's shoulder. "If he owed anybody money, they're gonna be outta luck and pissed off."

"Reverting to the mean," Beam said.

"Huh?"

"That's how most gamblers wind up."

"Oh, I dunno. You ever been to Atlantic City? Vegas?"

"Yeah," Beam said. "I left a little of me both those places."

"I hit for nine hundred dollars once on a quarter slot machine," Looper said. "Three smiling strawberries, straight across the pay line."

"That would suggest you've got some bad luck coming." Beam shut the drawer. "Let's go downstairs and see if Nell's got anything."

What Nell had was a short, serious-looking bearded man wearing khaki shorts, a sleeveless T-shirt, and rubber flip-flop sandals. He appeared to be in his fifties, and had medium length, unkempt gray hair. Despite his casual clothes, there was a professorial air about him. Probably because of the oversized wire-framed glasses.

Nell and the man were standing at the curb, next to a parked radio car with its red and blue roof-bar lights winking almost unnoticeably in the bright sunlight.

"This is Vash Kolinsky," she said, and introduced Beam and Looper.

"This is a terrible thing, this kind of violence," Kolinsky said, glancing toward the crime scene. He had a slight middle-European, or maybe Russian, accent.

"Would you repeat to these detectives what you told me?" Nell asked.

"You ask nice, not hit me, so sure." He was grinning—his idea of a joke. "I was playing chess on my laptop up there." He pointed to a third-floor balcony on a building diagonally across the street. There were potted plants on it that might block a view of anyone sitting there. "My opponent in the Internet chess club, a dummy in Vancouver, is so slow it bores me to play him, so I wait for him to move, and wait and wait, and happen to look over here, toward this building.

I see this policeman, and he was there when I first came out on the balcony half an hour before. There was something about him, like he was pretending to look into the parked cars. But I don't think he was interested in the cars at all. He was up to something, watching for something or someone. Me? I worry. I have family in Kiev. I didn't leave Russia under the best circumstances. I know policemen, and when something's not right with them. With this policeman, something wasn't right."

"Can you be more specific?" Beam asked.

"Mostly, the way he acts. Like there's more than one thing on his mind. And he had on a jacket, on such a hot day. And his uniform cap didn't look right, didn't fit him right."

"Did you see him go into the building?" Beam asked.

"No. But I look away, look back, and he's gone."

"Then what?" Nell asked. She was staring at Beam as if he should pay special attention to Kolinsky's answer.

"I move my queen's pawn two spaces."

"Mr. Kolinsky—"

"Then I hear a bang."

"Like a shot?" Beam asked.

"Could be like a shot. I didn't pay much attention. This is a noisy street, all the traffic, horns honking, and kids around, they bang on things. I see that dummy in Vancouver has already fallen into my trap, so I go back to playing chess. Then I hear sirens, hear them stop, look back outside, and see something is wrong. More police come. A crowd. I hear loud talk, people yelling back and forth, and I learn someone has been shot. Then I remember the bang."

"Do you remember the time?"

"Exact? No. About one-thirty."

"After you realized someone had been shot, did you continue to observe from your balcony?"

"Yes, I look, see everything. More police, ambulance. Saw the lady detective arrive, then you and you."

"The cop wearing the jacket, did you see him again?"

"No. He was there before the shooting. Not after."

"He could have left through the basement," Looper said to Beam. "The way we went in to get the super."

"That could be," Kolinksy said. "I wouldn't have seen him. I wasn't looking for him."

"Would you recognize him if you saw him again?" Beam asked.

"No. Someone in uniform, you see the uniform, not the face. He was average man. Not too tall or short or fat or thin. Average man."

"Hair color?"

Kolinsky shrugged. "He had on cap."

"Anything about the way he moved?"

"Like he's not supposed to be there. That's why I noticed him in the first place. I have an eye for such things." Kolinsky looked back up at his balcony. "King's knight," he said.

"Pardon?"

"I need to get back so I can counter the move of the Vancouver idiot."

"Certainly," Beam said.

He thanked Kolinsky for his help, then watched him cross the street and enter his building.

"Sounds like he saw the cop who was at Knee High's murder," Nell said.

"Someone who looked like him, anyway," Beam said.

Nell and Looper stared at Beam. "If he wore the jacket to conceal the bulk of a sound suppressor," Beam said, "he didn't use it. Kolinsky heard the shot from across the street."

"Might have been something else," Looper said. "Something not related to the murder. Backfire, somebody hitting something with a board or hammer. This is a noisy neighborhood that time of day."

"Kolinsky's a good witness," Nell said. "I'm sure he's heard gunfire before and knows what it sounds like. And there's corroboration. Two tenants on the first floor of Aimes's building also heard what might have been a shot, at about the same time Kolinsky heard it."

"Which would be about the time Aimes died," Beam said.

"Maybe Kolinksy just saw one of the uniforms we've got patrolling around here," Looper said.

"I checked," Nell said. "None of them were on the block at the time, and nobody was wearing a jacket."

"Maybe the guy Kolinsky saw wasn't a cop," Looper said. "A delivery man, maybe."

"Lots of maybes about this one," Beam said.

"But at least we've got a witness who saw and heard something," Nell said.

"There is that," Beam said. "Even if we don't understand it."

"Yet," Nell said, under her breath.

66

An hour later, in da Vinci's office, Kolinsky's name came up again.

Beam, Nell, and Looper were there, along with Helen. It seemed to Beam that the profiler was always in da Vinci's office these days. He appeared to be relying more and more on her.

"Somebody must have seen you three talking to Kolinsky in the street and found out where he lived," da Vinci said. "The man doesn't mind talking to the press anymore than to the police. I got a call a few minutes ago from the *Post*, wanting to verify that we now suspect the Justice Killer is a cop." He looked at his three detectives. "You should have conducted that interview indoors."

"They still would have gotten to him," Beam said, protecting Nell. "And when he isn't playing chess, Kolinsky likes to talk."

"The media's gonna be in swarm mode," da Vinci said. "Hell of a story, a cop who's also the Justice Killer." He looked over at Helen, who was seated slightly sideways in a chair and resting her chin on her fist.

"The odds are still against him being a cop," she said.

"This is a killer who figures screw the odds," da Vinci said. "Maybe one that's smarter than the cops trying to chase him down."

"That's what he wants you to think," said the imperturbable Helen. "He's trying to pressure you."

"He's doing it."

Beam thought da Vinci did look pressured. His hair was mussed, his eyes hollowed, and there was a slight razor cut on his chin, as if his hand had trembled while he was shaving this morning.

"And *he* feels pressured," Helen said. "From within and without. At a certain point, he'll want to be caught as badly as you want to catch him. Maybe more so."

"Psychology bullshit," da Vinci said.

Beam thought he was probably right. But Helen might be right about one thing: "There's no guarantee the killer's a real cop," he said.

"Since when's the media need a guarantee?" da Vinci asked.

"He's got a point," Helen said. "There'll be more pressure applied by the press and pols and NYPD brass to stop the killings. Might as well be ready for it. And we'll probably hear again from Adelaide Starr."

"Unless she's too busy writing her book," da Vinci said.

"She's probably got sample chapters by now," Helen said. "Somewhere in them she'll point out that the Justice Killer's achieving his goal. Since the deaths of Cold Cat and Aimes, potential killers will know it won't be only the courts weighing their guilt or innocence—or their punishment."

"They already know it," da Vinci said. "The assholes saying the city's safer are right. Latest violent crime statistics, the murder rates, everything's in free fall." Jabbing a finger at stat sheets on his desk that he'd ordinarily be proud of, he looked mad enough that Beam thought he might actually spit. "If it weren't for the Justice Killer, we'd hardly have any murders at all."

"Put us all out of work," Looper said.

Da Vinci gave him a black look. "Why don't you go someplace and smoke a friggin' cigarette."

"Andy," Helen said, "you've gotta take it easy, let things work for you. Remember, the killer's feeling the same kind of heat you are."

Beam was careful not to glance at da Vinci or Helen. *Andy?*

"I don't think so," da Vinci said. "Things seem to be going his way. The press, the public, they don't want this sicko caught. They're against us."

"Bradley Aimes was part of the public," Beam said.

"Who cares about that prick? He should've gotten the needle years ago. This killer's doing what his name implies. He's executing people who deserve it."

"What about Cold Cat?"

"That was Knee High's fault. And Knee High paid the price."

"I've been thinking about the cop who was spotted at the crime scenes," Looper said. "The jacket, the cap that doesn't fit right. Maybe the officer has breasts. Maybe the cap's too small or crooked because it has long hair tucked up under it."

"You think the killer might be a woman?" Beam asked.

Da Vinci was looking at Looper with cautious contempt. That the Justice Killer might be female was something they hadn't considered.

"Female cop?" Helen asked.

"Maybe, or a female civilian in a cop uniform."

"Not much chance of it," Helen said. "Serial killing is something women don't do. Something cops don't do. Not normally, anyway."

"Who's thinking about normal?" da Vinci said.

"All I'm saying," Helen said, "is the odds are so long it's not a hunch worth pursuing."

"There really isn't much evidence pointing that way," Nell said.

Da Vinci grinned. "So the two women present agree."

"What do you think?" Beam asked him.

"Helen's right. As usual. And as usual, Looper's—"

The desk phone buzzed. Beam thought it was a break for Looper.

"I know what that is," da Vinci said, "only call I'm letting straight through." He snatched up the receiver.

After a series of "yeahs" he said, "You're sure?" Then he grunted and hung up.

"More bad news?" Beam asked, looking at his face.

"I ordered a rush on the Aimes postmortem," da Vinci said, "told them to call me as soon as possible. That was Forensics."

"And?"

"Cause of death, a bullet to the brain, thirty-eight caliber. This bullet doesn't match the others."

"Shit!" Looper said. "He's switched guns."

"I'm sure he's trying to help us out, right, Helen?" Da Vinci slumped down in his chair and stared at nothing on his desk.

No one said anything. The silence took on weight.

After a while, da Vinci said again, "He's smarter than the cops trying to chase him down."

"He'll screw up," Nell said. "We'll be there."

"Then go there," da Vinci said dejectedly. "Find there. Go."

Beam nodded toward the door, then led his detective team from the office.

Behind them, Helen said, "Andy."

67

It was amazing how easy they were with each other now that the dam was broken. Nola enjoyed Beam's slow and attentive lovemaking, and the guilt he felt from being with a woman other than Lani had fled his mind.

Not that Lani didn't intrude in his dreams sometimes, as Harry must do in Nola's dreams. But Beam and Nola both understood that every day, when they were awake and alive and together, was precious.

Finally, for both of them, the present outweighed the past.

They lay side by side in Nola's bed, listening to New York slowing down outside the window. The scent of their love-making was still in the air despite the rose sachet Nola had dangling from the corner of her dresser mirror. Beam, who had always associated roses with funerals and death, now associated them with love and sex.

He had never talked much with Lani about the Job, but he did discuss his work with Nola. Especially the Justice Killer investigation. Part of it, he knew, was because he wanted her to better understand what he did for a living, a calling, so she might understand the symbiotic relationship between cop and snitch. Beam and Harry.

And now, Beam and Harry's wife.

But Nola was also part of the case. The Justice Killer had made her that, had used her antique shop, Nola herself, to divert the investigation and taunt Beam.

Nola smiled over at him and ran a fingertip down the ridge of his nose. "What are you thinking, Beam?"

"About what Helen the profiler said, that the killer taunts me because secretly, even to himself, he yearns to be caught. And the more he taunts, the closer we are to finding him."

Nola said, after a while, "Makes a crazy kind of sense."

A fly had gotten into the room. It buzzed the bed, then began flinging itself repeatedly against the nearby windowpane. They watched it.

"Frustration," Nola said.

"The NYPD with wings."

"I didn't mean the police. I meant the Justice Killer. He wants to kill, he wants to be stopped, he wants to be anonymous, he wants to be famous. He can't get enough of any of it. It must be making his heart beat faster and faster."

"That's more or less how Helen sees it."

"And you seem to be relying more and more on Helen."

"Because da Vinci is."

"Why?"

"He's frustrated, too," Beam said. "Like that fly and the rest of us only more so."

"Maybe he's afraid the killer will stop taunting and come after one of you."

"Helen said it isn't likely. We're his reason for being. Only she has a French phrase for it."

"*Raison d'etre,*" Nola said.

"Very impressive." Beam wasn't kidding. "She says we symbolize the system he's acting out against, so he wants to keep us alive."

"As symbols."

"Yeah."

"There are other symbols, like Adelaide Starr."

"The killer wants her alive, too" Beam said. "She's practically become his biggest asset. Helen says Adelaide's adding to the killer's celebrity and feeding his delusions. Besides, she's so cute, who could kill her?"

"Helen could be wrong about all that symbolism and its value to the killer," Nola said, "in whatever language."

"Da Vinci doesn't think so. Sometimes he says he does, but he doesn't. Not really. She's having more and more of an influence on him."

"You think they might be in love?"

"Might," Beam said.

Beam had lunch the next day with Cassie at a recently opened restaurant called Mambo, near the vast concrete and marble indoor park in the financial district. There were a lot of new businesses and new construction in this part of town, the city still coming back strong from the 9-11 horror. New York, the city that never sleeps and never surrenders. The city of scars with yet another.

Artificial potted palms flanked the restaurant's canopied entrance. It had a dance motif, life-size silhouetted figures on the walls doing what looked to Beam more like tango than mambo. There were more potted palms inside, lots of ferns, and soft background music that sounded like samba.

The food couldn't make up its mind what it was, either, though the menu was in Spanish. It wasn't bad, just not as good as one of Cassie's homemade dinners. And who was Beam to assume that Irish potatoes weren't eaten south of the border?

"Been a while since we've seen each other," said Beam's sister.

"As you might guess, I've been busy into the evenings." *With Nola. Missing Cassie's cooking so I could be with Nola. Twisting back and forth between man's two essentials:*

food and women. Beam knew that if Cassie or Nola could somehow know the thought had entered his mind, they might seriously injure him.

"Nola," Cassie said, pausing before taking a bite of something supposedly Latin.

Beam actually felt himself blush. He'd forgotten how preternaturally insightful Cassie could be. From the time they were children, she'd occasionally astounded him.

"She's forgiven me," he said

"Wonderful," Cassie said, inserting food in her mouth and smiling simultaneously. She'd said it as if she knew everything Nola's forgiveness entailed, and she probably did know.

"How's the investigation going?" she asked. Seeing that Beam was surprised by the abrupt question, she added, "I was sure you wanted to change the subject."

He laughed. "You should play poker for a living."

"It would bore me."

He brought her up to date on the hunt for the Justice Killer. As he talked, her expression changed from intensely interested to concerned.

"So Looper thinks the killer might be a woman," she said. "He didn't strike me as such an independent thinker."

"He's real independent on that one," Beam said. "Nobody agrees with him."

"You don't think it's possible the killer's a woman?"

"Possible. Sure. In the way that just about anything's possible. But what we know about serial killers suggests it's highly unlikely. Which camp are you in?"

"Not Looper's," Cassie said. "I don't see the Justice Killer as female."

"It's nice to have my opinions confirmed," Beam said.

"Shored up, anyway," Cassie said.

Beam recalled how she'd almost always won every game she played as a kid. How she consistently beat the other kids at guessing where someone would move a checker, which sweaty little clenched fist held the coin, which was the short straw, which cards would turn up.

"Maybe you really should play poker," he said. "It's only a game, but these days there's big money in it to go with the risk."

"Life's only a game, and it contains all the risk we need."

Beam raised his water glass and drank to that.

After the waiter brought them coffee, and bread pudding (was that a Latin dish?) for dessert, Cassie said, "You need to be careful."

"Of the bread pudding?"

"I'm serious."

"You think something bad is about to happen?"

"Yes."

"What?"

"I have no idea, bro. I'd tell you if I could. I'm not God."

"You're his messenger," Beam said.

"Trouble is," Cassie told him, "the message is always in code."

Despite the ordinariness of the rest of the food, the bread pudding was delicious. Better than Cassie's. Who would have guessed?

The next morning the *Times* ran a feature about Adelaide Starr being mistreated in jail. Beam sliced, toasted, and buttered a poppy seed bagel for breakfast, then poured a cup of coffee and sat at his kitchen table with the paper. He chewed, sipped, read.

Adelaide was a pest, but she sure had charisma, not to mention chutzpah. She was awaiting trial, like many of the other prisoners in the Bayview women's correctional facility, but her treatment was actually better. The food she complained was causing her to waste away was the same as the other prisoners', but because of her special status, she had a private cell. Under media pressure, she'd even been supplied with an electric typewriter. A hardship, she proclaimed, because she didn't know how to type. Why couldn't she have a computer she could talk to, like other writers? Or a tape recorder, so she could express her thoughts more completely to her editor, who had to type a lot of Adelaide's story herself, from interview notes and memory? The truth was getting lost here, Adelaide said. The truth was a victim again. And the place where they held her was noisy. It was heck for a creative person. How could she possibly write with such distractions?

On its editorial page, the *Times* suggested that Adelaide might be confined to a hotel room and wear an electronic anklet. Beam had to smile.

After breakfast, he went into the living room and switched on the TV, and there was Adelaide, being interviewed in her cell by a blond woman he recognized from local cable television.

Adelaide had apparently gotten permission to wear a frilly blouse, and dangling pearl earrings. Her bright red hair looked professionally mussed. She didn't appear to Beam in any way malnourished.

She twisted her lipsticked mouth into a sexy moue, her head cocked to the side, listening intently to her interviewer's questions.

I—Do you think justice is in any way being served by your confinement, Adelaide?

A—Oh, not at all. There's justice on both sides of the law. I think we've all learned that.

I—Could you explain that statement?

A—I mean, look at the statistics I saw in the papers. Since the Justice Killer has come to our city, it's become much safer. Women and majorities no longer have to fear for their lives every day.

I—You mean women and minorities?

*A—Them, too. (*Big smile.*) I love everybody!*

I—Do you even have love for the Justice Killer?

A—In a way, yes I do. I was taught as a child to hate the sin and love the singer.

I—"Sinner," you mean?

A—Of course. I'm sorry. (Sheepish grin. Cute.) *I guess I've been in too many musicals.*

I—Then you hate what the Justice Killer is doing, but for the killer himself, you do harbor some compassion?.

A—(Huge grin. Toss of hair. Darling.) *I try, I really do, but I can't hate anyone.*

I—How's the book coming?

A—Of course, it's a struggle. But I—

Beam had had enough. He aimed the remote like a gun and switched off the TV. The silence and blank screen were an immediate relief.

Some world, especially the New York part of it.

He balanced the remote on the arm of his easy chair, shrugged into his suit coat, and left to meet Nell and Looper in da Vinci's office. Maybe Helen would be there.

Helen was.

She looked as if she'd gone to the same beautician as Adelaide, only her red hair wasn't as brilliant, and she wasn't Adelaide cute. She was much taller and more the serious type, but not unattractive. If da Vinci was involved with her, Beam could understand how it might have happened. Beam, sleeping with his late snitch's widow.

They took the positions that had become habit—da Vinci behind his desk, Beam and Nell in the chairs angled toward it, Helen in the wooden chair used to work on the computer, off to the side. Looper pacing and patting his pockets.

"Anything new on the Aimes postmortem?" Beam asked.

"He was shot just behind the ear at point blank range," da Vinci said. "His hair was singed."

"I wonder if a sound suppressor could make for singed hair," Nell said, "even held close."

"I asked the ME that," da Vinci said. "He said it depends." Da Vinci glanced at the light breaking through the blind slats. He made a face as if it hurt his eyes.

Helen had on gray slacks today and was sitting with her chair turned around, straddling the seat and resting her bare forearms on the top of the wooden back. She had graceful but strong looking arms, as if she might play a lot of tennis or racquet ball. She was looking at da Vinci with a concerned expression. Then she looked at Nell in a way that puzzled Beam. Back to da Vinci.

"We've got a new development," da Vinci said. "A note from the killer. It came in the morning mail. The envelope was sent care of the NYPD, addressed to Beam."

68

"You opened the envelope?" Beam asked da Vinci.

"Yes. Only because it was from the killer"

"How did you know that beforehand?"

"I held it up to the light."

"But you were going to open it anyway."

"You were going to keep the contents secret?"

Leaning forward in her chair, Helen rested her chin on her muscular forearms and smiled.

Beam knew da Vinci was right to have opened the envelope. The Killer and his deadly games had them all edgy enough to play gotcha with each other, rather than with him.

"As you might expect," da Vinci continued, "paper and envelope are the common sort, not easily traced. The message was brief and printed in such a rudimentary way it doesn't provide much of a handwriting sample. No prints on any of this, of course, and no DNA sample on the stamp or flap. Our killer's as careful as he is vicious."

"He'll get careless," Helen said. No one seemed to have heard her. She was looking at Nell.

Da Vinci handed the folded note to Beam. It was plain

white typing paper, twenty weight, not quite transparent. Printed on it was a simple message:

For whom the bell tolls its death (k)Nell.
Justice

Beam read it aloud, complete with parentheses.

"Jesus!' Looper said. "He's coming after Nell."

"No question about it," da Vinci said.

"Telling us ahead of time." Looper's tone suggested he could hardly believe this. He touched all his pockets and picked up his pacing. "Some ego this bastard has."

"Taunting you again," Helen said. "Trying to rattle you the way you've rattled him. It's to be expected."

"You mean he might not mean it?" Beam asked.

"He means it," Helen said.

"What are we gonna do about it?" Looper asked.

"Let him come after me," Nell said. "Be ready for him." She sounded angry and confident.

"Don't doubt he'll come," Helen said.

"I don't," Nell said. "Unless he's using me as a diversion. Maybe he's really going after Beam."

"Or me," da Vinci said.

"He wouldn't lie in the note," Helen said.

Looper paused in his pacing and looked at her. "Huh?"

"He's essentially an honest man," Helen said. "A killer but, in his way, honorable. At least, that's how he sees himself. That ego you mentioned. The killer's locked onto Nell."

"Why me?" Nell asked.

"You're a woman. He sees you as the weakest link. The place to start. My guess is, if he succeeds with you, he'll come after Looper. Then Beam. Then Andy—Deputy Chief da Vinci."

"Working up the chain," Nell said.

"What about you?" Beam asked Helen.

She rested her chin again on her forearms, which were still folded on the chair's back. "He doesn't see me as part of the team. I don't strategize. I don't actively pursue him. I'm just a scientist. He has no more against me than he does against a tech in the fingerprint division."

"Even with all your face time on television?"

"The media have interviewed countless people regarding the Justice Killer. It goes on around the clock. Maybe you don't watch enough TV to know that, Beam."

"I hope not, having other things to do. Anyway, none of us has been on camera much since Adelaide came on the scene."

Da Vinci said, "Try not to mention that name in this office." He leaned forward, meeting Nell's gaze. "I think you should be publicly taken off the case, Nell."

"Seconded," Looper said.

Beam turned to face Nell directly. "How do you want to play this, Nell?"

She aimed her words at da Vinci. "I don't want to go anywhere. If I did, it'd only be delaying the inevitable. The killer would go after Loop, then Beam. Why not stop this before it picks up momentum?"

"Remember Knee High," Looper said. "Cheese in the trap."

Da Vinci looked away from Nell. "I put Beam in charge of the investigation. It's his call."

"You know my wishes," Nell said to Beam.

"And I know you well enough to figure there's something more to it."

"You're right. There's something about this cop costume thing that's eluding me, but I know I'll grab hold of it. And I don't like this prick thinking of me as the weakest link in the chain just because I'm a woman."

"You're a damned good cop," Beam said. "One of the best I've come across."

"And one who knows when she's being set up to get cut out."

"No," Beam said. "I think we should do it both ways. We'll announce you're off the case, that you've been put on indefinite leave and are no longer in New York. But you won't leave town. You'll live in your apartment, and leave it occasionally for routine reasons—to buy food, take a walk, maybe even meet someone for lunch. It will all look casual and unplanned. In fact, every step you take will be observed by undercover cops assigned to protect you, and to close in immediately on the Justice Killer when and if he appears."

"It can work," Nell said, too fast.

"We might be able to stop him in time," Looper said. "He'll have to move in on Nell. He kills at close range."

Beam thought about Aimes's singed hair around the ugly entrance wound, the smell of it in the stifling tile vestibule. *Close range.* "Loop's right. Other than shooting Dudman in a drive-by, he hasn't been a distance killer."

"You really think the asshole will go for this?" da Vinci asked.

"He'll go for it," Helen said. "He'll assume Nell wouldn't really leave town, and that he's outsmarting us. Winning the game. He'll try for her."

"Will he also know she's being guarded?"

"Probably," Helen said. "He'll enjoy the challenge."

"If we play it right, and make Nell's actions seem casual and spontaneous rather than planned out, he might have his doubts," Beam said. "He might get careless."

Helen nodded. "There's a chance. As I've been saying, he's coming undone, and he'll eventually take too large a risk, make a mistake. Accidentally on purpose. Deep down, but not as deep as before, he wants to be stopped."

"Why?" Beam asked, knowing the profilers' stock explanation involving the killer's inner conflict, but wanting

Helen to say it in all its pop psychology glory, for the record. In case this went horribly wrong.

But Helen knew a thing or two about Beam. She smiled thinly, not at all like the other redhead, Adelaide.

She said, "He believes in justice."

69

"Are you out of your mind?" Terry asked.

They were in Nell's apartment, where he'd come to see her after learning from the news that she was being taken off the Justice Killer case. He'd seemed glad about it until she told him her plans.

She was near the living room window, using a small green plastic pitcher with a long spout to water a potted fern. Maybe she could bring the damned thing back to life, now that she had more time to nourish it.

"I was so glad you were getting out of that madness," he said. He'd been working, and he had on jeans and a black golf shirt, brown leather moccasins. She knew he expected to shower and change here, then they'd go out, have dinner, maybe take a walk and have a few drinks someplace, and he'd spend the night.

"You're talking about the madness I'm trying to stop," she said. She put down the empty pitcher on the glass-topped table next to the fern. The plant still didn't look well, the tips of its fronds curled and tinged with brown.

"I'm talking about you risking your life."

"Everyone does that, every day. It's just that they don't always know it."

"Everyone doesn't play target for a killer," he said, pacing silently in the moccasins. "I thought you were really leaving the city, like they said on the news. I came by to see if you wanted to go with me to Cozumel. The airlines have a great special fare."

"There's always a special fare to Cozumel."

"I have a friend there who owns and operates a parasail business."

"Those things scare the holy hell out of me."

He stood still and held his palm to his forehead, had to laugh. "And you're not afraid of *this?* This thing you're doing?"

"Sure, I'm afraid. Like anybody who wants to continue breathing."

"Then *why* do it?"

"It's my job, Terry. I thought you understood."

"I try to understand, Nell. Honestly." He came to her and held her, kissed the top of her head. "I've found you. I don't want to lose you. That's what I'm afraid of. Simple as that."

"I'll have plenty of police protection." She extricated herself from his grasp and explained the details of the plan, how an army of uniformed and undercover cops would be stationed around her no matter where she went; how the Justice Killer preferred murder at close quarters, which would allow time for her protectors to move in, or for SWAT snipers to stop him from a distance with well placed shots.

Terry seemed unconvinced. "Your police protection won't be any closer to you than I'll be."

"No, Terry, that'd make him less likely to try for me. Or maybe he'd decide to kill us both. If we forced him to do that, he might think he has to do it from farther away, or maybe use some kind of MO he hasn't yet tried. This sicko likes to experiment. We think he's coming apart, that we have him on greased skids, and we don't want to slow him down till he hits bottom."

"If he's so unpredictable, why won't he decide to shoot you from a distance? Or plant a bomb in your apartment?"

"Even though he's varying his methods, we think he'll continue trying to kill close-up."

"But why?"

"He's enjoying it more and more. And even if he doesn't know it, he's a creature of compulsion."

"Oh, Christ! Who's doing all this psychoanalysis? Is it Beam? Is that what Beam thinks?"

"It's what we all think. Especially Helen Iman."

"Who is?"

"Police profiler."

"Good Lord! What can a profiler understand? It isn't like movies or TV, Nell. I know, I've done both. Every real cop I ever met thought profiling was a lot of crap."

"You haven't met them all, then."

"And now I've met one who's betting her life on pro-filing."

"It's more than that. It's what we all feel, what we know in the gut."

"The gut's gotten a lot of cops killed."

"You don't know that, Terry. You're talking bullshit. You've only ridden with cops for a while, and played a cop onstage."

"And slept with a cop."

"Well . . . that, too."

He paced around again for a few seconds, then faced her. "You're pissed at me for caring so much about you."

"Whatever the reason, I'm getting pissed."

What's with you, Terry? Why is this more difficult than it should be?

"I'll stay here with you tonight, Nell."

Tempting, tempting . . . "No, you have to leave and stay away. Until this is over."

"You're asking a lot of me."

"Don't think I don't know it." She placed her hands on his chest and kissed him lightly on the lips. "It won't be long, darling." *Try a little tenderness.*

He held her close, almost tight enough to hurt her.

When he released her, she saw the stress on his features, the now familiar vertical tracks above the bridge of his nose that told her he was thinking hard, agonizing.

Then she saw resignation.

A tenseness seemed to leave him all at once, changing the energy of his body though he hadn't moved a muscle.

"You're right," he said. "But even if you were wrong, it'd be your decision. I'm not going to oppose you on this, Nell. If I have to accept it, I will. I love you that much."

They kissed. Nell didn't want him to release her this time, ever; but when he did, the resolve in her tightened.

"Will you change your mind about tonight?" he asked.

"No. You have to go, Terry. And stay away for a while. I don't like that part of it, but it has to be that way."

"I suppose it does, if your mind's made up as only you can make up a mind. Did the police see me come in?"

"They saw you come in," Nell said, walking to the door and standing by it. "And now they'll see you go out."

As he left, he said glumly, "I think your fern is dead."

Terry had been gone less than an hour when Nell's cell phone chirped.

She went to where it was lying on the desk next to her purse, then picked it up gingerly and saw by the caller ID that it was Jack Selig.

The musical chirping persisted.

She laid the phone back down and didn't answer.

Beam sat in a battered white Chrysler minivan half a block down from Nell's apartment. The van had been confiscated in a Brooklyn drug raid last month and pressed into service by Narcotics. It had been used by the bad guys as a portable crystal meth lab, and there was still a faint chemical scent to its interior.

The evening was finally beginning to cool, so Beam had the engine and air conditioner off and the windows down. A pleasant breeze was moving through the van's interior. Traffic swished and honked in the background. Music was playing somewhere, wafting through the lowering dusk, a bastardized Beatles tune he couldn't place though it was hauntingly redolent of his past. Beam knew it was all deceptively reassuring. Mucking around in one's own contentment often ended badly.

But he couldn't help being somewhat reassured. They were as ready as they could be, for now. It would take a few days, and nights, to get Nell's protective net perfect, but he'd see that it became perfect. He could have stopped Nell from doing this—maybe he was the only one—so it was more his responsibility than anyone else's to see that nothing bad happened to her.

The way to do that was to make sure that when she moved around the city, pretending she was leading a normal life, out of the investigation and no longer a player, she was shadowed by undercover cops. When she was in her apartment, like now, the main thing was to keep track of everyone entering or leaving the building. Everyone.

Beam knew numbers were important, but they wouldn't get the job done by themselves. The killer might even figure out a way to use numbers against them. A lot of cops were a good thing, but they weren't necessarily a lot of protection; they multiplied the possibility of someone being spotted or identified as police, of making a mistake.

Usually a suspect couldn't afford even one mistake, but a mistake by the police could be rectified and might only delay the payoff. The Justice Killer had managed to reverse that dynamic, to flip the odds so they favored him. One mistake by the police, and Nell would be dead. And the stalker was choosing time and place, biding his time for a sure kill. He could wait. Numbers were no match for patience.

The patience of a hunter.

70

Like she hadn't a care.

Justice watched Nell stroll down the street toward a knot of people waiting to cross at the intersection, then stand on the fringes of the group. She was wearing Levi's, sandals, a gray golf shirt, and had her hair tucked under a blue Yankees cap. And she was carrying what looked like one of those collapsible two-wheeled wire carts many New Yorkers used to transport light loads such as clothes or groceries.

She's looking kind of yummy today, in those tight jeans.
Not that it matters.

West- and east-bound traffic squealed and rumbled to a halt, except for vehicles making right turns. The backup of people building at the intersection broke from the curb and began to cross. Some hurried, glancing warily from side to side, while others walked slowly and seemed casually unaware of traffic. Nell was a typical New Yorker and crossed briskly, her head up, her gaze shifting for oncoming traffic or other urban dangers.

For the urban danger standing unseen across the street, watching her.

Justice smiled. He wasn't at all surprised that Nell hadn't

gone to Los Angeles to visit friends, as the media reported. That had been a cover story floated by the police. She remained in the city, where Justice, unfooled, was supposed to discover her. A trap.

Unfooled and unfooled.

He stopped near a window display of electronics and observed the reflection of the street behind him.

There went Nell, into a D'Agostino's grocery store.

Justice studied the moving, reflected scene made vivid by bright sunlight. Who was the young tourist type, complete with jeans and backpack, who'd been walking behind Nell but now slowed down and moved back against a wall, then ostensibly began searching for something in his pockets? He finally found a map, unfolded it, and began to study it.

Did he glance at the casually dressed couple—the man with a camera slung on a strap around his neck—as they entered D'Agostino's? Did they glance back?

A green Ford Taurus slowed, stopped, then parked in a miraculously available space near the grocery store. It contained only the driver, and he didn't get out.

The police had quite an operation going. They were covering Nell very efficiently. Justice approved.

Fifteen minutes later, Nell emerged from the store with her wire cart unfolded and loaded with two tan plastic bags stuffed with groceries. The green of celery tops or leaf lettuce protruded from the top bag. There was a six-pack of something beneath the bottom one. Looked like Diet Pepsi. Justice was learning more and more about Nell.

She pushed rather than pulled the cart as she walked back the way she'd come. As it passed over seams in the sidewalk, the flimsy little cart bounced, and Nell had to use both hands to control it.

The young tourist with the backpack folded his map and stuffed it back in his hip pocket, then continued his stroll. The car whose driver had never gotten out pulled away from the curb. The middle-aged couple with the camera came out of D'Agostino's. Nothing in their hands. No paper-or-plastic dilemma for them. They began strolling side by side behind the youth with the backpack, who was behind Nell.

Nell walked leisurely along the crowded sidewalk, pushing the two-wheeled cart ahead of her. It looked as if there might be a wire attached to something in her right ear. Listening to music? Well, she was supposed to be unconcerned. To have assumed that the Justice Killer had put her out of his mind, out of the game, and she was safe.

She's turning in a pretty good performance, acting the unknowing bait. Even swishing her hips more than usual in case I might be watching. Those tight jeans are for me. That ass—

Nell stopped and raised a hand to adjust her earpiece. Probably not listening to music at all.

Justice watched her smile slightly, then bob her head as if in time to music. Nice touch.

She placed both hands on the cart again and resumed walking.

On the other side of the street, he followed.

Beam screwed the lid back on his nearly empty thermos and laid it on the seat next to him. He was parked near Nell's apartment in the white minivan. The evening was warm, so the motor was running and the air conditioner working away. He was parked on the other side of the street, facing away from Nell's building, but had its entrance under observation in the van's oversized left outside mirror.

Nell should be back soon.

A siren yodeled several times a few blocks away, making Beam squirm in the van's scuffed leather seat. The confiscated vehicle didn't have a police radio; Beam used his two-way: "This is Beam. What was the siren?"

"Ten fifty-three on Eighth Avenue," a voice said. Police

code for a vehicle accident. Could be a simple fender bender.

More sirens. Sounded like emergency vehicles.

"Code ten forty-five," explained the voice, before Beam could ask. An accident with injuries. An ambulance was needed.

"'Kay," said Beam, and got off the two-way.

New York being New York, he thought. Nothing to do with Nell.

He knew that officers Havers and Broome, borrowed from an SNE, a street narcotics enforcement unit, were posing as a tourist couple with a camera, keeping a tight tail on Nell. They had two-ways and backup mobile phones and would notify Beam if anything out of the ordinary was happening.

Beam sat up straighter. There was Nell in the van mirror, pushing a wire cart along the sidewalk.

He watched as she turned around and, moving backward, pulled the overloaded cart up the three steps to her building's foyer. The wide door, flanked by stone columns, opened, closed, and she was inside.

Safe at home.

Beam knew better, but he breathed easier.

A car's headlights flared in the mirror and momentarily blinded him. When the lights went out, he saw that a drab brown Chevy sedan had parked behind him, a vehicle as inconspicuous as the van.

Looper, here to take over until Beam returned at midnight. Excellent. Beam couldn't get the coffee taste from his mouth, and he had to take a piss.

He went back to the two-way: "All yours, Loop."

"She in?"

"Tucked away and secure, probably for the evening."

"No hot date?"

"Not unless it's the one we're trying to arrange."

Beam decided to take a turn around the block before

driving to his apartment, brushing his teeth, and trying to get some sleep. Looper would call him if anything developed.

He twisted the key in the ignition, and the starter grated, startling him. *Jesus!* He'd forgotten the van's old engine was already running.

His back ached as he put the transmission in drive and the vehicle jerked away from the curb, leaving Looper in the parked Chevy behind. Beam realized his legs were stiff from sitting in one position for almost two hours.

He was ready to be relieved.

The changing of the guard down in the street hadn't escaped his attention. He watched the white minivan turn the corner and disappear. From up here, the brown Chevy looked unoccupied, like any other parked car.

The police were good at their job.

Three o'clock in the morning. That would be entry time. Most of the cops he knew agreed that three a.m. was the optimum time for housebreaking if anyone was home and sleeping. That was when sleep was deepest, when dreams were firmly in charge, when things tended to happen.

He knew how to get on the roof of Nell's building from the fire escape of the taller building beside it. The top two floors of that building were vacant and being rehabbed. He'd scouted them, gained entry, and found a sturdy two-by-eight plank, part of a painter's scaffold, that would act as a bridge from fire escape to roof. In his dark clothing, he'd be difficult to spot from below even if someone happened to be looking directly at him. A shadow that moved. That would be him— a shadow that moved in the night.

There were ways to enter Nell's building from the roof. And there were ways to leave, to reverse his procedure, get clear of the area, and not be seen. This was a game he understood and was good at.

While the police were watching Nell's building, they

weren't as careful about watching this one. He'd gained entrance in late morning, made his way to the uninhabited floor where construction had been halted until inspections were made and permits were issued, and made himself comfortable amid plastic paint buckets and plaster dust. Lots of plaster dust. One of his biggest problems was not to sneeze and possibly draw attention to himself.

Seated on a folded tarpaulin, his back against a sheet of wall board, he occasionally nibbled a stale sandwich and sipped warm bottled water. He waited.

Patiently.

Three o'clock. That was what most cops said. He'd even heard one say it recently on a TV cop show. Called it magic time.

Truth and fiction . . . Weren't they running together these days?

Three o'clock in the morning.

When things happened.

71

Nell knew that the streets below, succumbing to the slower tempo of the night, were virtually crawling with NYPD. Beam was watching from somewhere outside, directing the operation. Uniformed cops were in the building, one stationed at the end of the hall outside her door. They came and went with some regularity. Undercovers were stationed around the block. Be they homeless, or drunken late-night revelers, or lovestruck couples strolling holding hands, they were out there, ready to become cops. A uniform was stationed in the super's apartment, off the lobby. Looper was nearby, cruising the neighborhood in an unmarked car. They all knew who and what they were hunting. They knew the danger.

As did Nell. She kept her nine-millimeter Glock in the nightstand drawer within easy reach, a round in the chamber, safety on.

After brushing her teeth and changing into her sleep shirt, she watched the late news on TV, then checked to make sure the apartment's door and windows were locked, the drapes closed.

Bedtime. Part of her regular life. Just like a normal person not worried about a madman bent on killing her at the earliest opportunity.

But she didn't switch on the bedroom air conditioner. The night wasn't so warm that she couldn't do without it, and she didn't want its background noise covering some other, more ominous sound.

She climbed into bed and read a *New Yorker* for a while, hoping for some help from the cartoons. But her sense of humor had deserted her.

A crossword puzzle in this morning's paper was a valuable distraction. It managed to frustrate her, which was better than being terrified. And when finally she did figure out a ten-letter word for *hypnotized*, she was tired enough to sleep.

Deliberately keeping her movements economical and balanced, so as not to jar herself all the way awake, she put down the folded paper, then her pencil, and managed to switch off the lamp and fall back onto the bed.

The dreams came, as she knew they would. The thin wire slicing deep into her throat, leaving her suddenly breathing blood; the silent bullet from nowhere, tumbling though her flesh, splintering bone.

Dark dreams from the darkest corners of her soul.

She slept with fear, but she slept.

At two minutes after three, beneath a moonless black sky, he worked the two-by-eight board out through the kitchen window of the soon-to-be-demolished apartment and wrestled with it until it was balanced on the fire escape rail. He squeezed between board and window frame, so he was outside, then maneuvered the plank so one end was still supported on the rail, and the other on the roof parapet of the building next door—Nell's building.

Mustn't waste time.

Switching off his fear, he stood up on the plank, fixed his eyes on the tile-capped parapet across the passageway, and began to walk.

A few seconds later, he dropped almost silently on the roof of Nell's apartment building.

He left the plank, knowing it was barely visible from below even if someone did happen to be in the dark passageway and glanced up.

The service door was unlocked, open about half an inch and blocked by a bent beer can. Apparently the super or maintenance crew didn't like the idea of possibly being stranded on the roof. Or perhaps kids playing, or lovers seeking a private, quiet place had left the door blocked. It wasn't uncommon in New York, to neutralize the lock on a roof door.

Odd, though, that the police hadn't spotted it.

He'd been prepared to pick the lock, had the equipment in his pocket. Much easier—and faster—this way.

He opened the small, heavy door, then ducked inside and switched on his small flashlight. It had masking tape over half its lens, making its narrow yellow beam even more precise. He was on a tiny landing, with wooden stairs leading down to an access panel that provided entry into a closet he knew held cleaning supplies.

In the closet, he had to be careful. He knew there were two plastic buckets, a mop and broom leaning against a wall, an ancient upright vacuum cleaner, cans and bottles of cleaning solvents and powders on a wire shelf. Mustn't make noise here. There was an acrid smell in the closet, some kind of disinfectant or insecticide. Very deliberately, he slowed down, slowed everything, even his heartbeat.

Quiet, quiet . . . keep movements small.

He opened the door gradually, stuck his head out, and peered up and down the dimly lit hall. It had a tiled floor but a wide rubber runner. He could move along it silently.

As he started to leave the storage closet, he saw motion at the far end of the hall. A uniformed cop, pacing almost lazily, pausing to gaze out a small window into the blackness of the night.

After scratching his left ear with violence and abandon, the cop moved on toward the stairs. Another uniformed cop came along, and he heard their voices, though not what they were saying. They were obviously going down the stairs together.

But they might not go all the way down. Or stay together. One or both might return at any moment.

That was all right. It would take almost no time to cover the twenty feet or so to Nell's apartment and gain entry.

But there was risk here. Undeniably.

His wild heartbeat was telling him that.

If I'm going to do it, the longer I wait before moving, the greater the risk. In this goddamned world there's risk in everything. So move! Swallow your fear and move!

He moved.

Nell was awake.

She didn't exactly remember waking up. It had been a smooth transition from sleep to consciousness, as if dimensions overlapped and a dream had somehow slipped into reality. Yet she couldn't recall her dream.

The clock's red digital numbers read 3:13 a.m.

She lay on her back, her neck muscles tense and her head barely denting her pillow. She listened.

Listened.

The apartment was quiet.

She realized she was thirsty. The bedroom was sweltering and her throat was parched. Her lips felt cracked. That was what had awakened her, the thirst. She swallowed. It made a sound like tiny bones cracking.

So thirsty.

She rolled to her side, then sat up on the edge of the mattress. Her bare feet found the floor and she stood up.

More tired than I thought. Dizzy.

She licked her lips, but even her tongue felt dry.

The bathroom, a glass of water, was only just down the hall from the bedroom.

But the refrigerator offered filtered cold water, with ice in it.

Definitely the kitchen.

She padded slowly and unsteadily across the bedroom toward the dimly outlined rectangle that was the doorway to the hall, then moved on past the bathroom, toward the darkness of the living room and kitchen.

In the van, parked near the end of Nell's block, Beam sat hunched low behind the steering wheel. He'd returned at midnight to relieve Looper, who'd taken a break and was again cruising the side streets. Beam was in the half awake yet alert mode of a longtime cop on stakeout. Like a hybrid car running on one system independent of the other, but always a second away from switching to maximum power and the hell with economy.

The van's dashboard was dark except for the faint green glow of the stock radio, tuned to an all-night FM station that played show tunes. The radio was on low volume, and couldn't be heard five feet away from the van even though the windows were down. Beam was listening—and not listening—to the orchestral score of *Phantom of the Opera*.

His slitted eyes took in the dimly lit street, the parked cars, the stunted, silvered trees that bent gently in the breeze, the infrequent headlights and passing of vehicles at the intersection. And Nell's guardian angels. The bulky bundle on one of the concrete stoops near Nell's building was actually an armed and ready undercover cop, not a drunk or a street person. Behind the windowed double doors of a brownstone apartment building was a tested and reliable uniform named Sweeney, using the vestibule as an observation post.

A violin solo began, rich even on the van's economy speakers, as subdued and melancholy as the night.

Light flared in the van's outside mirror as a car turned the corner twenty feet behind Beam. In the brightness wrought by the headlights, Beam glanced at his watch.

Three-fifteen a.m.

Looper, on schedule, in his turn around the block.

The dented brown five-year-old Chevy rolled past the van and continued down the street. Looper didn't glance Beam's way. Beam, barely aware of the violin, watched the Chevy's taillights, one brighter than the other, recede down the block, then merge and disappear as the car turned the corner. Looper would park not far down the cross street, and in a few minutes would drive another slow, circuitous route along the streets surrounding Nell's apartment.

The violin again, rich and expressive in tone, yet not much louder than a kitten's meow. Beam wished for dawn and a larger speaker.

Nell pressed the water glass against the refrigerator's ice-maker lever and cubes tumbled down into it. She switched the setting, gave the glass another shove, and purified water streamed over the cubes.

Three cool swallows brought her almost fully awake.

Almost.

She noticed a dim light coming from the living room and thought immediately that she'd gone to bed and forgotten to switch off the TV. She'd done it before. And she *had* been watching late-night news before going to bed.

Her fear still part of her dreams, she moved automatically into the living room, the glass in her hand.

Took three steps, then realized her mistake.

The light wasn't from the TV. It was from a flashlight. Held by a dark, unmoving figure standing just inside the door.

Nell's harsh gasp startled even her.

In the dimness, enough light from outside filtered in for her to recognize the man in her living room.

72

Rooted by astonishment and fear in the dim room, Nell said his name in a choked voice:

"Terry."

"I had to see you," he said. "I was so worried about you, Nell. Couldn't sleep. Wanted to protect you . . . *needed to.* I couldn't forgive myself if something happened to you while I was tossing and turning in my bed, close enough to help but not helping."

"How did you get in here?"

"I remembered some of the tricks I learned from my days riding with the police, so I knew how to get on the roof from next door. Then I came down through the service door. As for the apartment, I still have the key you gave me."

All the time he'd been speaking, he hadn't moved. Her fear was like a wall between them. A wall her love was trying to climb.

Nell wanted to believe him. Wanted to so badly. She knew he was leaving it up to her. Trust and terror. It would have to be one or the other for Nell. One direction or the other.

More awake now than she'd ever been, her mind raced as

she made the calculations, figured the gravity of her choice, and factored in the risk.

Decision time. The edge of the blade.

She came unstuck from her terror and indecision and ran away from Terry, toward the bedroom and her gun.

He was moving now, too. She knew he was close behind, heard the rush of his body, could even imagine she felt the heat of his breath. The gun in the nightstand drawer. That was what she concentrated on, what meant everything to her now.

The gun.

"I can't raise Garcia."

The voice came to Beam over his two-way, from the bundle of rags on the concrete stoop.

Garcia was Sergeant Wayne Garcia, the uniform stationed at the end of the hall outside Nell's apartment.

"Sir?"

"I heard," Beam said. He thought for a moment. The problem was most likely simple equipment failure. He couldn't imagine Garcia falling asleep. But there were other things he could imagine. "Let's go see."

He twisted the ignition key and heard only a low groaning sound. Tried again and got only a faint series of clicks. The van's battery was dead. It held enough juice to power the radio, but not enough to turn the starter and kick over the engine. Instead of driving down the street to the apartment building, Beam would have to walk.

Shit happens, he thought. Especially around three in the morning.

He got out of the van and began trudging down the eerie dark street toward Nell's building.

Ahead of him, the bundle of rags stirred and stood up.

* * *

Nell made it to the bedroom ahead of Terry and slammed the door behind her.

Almost immediately it crashed open, bouncing off the wall. Nell hadn't stopped moving. She dived onto the bed, lunged to the far side of the mattress, and fumbled to open the nightstand drawer.

"Nell!" he said behind her. "Listen, Nell!"

She yanked the tiny drawer too hard and it came all the way out and fell to the floor.

Damn it! Gun!

She couldn't see the gun.

It must be down there on the floor somewhere in or around the drawer. The drawer she couldn't reach.

"Nell!" Terry pleaded again. He was on the bed with her, his weight bearing down hard on her upper body. Her right bicep was clamped painfully in his powerful grip. "Nell, damn it!"

Terrified, she craned her neck to glance up at him.

Then froze.

Terry and Nell weren't looking at each other.

They were staring at the uniformed cop in Nell's bedroom. He was holding in his right hand a gun with something bulky fitted to its barrel.

Terry acted first.

He rose from the bed and flung himself at the figure with the bulky handgun.

And ran into an iron fist that struck his shoulder and staggered him.

He knew he'd been shot.

He took a few backward steps, still with the presence of mind to stay between the cop and Nell. The cop very deliberately edged to the side to get a better angle on his target.

And Nell's powerful Glock exploded the night's silence.

The bullet snapped past Terry's right ear and shattered the window.

"Get the hell outta the way, Terry!"

A faint sound came to Beam and the raggedy cop through the night, a flat *bam!* that reverberated only once, almost instantaneously.

More noise. Tinkling glass? A woman—Nell?—yelling something?

There was no doubt about the first sound. A shot.

Both men began to run.

In Nell's bedroom, Terry didn't get out of the way. He knew he couldn't let Nell have the shot without making her vulnerable to the cop. Keeping himself between the two, he backed to the bed, feeling his right calf contact the mattress and springs.

He whirled and scooped a pillow backward toward the cop, seeing Nell kneeling on the side of the bed, seeing a perfectly round hole appear like a magic trick in the wall inches from her head.

He dived across the mattress and her body folded down under him.

Nell was trapped in the narrow space between the bed and the wall, with Terry on top of her, shielding her with his body.

His hip was jammed against the wall, his left arm beneath Nell. She was squirming beneath him, breathing hard. Something—*her fingernails?*—was scraping on plaster. Pain was like a red tide assaulting his consciousness. Every muscle tightened in Terry as he waited for a second bullet to hit him.

It did. In the back of the shoulder that was already shot.

More pain erupted. He moaned but managed to remain conscious.

Nell squirmed even harder beneath him, her breath hissing between clenched teeth. Finally she gained leverage and mustered enough strength that she forced him above the level of the mattress, and he saw the cop bolting from the bedroom.

He must know the sound of Nell's shot drew attention.

The cop whirled, taking one more chance and trusting to luck. The gun made its muffled *pop!* The bullet went wild, hit the bedside lampshade, and made the lamp dance but not fall.

Nell was sitting up now, struggling to get Terry's weight off her so she could work herself up the wall to a standing position and give chase.

Then she looked down at the blood on her hand holding her gun. At the blood on the wall. On her nightshirt.

"Jesus, Terry. Is this from me or from you?"

"Don't know," he said. "Think it's all me. Hope . . ."

"Ah, your shoulder! That bastard!"

"Go get him, Nell."

"Screw him!"

She tossed her gun aside and reached for the sheets, anything to stop the bleeding.

They were in the lobby of Nell's building. Beam was aware of something, a faint stirring above, as if the shot had awakened every tenant, made everyone afraid in a way that was almost palpable.

Fear is in the building.

"Take the stairs," he told the bundle of rags that was a cop. "I'll take the elevator."

Rags pulled a Remington shotgun from beneath his worn raincoat and dashed for the stairs. Beam heard him going up, treading light, taking two, three steps at a time. Then Beam turned back toward the elevators. He'd already pushed the up button.

One of the elevators had descended to lobby level. The door opened, and da Vinci stepped out. He was in uniform, and holding a handgun with a sound suppressor fitted to its barrel.

He didn't notice Beam until he'd taken three or four steps. Then he stopped and made a half turn back toward the elevator.

But he was too late. The elevator door was just finishing sliding shut.

Beam stood between da Vinci and the street door.

Rags encountered no one on the stairs. He reached Nell's floor and slowed down, moving carefully now.

He edged open the door to the hall.

There was Garcia, sitting slumped against the wall. His mouth was gaping, and his chest and stomach were black with blood. His eyes were lifeless marbles.

Rags had gotten winded coming up the stairs. His breath seemed to him as loud as a steam engine as he stepped over Garcia's legs and made his way down the hall toward Nell's apartment.

At her door, he looked up and down the hall, but saw no one. The elevator should have beaten him up here. *Where the hell is Beam?*

Maybe inside.

He tried the knob, found the door unlocked, and went in fast, shotgun at the ready.

The living room was dim, unoccupied, but there was light down at the end of a hall.

"Who's out there?" a woman's voice called.

"Police!"

"C'mon back here. Come back here and help, damn it!"

Rags made his way down the hall, shotgun still raised and ready to fire.

He was slower going into the bedroom. Faint noise from in there, familiar, like bedsprings in shifting rhythm. *Someone having sex?*

Then he saw the man on the bed—looked like half his shoulder was blown away. Saw the bloody figure of Nell straddling the man, desperately using a wadded sheet in an effort to stanch the bleeding.

Rags glanced around. Nobody in the bedroom other than him and the two bloodstained figures on the bed.

"Goddamn do something!" Nell pleaded.

Rags didn't figure there was much he could do. "I'll call 911," he said.

"I already did," Nell told him. "See if you can help me stop this goddamned bleeding."

Down in the lobby, Beam understood it now, as he stared at da Vinci standing there in his old motorcycle cop uniform, the boots, the jacket that helped hide the bulky silencer, the cap with its eight-pointed wire frame removed, so it was worn crushed already and would fit beneath a motorcycle helmet.

The puzzle clicked into coherence: da Vinci's fuzzy familial past, the passion for justice, the questionably earned citations, the MRP cops with their crush caps and leather jackets, the frustration with the slow, slow wheels of the legal system that didn't grind exceedingly fine, the rapid advance in the NYPD at a comparatively young age.

Andy da Vinci, Deputy Chief da Vinci, was the Justice Killer.

* * *

"Surprise," da Vinci said flatly.

"Not when I come to think of it," Beam said. Sirens were sounding outside. Both men knew da Vinci wasn't going anywhere other than down or to jail.

"I got tired of seeing it," da Vinci said, "the scum of the world coming and going through the system, free to rape or kill again. After April—my wife, Beam—killed herself because the sick scum Davison went free, goddamned *free*, after what he did to our son, I decided to do something about it."

"About what?"

"The imbalance in the world. The unfairness. The way the wheel is rigged. So I worked for a while as a civilian in the St. Louis police department, then I joined the NYPD." He gave a tight smile. "You might say I advanced with a vengeance."

"You knew everything we were trying to do to nail you," Beam said.

The smile again, somehow infinitely sadder than a frown. "I controlled the investigation, saw that the controversial cases we investigated went back only ten years—not quite far enough to include Davison's trial and acquittal."

"Harry Lima's ring?"

"I knew about you and Nola. Had a duplicate of Harry's pimp-ass ring made in Toronto. Used it to point you in another direction and throw you off the scent. Being a cop, even a high-ranking one, has it's limitations, Beam. I was on a mission, and rules and regulations meant less and less to me."

"You took too many unnecessary risks," Beam said. "You could have kept coming and going as a uniformed cop, running the investigation of yourself. Helen was right. You wanted to be stopped."

"Helen? Maybe she was right. Could be the book on serial killers has them—us—pegged. Maybe I even assigned you to the case because I knew you'd eventually stop me. Maybe that was my way of stopping myself. After a while it became obvious to me that Nell was figuring out what was happening. Nell's smart. And dangerous. I had to kill her."

"Did you kill her?"

"No. She's alive. Lucky. I'm glad."

"But upstairs—"

"I wanted to prolong the game."

"That's what it was to you, a game?"

"Not only to me," da Vinci said. "And I wasn't the one who made it a game, played between cops and prosecutors and high-priced attorneys. But it *is* a game."

Beam wondered how far back da Vinci's own game went. "What about Rowdy Logan, in Florida?"

Da Vinci paused before answering. "The left-handed killer who murdered your son. His death wasn't a suicide. He was one of mine."

Beam held his breath. "And Lani?"

"I didn't murder your wife to lure you out of retirement for revenge. Or because I knew she'd talk you out of accepting the challenge. I didn't murder her at all. She must have taken her own life, Beam, for her own reasons. I'm sorry."

Beam believed he was.

"Some things you can never know for sure, Beam. Some things you just gotta let go of."

"Some things."

"You understand, the game isn't really about justice. That has to change."

The chorus of sirens grew louder, then stopped one by one outside the building. A glimpse of blue uniform. Someone was in the lobby beside and behind Beam. Sweeney.

"That has to change," da Vinci said again.

Behind him, the elevator door opened silently. Rags, with his shotgun. He stepped out of the elevator, the Remington leveled at da Vinci. Beam knew he'd been talking to Nell upstairs. Where was Nell?

"Game's over," Beam said, but he knew it wasn't.

Da Vinci made his last move, raising his silenced handgun to point at Beam. Beam saw that da Vinci's finger wasn't anywhere near the trigger.

Rags stepped to the side and let loose with the shotgun, spinning da Vinci completely around in a spray of blood. Beside Beam, Sweeney's nine millimeter banged away. The blue crush cap once worn by the young motorcycle cop went spinning into a corner.

Da Vinci was sitting on the floor, legs straight out in front of him. The back half of his skull was missing. He bent forward, as if he might attempt to touch his toes, then fell to the side.

Rags kicked aside da Vinci's gun, needlessly keeping the shotgun aimed at his fallen body. Sweeney advanced, still holding his nine in both hands, pointed down at da Vinci. Procedure.

Looper opened the lobby door and came halfway in, gun drawn, and scanned the scene, taking everything in.

His eyes lingered on da Vinci. "Holy shit!"

He holstered his gun, then signaled to someone outside, and came all the way in, followed by two EMS paramedics lugging equipment. They glanced at da Vinci's body.

"Not that asshole," Sweeney said.

"Upstairs," Rags said. "I'll show you."

Looper couldn't stop staring at da Vinci's corpse. "Jesus!"

"That thing still work?" one of the paramedics asked, pointing to the elevator door peppered with bullet holes.

"Try it," Beam said.

The paramedic did. It worked.

"What about Nell?" Looper asked.

"She's upstairs," Rags said. "She's okay. Somebody else isn't."

More uniforms streamed into the lobby. Two rode the elevator up. Others went thumping up the stairs. A crime scene investigation team would be here soon.

"We better get upstairs, see Nell," Beam said.

They waited for the elevator to return to lobby level.

"Helen will need to be told," Looper said, glancing back at what was left of da Vinci.

Beam was surprised by Looper's insight and sensitivity. Must have shown it.

"I think he was in love with Helen," Looper said. "And she felt the same way about him."

"They were in love," Beam said. "He must have known she was slow poison. It works that way sometimes."

"Well," Looper said, "she'll have to be told."

Barely five minutes had passed since da Vinci had been shot. Outside in the night, the city was alive with sirens.

"My job," Beam said.

73

The city soon became itself again, a sprawling construct of chaos seeking its own balances and levels. And justice. Business was conducted, for the most part legally. Trains and subways ran more or less on schedule. Trash was picked up on designated days, late or early. Crime was committed, collars were made, defendants cut deals or stood trial, and were convicted or walked.

Adelaide Starr was released from custody, as well as jury duty. Her book debuted at number three on the *New York Times* nonfiction bestseller list. Television talk show appearances led to the starring roll in a new musical about Evita Perón.

Helen Iman left the NYPD within a year and became a profiler for the FBI. She became involved with a former agent, and they bought a house together in Virginia, in a secluded, wooded area not at all like New York.

Terry Adams lost the use of his right arm, but he continued his acting career with more success, beginning with a role as an Argentine general who was Evita Perón's secret lover.

Nell and Jack Selig were at opening night, applauding.

A month after da Vinci's death, Nell quit the NYPD and

married Jack Selig. Nell had saved Terry's life, but not their love and trust for each other. She'd made her choice around three a.m. in the crackling darkness of her apartment living room, and she and Terry both knew it.

The Evita Perón play is still running, but with its third cast. The Seligs spend time in New York, but live most of the year in Europe. Selig manages his investments on his computer, and finances construction projects in France and Germany. Often he does this from an office on his yacht. Nell is reasonably happy.

Beam slipped back into retirement, and a deepening relationship with Nola. Neither of them fears or yearns for the past, but Beam spends much of his time at Things Past. He's developed a passion, and a discerning eye, for antiques. He and Nola expanded the shop, and moved into an apartment on the same block. They are more than reasonably happy.

While they deal in antiques, they live for the present and future, and don't do a lot of thinking or talking about Harry, or Lani, or Beam's former life as a homicide detective. They have friends, most of them in the antique business, or collectors. They meet at conventions or auctions, and now and then go out for dinner, or travel together. Their friends notice nothing unusual about Beam and Nola, other than they don't have a cute story about how they met.

Occasionally Beam wonders about the one Justice Killer victim, Bradley Aimes, who was shot with a bullet that matched none of the guns found among da Vinci's effects. But he doesn't wonder a lot.

Gina Dixon moved away to attend college in California. She majors in Criminal Justice.

Turn the page to read a preview of John Lutz's next thriller

MISTER X

Coming from Pinnacle in October 2010!

1

Quinn had found a box of paper clips in his bottom desk drawer and was just straightening up when the dead woman entered his office.

She'd startled him, the way she'd come in without making any noise.

She wasn't what you'd call beautiful, but she was attractive, with slim hips and legs inside new-looking stiff jeans, small breasts beneath a white sleeveless blouse. Her shoulder-length hair was brown, her eyes, a deeper brown and slightly bulbous. She had symmetrical features with oversized lips, a slight overbite. A yellow file folder stuffed with what looked like newspaper clippings was tucked beneath her left arm. Her right hand held a brown leather shoulder bag, the strap scrunched up to act as a handle. She'd said on the phone her name was Tiffany Keller. If she were still alive, Quinn thought, she'd be pushing thirty.

There was a kind of grim resolve to her expression, as if she'd just been affronted and was about to fire back.

The generous mouth suddenly arced into a toothy smile, and the dogged look disappeared entirely, as if a face like hers couldn't hold such an expression for long. Quinn was left with the impression that he'd momentarily glimpsed someone else entirely.

"Captain Frank Quinn, I presume."

"Just Quinn," he said. "Like the lettering on the door, Quinn and Associates, Investigations."

"I was aware you were no longer with the NYPD," she said.

"Want to sit down?" he asked, motioning with a paper clip toward one of the walnut chairs angled in front of his desk.

"I'll stand, thanks." Her smile widened. "I'm Tiffany Keller."

He continued staring at the woman while his right hand groped for the empty glass ashtray he used to contain paper clips. "You said when you phoned earlier to make this appointment that you were Tiffany Keller. Would you be the same Tiffany Keller who was a victim of a serial killer?"

"That would be me."

Unable to look away from her, he turned the tiny box upside down and dropped the paperclips into the ashtray, hearing the faint clickety sound that told him he'd hit his glass target. "Excuse me, but aren't you dead?"

"Not exactly."

Wondering where this was all going, Quinn tossed the empty paper clip box into the waste basket inside the desk's kneehole. It landed on recently shredded paper and didn't make a sound. "What is it you want, Tiffany?"

"I want you to find the Carver."

The Carver was a serial killer who'd taken five victims, the last five years earlier, and then suddenly ceased killing. In the way of most serial killers, he'd slain only women. His victims' nipples had been sliced off and a large X carved on their torsos just beneath their breasts. Then their throats had been cut.

At the time, Quinn had been laid up after being shot in the leg during a liquor store holdup and hadn't been involved in the Carver investigation. He'd followed it in the papers and on TV news with a temporary invalid's distracted interest. It had been one of his few alternatives to staring at the ceiling. If he remembered correctly, Tiffany Keller had been the Carver's last victim.

He leaned back in his desk chair and studied his visitor more closely.

She didn't wilt under his scrutiny.

"Actually I'm Tiffany's twin sister," she said.

"Then why the act?" he asked.

She smiled even wider. Lots of even white molars. Quinn would bet she'd never had a cavity. The large white smile gave her a kind of flashy cheerleader look. It would dazzle you even in the cheap seats.

"I thought one of the Carver's victims herself appealing to you to take this case might be more convincing," she said. She spoke with a hint of accent, her intonations flat and slightly drawn out. She wasn't from the Northeast. Probably someplace Midwestern. Corn country. "I'm Chrissie." *Ahm.* "Chrissie Keller. My twin sister and I were named after two of our mom's favorite eighties recording stars, Chrissie Hynde and Tiffany."

"Tiffany who?"

"She didn't use a last name. Some artists don't."

"Some artists I've met don't, either," Quinn said.

"Like pickpockets and confidence men and such?"

"Uh-huh. And impersonators."

"I didn't *have* to impersonate Tiffany," she said. "I just wanted you to think that maybe, for only a second or two, you were face-to-face with her. A victim asking that her killer be brought to justice."

"An emotional appeal."

"You got it."

"Justice is a hard thing to find in this world, Chrissie. Sometimes even hard to define. It can be a lot of work and expense, and then we might not like it when we find it."

"Or we might glory in it."

Never having been in her position, Quinn found it difficult to disagree.

"I have the means to pay you for your work," she said. "And what I want to do with my money is find out who killed Tiffany and make sure he pays for his crime. This might sound strange, but I think that's why I have the money. Why I won the Tri-state Triple Monkey Squared Super Jackpot." She shifted her weight in the stiff jeans so that she was standing hip-shot. "That's three monkeys in a row three times," she said with a note of pride.

"You did that?" he said, figuring she must be talking about slot machine winnings.

She swiveled back and forth on the foot her weight rested on, as if idly crushing a small insect. Her shoes were rubber sandals that looked as if they must hurt her feet. "I surely did. With a lucky quarter, and a good reason to win the hundred and thirty-nine thousand dollars." Her face broke into the big smile. "That's still a lot of money after taxes."

"Even here in New York," Quinn said. He leaned back again in his chair, farther this time, making it squeal a warning that it might tip and send him sprawling, make him pay for flirting with danger. He said, "Now you're on a mission."

"That I am, Mr. Quinn. Don't tell me to go to the police, because I already have. They're not interested. The Carver murders happened too long ago, and I got the impression the police don't want to be reminded of a serial-killer case they never solved."

"Bureaucracies hate being reminded of their failures."

"I'm not interested in what they hate or don't hate. I'm interested in justice for Tiffany."

Justice again.

"People on a mission scare me," Quinn said, thinking he had a lot of room to talk. But what he'd said was true. He sometimes scared himself. "You're not from New York."

She looked a little surprised and licked her big red lips. "It shows that much?"

"Not a lot," Quinn said. He tapped a forefinger to his cheek bone beneath his right eye and smiled. "Trained observer."

Chrissie pulled the chair closer to the desk and sat down. She crossed her legs tightly, as if she were wearing a skirt and not jeans, or as if she thought Quinn might glimpse too much denim-clad thigh and go berserk and attack her. "I'm from Holifield, Ohio. So was Tiffany, of course. It's a small town. Most folks work for the chemical plant or for Treadstrong Truck Tire Manufacturing. Tiffany worked in the plant for a while, then she came here to New York to try to become an actress. She got killed instead." A firm expression came over Chrissie's face. Her lips compressed together over her protruding teeth and paled, but only for an instant. "I want that rectified."

"Avenged?"

"That, too. You should know, Mr. Quinn, that when one twin dies the other also dies a little. And the way Tiffany died . . . Well, it's almost like it happened to both of us. Twins' deaths are special."

"Everyone's death is special to them."

Chrissie leaned forward in her chair, her hands cupped over her knees. She had long fingers, well-kept nails. No rings. "The police called the Carver investigation a cold case, Mr. Quinn. I want it heated up again. I want my mission to be your mission."

"You need to give this some thought," Quinn said. "The NYPD aren't fools. Most of the time, anyway. They couldn't solve the Carver murders five years ago."

"I've read about you, Mr. Quinn. When it comes to serial killers, you're smarter than the police. Smarter than anyone."

"Now you're making me blush."

"I doubt if much of anything does that," she said.

"Now you've reverted to insult."

"I didn't mean it that way. I was referring to your experience, the fact that you're a winner."

"Praise again. I'm getting whiplash."

"I'll put my faith in you, and my money on you," Chrissie said.

"Investigations go into the cold case file, time passes . . . They get harder to solve. I couldn't promise you much."

"I'm not interested in promises," Chrissie said. "Just results. Like you are." The smile came again, a red slash of amusement that broke into speech. "They say you're only interested in results, that you skirt the rules in ways an actual cop couldn't. That you're a hunter who never gives up." She edged even farther forward in her chair, as if she might spring across the desk and devour him with her big smile. "What do you say?"

"I give up. What do I say?"

"You say yes, of course."

"I guess I shouldn't have left it up to you."

He watched her pick up her worn leather purse from where she'd leaned it against the chair leg and reach into it for her check book.

He didn't try to stop her. For all he knew she was right. Right and lucky. That was why she'd won the Tri-state Triple Monkey Squared Super Jackpot.

What had he ever won?

2

It had all been so quick, and the eye could be fooled.

Pearl Kasner, acting as hostess, stood off to the side in the dim entrance alcove of Sammy's Steaks, unsure of what she'd just seen.

She'd waited patiently, making sure she was on the periphery of Linda's vision. A slender and tireless young woman with hair that dangled in natural ringlets around her ears, Linda was one of the busier food servers at Sammy's. The customers were crazy about her.

As she ran another diner's credit card, Linda casually drew what looked like a small black box from her pocket, laid it on the counter, and swiped the card a second time.

Back went the box into her apron pocket.

It was all done so quickly and smoothly that you had to be watching for it, looking directly at it, to notice it.

Pearl edged back completely out of sight and smiled.

She'd been right when she'd noticed Linda the first time. Whenever Linda was alone settling a diner's check, she would run the card twice, once legitimately, the second time to record the card's number in the device she carried concealed in her apron pocket. For several days, the customers' names and card numbers could be used safely to purchase merchandise. When, finally, the diners realized what was happening and notified the credit card company, they wouldn't be likely to connect the stolen number with a not-so-recent steak dinner at Sammy's.

Pearl left the foyer untended and weaved her way between white-cloth-covered tables and across the restaurant. She was slightly over five feet tall, with vivid dark eyes, red lips, and black, black shoulder-length hair. Pearl drew male attention, and when attention was paid, said males saw a compact, shapely body with a vibrant energy about it. Her ankles were well turned, her waist narrow. She had a bust too large to be fashionable, but only in the world of fashion.

No one who looked at Pearl was disappointed.

She approached a booth where a lanky but potbellied man in a wrinkled brown suit lounged before a stuffed mushroom appetizer and a half-empty martini glass. He was past middle-age, balding, and the day Pearl started pretending to be a hostess, he had started pretending to be a slightly inebriated customer who ordered appetizers as an excuse to drink alone. That was better than drinking at the bar, where the mostly under-forty club was watching and discussing baseball. Discussing it loudly and sometimes angrily. They could really get worked up over steroid use.

The solitary drinker was Larry Fedderman, who had long ago been Quinn's partner in an NYPD radio car, and later a fellow Manhattan South homicide detective. Fedderman, retired from the department, had been living in Florida when Quinn founded Quinn and Associates. Pearl had been working as a uniformed guard at Sixth National Bank in Lower Manhattan.

They'd both stopped what they'd been doing and went to work for Quinn as minority partners in Quinn and Associates, Investigations. They were the associates.

Restaurateur Sammy Caminatto had hired QAI to discover how his cousin's Visa card number was stolen, when the only place he'd used his new card and new number, before cutting the card into six pieces to keep it out of his new trophy wife's hands, was at Sammy's.

Quinn had assigned Pearl and Fedderman to the case, and they'd slipped into their roles as Sammy's new employees. Now it looked as if they'd found the answer to the riddle of the roaming card numbers. It was in Linda's apron pocket. Which Pearl thought was a shame, because she liked Linda, who was cute as puppies, naïve, and probably being used.

"Looks like Linda's it," Pearl said to Fedderman.

He showed no reaction but said, "I'm surprised. She seems like a good kid."

"Maybe she is, but she's going down for this one. Carries a mimic card swiper in her apron pocket."

"I watched for those and missed it," Fedderman said. "She must be smooth."

"You can tell she's done it before."

"Let's not spoil her evening," Fedderman said, sipping some of the martini that he hadn't poured into his water glass. "Let's let her copy some more numbers, build up the evidence against her."

"Watch her keep breaking the law?"

"Sure."

"Doesn't that kind of make us accomplices?" Pearl asked. Since becoming an associate and not having the NYPD to cover legal expenses, she'd become cautious about exposing herself and the agency to potential litigation. Or maybe this was because she'd become fond of Linda and didn't want to compound the mess the young woman was in.

"In a way," Fedderman said, "but nobody'll know but us. And you and me, Pearl, we'd never rat each other out."

"I suspect you're half right," Pearl said.

She waited till an hour before closing time to call the NYPD, and Linda was apprehended with the card recorder in her apron pocket. It contained the names and credit card numbers of five diners who'd paid their checks with plastic that evening. Damning evidence.

As she was being led away, Linda was loudly and tearfully blaming everything on a guy named Bobby. Pearl believed her.

"Men!" Pearl said, with a disdain that dripped.

Fedderman didn't comment, standing there thinking it was Linda who'd illegally recorded the card numbers.

A beaming and impressed Sammy told them his check to QAI would be in the mail, and Pearl and Fedderman left the restaurant about eleven o'clock to go to their respective apartments. They would write up their separate reports tomorrow and present them to Quinn, who would doubtless instruct Pearl to send a bill to Sammy even though it might cross with his check in the mail. Business was business.

Fedderman waited around outside the restaurant with Pearl while she tried to hail a cab. The temperature was still in the eighties, and the air was so sultry it felt as if rain might simply break out instead of fall.

It never took Pearl long to attract the eye of a cabbie, so they'd soon part, and Fedderman would walk in the opposite direction to his subway stop two blocks away.

Pearl extended one foot off the curb into the street and waved kind of with her whole body.

Sure enough, a cab's brake lights flared and it made a U-turn, causing oncoming traffic to weave and honk, and drove half a block the wrong way in the curb lane to come to a halt near Pearl.

"It might have been Bobbie with an *i-e*," Fedderman said, as Pearl was climbing into the back of the cab. "A woman."

Pearl glared at him. "Dream on."

She slammed the cab's door before he could reply.

Fedderman watched the cab make another U-turn to get

straight with the traffic. He wondered if Pearl had always been the way she was, born with a burr up her ass. She was so damned smart, but always mouthing off and getting into trouble. What a waste. She'd never had a chance to make it any higher in the NYPD than he had. Fedderman was steady, a plodder, a solid detective—unskilled at departmental politics and wise enough to stay out of them. Staying out of things was another of Pearl's problems. She couldn't.

Another problem was that Pearl was a woman, and she had those looks. Her appearance drew unwanted attention, and she'd always been too hotheaded to handle it. She'd punched an NYPD captain once in a Midtown hotel after he'd touched her where he shouldn't have. That alone would have been enough to sink most careers. It hadn't quite sunk Pearl's, but there was always a hole in her boat, and she'd had to bail constantly just to stay afloat. That was why she'd finally drifted out of the NYPD and into the bank guard job. She could be nice to people ten, twenty seconds at a stretch, so it had worked out okay for her. But she'd never been happy at Sixth National. She missed the challenge, the action, the satisfaction of bringing down the bad guys, even the danger.

The same way Fedderman had missed that life while chasing after elusive golf balls down in Florida, or fishing in Gulf waters and pulling from the sea creatures he didn't even recognize as fish.

Like Pearl, he'd been ripe for Quinn's call.

Fedderman smiled in the direction Pearl had gone and then walked away, his right shirt cuff unbuttoned and flapping like a white surrender flag with every stride. If he knew about the cuff, he didn't seem to mind.

He did kind of mind that there would be no more free drinks and appetizers at Sammy's.